Revelations

of

The Impossible Piddingtons

Adventures in Second Sight

Volume 1

Barry H. Wiley

"Think mindreading contrary to common sense. Wise provision of the Bon Dieu that we cannot read each other's mind. 'Twould stop civilization and everybody would take to the woods. In 50 or a hundred thousand centuries when mankind would have become perfect by evolution, then perhaps this sense would be developed with perfect safety to the state."

Thomas A. Edison

Diary Entry: July 16, 1885

Part 1

The Travels

Abilene, Kansas

Saturday, September 29, 1890

Kyame Piddington sat on a cushion that was on a board resting across two saw-horses on an otherwise bare stage. Her eyes were blindfolded, her sweat-soiled hands squeezed tight beneath the folds of her green silk performing gown. If she was careful, Kyame could see under the blindfold to pick up Papa's silent signals -- the signals she needed to instantly understand to be able convince their audience that she had the second sight -- that she could actually see with her father's eyes as he moved through the audience. Kyame couldn't really, of course, but she had to act like she could, so that she and Papa could eat. All the family's money had gone to doctors to fight Mama's consumption -- but now she was dead, and the money and the doctors gone.

Craven's Opera House smelled the same as other meeting halls, the mingling odors of coal oil from the lamps at the edge of the stage; of the stale sweat of the unwashed people in the chairs; along with the lingering taint of horse manure and urine from the busy streets outside.

The audience was already becoming more restless, muttering among themselves. Only fifteen minutes into their act, only fifteen and she was failing. Again. She wanted to run, hide -- and cry her heart out. She had failed Papa again. She had embarrassed him -- again.

Kyame had almost had it, getting his silent signals right, to apparently read the mind of a large woman sitting at the far end of the third row, where Kyame apparently couldn't see her at all.

She didn't understand yet how Papa could know what the woman was thinking, he would explain later, but just as she had said, "I feel four words" -- Papa had signaled the number four -- "You are visualizing ... seeing a ... a cloudy night ... a ..." when suddenly Kyame realized it hadn't been 'four' that Papa had signaled. Her heart went cold, as tears started. It had been *44* -- which meant a compact in their memorized list.

In their routine, once the item was identified from the list, Papa would then signal one or two additional details for Kyame to exploit. But she had it entirely wrong. She had utterly missed on the follow-up details as well.

Kyame wanted to die.

"No, child," the woman suddenly snapped angrily, her chair scraping against the floor as she stood, "I am not thinking of four words or a cloudy night. I am only thinking about the waste of money for a ticket to this ... this silly exhibition!" She looked back at the sparse and impatient audience. "We all should just leave. Don't you think? My husband and I have better things to do than watch a silly mindreading act that can't ..." Her last words were lost in the noise of the shuffling chairs. The abrupt hard sound of a chair overturning on the wooden floor made Kyame jump.

She easily heard loud comments as people moved away.

"Impossible Piddingtons? Impossible for them to get anything right!"

"My little son's card tricks are more mysterious than the Piddingtons."

She felt Papa at her side. He gently removed her blindfold and kissed her on her cheek as she dropped down off the board to stand on the stage.

He whispered, "I love you, Daughter."

But she saw how hard Papa was trying to hide his disappointment, his embarrassment, as the audience was laughing and leaving.

John Piddington smiled, a little, as he put his arm around her. "We must practice more, Daughter," whispered Papa, "just practice more. You will get it, just as Mama used to.

"And we must. Our money is running low." He glanced up at the hall manager coming up the center aisle to collect his rent. "There is nothing for us here … any longer." He paused. "Maybe," he said, "they haven't heard of our problems ... yet ... over in Kansas City."

Basil Craven put out his thick hand. "Fifteen dollars, Piddington. No excuses." The short heavy hall manager shook his head. "Pathetic, Piddington. Your daughter is a looker, couple more years every young man in town can't help but to notice her. But, my God, man, she just can't do the act. Second sight is a tough, tough act to do, I know that … and I'd heard good things about the Impossible Piddingtons; but I wasn't aware that your wife had died … and it wasn't the same act any more.

"I always get a cut of the ticket take above a two-thirds house, but" -- he tossed his hand toward the now empty hall -- "this was barely a third of a house. I could have rented it tonight for a lot more for a lecture on the Jesse James gang." After a quick count, Craven shoved the bills and coins that Piddington had handed him into his pocket. "I don't have to have second sight myself to see how much trouble you've got." As he walked away, Craven said over his shoulder, "Don't come back to Abilene any time soon, Piddington. You and her… Kai-ah-mee, that right? – you and Kyame will be laughed out of town. Impossible?" He shook his head, laughing.

Kyame wiped her eyes with Papa's handkerchief. She brushed her black hair from her eyes, and set her jaw. Now she was angry. No one could speak to Papa that way. Not some fat meeting hall manager.

"We'll come back, Papa," Kyame said, her voice cold, her moist green eyes polished steel, "and they won't be laughing at the Impossible Piddingtons. I'll scare them, Papa. Darn it, I will scare them down to their shoes!"

1

"We need a stunt, Kyame, that doesn't rely on our silent codes so that we can mislead reporters about what we are doing, and how we might be doing it ... and to give us a break in the routine. Something almost ... ah, casual ... without blindfolds and such. I have something in mind for our visit to the newspaper offices tomorrow." John Piddington grinned as he walked about their room at the Grand Hotel in Chillicothe, Missouri. They had three days at the local Farmer's Hall, with a fourth as an option if -- if the Impossible Piddingtons could fill the hall. Their yellow handbills had been distributed all over the town, particularly in neighborhoods near the four principal Chillicothe churches. Outraged ministers sermonizing about the evils of second sight always brought good crowds to witness the sin for themselves. Piddington beckoned to his daughter to join him at the table.

The debacle at Abilene was almost seven months in the past. His beautiful daughter of twelve, just twelve last week, had changed. The burden of losing her mother only a year ago, and the humiliations of her first appearances before audiences trying to take her mother's place in the act, had seemed to drive her deeper into herself.

Even he had experienced her withdrawals -- but Kyame *was* starting to get it, the silent signaling. As tough as a second sight act could be to learn, if it was done well, the act could make good steady money. And they needed the money, to eat and sleep -- and so that in a couple of years of saving he could send Kyame back to Boston to the best art school in the country. If only Laura could see their daughter's drawings now, their remarkable complexity.

Kyame was so much Laura, but now she exhibited an uneasy edge that, at times, transformed the laughing daughter that they had both so enjoyed, into almost a stranger.

She trusted no one -- only him. Kyame would sometimes sit and draw and redraw the same picture over and over. One time she had simply snarled to his question, *"Because,* Papa, *it is not right* -- not right!" Then she immediately dropped everything and ran to throw her arms around him, her hot tears on his cheek.

Now seated, Papa grinned at her. "Only one signal will do it. So, Daughter, here's the effect: you go out of the room with one of the reporters. After the door is closed, I have three or four numbers written on a slate or a piece of paper, doesn't matter, and totaled up. The slate is covered with a cloth and I leave the room. Once I am gone and the door closed, you come back in and with a bit of your smokey acting, and I love your expression" -- Kyame smiled, it seemed to describe everything; smokey, nothing real -- "you tell them the total of the numbers without ever seeing or touching the slate, or asking any questions. Then we repeat it, just to prove we can! Everything in silence and we are *never* in the room together during the effect." Papa raised an eyebrow. "What do you think? How do you think it is done?"

Kyame reviewed the routine in her mind, using the lessons she had been learning with so much difficulty. Only one signal -- but signal what? She nodded. "I like the effect Papa. It is simple, quick and very direct. The best kind. But," she smiled, "I don't see the gimmick."

"If you can't, dear Kyame, then no one tomorrow will. Here's what we will do."

As Papa laid out the routine, Kyame grinned, then laughed. Only Papa could think up something like this. Mama had once said, "You have a very devious, but very loving father, dear Kyame." Then she had laughed her beautiful bell-like laugh, so full of happiness. A happiness Kyame hadn't felt for over a year.

***

Kyame removed her blindfold and accepted the glass of water that one of the young reporters at the Chillicothe *Daily Tribune* offered her.

"Second sight must be thirsty work, Miss Piddington," he said. He was Tracy Ornum, with the paper less than a year. He had started asking her questions as the other three reporters had started talking with Papa. With the editors, the reporters, two type-setters and a visiting salesman, there were twelve men in the open area of the office. All the overflowing roll-top desks had been pushed back against the walls to provide a completely open space so that the newspapermen could surround the Piddingtons.

Good, she had thought. They needed at least ten men to work the new stunt.

The editor, Albert Baker, had a closely trimmed white beard and mustache, a bit out of style, but Kyame thought it looked elegant with Baker's red brocade vest and cravat. He had been very polite to her, commenting that he had a granddaughter up in St. Joseph just her age.

She had nailed the first two stunts, blindfolded. She had easily read Papa's silent signs and felt a cool sharp boost of confidence. Kyame could see her smokey acting had hit home when she removed her blindfold. The men were talking so earnestly with each other as Papa stood off to one side.

Like other men at the public performances, Ornum and the other reporter had been uneasy about tying the handkerchiefs over her eyes too tightly about her head, not wanting to hurt her, but still had to tie tight enough not to look foolish. She had only smiled and urged them to tie the knots tighter.

"May I borrow that slate over there, Mr. Baker?" asked Papa. "And Mr. Ornum, would you please escort Kyame out of the office and close the door behind you?" As each man moved to respond, Kyame said, "Thank you, gentlemen." Ornum opened the door, waited as she passed through, then closed the door securely behind them.

The reporter started to speak, then went silent when Kyame closed her eyes, touching her temples with the tips of her fingers of both hands. She breathed deeply, slowly -- to help sell the process -- as Papa called it.

At Piddington's request, four men had written numbers on the slate, the total coming to 28. "Now please turn the slate over and cover it with a cloth so that the numbers and the slate cannot be seen. And, Mr. Baker, would you please hold the slate when my daughter re-enters the room? Thank you." One of the reporters took Piddington by the elbow through a door into another office, and closed the door, even locking it behind them.

"Tell Ornum to bring the girl in," said Baker.

When Kyame appeared, the editor asked, "Could you hear anything of what went on in here, Mr. Ornum?"

"No, sir. And Miss Piddington didn't say a word ... even had her eyes closed all the time."

"Miss Piddington, I am holding a slate with some numbers written on it. Can you tell me the total of those numbers without asking any questions?"

Kyame smiled her smokey smile, a half-smile with a mischievous cock of her head. She raised one hand to her forehead as she passed her other hand over the cloth-covered slate. She knew the number, 28, the moment she walked into the room. But it was process, the smokey acting that sold the effect.

"I ... won't ask anything, Mr. Baker. I must feel my father's presence before me, seeing into his mind, not into yours. Into his ... mind ... his eyes." Her voice went soft, drifting off. "Two digits ... I sense, see the total to be twenty ... twenty-eight." She looked directly into Albert Baker's questioning brown eyes. "The number you are holding, sir, is twenty-eight."

Baker's jaw dropped. "My god, girl, you are right! You are exactly right. How ... how could you have known?"

The editor's jaw dropped even further the second time when she announced, "Thirty-three." One of the type-setters was holding the slate while Baker had stood just on the other side of the door that was closed behind her, hearing nothing.

***

With a small sketch of Kyame in the center, the front page description of the Piddington exhibition in the *Tribune* offices filled the hall that night -- as Papa had predicted.

At no time, Tracy Ornum had written, had either John or Kyame Piddington spoken to each other; at no time had they even *seen* each other. The numbers had been chosen by the men in the office, even changed at the last moment without warning. How the father had transmitted the number to his daughter was a complete mystery, Ornum assured his readers. A complete mystery -- or -- or, maybe *it really was* second sight!

***

Returning to their room from the *Tribune* offices and once the door was closed, Kyame had started laughing. "I think we scared them a bit, Papa. A bit, but still scared."

Papa kissed her on her cheek. "We did, or you did. I was behind a door at the time. And, Daughter, I think our great powers have earned us each a piece of cherry pie in the dining room."

As Papa had explained the night before, regardless of how the reporters and editors might be standing when the Piddingtons entered the newspaper offices, the men would be silently counted, left to right, as one to however many but at least ten. The men would each keep their number regardless of how they might subsequently move around the office.

Kyame and Papa agreed the first totaled number would be in the twenties and the second in the thirties. Adding to himself as the numbers were called out, Papa would stop when the numbers totaled in the twenties, or in the second test, the thirties. He then turned the slate over, covered it with a cloth and handed it to whichever of the men was numbered appropriately. Baker had been the eighth man, numbering from the left, when they had arrived at the office, so Kyame, knowing that Papa would keep the first total in the twenties, knew the number was 28 the moment she saw the editor holding the slate. The one sign, Papa had said, was who would be holding the slate. The typesetter, Donnie, holding the slate had been number three, so the second total was thirty-three.

Then Kyame had to sell the process, to convince the reporters that there *was* a process, a studied process with no guessing -- hopefully leaving second sight as the most likely, even legitimate explanation

2

The boarding house dining room couldn't tell Kyame Piddington where she was. The picture of President Benjamin Harrison, the oval picture of the heads of three galloping horses -- all much the same whether it was up the dusty road in Dodge City, or down here in Ellsworth.

She looked at Papa across the table through the steam rising from a pot of meat stew. There were three women, two men, Papa and her at the table. Kyame searched their faces as she waited for Papa to start their routine. Papa had learned that the Reverend Harold Blacker always took his meals here, so that was why he took their room here.

Papa suddenly hunched his shoulders as he spoke with the hard-faced shopworn lady in rusty-colored silk to his left. The signal -- she would be the one, then. The lady was probably telling him her whole life. Women would when Papa smiled, Mama had once confided to her.

Kyame couldn't have said 'shopworn' in the past without a mild scolding from her mother, but Mama was gone now. With Mama gone, Papa would sometimes act shopworn so Kyame didn't say the word any more. She only thought it.

With Papa's ready sign, Kyame went tense, her heartbeat jumping. She just couldn't miss. She had to read Papa's signs accurately or no one would come to their evening performance tomorrow night or to the press review tomorrow afternoon.

With extra practice, Kyame now almost always got Papa's silent signing right. But her heart continued to pound.

Mr. Dobie, a whiskey drummer, a man with a dirty yellow mustache, dirty fingers and sagging blue eyes sat across from her. His green silk vest was stained and poorly patched. Kyame thought for a moment of how Papa would 'send' him with their silent signals, then she took a mouthful of mashed potatoes. He winked at her, grinned, then reached up and pulled out his grin and laid it on the table.

Her stomach flipped and surged.

Dobie took his napkin and began to polish the false teeth, cleaning off mashed potato residue.

The uppers had two gold teeth in front; the lowers had one tooth missing in back.

"Can't sell much without a bright smile," he chuckled, his smile an empty chasm as Kyame's stomach churned again. He started polishing the lowers after dipping them in his glass of water.

Oh ... all thought of their routine was gone. Kyame looked desperately at Papa, just as he turned away from the lady. Seeing Kyame, his smile vanished and he started to rise but it was too late. She frantically held her napkin to her mouth as she heaved out her mashed potatoes and stew. In a moment her father was at her side as the people on each side pushed away from the table.

She heaved again.

"Kyame, Kyame ... easy, daughter." Piddington took away her bulging dripping napkin and gave her his napkin which she used to wipe her mouth.

"Thunderin' ...." said Dobie, shoving in his uppers. "She got something bad? Smells like spoilt cream."

"Yes," agreed Miss Randolph, a school teacher, who had been seated next to Kyame, but who now stood away, safely behind her chair. "Why would you have her with you, Mr. Piddington, when the child should be in school?"

Her stomach quieting, Kyame wiped her mouth again with Papa's napkin. She couldn't look toward Mr. Dobie. She knew she would start heaving again.

"Kyame works with me, Miss Randolph. But I intend for her to be at the best Eastern art school money can buy."

"But what can a girl of twelve do, Mr. Piddington?" asked Rev. Blacker, standing at his chair at the far end of the table.

"Kyame can listen to my thoughts, Reverend, like her mother did before her death."

"That girl has the second sight?" Startled, Blacker frowned and gripped his chair tighter. The others drew further back from the table. Even stocky Mrs. Rudabaugh, the owner of the boarding house, moved half a step distant. "She must be prayed over, Mr. Piddington. God must be petitioned to release her from such sin. Leviticus nineteen teaches that ...."

Kyame was angry. She wasn't sinning, just heaving. She had heard Papa lectured at before about her, but as much as those people might care, they just didn't understand. She wiped angrily at her mouth and started to speak.

Papa touched his sleeve. To touch cloth -- the signal for silence. Kyame instantly obeyed.

"We entertain, Reverend. We ...."

Dobie's eyes lit up. He pointed at Piddington. "You're The Impossible Piddingtons!" he announced. "Your yellowsheets're up all over town. I thought your partner was a grow'd woman, not a little girl. I didn't connect ...."

"And those playbills," interrupted Blacker, "are being torn down just as quickly by God-fearing folk. It is sinful, entertainment or not, and particularly involving a young innocent girl kept up at such late hours in ugly places reeking of Babylon."

Miss Randolph backed further away. "You're ... you're *theater* people?" she asked, as she looked anxiously at Mrs. Rudabaugh. "You would allow *theater people* in your rooms? Next to us?"

Mrs. Rudabaugh took a step toward the school teacher. No one challenged her in her own boarding house -- no one, by God.

"Theater people must always pay in advance, Miss Randolph. Mr. Piddington and his daughter are welcome here. They have caused me no trouble."

Kyame started to stand and -- but Papa touched the tablecloth. She sat back and was silent. But then he touched his right ear with two fingers, as he shifted to his right, his left hand brushed against his belt buckle. He coughed. She continued to read his movements carefully doing her silent count while apparently looking up at the ceiling then down at her feet.

She was ready. She knew she was ready.

When John Piddington suddenly turned his back and walked silently away into the parlor, Kyame stood up. Everyone backed away another step. She brushed her long black hair away from her face, pointed at the lady with whom Papa had been speaking, and then dropped her hand.

Kyame knew everyone would later confirm that she could not have overheard anything, particularly with her heaving.

"Miss Kelly," said Kyame quietly. "Miss Angela Kelly, but that is not your real name ...."

The woman started, her hand at her throat, her eyes went wide.

"You carry a concealed silver-plated two-shot derringer. It is loaded." As she had practiced, Kyame let her eyes go wide enough to show the whites all around her green pupils. "You are anxious, in fear of ... Emmett returning for money, and ...."

Angela Kelly screamed and ran from the dining room. A moment later the front door slammed.

Rev. Blacker paled, then backed away toward the entry hall. "I will warn everybody of you, Piddington," he said. He frowned down at Kyame. "Who has your soul, child?"

She looked at Papa who had returned to the dining room but he held his handkerchief. She obeyed and didn't speak.

Blacker waited for a moment then vanished into the entry hall. "I will warn everybody," he shouted as the door closed hard.

Good work, Darling, Papa signed with a brief tight right fist.

Kyame smiled, and, if she didn't look at Mr. Dobie who was edging out of the room after Miss Randolph, she could be hungry again.

3

John Piddington drew the covers up to Kyame's chin.

"The initials on her hand-bag didn't match with Angela Kelly," he said, "so something was wrong, and Emmett Jones or Janes or something was written on a well-read letter. She had mentioned having some funds at risk.

"You matched things well, Kyame … your mother would have been impressed. As I was. You are reading the silent code now almost as well as your mother did.

"And thanks to the Reverend Blacker, the hotel will be full tomorrow afternoon for our press demonstration. I didn't plan it exactly the way it went, but it worked just the same."

Kyame smiled. Mrs. Rudabaugh had made her some eggs in the kitchen and she was pleasantly full. Papa kissed her forehead.

"Dream of Mama," he said. "I will be." *Good night*, he signed, as he closed her door.

***

Kyame was dressed in white lace with a blue ruffled skirt that almost touched the floor. It had been made by a seamstress in Kansas City from one of her mother's dresses and was reserved for performing only. As Papa had proposed to the audience, she sat on a pillow on a wide board placed across two saw-horses positioned near the row of unlit kerosene lanterns set across the edge of a low stage at the end of the hotel ballroom.

The sunlit room had been cleared by the hotel staff to allow for the eleven men and women sitting in two rows in a semi-circle around her. A reporter from each of the Ellsworth newspapers, the *Reporter* and the *Messenger,* Sheriff Charlie Emerson, two local physicians, the Rev. Blacker and three women from his church, the hotel manager, and Jamie Glasgow, the owner of the Ellsworth State Bank directly across muddy First Street from the hotel -- and also an elder in Rev. Blacker's church.

As Papa had explained, if these people were impressed, they would talk which would bring large audiences to their four planned evening performances at the Ellsworth Meeting Hall.

At Papa's request, the two reporters had come up from the audience to blindfold her with two red kerchiefs. Her stomach churned for a moment when the men surrounded her. Their breath and clothes were a cloud of fusty whiskey and coal-oil.

But they were like the others in other towns who had come up, afraid to hurt her by tying the kerchiefs too tightly, but afraid of looking foolish if they didn't. Didn't really matter, Kyame could see anyway no matter how tightly they tied her. She frowned deeply as they tied. Then by raising her eyebrows, after the reporters had left the stage, she lifted the kerchiefs enough to enable her to see clearly down the sides of her nose. Seated up high on her perch she could see out almost to the second row of assembled chairs in the room.

She signaled the limit of her range of view to Papa by coughing at the point when she could no longer see his shoes as he walked slowly up the narrow center aisle introducing their performance.

Townspeople always thought that putting her up on that board where everyone could watch her, guaranteed she couldn't get any help from anybody and certainly not from her father. But if she wasn't up there, Kyame couldn't see far enough beyond the edge of the stage to do anything.

When her mother was alive, Kyame would sit at the far end of the front row and relay the signaling when Papa was out of Mama's view. No one ever suspected an innocent little girl and afterwards the three of them would sometimes laugh about it when the audiences would be scared by the strange phenomena they had just witnessed.

4

Reading Papa, Kyame said: "It's a picture, in a very fine silver frame" -- a woman gasped -- "of a handsome young man. Your son, who is ... oh, I am so sorry, who is dead ... killed in the war between the states."

"Oh, gracious Lord!" the woman cried out. She looked over at Rev. Blacker seated next to her. "How could she ...?"

Kyame just glimpsed the woman's hands shaking. She always had to be careful not to let her head tilt back too far to try to see more. That might give the blindfold away. Papa always watched her closely on that. It wouldn't necessarily give the act away, but could trigger awkward suspicion.

"Yes, child," the woman said through her tears, "you are right, but how could you know? All I showed your father is the picture."

Kyame could feel the audience stirring nervously in their chairs. This was going good, but Papa had signaled he wanted her to miss on the third one coming.

"I just felt your love for him, Ma'am." She glowed when Papa briefly squeezed his right fist. Papa would tell her later how he had found out about the boy -- part of her continuing to learn Mama's job.

The woman sobbed again. "Bless you, child."

***

Kyame's back began to ache. It was almost time to finish. Through the wide cracks in the stage planking, Kyame suddenly saw lights moving about in the basement below her. The audience was buzzing because, on signal, she had just incorrectly described something round and shiny as a watch when it was a woman's compact. It helped to miss, intentionally, every now and then. It made things look more real. Papa was speaking to give her a brief rest before their finish.

She relaxed by looking down at the floor. Through a wide crack she could see someone under the floor was carrying lanterns. She glimpsed blue bandannas on men wearing shiny black coats. Then light reflected from pistols and a long rifle barrel ...

Kyame interrupted her father. "Oh, Papa, something bad is going to happen!" Her voice shook. "Something bad with men in blue bandannas and black rain slickers."

Bank owner Jamie Glasgow and Sheriff Emerson were immediately on their feet. Others quickly joined them. The rest of the audience shifted anxiously in their chairs.

"Blue bandannas?" a reporter shouted. "What is she saying? The Dalton Gang wears blue bandannas and black slickers."

"Can't be the Daltons," the hotel manager challenged, coming to his feet. "Man, your own paper said they robbed a train way down in west Texas only last week,"

John Piddington turned to stare at his daughter, her open hands raised toward her face. It was real -- the signal for trouble. He started for her.

"They're coming, Papa!"

Kyame could see men moving below her. She was afraid they could look up and see her. Her stomach began to churn.

Sheriff Emerson strode heavily toward John Piddington.

"This a stunt, Piddington?" he snapped. "We had some nasty trouble with the Daltons a couple of months back and we ain't in *no mood* to laugh."

Kyame saw the lights go out below her.

"Papa," she cried, pulling the bandannas from her eyes, "they're out there." She pointed toward the front of the hotel. "They're going that way." She jumped down from the board and ran up the aisle to him.

"No stunt, Sheriff," Piddington said. "I don't know what's going on, but men in blue bandannas are out there if Kyame says they are."

The sheriff's hard glance was frightened but he pointed toward the reporters as the audience began to mill toward the door, chairs toppling in loud crashes.

"Get to my office for the deputies," he shouted over the growing noise. "If it's the Daltons come back again, then by God, we shoot to kill." His face twisted, Emerson looked back again at Kyame. "Girl, if you're playing with me ...." He

26

turned to push his way through the frantic people. "Jack," he yelled. "Hold the men at the porch!" As the Dalton name swept instantly across the lobby, the tide of people fleeing the lobby jostled against those coming out of the ballroom. The swelling humanity at the doors resisted the sheriff as he elbowed viciously through the crowd.

Kyame followed Papa back to the stage. She quickly whispered what she had seen.

Piddington nodded. "The show's over, Kyame. Let's get back to our room at the boarding house. It will be safer there."

5

When the Piddingtons reached the porch of the hotel they heard three shots fired in the bank across the street. The large gold-lettered bank window shattered, scattering glass shards across the sidewalk. Then two more shots, as the doors of the bank flew open and four men in black slickers and blue bandanas rushed out. Three held pistols, one held a rifle. Kyame started as one of the men looked over at them, raised his gun toward them, then ...

"Inside quickly, Kyame!"

She felt Papa's hand squeeze her shoulder. As Kyame lifted her skirts to run, she froze, the scene etched in her mind. A deputy had fired and missed, as the man in the slicker whirled toward him, firing once, twice, and then pulled himself up on a horse. The deputy went over backwards as if hit by a train, sprawling across the dust and didn't move.

Two of the Daltons were already away, at a full gallop, their black slickers flaring out behind them. The other two raked their spurs along the flanks of their horses, as the animals leaped ahead.

Two more shots were fired by Sheriff Emerson as he ran toward the bank. One of the robbers slumped in his saddle but held on. The four disappeared around a corner and were gone.

Trembling, Kyame held Papa's arm tightly with both her hands. In their travels, she had seen death before, but not like this.

"Get a doctor! A doctor!" A man had come to the door of the bank. "There are three men down in here!"

John Piddington hesitated, then taking his daughter by the hand, started toward the bank. "There may be something for us," he whispered to Kyame. As hard as Kyame tried, filling the meeting houses and town halls had been difficult since Laura's death; he needed something to catch the fancy of the people, to unsettle them, to scare them, more than just baiting a fiery minister like Blacker.

***

Inside the bank, three men were on the floor, large pools of blood forming under them. One had a large wound in his chest, the other face down with two wounds in his back, the third, Kyame could see, had been shot in the back of the head. She recognized the doctor leaning over them. He straightened and turned to the sheriff standing by the teller's window.

"Dead, all dead, sheriff. The three of them." The doctor turned back, bent down, "Look. Daltons must have had an arsenal with them. Those two were hit with three, maybe four forty-four slugs, but this head wound's smaller. Maybe thirty caliber. A .44 at that range would have blown his head off. See the powder burns?"

Sheriff Emerson stepped over beside the doctor and knelt down to get a better look. He nodded. "Don't know the head wound. Other two are farmers from west of town."

Catching Kyame's eye, Piddington signed silently: Did you see the robbers with a small caliber gun? Kyame possessed a vivid graphic memory, a gift from her mother.

Kyame turned, touched her waist, spread her left hand, and then moved her right hand behind her. No, she responded – only had big pistols and a rifle.

Piddington knew she had her mother's picture memory. He decided to trust it and make his play. If he was wrong, they would have to leave town and try again somewhere else down the road. Each town was becoming smaller, more difficult to find a good audience for their second sight act. But – if his hunch and his daughter's remarkable memory were right, The Impossible Piddingtons would be on the front page of every paper in the territory.

It was a necessary gamble.

"Sheriff, the Daltons didn't kill the third man. Someone else did. My daughter did not see the Daltons carrying any small weapons in the bank."

Emerson looked at Piddington for a moment, frowned. "Her? She wasn't even in the bank. How could she know?"

Taking Papa's cue, Kyame stood in front of Emerson, widened her eyes, the whites encircling her deep green pupils.

"Because, sheriff, I *saw them*," she said, her voice became softer, like she was under a compelling spell.

The bank suddenly went quiet.

Sheriff Emerson looked hard at Kyame, then at Piddington. "You people better not be playing with me. I never put a child in jail, but I sure as h… can put your papa behind bars."

Bank owner, Jamie Glasgow stepped from behind the sheriff, pointed at Kyame who was now alone in the middle of the bank, the bodies on the floor behind her, the room filled with the coppery odor of fresh blood.

Everyone had silently backed away, up against the walls.

"Child, who did kill the man, then? If you could see into the bank from the hotel, you certainly saw who shot that man there."

Emerson whirled to stare at the bank owner. "Glasgow, are you …?"

Papa rubbed his neck to sign: stall, Daughter.

Kyame was silent; her eyes half-closed, her head back slightly as though searching for something, straining for a scent – waiting for Papa to cue her. Never, he had instructed her in her training, never be afraid of being silent, of doing nothing. The people don't know what to expect anyway.

Then Papa began to sign.

She opened her eyes wide, raising her hands, fingers spread, reaching toward the teller's cage, her ensorcelled face causing a low murmur in the people crowded at the bank's doors.

"The killer," she whispered. "The killer," she repeated louder, "had dark hair, was dressed in a dark blue business suit. A moustache." She paused.

"That'd fit a dozen or more people ...." Emerson started.

"But only one had to kill," Kyame answered. "And he, he *had to kill* ... now!"

There was a scuffling near the door of the bank.

Papa signed, yes.

Kyame pointed at the man trying to squeeze through the crowd at the door. Dark hair, dark blue business suit, moustache – and a derringer in his hand.

She pointed. "Him!" she cried. "Him!"

Emerson lunged after the man, catching his arm as the small pistol went off. The sheriff drove his fist into the man's face, sending him reeling against the door frame. Two men grabbed at the derringer, knocking it to the floor, as Emerson kicked the legs of the man out from under him.

"Ain't goin' no wheres, Bascom. No wheres but my jail."

***

James Bascom was the bank manager, Sheriff Emerson explained to the Piddingtons, when he returned to the bank. The man Bascom had murdered was a state bank examiner on a surprise audit who had just introduced himself when the Daltons had come blasting through the door. Bascom had been embezzling funds. Desperate, he had tried to use the Daltons as cover for killing the examiner with the small thirty-two caliber derringer that Jamie Glasgow insisted all his employees carry.

When Glasgow and the sheriff finished explaining, the banker put his hand on Kyame's head.

"Beautiful hair, Miss Kyame. Like your mother's?"

"No, sir. Like my father's, back when he had some."

As the men laughed, Kyame saw Glasgow give Papa an envelope as they shook hands.

The reporters insisted on questioning the Piddingtons as they came outside the bank, on what was it like to have second sight, were they Spiritualists, and the other standard questions that Papa answered with his mysterious ways, while Kyame watched, waiting to be cued if necessary -- and listened, to learn the answers.

John Piddington took Kyame's hand as they returned to the parlor at the boarding house. With the parlor door closed, Piddington sat his daughter next to him on the couch.

"You did fine, dear Daughter. Truly fine. Your mother would have been so proud. You read beyond the signs like I hoped you would."

"How did you know, Papa?"

"That Bascom was the killer? Well, all the men working for the bank all had mustaches and wore about the same thing, we saw that yesterday when we arrived, so your description of the killer would naturally be correct, so far as it went, since someone working at the bank had to be the killer.

"The teller was still in the cage behind the counter, only Bascom was in front of the railing, apparently meeting the bank examiner, and would have been close to him as the Daltons came in. The killer had to have acted without any planning. Bascom must have been frantic trying to think of a way out of the surprise audit, when the Daltons suddenly marched in to give it to him. At least Bascom thought anyway.

"Let's see if Mrs. Rudabaugh has anything to eat."

As her tension relaxed, Kyame suddenly started to weep.

"So many dead, when there is no reason ... no reason ... why, Papa? Why?"

He wrapped his arms around his daughter and held her without speaking.

***

Sheriff Emerson removed his hat when he came into the boardinghouse parlor. Kyame sat next to Papa, his hands tight in hers, her sleeves wet from her tears. Mrs. Rudabaugh had brought coffee, a glass of milk and two pieces of apple pie.

"Mr. Piddington ... Girl ... a lot of people'll want to thank you. A lot were hurt by Bascom's stealing. You spooked Bascom enough he tried to run. He's still spooked." He put on his hat but didn't move. "Daltons got away ... but I think we put some holes in the hide of the last one. But you Piddingtons" -- he hesitated -- "what are you? Never seen anything like you before."

Kyame slid off the couch. She smoothed out her lace dress, then looked up at Papa.

He winked.

Kyame wiped her eyes, then smiled. "We let people figure that out for themselves, Sheriff," she said.

6

"Live your life as richly as you can, Miss Kyame," he said, his mouth a slight smile. "When life is over there is nothing, just nothing … like falling into a final endless black sleep. Those religioners may be right … that there is a heaven or a hell of some kind, but they can never prove it; and you will never know until you get there … so, dear girl, live as though neither place exists and all you have is what is in your hands now, this moment. There is no assured tomorrow." He leaned back into his seat as the train swayed and rattled. He started to smile, then the smile slid into a smirk. "Even the Scripture, Miss Kyame, Psalm 144, says that 'Man is like to vanity: his days are as a shadow that passeth away.' Just a shadow … with no promises."

Kyame Piddington let the rhythmic jostling of the train rock her gently. They were on their way back to Abilene. It had been almost a year since that ugly humiliation at Craven's Opera House. But now she was ready.

The clean shaven thin-faced man sitting across from her in the crowded passenger car,

Solomon Royale, wore the shabby black uniform of an itinerant preacher, like so many she had seen in the towns and crossroads that she and Papa had passed through in the past months, across Kansas, Missouri, Nebraska and once up into Illinois. But his brown eyes were alive with interest -- when most preachers' eyes that she had encountered were angry -- and sometimes fearful.

"But," she said, frowning, "aren't you a preacher? Isn't that your job to convince people there is a Heaven and scare them with Hell?"

Royale laughed, displaying a ragged mouth with many teeth missing.

"Ah, scare them with Hell. Dear girl, you've heard one too many passionate reverends. Once," he said, "when I was your age, Miss Kyame, I believed with all my heart that God and all the saints were waiting for me just behind the clouds, their arms outstretched with smiles on their faces." He shook his head. "But that was many years ago. Too many disappointments and unanswered prayers have ground away all that faith. I don't pester God anymore with prayers and I hope He doesn't pester me when things are over.

"I wear this rig because I don't have the money yet to buy something more honest." He shrugged, grinning. "Wearing the collar, however, has brought me food and a bed when there were no coins in my pocket."

Royale arched his back, stretching his arms, and then he leaned forward, his elbows on his knees, his chin resting between his fists. "There are people who believe carrying a bigger Bible makes them appear to be more holy." He shook his head. "I can still say the holy words; I still remember the scriptural references; and I can deliver a grace at a table to curl your toes and to grab for the dessert." Leaning back into the seat, Royale shook his head. "Yes, I can fake it with the best of them. Because … now … I, too, am only a fake."

Royale's eyes softened, becoming gentle as he looked at Kyame. "Dear girl, let me pass on one thing from my ministerial experience. After one of my better sermons where you could feel the flames of Hell licking under each of the pews, a member of my misguided flock, a Russian farmer, pulled me aside. He spoke with a respect I didn't deserve, and explained that in Russian there are two words for truth: *pravda,* the everyday kind of truth; and *istina,* the core truth that lies behind pretense, behind blind certainty. I needed, he instructed, to understand which kind of truth I was speaking.

"That Russian was right. There *are* two kinds of truth, Miss Kyame, not just the one truth of the religioners." Royale leaned back into his seat, glancing out at the endless prairie lands flowing by, a realm so flat it seemed that its only defining feature was the curvature of the earth.

Kyame fumbled with the pronunciation of the two words.

Royale repeated them slowly, then nodded when she got them right. "You know, Miss Kyame, it was the British writer, Christopher Marlowe, who wrote back in the sixteenth century:

I count religion but a childish toy,

And hold there is no sin but Ignorance.

"Now, you can speak some Russian which immediately sets you apart from everyone else in this car."

Kyame looked over at Papa who smiled. "I can speak some Russian, Papa," she said, repeating the words for truth.

Rousing from beneath the newspaper that he had covered his head with for a short nap, John Piddington put his arm about his daughter. "So", he asked, "what line of life are you looking for now, Mr. Royale?" Abilene, he noted, was about a half-hour away.

Kyame shifted to lay her head on Papa's shoulder and looked at the counterfeit preacher through her black hair that slipped down across her face. She liked Solomon Royale, but didn't know why. Maybe because he was the first preacher that didn't look down on her as *only a theatre girl*. But then, she reflected, he wasn't a preacher anymore, anyway -- so he didn't count.

"I plan to ..." Solomon Royale hesitated. "I plan to get a job somewhere as a newspaper reporter and writer, Mr. Piddington. I know words ... and I know how to keep secrets." He smiled, a small cautious smile. "But first I need to change this costume into something more authentic in keeping with my new role as an unquestioning agnostic ... to use Professor Huxley's descriptive word."

"How then, Mr. Royale," Kyame murmured as the rocking train lured her to drift off toward sleep, "will you make money to buy new clothes? It is cold outside."

"By shooting pool, dear Kyame," Royale said, flashing his ragged smile. "Shooting a progressively better game of pool … and leaving with the sinners' cash. I plan to be dressed warmly within a day or two."

7

Kyame sat on the bed, carefully studying her father walk toward the dresser then stop, shift his shoulders to settle his suit coat then walk back to the door of their hotel room. He hesitated, then turned toward her.

To anyone else watching, he did nothing but walk, but Kyame, reading his movements, said, "A bald man with black hair is sitting next to a woman with dyed yellow hair and a red stripe down her nose." Kyame laughed at the image but her father did not.

"A green stripe, Kyame. You're off a beat," he said. He carried a chair over to the bed where she was sitting.

"I'm sorry, Papa. I thought I had it this time."

"You're getting more of the code faster each day, Daughter, and an occasional miss adds to the realism of our second sight, but the misses must be planned for effect, not genuine mistakes." He sat down in front of her. "Of course, Mama would sometimes miss, as do I, but it can't happen very often."

Kyame felt his hand gently on her head, his handkerchief wiping away her ready tears. She thought she was ready, but ... She raised her head. Papa signed, she obeyed and began the silent count.

"Five," they said together.

Good, he signed. Again.

"Seven." And again. "Twelve."

She glanced at the open window at the sudden sound of children's voices. "Four," she said a moment before Papa -- and felt sick again.

He smiled and wiped his handkerchief over his damp brow and back over his balding head. "We cannot miss, Kyame. We cannot. To convince audiences to spend their money to see our demonstrations of second sight, we can only miss *when we want to* ..." He stopped and looked over at the window.

"Even with the chill, you can smell the sweat of the horses down on the street and the winds still blow the stench of the stockyards across town. Why don't you go play outside with the other children until dinner, then we must go the meeting house for our performance."

In each dusty town that they visited, the mothers would not let other children play with her. Kyame was a theatre girl, one of the *show people,* and not to be trusted, they whispered. But the older boys would look at her in a strange way that Mama had said she would explain later, but Mama was dead now. Papa had been so burdened with paying for Mama's long illness that Kyame didn't want to ask him. She gathered her drawing materials.

"Papa," she asked, turning to him, "is what we do ... right?"

John Piddington started as he replaced the chair. "What do you mean, Kyame?"

"Our second sight performances ... if you were a traveling blacksmith or a gunsmith I could play with the town children ... but I can't because their mothers believe I can see into their heads. Is it right to make people think that?"

"Yes," said Papa without hesitation. "Because when people hurt emotionally, or even physically, they want thrills to distract them from their hurt. We give them that … the feeling they are seeing something strange and a little frightening … a thrill. It helps them live their lives, richer lives … and ours as well."

Kyame had her drawing box under her arm as she walked toward the door. But rich or not, the children still wouldn't play with her, and the older boys always wanted to touch her dress.

8

Kyame passed the Abilene National Bank on Texas Street to reach the corner hardware store where she could sit and draw the passing traffic. Blowing on her fingers to loosen them against the chill, Kyame arranged her sketchbook. It always felt -- safe, to lose herself in her drawing, to keep trying to make the images ever better.

She overheard men talk of a financial panic "back East". Papa promised she would go "back East" to art school, when he had the money. But could she if there was panic? What was "back East"? Where really was "back East"? She had studied a geography book Papa had found in the lobby of a hotel in Kansas City, so she knew names and states and foreign countries. And like most books she had a chance to read, Kyame had memorized the book so that she could study it at other times.

"Back East" seemed to be mostly colored pink for some reason.

Kyame began to draw a carriage with two matched chestnut horses. After a few strokes she ripped it up and started again. Without Papa she could never go on a stage in front of strangers. Kyame started on the carriage again, but there was an odd crowd down near the dry goods store. Maybe some interesting faces. She just couldn't get anything right on the carriage.

Kyame normally drew from memory, an almost picture perfect memory, like Mama's -- maybe the carriage would come better later. She felt calm, secure, drawing, and drawing.

The Miraculous Maid!!

-- Mollie Fancher --

The World Famous

Brooklyn Starver!!

A corner of the red and blue banner had broken free to snap and flap in the breeze. Kyame edged past the shifting line of people to look in the store window. A small wooden sign said: 13 Days of Abstinence. The '13' was painted over a faint '12'.

In the window a pallid, shallow-cheeked blonde haired young woman languished on a couch, a light pink coverlet over her, her right arm laid back above her head while with the fingers of her left hand she reached out to touch the hands of those people filing by. Women turned ashen at her touch, men forced smiles, but Kyame noted that they all dropped money into a wooden box and some left packages by the couch. The sickly woman moved only her left arm, her dark eyes half closed.

"What is happening?" Kyame asked a woman with a baby in her arms who pushed by her.

"It's the Starver, girl. Gives you the shakes to think you can actually touch her in a few minutes."

"What is a Starver, Ma'am?"

The woman glanced down at Kyame with some impatience and pointed at the smaller sign.

"Thirteen days she's gone without any food here. They say she's gone six, maybe nine months or more back East. Could see visions, could see without her eyes, blindfolded … once her bondage to her flesh was broken."

The woman walked on hastily as her place was taken by others pressing in behind her.

"Fed by the angels, that's what," said a tall dark-haired woman leaving the store behind Kyame, another woman beside her.

"Must be the angels," her friend agreed, as they walked away.

"Can't be any other way, Clara."

Thirteen days without eating! Why would anyone want to do that? "Back East" again. Kyame loved to eat. Visions and blindfolds. Kyame could see while blindfolded -- that was part of their act. Some people thought she could see visions as well -- she frowned -- but only if she had read Papa correctly.

A bearded man in a travel-worn black suit appeared in the window. Kyame had seen him standing in the line ahead, a leather bag held closely to his chest. He was heavy in his shoulders, but seemed to waste away into his legs. He stepped slowly to the Starver and held out the large bag toward the almost comatose woman, saying something that Kyame could not make out.

The Starver stirred from her languor, reached out for the bag with both hands. She drew it to her lips for a moment in a kiss of blessing -- and then let her arms fall back to the couch as he took back the bag.

The man bowed gravely and placed the bag near the money box and left. His place was taken by a woman with a large bouquet of flowers. A uniformed nurse stepped forward to take the flowers.

The Starver's eyes slowly looked over at her without focus, then, just as she closed them, Kyame caught a quick flash in them. The people kept touching the limp fingers and dropping money into the box. Kyame watched the woman she had just spoken to lay a bulging purse on the Starver's lap, which the nurse seized and placed next to the money box.

9

When they returned to their hotel room following their evening performance, Kyame sensed Papa was worried. He slumped into one of the chairs without removing his coat. The meeting house had been only half full which she knew meant little money left for them after the rental fees. The audience did not react to her as in other towns even when she told a man he would come into a great fortune only to lose it again.

"Starver's already told me that, Miss Kyame, but she said I wouldn't lose it," he had responded. The audience had laughed and Papa was not pleased -- but he had told her she had handled it well -- and her silent counting had been exact.

"Is...?" started Kyame.

Papa interrupted. "The Fancher woman is cutting down our audiences. So we have a choice: we can quit now and move on, or we can expose her sham, or ..."

His voice drifted off.

"The Brooklyn Starver really eats?" asked Kyame.

"Of course, Daughter. No one can live without food. Even the saints ate something. She gets her nourishment in the same way a magician gets the rabbit from his hat. He puts it into the hat first without the audience realizing it. The Starver is fed without any one realizing it. Most probably at night." He stood up, his face drawn tight. After a moment, he jammed his fist into his other hand, his jaw set. "We are going to stay ... she might show up again in another town. And I have to find a way to ... to completely defeat her, so that she will avoid The Impossible Piddingtons in the future."

"But she seems such a sad lady, Papa. Do we have to hurt her?"

Papa frowned. "There are only so many dollars available to us in each town, Kyame. If she takes too much, then there isn't enough left to save for your school. And, Daughter, you need to learn just how sad and helpless she really is."

"If she isn't real, is what she does right ... like us?"

Papa hesitated as he removed his suit coat, his eyes holding hers for a brief moment. "Get some rest, Daughter, while I do some thinking."

Kyame nodded. But then the Starver can't play with the other children either. As Kyame drifted into sleep, she heard Papa leave their room.

10

"The Starver is dead?"

Kyame looked up from her breakfast porridge at the man sitting across from Papa whom he had introduced to her as Marshal Winlock Toledo.

The man wore a glistening five-pointed tin star on his vest with Abilene Town Marshal imprinted in black enamel on it. He had a small gun with a polished ivory grip in a holster under his left arm hidden by his suit coat, but his coat had hung open as he reached for his cup of coffee.

The hotel dining room was barely half full at seven in the morning. Kyame hadn't heard when Papa returned to their room. Papa looked so tired.

The marshal's face tightened. "She was poisoned by someone who knew her tricks," he answered, looking down at Kyame, then across the table at Papa.

"But she didn't eat anything. How could she be poisoned?" Kyame asked, apprehension beginning to spread through her as she looked first to the marshal then to Papa. "I thought she was fed by the angels. That's what they said. Are there bad angels, Papa?"

John Piddington smiled at his pretty black-haired daughter with the small clump of porridge on her chin. He gently wiped it away with his napkin.

"Sometimes, it seems, there can be, Daughter."

"But she didn't do anything, except just lay there. Why would anyone want to hurt her?"

The marshal looked intently at Papa. "That's what I want to know, too, Piddington. Why?"

***

After the marshal had excused himself, telling Papa they couldn't leave Abilene without his permission, Kyame and Papa had gone back to their room to rest. Papa said they wouldn't do a performance tonight, because of the Starver's death.

Kyame collected her drawing box and her coat. As she walked out on the chilly early morning street, Kyame caught a glimpse of

Solomon Royale going into a hardware store. He no longer wore the preacher's garb, but a fur-trimmed cattleman's jacket. His face was shadowed with unshaven whiskers. Frowning, Kyame was disappointed to see that Royale wore a large revolver on his hip. Was that the opposite of believing in God, become a pool-shark and wear a gun?

She watched the marshal speaking with two men, one of whom was pointing toward the dry goods store. The other was nodding vigorous agreement. He wore a shabby black suit.

Kyame knew the man in the black suit was the same man who had given the money bag to the Starver for kissing -- but, now, he didn't have a beard.

She recognized his nose, ears and the set of his eyes. She settled onto a bench in front of the bank and began to draw the man, first with a beard -- then without. It was easy, his features were clear in her mind.

The marshal's face clouded over as he turned away from the men. When he saw Kyame drawing, he nodded toward her, touching his hat, and then strode down the street toward the hotel. Without changing his long stride, Winlock Toledo dodged around over-loaded buckboards and hitch carts that moved slowly along the crowded street. When he saw John Piddington coming out of the telegraph office, he changed direction.

Kyame finished her sketches, closed her drawing box and started for Papa. A great fear was building in her, fear for Papa.

"Piddington! Hold up a minute." The marshal lengthened his stride, shifted to a loping run.

Papa turned toward the marshal, stopped and waited.

The marshal pointed toward his office that stood between a dress shop and the telegraph office. A stone jail rose in back.

"In there."

Kyame followed the two men.

11

Once inside, the marshal told a deputy to stand by the door.

"Piddington," said Toledo, "I have two witnesses that put you behind the storefront that the Starver was using at about one this morning. Said you were sneaking around like a thief in the night. The Starver had cut into your take from your second sight act, that's been obvious. Then, suddenly she's dead." He pointed at Piddington. "Why shouldn't I put you in jail right now?"

Kyame gasped and jumped up from her chair. "No!" she cried.

Papa put his arm around her. "That's all right, Daughter. Marshal Toledo is only doing his job, dear." He turned to Toledo. "I wanted to understand who this woman was, Marshal. I telegraphed a newspaper friend in New York City last night to ask for a description of Mollie Fancher. I got my answer this morning."

Piddington handed the telegram to the marshal.

"Mollie Fancher still hasn't eaten in two years," said Piddington, "and is still in Brooklyn. She also is dark-haired, not a blonde like the dead Starver here."

Piddington got up, shifted his suit coat and walked toward the front window of the marshal's office to look out. A deputy moved away to the other side near a rifle rack.

Kyame caught Papa's ready signal. *I saw ... man,* she signed. *Had beard yesterday ... not one today. He one witness.*

Papa turned toward her without speaking. He touched his belt for a count of two, then coughed, then....

When ... first see him? he signed.

He gave bag to ... She hesitated, trying to think of a means of sending Papa the word Starver. She managed *not-eat* by shifting her skirt with both hands while leaning awkwardly against her chair.

Papa turned away from her, their entire silent conversation had taken less than a half a minute.

"Marshal, I was where your witnesses say," acknowledged Papa. "The Starver was being fed, somehow. There are a number of ways that has been done. I thought it would be sometime at night, but I was wrong unless at least a dozen of your people have been paid off. There are local guards that block any entry to her rooms."

John Piddington returned to stand beside Kyame's chair.

"The Starver and her people, however many there actually are, wouldn't take that chance with their payoff obviously being so good here. There have been three or four Starver exposures back East, which included in one case bribing a local doctor who was supposed to be supervising the whole situation.

"Where did the Starver come from," asked Papa, "before Abilene?"

Kyame watched the marshal fidget with a pair of handcuffs, then drop them back on his desk.

"Down Oklahoma Territory," said Winlock Toledo. "And Texas before that ... according to what they told me when they were setting up at the empty store.

"They brought her in a heavy wagon fitted out with a special bed. Fancher looked like she was about to die.

"Don't travel too well, I guess."

Papa looked at Kyame, then asked, "Have you confirmed where they say they've been, marshal?"

"No, no need to."

"Why not look into it?" asked Piddington. "By the way, what are the names of the witnesses? Do you know anything about them?"

Piddington walked back toward the gun rack. A deputy shifted his feet nervously.

"Doyle and Symington. Doyle is a druggist, down the street, but Symington is new to me."

"What were *they* doing at one in the morning behind the Starver's place?"

"Wait a minute, Piddington," snapped Toledo. "Only reason you aren't in a cell right now is because of your little girl. She's my daughter's age and I don't want to hurt her, but ...." Winlock Toledo shrugged -- then tossed his hand. "Let them go, for now, Deputy."

12

Papa led Kyame away from the marshal's office. "We need to find out where the Starver has been," he said, his words misting in the cold air. "We've traveled all over Kansas and Missouri in the past months and never heard of the Starver, so where did they come from?

"There's a crowd around the Starver's window, Kyame. Go over there and listen. We need to understand who this Symington man is, with and without his beard. I'm going to send some telegrams."

Before Kyame started away, she explained to Papa what she had seen in the Starver's eyes.

Papa nodded. "She was acting and relaxed for just a moment. Not many could catch what you've seen, Daughter."

He clinched his right fist momentarily and then relaxed his hand. His signal for when she had been "very good".

Kyame glowed inside, then with her drawing box under her arm, she walked toward the small crowd, as Papa turned toward the telegraph office. She recognized three of the women who had been in the line the day before, along with Doyle, the druggist. He had been inside with the Starver when Kyame had watched through the window.

She settled onto a bench and began to sketch Doyle while she listened.

"Poor Mollie's going to be shipped back East for burial, I hear, Clara. Family's back there near New York."

"Who could want to hurt such a harmless person, she only wanted to help people." Clara turned toward Kyame. "There's that strange Piddington girl. They think her father killed the Starver. Isn't that right Mr. Doyle?"

Kyame started to respond, then restrained her temper. Listen, Papa had said. Only listen. She went back to her sketching.

Doyle walked nearer to Kyame. "I'm testifying against him and so is Mr. Symington. We both saw him snooping around out back like a thief.

"Here!" Doyle suddenly turned pale. "Why are you drawing me, girl?"

Kyame smiled as sweetly as her anger would allow. "Because you have an interesting face, sir ... so does Mr. Symington ... without his beard."

Doyle started. The druggist frowned, and flushed red when he looked down at his face on Kyame's paper. His hand shot out to tear the sketch away.

"Not unless I say so, girl, you don't draw me or anyone else!" Doyle shouted, "Get away from here, confound you … you little witch!"

He crushed the paper, throwing it out into the street under the wheels of the passing wagons.

Kyame quickly closed her drawing box and edged backward from the red-faced man shaking his finger at her. She saw the man Symington come out of the building as the three women walked away, glancing back over their shoulders at her.

Mr. Symington looked worried, Kyame thought.

Doyle walked over to Symington, took his arm and pulled him away. He pointed back at Kyame.

***

Kyame found Papa in their hotel room counting their money. She dropped her drawing box and coat on the bed. He smiled and stretched out his arms to hold her close. He kissed her forehead.

"Just thinking about Mama. I so miss her," he said. He collected the few coins and bills back into a black wallet.

Kyame leaned against Papa's chest. "Why would the Starver kiss a leather bag, Papa?" She told him about her encounter with Doyle and Symington.

"When did she kiss a bag?"

"Mr. Doyle gave it to her. A woman next to me thought the Starver was blessing the bag."

"Did Fancher hold the bag?"

Kyame nodded. "Yes, with both hands."

Piddington leaned back in his chair for a moment, then grinned.

"Out in the daylight, in front of everyone. Brilliant!"

Kyame looked up at Papa, an eyebrow raised.

"That is how they fed her." Papa explained. "There was something in the bag, a tube, that she could slip between her lips just for a moment, then she squeezed the bag to force out a mouthful of soup or soft stew … probably some kind of clear soup so it would look like water, if it dripped on her. They openly gave her small amounts of water. So Doyle is in on the humbug. Symington must be, too. That was why they were there at one in the morning."

A sudden hard knock at the door caused them both to jump.

Kyame opened the door. "Telegrams for Mr. Piddington," a young boy said, holding out two envelopes.

Papa reached over Kyame's shoulder for the telegrams and gave the boy a coin.

Kyame pushed the door closed.

Piddington tore open first one telegram, then the other. "No Starver of any name has been in Oklahoma and no one in the Texas Panhandle has gone through doing that act, but there was a conjuror, the Great Silverman, with a floating woman who also did second sight, but a mail robbery at the Oklahoma City train station caused them to shut down and leave town.

"Kyame, remember, it always pays to have friends at newspapers." He put on his suit coat. "Let's go visit Marshal Toledo."

13

Winlock Toledo sat quietly after Piddington had explained. He looked at Kyame. "Let me see your sketches of Symington ... please."

She opened her drawing box, pulled out a sheet and gave it to him.

After a moment of study, Toledo placed the sheet into the drawer of his desk. "I'd like to keep it for a while, if that is all right."

Kyame nodded.

"I also have contacts in Oklahoma and Texas, Piddington. They confirm what you say. So, just where *did* this Starver come from, and what is this thing all about? I'll buy your explanation of how she did it. Da" -- he looked at Kyame -- "... darn clever!

"I'll buy their getting Arthur Doyle involved. He's been a big loser at cards, last two, three weeks. Probably would do anything to pay off some heavy debts to some mean people.

"Starver act was making good money from all the attention it was getting." The marshal tapped his desk with a pencil. "They put everything into the bank at the end of each day. Bank won't tell me how much without a court order, but every day had to be adding up. So, why would someone kill her and cut off the money flow?"

He looked at John Piddington. "You and the girl do visions too, so you tell me."

"Yes, sir," said Kyame, smiling. "But only under the right conditions, when people are ready."

Looking at his daughter, Piddington smiled. "Marshal, who opened their account at the bank?"

Toledo frowned. "Didn't think to ask. A good question. Let's get it answered."

***

"Arthur Doyle opened the account, Marshal, since he was already a depositor, a respected local citizen. We don't," the bank manager, Eric Dixson, frowned at Papa. "This bank don't accept accounts from traveling show people."

Kyame felt anger start to rise, but Papa's hand touched her shoulder, once, twice, pause, again. Ready.

Piddington asked, "Where were the gifts to the Starver taken?"

"The gifts in kind are given to the churches for dispersal to the poor," said Dixson. "The cash is deposited here in the bank."

Toledo asked, "Why Doyle? What's his connection to the Starver crowd?"

"Said he knew one of the men from Kansas City, a Mr. Symington, and wanted to help the Starver in her difficult and charitable work. Said he would guarantee Mr. Symington's honesty."

Kyame backed slowly away. Papa had signed he wanted her to look at the papers on the bank manager's desk -- to memorize them. One of the clerks held up a piece of hard candy from a jar on his desk. Kyame walked over to take it, nodding her thanks. She unwrapped the chunk of peppermint and put it into her mouth.

As Kyame turned away, the clerk reached out and pulled gently on her skirt, lifting it slightly.

A hard chill went through her heart. She almost forgot to examine Mr. Dixson's desktop as she walked back toward Papa. She wanted to spit out the candy. She had memorized the papers on the clerk's desk as well.

The name Richard Symington had been written across a file.

14

They returned to their hotel room after leaving the bank. Papa had explained she needed a rest and Marshal Toledo had only nodded as he left them.

As they walked, Kyame spit out the candy as soon as she was sure no one was looking. She would never like peppermint again.

With their door closed, Kyame quickly took several sheets of paper from her drawing box and began to sketch out what she had memorized, first on the clerk's desk, then on Dixson's.

Papa watched silently after putting a glass of water on the table next to her. She drew, sipped water, then drew again. Each number, each page, each symbol, each name. After almost half an hour she looked up.

"Finished, Papa."

Papa kissed her on her forehead. "Wonderful, Daughter. Mama would be impressed, as I am."

Kyame recalled Mama laughing so happily when Kyame had corrected her recall of a long series of playing cards. Mama had miscalled two cards out of fifty-two, but Kyame had been perfect. "Wonderful, my dear Kyame," Mama had said, kissing her forehead. "John, she truly has her grandmother's memory." Kyame's eyes misted. That was so many, many months ago.

John Piddington examined the eight pages reproducing the desktops of each of the two bankers, placing the sheets one at a time back on the table.

He stopped.

A partial list of deposits by Symington -- the full list was concealed underneath a letter that Kyame had drawn so vividly that it looked real enough on the page that you could almost push it aside to see under it. The letter was unimportant. But the $6,000 deposit by Symington four days earlier, three days before the Starver was killed, then, $1,400, $1,500, then another of $9,000 the day just before the Starver died. The best daily take for a Starver act that Piddington knew of was $1,100, once in Cincinnati.

Piddington looked up at Kyame, who was watching him intently. He smiled. "We have something, Kyame." He explained

She relaxed, grinned. "Papa, now I'm hungry."

Kyame decided not to say anything about the clerk pulling on her dress. Maybe whatever Papa had seen in her drawings would get that man into trouble. She hoped it would be a lot of trouble.

Papa laughed. "I think we can find something downstairs in the dining room, Daughter."

***

Kyame closed her eyes for a moment, took a deep breath, then opened her eyes wide, letting the whites show around her green pupils.

Marshal Toledo frowned, glanced quickly over at Papa who stood with his back turned at the other side of the Marshal's office.

The two deputies edged back a step.

Kyame raised her hands, extending her fingers, then brought her hands slowly together.

"I see papers with numbers, numbers and more numbers. I see the name on the papers ... Symington, Richard Symington. March 17.

"A large number. $6,000."

"What?" Toledo stood up.

Piddington remained silent, his back to his daughter.

"I see $1,400 on the 18th," Kyame continued, "then $1,500 ... another large number. Eight ... no, nine thousand dollars on the 20th."

"The day before the Starver was poisoned, Marshal," said one of the deputies. "Sir."

"Almost $18,000 in four days? Not possible." Toledo shook his head. "Not enough people in this town going through that store to leave that much cash. They would need a wheelbarrow for that much."

He turned to Piddington, his mouth drawn tight.

"She really can see into the bank? You playing funny games with me, Piddington?"

Papa turned, looked at Kyame, squeezed his right fist, then looked back at the red-faced Toledo.

"If Kyame says she sees it, Marshal, she does. She does not miss."

Kyame was elated. The bitter memory of the clerk faded. Papa had told her many times that it was her acting, her smokey acting that sold The Impossible Piddingtons. Getting and knowing the information was critical, but unless Kyame sold the result, there was no mystery and no income. She could see that the deputies were uneasy, looking at her, even scared. Scaring Abilene -- a good start to her erasing the bitter memory of Basil Craven.

"I go to the judge for a court order saying my evidence is from a girl with second sight, he'll throw me into a padded cell somewhere." Toledo shook his head as he stood, pushing his chair back against the wall. "Have to rob a bank to get that much that quick."

He turned on one of the deputies. "Mack, how much was stolen in that Oklahoma train station mail holdup?"

"I'll check, to be sure, Marshal." The deputy went to a wooden filing cabinet, thumbed through a number of papers. "$29,000, Marshal. Mostly gold."

"There could have been an earlier deposit that Kyame couldn't see, for some reason," suggested Piddington. "She can't always see everything." He jabbed his forefinger at the marshal. "Or ... maybe there is still more to be deposited. Need a strong wagon to carry that much gold."

Kyame sat down next to where Papa stood.

Marshal Toledo remained motionless, his eyes went suddenly wide. "They bring in the gold in the heavy wagon with the Starver's bed, the gold hidden somewhere inside, then transfer the gold each day with the day's contributions to their bank account where it becomes, well, almost legal."

He started to say something, then saw Kyame. "Ah ... darn it! They could then leave town with a bank draft tucked in their pocket for the whole thing and it would look all legal."

"Where is their wagon?" asked Piddington.

Toledo pointed at his deputies. "Find that wagon, boys, and search it for a place to hide a large pile of gold coins."

***

Arthur Doyle sobbed as Marshal Toledo closed the handcuffs on his wrists.

"Had to do it. Had to. No other way to keep my store, pay off my debts. Didn't want any part of any killing," he sobbed. "Only two more days, one more deposit ... and I would have had all I needed. And they would have left town clean with a bank draft. Then that cursed woman demanded a bigger cut for doing her sick act, and Symington ..."

Doyle looked over at Kyame who sat near the marshal's desk. "Mollie said you would be trouble, girl. She saw it in your green eyes ... the eyes of a hawk. Said you don't miss nothing."

The Oklahoma City police had confirmed to Toledo that the Great Silverman had worn a beard while performing in town. The description matched Kyame's drawing of Richard Symington with a beard. The sack of gold coins found hidden in the springs of the Starver wagon by the deputies sat on Toledo's desk.

Piddington asked, "What cut was Fancher taking?"

Doyle looked at Richard Symington grinning at him from behind cell bars. "Ten percent, then she upped it at the last minute to twenty-five. He" -- he pointed at Symington -- "he told her it was okay. They would just take it out of my share. Not fair! They wouldn't have had the bank account without my guarantee."

Symington laughed. "Just look for the biggest chump in debt. Everyone in town told us about the dumb druggist who thought he could play poker with real men. The easiest setup we ever found."

Doyle lunged away from the deputy to throw a lighted lamp at the laughing Symington. The lamp shattered against the iron bars. A deputy quickly threw water on the flames that leapt up.

"Enough!" snapped Winlock Toledo. "Put Doyle in the back cell, Mack."

15

Marshal Toledo walked back to their hotel with the Piddingtons. The grey skies had almost cleared with the low sun creating pleasant warmth. Symington, he explained, had progressively poisoned the Starver with white arsenic in the clear soup he had fed her. She wasn't supposed to have died so quickly. Was supposed to die once they had left Abilene, but her system had been too weakened with the Starver act.

"Doing a show tonight?" Toledo asked as he shook hands with Papa, then tipped his hat to Kyame. "I'm coming. After seeing you in action, Miss Kyame, I want to see the whole show."

Kyame did a small curtsy, then smiled her smokey smile, "Sit up close, Marshal, so you can see everything ... and just maybe I will see something in *your* life."

Toledo stopped, his eyes widened. "I'm not sure just how much I would want you to see ... Miss Piddington. I think the people in Abilene just might get pretty antsy, once they learn more about what you can do."

Scaring the life out of Abilene right down to their shoes -- just what Kyame wanted.

***

Solomon Royale's ragged smile quickly faded when he saw Kyame's disapproval in her eyes. He had come to the train station to congratulate the Piddingtons on their successful run at the meeting house.

Even Basil Craven had been in one of their audiences. Kyame had glowed when she glimpsed his wide eyes and obvious discomfort when she had nailed the number of a folded ten dollar bill that she could not have seen, even without a blindfold. The publicity from Marshal Toledo helped push the audiences to standing along the sides of the meeting house.

Royale had gotten a job at an Abilene newspaper, not much pay but a start on a new life. A few games of pool could fill in the cracks -- but once Kyame saw the gun on his hip her expression had changed to disapproval -- no, more of disappointment.

"There are so many guns, Mr. Royale. Even if God, even if your teaching has failed you, why have you put more death on your hip?"

"I have no adequate answer for you, Miss Kyame. I could plead self-defense, but that would be false. Your condemnation hurts deeply. And," he paused, "and you are right. You are gifted to see more than most, and you see the fraud I still am."

As the conductor signaled all-aboard, John Piddington put out his hand. "Good luck, Royale."

"Come back, Piddingtons, and I will write you up like you have never seen before."

Kyame turned to look back at him from at the top of the steps, the conductor starting to climb up. Her wave was small, but it was her gentle smile that hardened his resolve. It would be a new life, a *complete* new life -- no more frauds, no more easy slippery words -- not anymore.

As he left the station, Solomon Royale unbuckled his pistol belt and dropped it and the gun in a trash barrel. He suddenly felt more alive than he ever had before.

***

At Papa's voice, Kyame looked up from the book Winlock Toledo's wife had given her, Alexandre Dumas' *The Three Musketeers*. The train clattered across switch points, the car swaying as the engine gained speed, gray smoke roiling across her window.

"Kyame, you must be careful," said Papa. "You are starting to show that same strange way that Mama had ... of being a life-shaper, of causing people to change their lives to please you, even if you are not asking them to. I could see that in Royale's eyes. He is still a confused man, seeking his way, his reason for being. You may ... you may have given it to him." Papa hesitated. "But that way can bring terrible responsibility, even if ..." His voice trailed off. Papa smiled. "You become ever more like your mother each day, Daughter."

Kyame felt warm inside. To be compared to Mama. That meant everything. She nodded and turned back to the gallant d'Artagnan.

16

Solomon Royale thought of her eyes. Beautiful green eyes that, as Kyame grew older, could captivate any man she chose. But it was the disappointment so evident in those eyes as the train had drawn away, even a sadness, that continued to haunt him. As though she were searching for someone and, thinking she had found him, yet found him lacking, disappointing, a hollow fraud.

When he had dropped that gun into the trash barrel, Royale had felt his life open up as it had never before -- he smiled, he had even wanted to run back to the tracks to tell her -- but naturally Kyame was already gone.

Without a gun on his hip, Solomon Royale was no longer a focus for manly challenges from drunks with no souls or any further reason for living, except to make it to the next Saturday, to spend their money losing their very being in raw spirits -- "hot as Satan's hoof", as one drunken young banker had quoted Herman Melville before collapsing on his face in the mud.

Royale leaned back in his cane chair in the second floor newspaper office, his weekly column for the Lawrence *Journal* already completed, some drivel about seeking political help at the state house for something that had, to him, suddenly become uninteresting and unimportant. The reporter job in Abilene had lasted a couple of weeks, but he realized he needed a truly fresh start and had taken the train east to Lawrence, took a room at the Eldridge Hotel to start his new life -- again.

He thought about people like the Impossible Piddingtons, traveling through the country making a living by convincing other people that they had a power that others didn't. Their life lived precariously on a fine edge, where, if their methods were exposed, they lost everything. What was it like to bet everything *every day*? Royale shook his head. He couldn't imagine living like that, under that kind of hassle and burden. What would happen to a young girl like Kyame after years of such relentless stress?

Royale stood, stretched his back and looked out the window down on chaotic muddy streets below him. No one down there lived at the edge, unless they were crooked in some way. Why not write about people living at the edge? He nodded.

There was a woman in town, just arrived from Kansas City, Missouri: Madame Pearl Tangley, The Mental Marvel, who claimed to be a seer, to see beyond "the trials of daily life". He would write about her, someone at the edge.

And he would write about belief, why someone could believe in something that, on the face of it, was utterly impossible. Maybe even a book on people at the edge and how others can believe the impossible, believe *in* the impossible, about the men and women who led them to those beliefs -- had   led them to the edge.

Royale grinned. Religion dealt with the impossible, with the eternal unanswerable questions. Was he slipping back?

A thought struck him -- something that the Roman orator, Cicero, had written about belief. He had once had that book in a small bookcase in his bare office at his last church. It had been in Latin, which a deacon of his congregation had thought the preacher would enjoy; though the member didn't understand Latin, she had only recognized the name, Cicero. And the book had been bright red.

He put on his hat. Maybe that new librarian just arrived from Philadelphia could help. Spirits, Royale shook his head, spirits. He wished he could interview the Piddingtons, but Tangley would do for a start.

***

Kyame wasn't sure about spirits, whether they really came back from the dead to pound on a table in the dark, to communicate some silly trite messages as she and Papa had seen in some of the towns and cities in their travels. When Papa and Solomon Royale had talked about spirits and such, the former minister had only mocked the Spiritualist beliefs -- but then he seemed to mock most beliefs, since he had none himself, it seemed, anymore.

A chill ran down her spine as she watched the slim mustached -- and handsome -- young man with a thick mane of black hair, which he would run his hands through at times as though trying to physically pull thoughts from his mind. Were his effects the real thing, really a spirit presence? Kyame knew how to cast the glamorie, to raise a psychic illusion through her smokey acting -- but this?

The young man suggested the effects were real, that they were "experiments in phenomenal psychology that demonstrate the reality of an unexpected human capacity"; but at the same time he claimed that he wasn't a medium for the spirits, just an objective investigator of what might lie beyond normal experience.

He used a word Kyame had never heard before: paranormal. Para, he said in his attractive mellow tenor, in Greek meant 'contrary to', so the region beyond that "enchanted boundary" between the daily experience of here and now, and what might be out there, could be called the paranormal world. The question, The Eternal Question, as the young man styled it, was *where was* that boundary? And -- did it actually run through this room, now, tonight?

His name was Theodore Squires from back East, from New York, his handbills said. He moved gracefully, but then there were times when he hesitated, as if he didn't seem to know where he was, where his next step should be, like someone waking up from a deep dream. Sometimes Squires would just stop, his hand to his forehead, like ...

Kyame knew what that felt like. She would sometimes wake up in the night in a hotel room and could not readily recall just where she was. All the travels of the Impossible Piddingtons -- yet so much of it *was* the same. Papa had warned her against feeling like that about audiences -- they were never the same. It meant trouble if she began to believe they were.

Papa was sitting next to her and was smiling. The Squires lecture on 'The Eternal Question' had been advertised at their hotel with tickets for a dollar. They were stopping in St. Louis for two days waiting for confirmation of bookings in other surrounding towns, possibly as far north as Chicago.

"Is he real, Papa?" Kyame whispered. "He bothers me."

Papa shook his head. "But very convincing, Daughter," he murmured in agreement. "Watch how he lets the audience draw their own conclusions, and not hit them over the head like some of the magicians we've seen trying to work their spook tricks."

"I need a helper, a volunteer, perhaps," Squires said, "perhaps the pretty young woman there in the fourth row would honor me." He bowed to Kyame and beckoned.

Kyame glanced at Papa who nodded.

The audience of thirty-one -- Kyame had developed the habit of counting groups wherever they were. Papa had grinned when she told him. "Counting the house. You are becoming a professional performer, Daughter."

When Kyame stood next to Squires, he asked, "May I ask your name, Miss, so that I may address you properly?"

She smiled. "I am Kyame Piddington, sir."

"I am Ted Squires." He took her hand only after she had first extended hers. "I want to try to touch that boundary again. We have never met before have we?" he asked, then bowed to her. "I know that I could not have forgotten you if we had."

Kyame blushed as some of the women giggled. "Ah, no, Mr. Squires … we have not met before."

Squires picked up a square of paper from the table behind him. "Please write the name of someone that neither I, nor anyone in this room could possibly know. Someone who has affected your life … but unknown to any of us."

"Do I have to like the person?" asked Kyame. The audience broke up laughing. She saw Papa laughing.

Grinning, Squires shook his head. "No, you can hate the person if you wish, Miss Piddington. Here is a pencil." He turned his back.

She wrote the name, Basil Craven.

Turning back, he said, "Please crush the paper into a pellet." Kyame gave Squires the pellet when he put his hand out. "Where do you want this pellet placed … anywhere in the room, preferably in the clear view of the audience."

"On the top of that piano … there, next to the window."

Squires, holding the pellet at the tips of his fingers, placed the pellet at the corner of the piano. "Can everyone see Miss Piddington's paper?" There was a general mumbling of agreement from the audience.

Taking another square of paper from the table, Squires took the pencil back from Kyame. "By the way, have you ever met the person whose name you wrote?"

Looking up into his soulful dark eyes, Kyame nodded. "Yes, I have."

Squires wrote on the other paper, crushed it into a pellet and walked to the end of the front row. "Please hold my paper, sir, if you would." When the spectator took the paper, Squires spread the fingers of both hands, clearly showing that his hands were empty.

Kyame glanced back at Papa. She frowned. What was going on? Papa grinned.

Squires smiled at Kyame. "I am not going to pretend that I read minds or anything like that, Miss Piddington. I don't even know if that is possible. You have written a name, over there" --

he pointed at the piano -- "and I have written a name, over there." He placed his fingers against his forehead for a brief moment; his eyes closed, then looked around at the people.

"I had planned on demonstrating one or two more challenges, but I have grown exhausted from my traveling from the east in the past few days. I arrived late last night. Let me conclude this evening of investigating 'The Eternal Question' with my beautiful volunteer, Miss Piddington."

While Kyame stood, a half-smile across her face, intently watching his every move, Ted Squires walked to the piano, with his fingers wide to show he had nothing in either of his hands, he picked up Kyame's pellet, opened it, paused, then rotated the paper to apparently get Kyame's writing upright. "Basil Craven," he read, raising his voice. "That is the name you wrote a few minutes back, is it not, Miss Piddington?" He wadded the paper and dropped it into his pocket.

Kyame said, "Yes." She brushed away a curl of black hair that had fallen over her right eye. "Yes, it is."

"I am not sure how all this works, ladies and gentlemen, but it often does, and I leave it to everyone here to help me understand." Squires turned to the man at the far end of the front row. "Sir, what name did I write on my paper?"

Squires walked over to stand a few steps from the spectator as the man stood and carefully opened the paper.

"You wrote ... Basil Craven. Mr. Squires! By God, you have!" The man's eyes were wide as he handed the paper back to Squires. "How?" He looked back at the rest of the audience which had gone completely silent. "How?" the spectator repeated, and sat down.

Ted Squires bowed Kyame back to her seat as the now animated audience applauded. He took out a handkerchief to wipe it across his forehead, as he nodded to the audience which was beginning to break up. The room had begun to fill with voices and scraping chairs.

"Papa?"

He helped Kyame into her coat. "A very nice presentation ... with an original style. And no

I don't know how Ted Squires did the duplicated names. Very simple, very effective. Wouldn't mind having that in our repertoire for pressroom demonstrations.

"Wonder," said Papa, "if Squires would consider talking about it ... selling the routine?"

Kyame followed Papa as he walked through the crowd toward Theodore Squires.

***

Pearl Tangley had been a disappointment. As Solomon Royale walked in the light rain back to his room at a boarding house two blocks away, he reflected on their discussion at her room on the third floor at the Eldridge.

He turned the copper token she had given him over and over in his pocket. The token was to be sold for 25¢ at her performances as a good luck piece. It was thin copper, stamped with her name and some odd symbols that had no meaning that he could discern. And, Norman Baker, her short sharp-eyed manager, bearded and bald, had grinned. "The piece sells very well after every performance," he had assured Royale. "Always does to the believers … and, believe me, Royale, everyone in the hall is a believer when Pearl walks off that stage."

Royale abruptly changed directions, and started back down the street on the other side.

Tangley was young, very attractive, dark haired, gentle blue eyes, poised and practiced with a sheen of -- defensiveness about her -- no, it was more rigorous caution as she evaluated him and what he might write. So far, he was just a harmless local reporter, and no further, she seemed to have concluded.

There had been two men in the room when he arrived. One was her manager, and the other an assistant, Jeremy Brin. Brin was closing up a large notebook and left after they had shaken hands. Royale would do some checking on Brin. He looked vaguely familiar.

He didn't really care about how Tangley did her tricks of mind reading; her seership, as she called it. But what connected her to the beliefs of the audience? That was his focus.

He recalled watching the audience one night in Abilene as the blindfolded Kyame Piddington convinced the men and women that she could see what clearly she could not see, by any normal standards. The people sitting around him that night were convinced that the green-eyed girl on the stage was the real thing, a genuinely psychically gifted young woman.

And they had been afraid -- not just scared, but deeply afraid.

Solomon Royale walked faster as the rain strengthened. He laughed at the old barroom question. Do you get wetter running in the rain, or by going slower?

***

A short, but heavily muscled David Ruly held the Tangley token up to a magnifying glass. Ruly and Sons, Co. tool and die makers since 1870, stood just off the far end of Main Street on Oak Avenue. Royale was now wet regardless of how fast he had been moving. Ruly had invited him to stand by the forge to help dry off.

"How much would it cost to make a token like that, Mr. Ruly?" Royale had implied he was interested in doing an article on the Ruly family who had been in Lawrence for three generations. Ruly had immediately smiled. When Ruly held the token up, Royale noted his long graceful fingers, the fingers of a violinist not a machinist or a blacksmith, except for the cracked knuckles on both hands, and one finger that had been badly broken.

"How many you talking, Mr. Royale? This kind of copper, or something of better quality? That would determine the quality of the die setup."

"That copper, and say about 5,000 to 10,000 tokens. That range, anyway."

"You want it in writing, or just a quick estimate?"

"Just a quick estimate, for now."

Ruly beckoned Royale to sit down at his desk. "Tea'll be up in a few minutes. My grandfather came over from Scotland, just north of Edinburgh, so the Ruly family drinks tea, not coffee." He half-smiled. "These queer symbols mean anything? They look like black magic. Had an aunt once who had the second sight. She was from the Highlands out in the hills where the folk have that power sometimes. Didn't do anything for her ... except drive her crazy."

"I don't know their meaning, Mr. Ruly," said Royale, "but I suspect they are only for effect and mean nothing."

Ruly raised a thick eyebrow and shook his head. "Don't you believe that, Mr. Royale. You're asking for trouble if you dismiss the black arts that way, with disrespect.

"So," said Ruly, "the die that made this token is showing some late wear, here you can see how the edges of the letters and symbols are sloping and irregular. Not well defined." He handed the magnifying glass and the token to Royale. "This tool would be good for maybe another thousand or so tokens before the die needs to be refinished, or a new die is used.

"A die for this size, softness and thickness of copper would run about $175 and would punch out about 8,000 tokens before the end products couldn't be used any more. That's probably how many they got out of this die." Ruly turned, glanced over at tall young man carrying a tray with a teapot on it. "Just put it there, Joseph, on the table. And thanks to your Mom." He turned back to Royale. "Piece-part price including set-ups would probably run about a penny, maybe a little less if you did the whole eight thousand at one time." He handed the token back to Royale. "That what you need?"

Royale sucked in his breath. He quickly worked the math. Selling eight thousand tokens at 25¢, as Tangley apparently had done, would generate: $1,920 in net profit! That was nearly four years salary for him at the paper -- off of a fake good luck piece! No wonder Norman Baker had been so relaxed. Tokens, tickets and maybe some expensive private readings -- income from the Tangley operation could be substantial, very substantial. Beyond anything that Solomon Royale had ever dreamed possible -- short of robbing a bank.

"Yes, Mr. Ruly," he said, accepting a steaming cup of tea, "that is what I need."

***

"Your offer is very generous, Mr. Piddington, and of course, I have heard of the Impossible Piddingtons." Ted Squires smiled, nodding to Kyame. "But I must decline your offer."

All of the audience had finally left. Several of the women had lingered to ask questions of the "strange and so handsome Mr. Squires" as Kyame had overheard him described. Once the room was completely clear, the three of them had walked to a quiet corner of the hotel bar.

Kyame drank a cup of tea as Papa and Squires drank mugs of beer -- and listened.

"I understand, Squires. Would you object if Kyame presented the same duplicated name effect using her own method?"

Ted Squires looked at the steel-green eyes of the beautiful young woman sitting next to him. "If Miss Kyame, with her presence, were to perform the effect as well as I suspect she could ... using whatever method ... she would make believers out of everyone in the audience ... including me."

Kyame blushed and smiled. "Thank you, sir. That is most generous."

Squires raised his mug in salute. "Yes, Mr. Piddington, you are free to use the effect with your own method ... so long as we are not in the same town at the same time."

"Of course, that condition is understood." John Piddington put out his hand. When Squires took it, Kyame placed her hand on top of the men's hands to signify her agreement as well. Squires' hand was sweaty, his dark eyes drifting as in struggling with some suddenly tenuous thought. Kyame wondered if she would ever see Ted Squires again.

But, how to do the Squires effect that seemed to her to be an absolutely genuine demonstration of -- the paranormal, whatever that was. How?[1]

---

[1] See John Piddington's notes in the Appendix.

17

"Your mind is capable of astonishing feats, even without considering telepathy or second sight," said John Piddington to the group surrounding him, tapping on the table for emphasis. "Your greatest power lies in your memory ... if your memory is properly and carefully trained and disciplined. In a moment, I am going give you a simple demonstration of what a disciplined memory can do.

"Naturally," he said, bowing his head toward the three women seated at the table across from him, their faces expressionless, "I don't mean to suggest, ladies, that playing cards are necessary to learn the amazing secrets of Mnemosyne, the ancient Greek Goddess of Memory. They are simply a convenient means of demonstration."

Piddington breathed easier when two of the bonneted women acknowledged his subtle apology with a small nod. The small smile of the third woman in a red bonnet was challenging and mischievous.

The three women were the key, as wives of prominent citizens of Coffeyville, Kansas, talkative citizens, hopefully, of the beneficial power of a well-trained memory. Their instruction would be free.

The men would follow the women into the course, if it appeared socially safe. One of the men, identified as Frank Olsen by the desk clerk, was a reporter for the Coffeyville *Journal*, while three of the men standing in the group had not been recognized as locals by the desk clerk. Just commercial travelers, he thought.

At the bottom of the yellow Impossible Piddingtons handbills, pasted up around the town by hired boys, listed below the announcements of their performances at the Music Hall and the memory course, was the promise that, along with learning to memorize greater portions of the Bible, lists of market goods, favorite poems, etc., John Piddington would also teach how to quickly memorize a deck of playing cards to facilitate the "enjoyment of family games". Most men would understand which family games the handout was referring to.

Piddington glanced over at Kyame, who hovered innocently at the edge of the group surrounding him at the table. Dressed in an almost new dress of pink and green, she walked, apparently aimlessly, around the group and then toward the registration desk and back. Piddington could see her lively green eyes scrutinize each of the nine men and women surrounding him, pillars of the community, of -- Piddington had to pause a brief moment to recall just where they were this week.

The various towns in the travels of The Impossible Piddingtons through the West could begin to all look and smell the same as they moved ever Westward, following the flow of people toward the Pacific Coast, the flow of the money. But it was critical that the audiences did not look the same from the stage. That would invite carelessness and guarantee trouble for their second sight act.

Coffeyville, Kansas, close on the Oklahoma border, was growing with sawmills and a brick-making plant; and the livestock auction next week would draw more activity -- and cash.

Piddington smiled and would have laughed at the absurdity of his forgetfulness, since he was in the process of demonstrating the power of the trained memory, but took a swallow of coffee instead from the cup at his elbow. Kyame would enjoy hearing about his lapse later when they could laugh.

John Piddington was demonstrating his memory in order to sell the idea that some of those at the table and their friends should sign on for the course of five lessons of memory training for ten dollars that Piddington was advertising as a complement to their second sight performances at seven o'clock at the Music Hall each evening for the next week.

They needed the extra money to save for Kyame's art school. Audiences had been thin in Kansas City as the Pearl Tangley, The Mental Marvel, troupe had soaked up most of the town money only a few weeks before. He could only add $20 to their savings after five days work in KC. It wouldn't be fair to Kyame to ...

His memory demonstration this morning would be faked[2], this time; though Kyame's

---

[2] See Appendix for John Piddington's notes on fake memory demonstrations.

memory feats were always genuine, a stunning power she had inherited from her late mother and grandmother.

But this was his sell, not hers.

The struggling fireplace at the far wall of the lobby hardly touched the chill of the early spring air. It burned only wood, not coal, so the chill was going to stay. And each time the main double doors of the Grand Hotel opened, a draft swept across the lobby, even to the corner where Piddington was shuffling a deck of hotel-labeled cards, displacing whatever heat had formed.

***

Kyame knew that after their first performance tonight, the town mothers would not let her play with their children. They would look with hostile suspicion on the psychic theatre girl. *Only an untrustworthy theatre girl,* they would whisper together behind their hands as Kyame would walk by. She had heard those whispers before in other towns. It had always hurt, but now it seemed to hurt more. She would glance into windows of houses as she walked by on her way to the theater or hall for the night's performance to

111

see families gathered around a table at dinner. Kyame wondered what that kind of life would be like. She smiled slowly. Probably pretty dull.

Maybe.

Papa understood, as she understood Papa's effort to raise the money for her Boston school -- though the thought of separating from Papa always hurt. She wondered if she could actually do it. Papa had said he would go back into banking where he had been when he and Mama, and her, had first gone on the road as The Impossible Piddingtons. But that was over three years ago and Mama was gone now.

Kyame walked toward three men speaking together near the registration desk, to listen without appearing to. She would then circle back to signal Papa whatever details he might be able to use.

***

Jim Hardesty, a lawyer in a black suit with a green satin vest and black boots, leaned over to spit a blob of tobacco juice into the brass spittoon near the registration desk. He noted the black-haired girl in pink walking around the lobby, now approaching the desk for the second time.

Had never seen her before. Tall for her age, maybe thirteen, fourteen or so, and very pretty -- and trying to look only curious, but really observing everything closely with her keen eyes. Her poise was almost like a grown woman in the body of a girl. Odd. His own daughter of similar age could never reflect that maturity.

He turned back to the other two men.

"Naw, Juice, no Indians are going to go on any warpath," Luke Neel was saying, "but if they do, I hope they run through the Capital in Washington. Maybe scalp a few Congressmen, the way those crooks are stealing out of our pockets, destroying the economy, like that cussed Senator standing over there in that group in the corner." He squinted. "What they doing over there, anyway?"

"What Senator, Luke?" Hardesty turned to look.

"Albright, Fred Albright, there, in the grey derby. He's up for re-election over in Missouri this year. Been promising the moon to anyone who will listen … but Kansas City papers are sayin' he may be indicted for embezzling from some land company.

"What about it, Macallen?" said Neel, turning to the short man at his side, who was just turning back from the spittoon. "You're a local cop."

Deputy Marshal Juice Macallen shook his head. "Not talkin', Luke Neel, not about no U. S. Senator. Say the wrong thing and I'm out a job and a reputation. He's not in my jurisdiction anyway.

"But, if he were runnin' in Kansas?" Macallen shook his head again and leaned toward the spittoon. "I wouldn't vote for'm." Relieved, Macallen said, "Let's get a beer, gents. I have honest work to do, even if you two lawyers don't."

Hardesty watched the green-eyed girl walk back toward the crowd in the corner. He turned when Macallen took his arm.

"Comin', Jim?"

The lawyer watched the girl stop for a moment, then just sort of fuss around. He shrugged, following Macallen toward the barroom. Something about that girl.

"Yes, Juice, a beer would help wipe away some of the politics for a while."

***

Kyame walked briskly back toward Papa. When she caught his eye as she approached the group, she touched her chin, their agreed ready signal for today.

Kyame slowed her step, casually brushing her short girlish skirts aside with her right hand while looking to the left. *grey -- derby.* She smiled, brushing her fingers across her nose, then back against her ear. The signal for the number 130 in their memorized list of objects. *U. S. Senator.* Kyame turned sharply, her skirt flaring out. She looked down. Number 24. *Missouri.* She coughed into her raised hand, looking up to the right. *thief.* Then she added, compressing her lips. *maybe.*

As she touched her chin, to signal *finished,* Kyame glimpsed a man seated across the lobby watching her intently through black-rimmed glasses. He had a satisfied smirk on his face, as he pulled a notebook from his suit-coat pocket and began to scribble rapidly.

Kyame felt a stab of dread down her back.

John Piddington saw the look of concern on Kyame's face, but had to focus on the people in front of him. The Senator from Missouri stood to his right. Thief?

He accepted the shuffled deck back from Jack Olsen on his left. "Thank you, sir," said Piddington. "Now if you will give me a few seconds to memorize the deck, the exact position of all 53 cards in the deck." He flipped slowly through the deck as though noting each card, actually remembering only the top card, the Jack of Diamonds.

"Now, Ma'am, would you cut the deck and place the top portion in front of you."

The red-bonneted woman complied; her dark eyes alight with interest. "I am Mrs. Janet Macallen, Mr. Piddington. But shouldn't you already know that? Reading my mind, or something?"

"Thank you, Mrs. Macallen. I never mention a woman's name unless she honors me with it first."

Janet Macallen tilted her head with a raised eyebrow. "Very neat response, sir. Better than the last mindreader that came through here a couple of months back. Claimed he was a Hindoo from Tibet, but he sounded Brooklyn to me. And there aren't any Hindoo's in Tibet, anyway."

Piddington laughed with everyone else. He knew who she meant, Simeon the Great -- and he was from Brooklyn. Joe Schwartz. Simeon was a competent performer but he tended to believe that everyone in a small town was dumb and easily fooled. Many magicians and mind readers frequently didn't allow for the intelligence of their audiences. A mistake the Impossible Piddingtons would never make.

"My daughter and I are from Ohio, Mrs. Macallen, which can be a mystical place, but no mountains."

Janet Macallen bent her head in acknowledgement. "Nice." She put out her hand to indicate he should continue. "My apologies, Mr.

Piddington, for intruding in your fascinating demonstration."

Barely lifting a corner, Piddington glimpsed the top card of his portion. He focused his eyes on the pile in front of him. After a few seconds, he said, "From the card I noted and estimating the number of cards in front of me," -- he paused --"I believe your card is the Jack of Diamonds."

The group gasped as the eyes of Janet Macallen widened. She turned over the Jack of Diamonds.

Piddington repeated with another card with another woman cutting the deck. It was the Ace of Spades. Next time would be different.

When Piddington said Six of Clubs, the woman turned over a King of Hearts.

"My mistake, Ma'am, I missed my estimate by one card. The next card down is the Six."

When the Six of Clubs appeared the group broke into applause, to which John Piddington bowed his head. He collected the cards and pushed them to one side. Time for the sell as the applause drew more people from other parts of the lobby.

He caught Kyame's signs. *red-bonnet wife Deputy Marshal.* Then he saw the man with black horn-rimmed glasses say something to her and walk out the double doors. Piddington could easily see his daughter's quick temper flaring.

***

"I have you, young lady. You won't be such a smart-alecky girl when I get through," he had growled to Kyame as he passed.

She clenched her fists, infuriated by the man's supercilious sneer, but turned away as Papa would want, squelching her steaming anger.

Kyame prayed the man would break both his legs going down the steps outside; she would have liked to help God along by giving the miserable man a little push. Solomon Royale would have laughed at her theology. They had encountered him briefly at Lawrence just before they had caught the train for Coffeyville. Kyame had been glad to see that he no longer wore a gun and was doing well at the Lawrence newspaper.

"I'd write up the Impossible Piddingtons like you were the Second Coming," Royale had laughed up to them as their train pulled away.

Turning back, Kyame saw Papa look concerned. She smiled to reassure him. He was too busy for her to burden him.

She turned to walk to the bellboy. His drooping leather name tag said, Johnny. Cultivate the invisible people, Papa had instructed her, they see everything.

"Johnny, hello," she smiled. "Could you tell me who that was in the black glasses? He isn't nice." Kyame could see the boy's eyes light up as she approached.

He would be an easy read. She had seen that light in other boys' eyes.

"Why that's old William Brockway, the editor and owner of the *Journal,* Miss. He doesn't like mind readers or spirit mediums. Thinks they're all crooks and evil as sin. Ran the last mindreader out of town, exposed everything that Hindoo could do." He laughed at his rhyme. "One of his reporters is over in that group in the corner."

Kyame made a small curtsy. "My thanks, Johnny."

She walked back toward Papa who was shaking hands with the men as the group was breaking up. The Macallen woman was lingering behind and Papa clearly enjoyed her company which made Kyame uneasy

18

"I believe that quotation you are looking for, Mr. Royale, is from *De Divinatione,* Cicero, 45 B.C." The librarian, Patricia Reese, then read the quotation on the first page: "Now I am aware of no people, however refined and learned or however savage and ignorant, which does not think that signs are given of future events, and that certain persons can recognize those signs and foretell events before they occur."

"That's it, Miss Reese," said Royale. She was an attractive blond-haired tall woman with questioning eyes. He had been impressed the moment he had walked into the library.

"And Cicero also points out, sir, that: 'A really splendid and helpful thing it is -- if only such a faculty exists -- since by its means men may approach very near the power of gods.'" She smiled wistfully. "The power of gods ... how many lives have been lost because someone thought they had found just that?" She pushed the book across the counter. "Do you wish to borrow the book, Mr. Royale?

"We both know, I believe," she said, "that Cicero actually didn't say all that. In his dialogue in the first part, he has Quintus, his brother, say all those things in support of divination; while Cicero himself, in the second part of the book, thought such arcane arts were really garbage ... or pretty close anyway." She smiled, laughing. "Though it all does sound more authoritative in Latin, doesn't it."

Solomon Royale grinned. "Yes, I would like to take the book out ... and you, Miss Reese, to lunch at the Eldridge. For more Latin translation ... naturally."

Suddenly, beliefs and mind readers didn't seem so immediately important, but pleasing this one woman did.

***

"What in hell is this, Royale?" Norman Baker angrily demanded, throwing the folded newspaper on the desk. "Why are you trying to queer our spiel? We don't hurt no person. We give'm a good time." Baker paced up and down in front of him. Then he turned, leaned over the desk and shook his finger at Royale. "By God, I'll see

that you pay for this -- and pay good and solid."
Baker turned and stomped out of the news room.

The other reporters were grinning.

The profits from the lucky pieces, with David Ruly quoted as the authority, were revealed in Royale's front page article, "Pennies from the Spirits". He added in the dream books and the ticket sales to give an estimated total of what The Mental Marvel could clear in a week. "I don't care what trickery Tangley may use," he had written, "or if she is actually genuine. But why should someone telling fortunes make more money in a week than most of us can in six months?" There were some valid positive answers to that question, but they were beside the point he wanted to make.

He had thought first he would write up the Tangley operation in a positive mode, after all no one was getting defrauded or hurt -- but then after the two hour lunch with Patty Reese, he knew he couldn't. She had no tolerance for any chicanery, even in the name of entertainment. He just couldn't let Baker and his crew squeeze innocent people.

But, was he wrong? He watched Baker slam the door and briefly relished the small cheer that went up from the others; but suddenly he had a dark feeling. Queering Tangley, and others like her -- would that include the Piddingtons? -- where could that lead?

Solomon Royale went for a walk in the rain.

19

Returning to their room, Kyame was delighted with Papa's happy eagerness.

"Signed up two of the men and, of course, the three women," said Papa. "Mrs. Macallen is going to suggest her husband attend as well. A trained memory is good for a policeman."

Kyame quickly explained about William Brockway and his threat.

Papa nodded as he dropped his suit coat over a chair. "You did right not to respond. Brockway won't do anything until after our show tonight … sort of give us the rope to hang ourselves.

"Exposers can be useful, Daughter, handled properly. Remember that magician in Topeka who tried to ruin our act … and made a fool of himself trying?"

He explained the Brockway exposure of Simeon the Great.

"Simeon's methods were crude, straight out of a magic dealer's catalog. His act has been exposed before, on the West Coast somewhere."

He stretched his arms and yawned. "Been a busy morning. Let's get some rest and some lunch.

***

The rattle of chairs and the rising bustle of excited voices from the Music Hall became clearer through the walls as Kyame sat with Papa back stage to review the town information he had "dredged up" in their previous two days in Coffeyville. Kyame liked the expression and always smiled when Papa used it.

It sounded so happily illegal.

"We must be careful with Marshal Macallen, Daughter," said Papa, sorting through his notes. "He may react too strongly to everyone hearing of his brother's arrest in Wichita for robbery. I may use that only if we need a punch to close strong … but there is enough here for tonight and tomorrow without it."

"The cattle buyer, Mr. Welsh, knows Mr. Vicks the jewelry salesman, Papa," said Kyame. "Why do they act like they don't?"

Papa looked up from the notes, an eyebrow raised. "How do you know that, Daughter?"

"Welsh made a secret nod to Vicks after Welsh had been in to talk with the hotel manager. I saw it."

"A secret nod?"

"Like you do, Papa, when you shift the signaling to the backup numbers."

Papa laughed. "Kyame, your powers of perception are becoming extraordinary. But, no, I don't know why they would conceal their association" -- he paused -- "unless ... unless they are hotel thieves. Hotel thieves generally work in pairs; and with the regional livestock auction coming next week, there will be a lot of cash floating around. And Welsh and Vicks may not be the only thieves coming to town." He looked over at the glistening sea-green eyes of his daughter. "Do you know their room numbers?"

"309 and 308. They checked in two days apart."

Papa grinned at her. "You memorized the registration book?"

Kyame nodded as she wiped her nose with a handkerchief.

"Only took a couple of seconds, Papa."

John Piddington stood up, shrugged, touched his belt and turned toward the stage. *Ready?* he signed. I-love-you-daughter.

Kyame laughed. I-love-you-Papa, she signed in response.

After their show, John Piddington decided they would inspect the doors of the rooms on the third floor. If Welsh and Vicks were hotel thieves, then there should be some evidence. They could use that information to spice up their show tomorrow night.

But now for tonight.

20

As they climbed the stairs to the third floor of the Grand Hotel, Kyame asked, "Why would they steal on their own floor? Wouldn't they want to steal as far away as possible?"

Their evening show had been satisfactory with the Music Hall almost filled with an active responsive audience. Walking on stage, Kyame had searched immediately for William Brockway. She located him sitting at the end of the fourth row on her left. Papa promised that the editor was one of the people who would be touched tonight by the Impossible Piddingtons.

When Kyame, following Papa's signing, began to explain how Brockway had cheated a brother-in-law out of a piece of family land, the editor had gone pale, slapped his notebook shut and stormed out of the hall to the raucous laughter of the audience. That was the most fun of the night.

Almost as good as pushing Brockway down the steps.

"Because, Daughter," Papa was explaining, "with the regional livestock auction next week, the hotel is adding more guards and house detectives for each of the floors. If the thieves steal on another floor, the guards would see them going from floor to floor which could queer their setup. Stealing on their own floor means the guards at the landings would see nothing."

Papa had brought a small oil lamp with him that he now lighted as they started down the third floor. There had not been a guard placed on the third floor landing yet. Kyame had reviewed the registration book in her mind to determine which rooms were empty as of the late morning. Papa was interested only in empty rooms. There were five empty rooms on the floor, 301, 304, 305, 307 and 310. There was no 306, as that room was being used as a storage space.

Piddington knelt at the door to 301. He held the lamp close to the lock and doorknob. After a moment of examination, he said, "Here, Kyame, look closely. There, just above the lock."

Kyame could see what looked like a small hole in the door filled with a white paste or putty, almost invisible against the white door. "What is it, Papa?"

"I'll explain later, but that is evidence that the two men are professional hotel thieves. Let's check the other empty rooms, then go back to our room upstairs."

All the empty rooms except 310 had the same small hole filled in with putty.

***

They sat at the table in their room, Kyame holding a glass of water. Taking two sheets of her drawing paper, Piddington drew the cross-section of a door, sketching in the lock and the inside bolt.

"First, Kyame, they open the door using a bar-key, which looks something like this." He drew the outline of a key, but without the flag-like bits at the end that actually operate the levers of the lock. Then he drew four shapes of lock bits. "Since the rooms are empty, the door is only locked, if it is, from the outside. By fitting the various lock-bits into the bar-key, the thieves will find the bit that will later open the lock."

"They make their own key to the door?" It had never occurred to Kyame that someone could do that.

"Yes, exactly. And since hotels tend to use the same style of keys and bolts in all their rooms, once the thieves know one, they know them all.

"So," he said. "They go in … one stands lookout, while the other looks over the bolt and lock setup. Once they know how the doors are secured, the thief drills a small hole through the door above the level of the bolt to allow a thin rod with a movable piece at the end ... like this. They call it faking a room."

Piddington drew a small circle, then a long line with a short line attached at the end.

"This short piece of rod is loosely secured by a screw to the end of the long rod. It can be bent at an angle at the end and a string is attached to the tip of the short end. So, the door is closed locked and bolted on the inside. The rod is pushed through the drilled hole, then the string is pulled to draw down the short piece at the end to make an L-shape. And, holding the string taut and using the loop here at the end of the rod for leverage, the thief just rotates the rod which catches and throws back the inside bolt. He pulls out the rod, then picks the door lock with the bar-key and the right bits. Everything takes only a few seconds.

"The thief enters and in five minutes quietly goes through the room and the luggage, even under the pillow; then re-locks and bolts the door when he leaves. He refills the open hole with the putty again.

"The thief who goes into the room only wears wool clothing because linen or starched cotton can make too much noise in the room, especially if they are robbing a woman.

"That's how they do it." He looked up at Kyame's inquisitive eyes.

"I understand." she said. "That could panic the victim since there would be no easy explanation of how he could have been robbed when the doors and windows were still locked from the inside." She looked up at Papa. "That would take a lot of nerve to do. Do they risk robbing more than one room a night?"

"Yes," said Piddington, "they will hit as many as three or four rooms in a single evening if the opportunities are there. But, you are right, at that point the operation becomes a serious risk."

Piddington wadded up the papers and threw them into a wastebasket. "The thieves take turns in the lobby or the dining room," he said, "to watch the travelers who check in after them in order to select the most prosperous on their floor and pick them clean. The thieves return separately to their own rooms on the same floor without anyone, including the guards, seeing or hearing them.

"So, Daughter," Piddington said, "I was looking for the small hole, the gimlet hole they drill. Now we know they are here."

"But how do *you* know all this, Papa?" Kyame's voice was strained with concern.

John Piddington reached out to hold his daughter in his arms.

"When we still lived back in Warren, Ohio, and you were only about eight or nine," he said, "before we left to go on stage, a Pinkerton operative, Kate Wayne, from Chicago visited the bank where I worked. Miss Wayne was looking for information on a series of bank robberies.

"Over lunch, Miss Wayne told me all about her adventures trapping hotel thieves because they never suspected a woman operative. She gave me a quick education in how to rob hotels."

Kyame laughed, laying her head on Papa's chest. "Now you've educated me, too."

***

John Vicks looked over the dingy alley. The hour was early, the sun barely up. The alleyway stood empty and silent but for a few birds. There were no windows opening onto where he stood. But they had to be quick.

Their connection would be only a two-three minute period to establish when and which room, after which they wouldn't be within fifty feet of each other until they lifted the patients, the victims, in the selected rooms. They would split the money in his room and check out separately a day apart to meet later in Kansas City.

Desperately sucking in air, Alexander Welsh suddenly rounded the corner, his flaccid face moist with sweat. He brushed his thinning grey hair back and adjusted his rimless spectacles.

After two deep breaths, he looked up at Vicks. "Tied up with Marshal Macallen for breakfast, for God's sake, of all people," said Welsh. "Had to finally cut him short. Kept asking me about livestock auctions, what happens, how the money flows. I'm supposed to be a cattle buyer … but what do I know about auctions?"

Welsh's tardiness only added to Vicks' growing uneasiness about his partner of two years. There had to be total trust, or there would be real trouble. Welsh was his lookout, the man who guarded his back. Vicks was the shadowy thief in the room.

"Fine. That's all we need," Vicks snapped. "Now … I see 305 and 304, the doctor from St. Louis and the lawyer from Chicago. Both are early sleepers with large rolls."

"Agreed," nodded Welsh. He wiped his face with the sleeve of his coat. "The hotel will be putting guards on the landings in two days, according to the hotel manager." His breathing was returning to normal. He brushed at his dusty trousers.

"We need to move before then," said Vicks. "I saw Sour Jack Bidwell going into Isham's hardware store next to the First National Bank just before dinner last night. We need to score before Bidwell and Henry Gadsby connect to make their move. Could seriously mess up everything if we get in each other's way. Queer everything."

"That Juice Macallen is no fool, Vicks. He told me there was even a Pinkerton operative in town only last week." Welsh shook his head. "God knows how many thieves and such will be drawn by that auction next week … and we don't want to get caught in that net."

"Nine, then? 305." Welsh turned to go.

"Nine, tonight. 305."

21

"Thought I would deliver this myself, Piddington," sneered William Brockway in a loud voice. He threw the morning *Journal* in front of John Piddington, scattering his breakfast over the table. "Had a belly full of you two last night and this challenge will take care of you." He pounded on the table with his fist. "If I don't get an answer by noon, I'll publish so many of your tricks you couldn't get an audience anywhere north of the equator."

He turned, glowered darkly at the waiter who stood in his way. The waiter immediately stepped aside as Brockway strode loudly away with all the eyes in the dining room on him.

"Fake Mind Readers! The Impossible Piddingtons Challenged!" shouted from the top of the paper. Kyame watched Papa read for few moments, then he looked up, smiling.

"Perfect, Daughter. Brockway is using the wrong explanations for how we do it. Probably got his information from reading that short book by Washington Irving Bishop that's been out for three or four years."

"What is his challenge, Papa?" Kyame didn't like the sound of any of it.

"Brockway declares in capital letters that we can only 'communicate' when we can physically see each other; then he gives the stuff from Bishop including something on fake blindfolds," said Papa. "His challenge, therefore, is for me to be locked in a safe in the lobby of the C. M. Condon & Co. bank while you are out of the room. I am not to be given the safe combination until after you are led from the room and cannot see or hear me. Once you are gone, the bankers demonstrate what the combination is and that the lock is operable. I would be locked in and then you would be brought back to open the lock based on reading my mind.

"I would have three minutes of air before suffocation."

"Papa!"

People at the other tables immediately stopped talking to look over at them.

"Let's go to our room. I'll explain. It will depend on your memory, dear Kyame ... on the ghost of Mnemosyne."

140

The lobby of the C. M. Condon bank was jammed to capacity while the windows on all three sides of the bank were filled with faces smudged against the glass. The outside plaza formed by the triangular junction of Union and Walnut Streets was filling as well, stopping all downtown traffic.

Standing against the polished bank counter was a black Herring, Hall & Marvin burglarproof safe with a flapping American flag outlined in gold against a blue sky painted across the steel door. It stood about four-feet tall and three-feet wide on large wide wheels.

"A death trap." Kyame heard someone say. "Can't believe they're doin' it. The Piddingtons only do an act, for God's sake … shouldn't have to be life and death."

"Yes," a woman said, "that poor girl must tearing herself up inside. Our Sarah could never stand this strain."

Kyame wasn't sure she could either, but Papa had explained very carefully. She knew she could do it -- if, if she didn't lose her nerve.

Brockway had agreed to open the safe, one way or the other after four minutes; until Janet Macallen looked like she could kill him. He changed it to three minutes and thirty seconds.

Brockway raised his hands to quiet the thick assembled audience jostling and elbowing for a view of the safe.

"Here is what will happen," declared the editor. "Deputy Marshal Macallen will escort the Piddington girl out of the lobby to Mr. Condon's private office and close the door ... and will remain with her until she is called.

"Further, I will blindfold the girl to ensure that only the two minds of the so-called Impossible Piddingtons can be used ... and I know fake blindfolds, wrote about them this morning in the Coffeyville *Journal*."

Piddington stopped as he was removing his suit coat. "Wait a minute, Brockway," said John Piddington, raising his hand. "There is nothing in your public challenge about blindfolding my daughter. All she will be able to see is the safe anyway."

Several women raised their voices in protest to complain about harming the girl, but then Kyame stepped up to confront the editor and said in a soft voice that carried throughout the lobby.

"Blindfold me, Mr. Brockway, anyway *you want,*" she snarled. "I challenge you. And," she spoke louder, her hands on her hips, "you haven't said, publicly, what you will do when Papa and I defeat your silly challenge."

Papa had instructed her to ask that when she had the chance. It would make Brockway look smaller to the people if Kyame challenged the editor rather than him. Kyame loved that idea -- but not much of the rest.

Immediately, the collected group began to demand Brockway's payoff if he lost.

Now John Piddington stepped forward, his suit coat thrown over one shoulder. "Here is what William Brockway will do when he loses. If he doesn't, he should be forced to leave Coffeyville. This city has no room for cheats and swindlers."

Loud cheers went up from the crowd.

"Brockway will print his apology on the front page of the *Journal* in the same size typeface as he used for his challenge this morning and say 'I was wrong!'. He will, as well, publish each day, at no cost, so long as the Impossible Piddingtons are in Coffeyville, a full-page advertisement for us in which he will repeat his apology." Piddington turned on the editor. "Agreed, Mr. Brockway?"

Brockway's face sagged and didn't answer.

"Hey, Brockway, you quittin' already?" shouted a man that Kyame recognized as the thief, Vicks. Strange he would be here.

"No!" Brockway roared. He pointed at Papa. "I will print the Impossible Piddingtons, *even if* it is only *his* obituary!" He turned to Macallen. "Hold the girl, Marshal, while I apply her blindfold."

Good job, Daughter, Papa signed, squeezing his right fist.

Kyame pursed her lips, took a breath, and said," Yes, Mr. Brockway, time to stop *your* talking and stalling."

"What pluck, that girl!"

144

"More grit than that ink-blotched editor!"

Brockway took out a silver half-dollar, placed it against Kyame's right eye and taped it in place with surgical tape, the tape running vertically down her face. He did the same with the left eye, then placed two strips of wide adhesive tape across her taped eyes.

"My God, Brockway. That is cruel!" Kyame heard Mrs. Macallen protest.

"It is the challenge," Brockway insisted.

Kyame felt the Marshal's hand on her shoulder. "Let's go, young woman. You've got more guts than any man here."

She relaxed her intense frown and raised her eyebrows as high as she could. The tape stretched, then loosened, opening a clear view down the sides of her nose and under the coins to about two feet around. The radius that they had assumed in their practice.

That was the easy part.

Kyame closed her eyes so she could stumble convincingly. Papa always warned her that persuasive mistakes are difficult to fake.

***

Seeing Kyame disappear through the door, John Piddington turned to C. M. Condon, the bank's senior partner. "Show me the safe, sir," he said.

Condon, tall, white-haired with a bemused expression across his full clean-shaven face, with large wispy side-burns that haloed his features, nodded, and stepped to the safe. "Strangest thing I have ever been involved with." He pulled the door of the safe open. "Three minutes maximum of breathable air, Mr. Piddington. I pray you and your remarkable daughter know what you are doing."

"Mr. Condon," said Piddington, his voice carrying throughout the crowd. "I publicly absolve you personally and your bank of any liability for might occur here this afternoon."

"Thank you, sir. That is most gentlemanly. Now, here is the combination." Condon knelt down and twirled the dial to the right, then stopped it at 6; two turns to the left, stop at 36; one turn to the right, stopping at 43, and finally one turn back to 6. He pulled the handle of the safe. The locking cylinders retracted smoothly to allow the safe door to open.

Condon rose and stepped back to allow Piddington to confirm the combination and the door operation himself.

"I have it, Mr. Condon," he said. "Thank you."

"You may not write anything, Piddington," said Brockway from behind him. "Use only your memory ... about which you claim so much knowledge."

"Not necessary, Brockway. Ladies and gentlemen, please give me a moment or two. I need to concentrate, to be able to reach out to my daughter behind those doors and walls."

John Piddington began to walk about the limited open space in the lobby, stopping, frowning, then walking a few steps, stopping again. He stood with his eyes closed. The bank lobby was silent. Even the crowds outside had gone quiet. Piddington looked up, grimaced, then walked back toward the safe.

"Mr. Condon, I want my daughter brought back the instant that door is closed on me."

"I will see to it myself, Mr. Piddington." Condon extended his hand. "Even if old Brockway over there won't, may I wish you and you daughter the best of luck." The audience responded with enthusiastic applause.

William Brockway stood glowering at Piddington.

John Vicks stood, disbelieving, and queasy. Genuine mindreaders were not good for his business.

Piddington removed his tie and collar and left them on top of the safe. He squeezed himself down inside the safe, shifting his shoulders to relieve a cramp and to allow easier breathing with his legs pressed up against his chest. He took one deep breath, then a second, then, "Close!"

Condon pushed the door shut, twisted the large polished handle, and spun the dial.

"Mr. Piddington is entombed in the safe!" Condon announced.

Only whispered quiet prayers broke the stillness. A horse neighing in the street sounded like thunder.

***

Marshal Macallen, with C. M. Condon beside him, led Kyame to the front of the safe. The two men stood back. "The safe is two feet in front of you, Miss Piddington," said the Marshal. "You have two minutes and fifty-five seconds. I will announce the time at thirty-second intervals."

"Thank you, Marshal, for your kindness," Kyame said.

The first number was six. That had been easy. Their plan was that Papa would leave clues around the lobby in a sequence that she would follow, while looking down her nose.

She turned away, raising her hands, palms toward her, as she bowed her head. Kyame walked slowly, then turned and stopped. She compared what she could see with what she had memorized when they had first entered the lobby. Whatever was different was the signal, part of their regular number code system.

Thirty-seven. The chair had been moved and rotated. She could see the legs.

The crowd was murmuring, with others shushing them, pleading to give the girl a chance.

She ran her hand along the railing around the desks. Nothing had changed! A stab of fear went through her. This was where the third number was supposed to be!

Kyame continued. Brockway may have guessed the plan and had tried to interfere with the signals. Papa would leave two signals for each number, in case she missed one. She leaned against the railing.

"Two minutes and thirty seconds, Miss Piddington."

She took a breath, pushed both hands through her hair, pushed away from the railing to continue walking. She saw it! Forty-three. The wastebasket was rotated, pressed up against the fourth vertical railing. Four and three.

She nodded. "My time, Marshal, I am losing track of the time … please!"

"Two minutes and twenty seconds."

"My thanks." She walked back in the direction of the safe.

One more number to kick that editor in the pants. She extended her hands, hesitantly, then, not locating the safe, turned again, reaching out with both hands.

"Don't help her, Marshal, no one touches the girl," growled Brockway.

Didn't matter. She knew exactly where the safe was. She could see its wheels down the right side of her nose. Just to add to her apparent helplessness.

Six!

"Two minutes."

The mark in the dust of the safe's wheels when it was brought in. Papa had scuffed it twice.

She took a step, another. Touched the safe.

"I cannot see through the blindfold to turn the dial. Please remove the tape, quickly please! I must save my father!"

The audience groaned at the sound of the tapes being stripped from her face. She cried out the tape was peeled away from her right eye. She blinked her eyes as though to focus them.

Kyame knelt at the safe, twirled the dial, stopped, then turned, stopped, turned back, stopped, turned stopped. She pulled on the handle. But nothing happened!

"Oh, Papa, help me! Help me!" Both her hands were flat against the safe, as though to feel her father's presence.

Several women screamed in terror. "Her father is dying. Help her!"

"One minute, thirty seconds. Still time, Miss Piddington, still time." The Marshal's calm voice steadied her.

Kyame twirled the dial again. She hadn't faked the miss. Papa had planned for her to miss the first time, but this was no fake.

She squeezed her eyes shut, letting her head rest against the safe door, and walked again through the lobby in her memory sorting again before and after.

Six. Thirty-seven. Forty-three. Six.

Couldn't be anything else. She went through the secondary signals. Six.

"One minute."

Six. Thirty ... thirty-six. Thirty-six! Stupid over-confident fool! She had missed it! She hadn't detected that the first signal hadn't matched the second. Something, probably Brockway in some way, had altered the first signal. Or maybe just an accident.

Too easy. Too stupidly easy. She squelched her anger at her foolishness.

Kyame raised her head, took a breath, and began to rotate the dial -- then with both hands, pulled down on the handle.

"Thirty seconds."

A hard solid sound -- of metal sliding, rubbing against metal. Kyame pulled hard. The safe door swung open to the immediate cheers of the audience.

Several people ran outside to announce, "The Piddingtons did it! They did it!" The cheering spread to the crowds gathered outside the bank on the plaza.

John Vicks slid out the back of the crowd. He wanted nothing to do with the eerie Piddingtons. They could be reading his mind even now.

22

When the Piddingtons walked on stage that night, the audience rose as one to applaud. Kyame could feel the wave of sound pass over her, like nothing she had ever experienced before. Lots better than sitting at a family dinner in a house.

She had fallen sobbing into Papa's arms when he uncoiled from the safe and stood. His own eyes had been moist as he had squeezed her to him.

The audience had been responsive, laughing at all the right times, but now Papa had signaled number 212, "thief".

Kyame stopped immediately. She had been in the midst of describing the contents of a man's wallet, the bills and the picture of a child and had started describing an envelope.

She suddenly turned away, to face away from the audience toward Papa.

"Robbery. Papa! I see a robbery." Kyame waved her hands to the left. "Out there. There at the hotel. Tonight? Is it tonight?" Then making fists with both hands, Kyame suddenly shouted:

"There will be a robbery ... tonight at the Grand Hotel!"

John Vicks turned the thin rod, felt the bolt slide smoothly back. He inserted and turned the bar-key. The lock silently opened. He glanced back at Welsh who nodded and stepped closer with the putty, ready to immediately refill the access hole.

The doctor was sleeping heavily, a soft gurgling sound from his throat.

Vicks dropped to his knees and crawled into the room. If the doctor should wake and look around Vicks would be under his line of sight.

His expensive clothes were laid carefully across the corner chair. Nothing in the pockets but loose change, a couple of gold coins.

The vest was missing -- that meant the mattress.

Vicks whirled around to creep back to the bed. The lower sheet was loose from when the doctor had put his roll under the mattress. Pulling his wool sweater back to bare his right arm, Vicks slid his arm under the mattress, touched the vest and gently pulled it toward him.

The doctor shifted to one side. Vicks froze for an instant, then steadily withdrew the vest. A wallet was wrapped in it. Vicks emptied the wallet, the roll of bills was thick. He slid the vest and wallet back into place.

A faint shushing at the door. The signal that Welsh heard steps on the stairs.

Vicks crawled rapidly back through the door as Welsh drew it shut behind him. It took only a few seconds to relock the door and re-putty the hole.

The two men split.

Three minutes.

***

Kyame stopped, shook her head, the audience still murmuring with excitement. "I think ... I believe, I see the robbery will be on the third floor in a room with an odd number." Three of the four identified targeted rooms were odd-numbered -- should be a good chance.

The audience rustled with noise as all eyes turned toward Marshal Macallen and his red-bonneted wife in the front row.

Papa signed, *enough -- continue.*

Kyame lowered her head. Then raised it to begin to describe a child's toy at the back of the Music Hall, a toy she couldn't have seen even without the blindfold wrapped around her face.

23

Brockway's apology was on the front page and in the full page advertisement. It was a grudging piece of writing, but Piddington grinned as he passed the paper to Kyame.

"You beat him, Daughter. Beat him good."

Kyame read for a moment. It was even better than pushing the man down the stairs. She looked up. "Papa, I couldn't have lasted even a minute inside that safe. A minute would have felt like an hour. I was so scared that I had, had ..."

"Kyame," Papa reached his hand across to hers, held it for a moment. "I was never in doubt that you could do it." He grinned. "I held my breath for almost a minute at the beginning, so I could have lasted four minutes if you wanted to work up the audience a little more."

Smiling, Kyame looked up to see Deputy Marshal Juice Macallen coming toward them. He acknowledged Kyame with a tip of his hat.

"May I join you, Mr. Piddington, Miss Piddington?"

"Certainly, Marshal," said Piddington. "Please help yourself to some excellent muffins and coffee."

"Wish I could, but I have two serious problems, and, my boss, Marshal C. T. Connelly, won't return for another day."

"How may we help, Marshal?" asked Kyame. She liked the Macallen's. They cared.

"That robbery you saw last night, Miss Piddington. What did you see? Did you see who did it? It was room 305, just as you predicted. A doctor from back East was robbed of over two thousand dollars. Was coming to buy a horse for his granddaughter." Macallen shook his head as he reached for the coffee. "Darnest thing. The door for 305 was still locked from the inside, as were the windows."

"What is your other problem?" asked John Piddington. He squeezed his right fist as he glanced at Kyame.

Kyame was a little amazed herself. There had been more odd-numbered rooms fixed by the thieves than even numbers, so she and Papa were just going with the odds -- but she *had* hit it.

Marvelous.

"I have a murder on the same floor," said Macallen, finally sipping his coffee. "A Mr. Welsh, a cattle buyer, in room 308. Found this morning, in bed with a knife in his chest. His door was locked *and* bolted from the inside, as were the windows.

"And that's not all. Welsh told me yesterday at breakfast that he was a light sleeper and always slept with wadded up newspapers spread all around his bed ... you know the old traveler's trick to be sure you can hear if anyone comes into your room. Was nervous about being robbed, he said. The wadded newspapers are undisturbed, too." Macallen held his cup in both hands. "I'm stuck. I can't see any way that either crime could have been done ... so my wife suggested I come to you. Said if you read minds inside of a safe and predicted the robbery, maybe you could see more."

Macallen compressed his lips. "Can you?" the marshal whispered.

Kyame signaled, *ready*, not knowing what Papa might want her to do. She understood the robbery, she thought, but the murder?

"Marshal, Kyame and I will help anyway we can. Come, Daughter, let's go with the Marshal up to the third floor." As he walked, Papa signed, *Vicks -- look -- out -- him.*

"Papa, I will come up in just a moment."

As the men went up the stairs, Kyame walked toward the bellboy who grinned at her.

"Wow, Miss Piddington, you and your father can do some amazing things. You were just great last night. Bought a ticket with my own money ... not my parents."

"Thank you, Johnny." He was a nice boy, but ... "Have you seen Mr. Vicks this morning?"

"Vicks? Yes, his luggage is stacked over there. Leaving on the 10:25 train for Lawrence, heading on toward Leavenworth. Goin' to come down for breakfast in about fifteen minutes, he told me."

Kyame eyes glittered as she did a small curtsy. "My thanks, Johnny."

She ran to the stairs with Johnny, longingly, watching her blue skirts fly.

***

Juice Macallen stood back, his eyes wide. "Never saw anything like that, Mr. Piddington. Never. Little holes in the doors all puttied up? That's just crazy." He turned to Piddington. "This will be the first regional livestock auction we've had in Coffeyville. Town spent some serious money to set up facilities, expand the train station. With the changes everybody expects in the Cherokee Strip down in Indian Territory, Coffeyville will become a major town, a railpoint for the area.

"But we've never had professional hotel thieves like this before. Janet was right about asking you."

John Piddington glanced back at Kyame who suddenly appeared at the stair landing. She had obviously been running.

She stopped, then walked slowly toward him down the hall, signaling, *Vicks – leaving – today – first – train.*

"I suggest, Marshal," said Piddington, turning back to Macallen, "that you keep Mr. Vicks in town for another day or two. He may prove to be of importance in your murder problem. I sense that he is planning to leave on the first train this morning."

"What? Why Vicks?" asked Macallen. "He was with me when we broke down the door to get into Welsh's room. Was staying in the room across the hall. Vicks said he had seen Welsh around the hotel but had never talked with him."

"Because, Marshal," said John Piddington, "Vicks and Welsh are very likely the pair of hotel thieves who robbed room 305."

***

John Vicks made a face when Deputy Macallen told him to stay in town for two days. "Don't know Welsh, never saw the man before coming here, Marshal." Vicks' face grew red. "I don't know what you are talking about or understand why I am to be inconvenienced. I have customers to call on. I have a living to make." He blanched when John Piddington appeared behind the Marshal. That queasy feeling again. Could Piddington see into his mind?

"I will see that your luggage is returned to your room, Mr. Vicks," said Macallen. "May I have your ticket on the 10:25? It will be returned. The station master will be instructed not to sell you another without my prior written permission."

How? Vicks removed the ticket from inside his suit coat. No one had seen him buy the ticket. How? Then he caught the bright green eyes of the daughter standing beside Piddington.

Her eyes were like ice.

24

Deputy Marshal Macallen grinned. "Your idea, Piddington, was a good one. Jack Nardone, teller at the First National, confirmed that John Vicks bought a bank draft for $2,300 with hundred-dollar silver certificates when the bank doors first opened this morning. Draft is drawn on the First National up in Lawrence.

"Jack said he was glad to get the extra cash to help handle the press of business expected next week."

John Piddington leaned forward on the table in the Marshal's office. Kyame was out walking around the hotel. She'd had an idea for the murder and wanted to see if it was possible. He had kissed her on her cheek and sent her off.

"Stands to reason, Marshal, that the thief would convert that bulk of cash into something easier to carry. Saw that done by thieves in Abilene several weeks back. Vicks probably worried about getting robbed himself. How much did the doctor lose?"

"$2,100 in hundred-dollar silver certificates. Had some gold coins in his pockets, but the thief didn't touch it."

"Did he record any of the serial numbers … or maybe write something on any of the bills? An address or something?"

Macallen raised his eyebrows. "You done police work before, Piddington? You've got the right kind of suspicious mind."

***

Kyame walked into the alley at the rear of the Grand Hotel. If the door to Mr. Welsh's room was locked from the inside and there was no little hole in the door, then it seemed logical that the killer had come from another direction.

She looked up at the backside of the hotel. There was a fire ladder running up the wall to the fourth floor at each end of the building, then the ladder was extended with a handrail from there to the top of the building. She walked to the far end where Welsh's room was located.

Other than two mongrel dogs yapping at each other, fighting over a chunk of green something, there was nothing moving in the alley. The dogs stopped to sniff and growl at her as Kyame ran by to the base of the ladder.

A chill breeze swept across her face. Some dark clouds were gathering to the west. Some talk about maybe a storm moving through. Kyame needed to hurry. She didn't want to be on the side of a building if any rain started.

She pulled a long piece of twine from her pocket, wrapped and tied it around her skirt to keep it from flapping in the breezes as she climbed the ladder. She wanted to see if the third floor window next to the ladder was Welsh's. It had to be the window if the door had really been locked -- only logical.

She jumped, caught the bottom rung and pulled herself up as she braced her feet against the cedar siding and brick of the hotel wall.

The rusted screws holding the rungs were loose and wobbled as she climbed cautiously up the side of the building. There was a small ledge at each floor, barely wide enough even for her feet.

She looked into Welsh's room. The bed, with the bloody sheets thrown in a pile along the wall and a large blood stain across the mattress where the body had been dragged off the bed, was only about two feet from the window. Some of the wadded newspapers were still scattered around the floor.

Kyame pushed up against the window. It moved. On tiptoes she raised herself up and out to see the window lock. The lock was broken. It looked locked -- but wasn't.

"Hey you, girl! Whad're you doin' up there?" A man shouted suddenly from below. "Get down from there. Break your silly neck! You peeking at people, girl?" He was in shirtsleeves with no collar and patched work-pants with a black sickle in his hand, a stub of cigar in the corner of his mouth.

Kyame slowly stepped down the ladder, until she came almost level with his face.

"No, sir, I was not peeking at anyone. I was learning how to kill a man," she said gently. "Do you know about killing a man?" Kyame dropped from the last rung to the ground. "I do now."

He took two steps back, his lips curling into a sneer and walked away, his cursing just audible.

Kyame pulled the twine loose from about her skirt. A quick survey of the alley, she began to search behind the boxes and trash piled in the alley on both sides. It took about five minutes. She grinned when she found it.

Just like Mama had used.

25

Piddington was laughing when Kyame came through the deputy's office door carrying a broomstick and a loop of cord.

"Not really a suspicious mind. I worked in a bank in Warren, Ohio, Marshal, before we went on the stage. I remember seeing all kinds of notes and even pictures drawn on paper money. Just a possibility."

"And a good one." Juice Macallen pushed his chair back. He tipped his hat to Kyame as he left.

Waiting until the door closed, Kyame said, "Papa, I think I might understand the killing. Remember back home when Mama tied a knife to a broomstick to get at a big rattler that had gotten under our porch? I thought that if a window in the room could be opened, then the killer could do the same to Mr. Welsh. His bed is near the window. I just checked that. Then the door could be locked and bolted, the windows locked and the newspapers untouched. The killer just speared Mr. Welsh through the opened window, slipped the knot leaving the knife in Mr. Welsh and left.

"Mama used a slip-knot so she only had to jerk the rope and the broom stick came loose, and left the knife in the snake. It was a real big one. Mama didn't want to get filthy under the porch to haul out the dead snake. She was leaving that for you. It did start to stink a little."

"Good thinking, Daughter," said Papa, his eyes becoming moist in remembrance. "Yes, I remember. That snake was big, almost six feet long, and Mama had skewered him right behind his head. Mama wasn't afraid of anything." He grinned and squeezed her arm. "And you're right. It did stink."

"But," he said, "the windows were also locked from the inside in Welsh's room."

Kyame sat in the Marshal's chair, spreading and smoothing her skirts. She frowned, then grinned up at Papa. She shook her head.

"I found this broomstick and the cord to tie the knife. They were stuffed in some empty boxes behind the Read Brothers dry goods store next to the hotel.

"And," she said, triumphantly, leaning toward Papa, their faces only a few inches apart, "the window lock in Mr. Welsh's room is broken. It looks locked but it still opens. The killer may not have known that, but it wouldn't matter. Locked or unlocked, the window could be opened from the outside. There's a fire ladder right there.

"The window lock could have been made to look locked by the killer when he returned to Mr. Welsh's room with the Marshal to help discover the dead body. He would have had to be one of the first ones into the room; and no one would notice anything he was doing, not with a bloody dead man staring at them. Would they?" she smiled, her head cocked to one side.

"Let's find the Marshal, Kyame," said Papa, standing. "Good sound thinking. I think you've hit it. And bring your broomstick and cord."

**

With the doctor's acknowledgement that he had drawn a quick sketch of a unique buzzard he had seen from the train a mile or two outside of Coffeyville on the only paper he had available, the back of a silver certificate, and the finding of that bill by bank manager, Jack Nardone, John Vicks confessed to the theft.

But it was when Kyame confronted Vicks with how he had murdered his partner that froze him in place, his face turning the color of cold ashes. It was like she could see into his mind with those chilling green eyes.

"My God, do you see everything, girl? Are you human?"

***

Slumped into a chair in the Marshal's office, John Vicks said, "Yeah, I should have waited until we'd left Coffeyville, but... but I just couldn't trust Welsh. He was getting shaky, losing his nerve. Thought he'd try to run off with the money, or maybe trip me up next time and take everything. Thought *I'd* be out of the state by the time anyone could figure the killing and the robbery... if anyone ever did.

"Read about a man killed that way up in Nebraska. They never caught the killer. Police up there never figured how it was done."

"But," said Juice Macallen, taking cuffs from his pocket, "that killer didn't have to face the Impossible Piddingtons."

The Deputy snapped the cuffs closed.

***

The platform of the Coffeyville train station was thronged with men and luggage, shouts and laughing. Kyame listened to the loud accents of the surrounding states. She loved the excitement of the start of the auction -- like a county fair for adults.

Red-bonneted Janet Macallen gave Papa a basket. "Some baked goods for you and Kyame for your trip north, to help remember us … that's from your lessons, remember. And, sir, you will be happy to know that I easily remembered my lesson for Sunday school and my shopping list, thanks to your introduction to the mysteries of Mnemosyne."

Macallen stood with his arm around the waist of his smiling wife. "You two are welcome to come back any time … even if you aren't performing. I could use more help with my memory. And my boss could too." He grinned. "Not this lovely boss, my other one."

"We would like to, Marshal," said John Piddington. "You and your wife have been most hospitable to us."

The loud whistle and the shushing burst of escaping steam of the locomotive made Kyame jump. She squeezed Papa's hand tighter.

"And, Mr. Piddington," said Janet Macallen, as the four of them walked to the train, "with your remarkable daughter and the strange knowledge you have acquired ... have you ever considered starting a new religion?"

Stunned, Kyame stopped breathing for a moment and looked up at Papa who only shook his head without smiling. Then he glanced over at his startled daughter and winked.

26

Kyame reflected as the train rumbled on, the passenger car had become progressively more silent as the day lengthened into dusk, the glowing sunset obscured by low rain clouds in the distance. There would be a brief stop for dinner somewhere ahead, slabs of grilled pork, soup of some kind, bread, coffee or milk and then back onto the train. If you missed the train, as Papa had warned her more than once, very likely you would then sleep the night in the train station -- and hopefully be able to catch an early morning train in the right direction.

She thought about looking at the windows that revealed families gathered together around the evening meal -- and that instant pang of longing she had felt. Papa was lost in a book when Kyame glanced over. But the Impossible Piddingtons just kept moving, always outsiders just visiting for a few days and moving on to yet another place.

And, yes, she admitted, smiling, that she had caught herself thinking of the audiences as all the same, a feeling that was quickly corrected, usually only a few minutes into their performance.

But, how long can this traveling life last? Or, as she frowned, how long did they really want it to? Mama had said something about the second sight would be for only a few years to build up their savings for her school, then -- but Mama never finished. They had to get ready for the show, always the show.

But as Kyame shifted to a more comfortable position, without the traveling she would not have the unique friends in her life now, like Marshal and Mrs. Macallen back in Coffeyville, and others, remarkable people she would never have encountered by staying in one place and gathering around a family table for dinner every night.

She stretched as the train began to slow.

Kyame smiled -- she did like scaring people -- but why would grown people want to believe that something like second sight was real? It wasn't that they just believed; it was that they seemed to *need* to believe. Why? That was a question she needed to answer -- in the towns ahead.

"Looks like time for dinner, Daughter," said Papa, closing his book. He paused, then, "You look as if you have been thinking. What about?"

"A slab of pork that maybe will be cooked right this time, Papa," she replied, laughing.

That feeling, just before she walked out on the stage -- that combination of fright and anticipation that always set her heart pounding. How else could she ever experience that exhilarating feeling pouring through her body, down to her toes, that growing sensation of implacable determination that she *would* prevail -- that she would scare them into belief. It was that belief, Kyame realized as she stood, that brought in the dollars for the Impossible Piddingtons. And, she realized, that during her time on the stage, she had to believe in second sight, too.

As Papa took her hand, Kyame felt -- older.

***

Solomon Royale had suddenly recalled who Jeremy Brin was, though that wasn't his name at the time. He was a con man, Tom Hugard, who had escaped a conviction back in Kearny,

179

Nebraska, his last church job, when witnesses had suddenly disappeared or couldn't remember.

He had seen Brin once, when he was getting on a train laughing as the people he had cheated shouted and yelled hatred after him. When a pistol shot was heard, Brin quickly ducked inside the slowly moving passenger car and was gone.

Pearl Tangley, The Mental Marvel, had been gone for three weeks. Patty Reese had been proud of him, which had caused him to glow inside as he had never experienced before -- but then she had frowned and asked, "Solomon, in diminishing Tangley you have crushed the beliefs of many people ... aren't you now obligated to give them a belief of at least equivalent value to replace her?"

He knew the honest answer was yes. Just ripping up people's hopes did not accomplish anything -- just transformed him into a different style of fraud -- regardless of the cheers of the newsroom.

But Brin stood in front of him now, Solomon's back against the wall, in the rain and mud behind his boarding house. "You are done queering honest people's play, Royale. You are done."

Snarling, Brin swung a wooden club. Hard. Again and again.

27

When the yellow-robed snake charmer raised the lid, the glistening brown cobra rose slowly from the woven wicker basket, its forked tongue flicking rapidly in and out, its cold unlidded eyes, they looked coal black to Kyame, reflected no fear at the raucous crowd gathered around it. As the snake spread its hood, the black and white spectacle design on its back became visible -- just as the books Kyame had read said it would.

A fabled killer snake from mysterious India -- she was fascinated by how easily it moved, smoothly shifting to keep the growling bull terrier centered that was held by its owner three or four feet away.

The growling whining small dog twisted in the man's hands, scratching at the wooden floor, eager to attack. As Kyame had pushed and elbowed her way through the rowdy throng gathering in the Acme warehouse, she had heard that the terrier's name was Buck, a locally famous snake dog used to help flush out rattlesnakes in the countryside around Julesburg, Colorado.

"Ol' Buck likes fresh snake meat."

Kyame glanced over her shoulder. Two older boys were laughing while mimicking a hooded cobra with their weaving hands. Ignoring their stare, she pushed closer to the cleared area.

"One bite from that slimy cobra and you're right dead, what I've heard," a man standing behind Kyame said. His companion, a well-dressed businessman, grunted agreement and edged back another foot.

Someone else behind Kyame muttered, "Snake's harmless ... probably had its fangs pulled. Heard that was what the snake charmers do in India. Nothing's goin' to happen 'cept that dog'll chew it up for a bit, maybe have the thing for dinner."

Kyame Piddington glanced over at the rest of the Hindoo troupe pressed against the back wall of the warehouse. One dark-skinned man in a loin cloth with a loose brown robe thrown over his shoulders, wearing a soiled green turban slouched carelessly against the wall. Standing apart, his hands held primly behind his back, the other, a taller man, was elegantly dressed in a tightly bound white turban with a tufted gold aigrette, an embroidered blue silk jacket and white leggings.

In contrast to the drawn emaciated face of the smaller man, the one in blue had striking charismatic features, his smooth olive skin polished with perspiration from the rising warmth in the crowded boisterous warehouse.

To Kyame, the dull-eyed man appeared indifferent to the cobra-dog battle, while the blue one was obviously afraid of something. His dark eyes never stopped searching the crowd. When his eyes suddenly met Kyame's, he immediately looked away.

Kyame turned back to the impending battle. She had been the only girl to enter the Acme warehouse after paying the 25¢ entry price about twenty minutes before. Initially, there had been some muttering about it not being a suitable place or experience for young females. But once the impassioned wagering on the cobra-dog fight had begun, Kyame was ignored as wads of cash and gold coins rapidly changed hands on the outcome of the fight.

Kyame had told Papa she was going out to draw, while he remained in their hotel room completing arrangements for their performance that night. After picking up one of the Hindoo Troupe's red handbills lying outside a tobacco shop, Kyame had followed some men to the warehouse looking for exotic Hindoos to draw. Snakes, jugglers and a Brahmin Jadoo-Wallah, a magician.

Kyame held her drawing box close to her chest as the men around her pressed forward for a better view. The images of the snake and dog, the fierce anger in the face of the Hindoo snake charmer, the wide eyes and eager mouths of the men sensing a sure thing at three to one odds -- she would have a whole portfolio to draw.

The near-naked snake charmer crouched behind the weaving cobra, which had now raised its head to almost two feet from the ground. The Hindoo did not move, only pulling his yellow robe more tightly about him. His lean brown face was drawn into an angry smirk. He appeared to have understood the comment about the cobra's fangs.

"Let him go, Max! Let Buck get at that heathen snake! It's time to collect our money from these black foreigners and send them on their way."

The crowd erupted in laughter and happy shouts of "Now! Now!"

Tom Leysen, the short dark-haired burly manager of the Royal Band of Elite Hindoo Faqeers, as their red handbills had announced them, stood at the edge of the crowd with both hands bulging with bills and coins, some bills protruding from his jacket pockets. He shouted above the growing noise. "Odds of three to one, three to one the snake will kill the dog! Any more takers? Any more takers?"

Two men pushed toward him through the crowd.

Quickly closing the deals, he looked up. "Any more? Any more?" Leysen shouted. When there was no further movement around him, Leysen nodded to the man holding the dog.

"Let'er rip, Max!"

Snarling, its fangs bared, the terrier was across the floor and at the cobra in two jumps. As the dog left the ground in its final leap at the snake, the cobra suddenly struck, its head darting just under the lower jaw of the dog to bite into the dog's throat.

The terrier flopped over on its back, thrown off balance in mid-air by the cobra's swift hard thrust. The snake threw a heavy coil around the dog's hind legs. Buck struggled, rolling frantically to shake the snake loose, to free its jaws, to get its teeth into his attacker. But the cobra remained fastened to the dog's neck.

"Get'm Buck! Get'm big dog!" The shouting became more frantic as the dog thrashed about, brown coils tightening around it. "Get up Buck, get up!"

Kyame saw a thin smile appear on the charmer's face as the dog's eyes went wide and its movements became slower. Unable to dislodge the cobra at its throat, venom spreading through its body, the terrier desperately gasped for breath.

She glanced over at the two men against the wall. One remained indifferent, his eyes half-closed. The elegant one in blue appeared more fearful.

The warehouse went silent.

After a slight whimper, the terrier's legs quivered, then the dog lay still, the coils of the cobra drawing still tighter, its jaws still fastened to the dog's throat.

No one in the crowd moved.

The snake charmer pulled a short wooden rod forked at one end from the bag beside him on the floor. As the cobra relaxed its jaws and began to uncoil and pull away from the inert dog, the charmer reached out to imprison the snake's head in the fork and press it against the floor. Cautiously grasping the cobra just behind its head while firmly gripping the writhing snake about halfway down its body with his other hand, the charmer lifted the serpent up. Carefully, gently, he pressed the coils down into the basket. With the lid in one hand positioned over the basket, the Hindoo slowly pressed the cobra's head down; then jerking his hand free, he quickly fitted the lid back in place. There was a noticeable sigh of relief from the crowd.

Kyame took a deep breath. From the moment the dog had charged she had been holding her breath, her moist hands trembling as she gripped her drawing box against her chest. The amazing sudden deadly strike of the cobra was fixed in her memory. That would be the first of her Hindoo drawings. The frightened man in blue would be the second.

"No fangs, huh," said a man behind her. She turned to see a well-dressed businessman. "Damn, Calhoun, that snake is a faster killer than any rattler I ever saw."

Jeffery Calhoun grunted agreement. "Yeah. So, Mitchem, why does the sheriff allow a killer like that in the town? That thing gets loose, somebody is going to die."

Henry Mitchem nodded agreement. "True. I intend to talk to Sheriff Layne. Have to evacuate the town if that cobra ever runs loose."

As Kyame left the warehouse she overheard one loser complaining, "Out ten bucks. Okay, I can stand that, but so darn quick. A cock-fight's more exciting. At least I would get something for my ten bucks."

John Piddington leaned back smiling as Kyame concluded her wide-eyed description of the cobra and dog battle. "I want to see your pictures when you finish, Daughter," he said. "What happened after the snake was put back into the basket?" He could not scold Kyame for going. The Acme warehouse was the wrong place for an ordinary girl, but Kyame was far from ordinary and even at just thirteen, had the maturity of a young woman.

"Mr. Leysen, the manager of the Hindoos, announced their next show would be behind the Julesburg Hotel tomorrow, Saturday, at noon. When I left the warehouse, I heard one of the men say that Leysen must have made a couple of hundred dollars from the betting.

Returning to the hotel, Kyame had done a fast calculation. Over two hundred dollars in less than five minutes – that's $2,400 an hour!

"Papa," she asked, "should we get a snake?"

***

"Keep that slimy thing away from me!" snarled Tom Leysen as the snake charmer placed his wicker basket on one of the troupe's red traveling trunks with "Hindoo Faqueers" in bright yellow painted on each side. Like the other towns, no hotel in Julesburg would allow the Hindoos into a room. Consequently, Leysen had rented an empty storefront at the far end of Main Street. The simple bed rolls for the two *dacoits*, Ashok, the snake charmer, and Nagpal, the juggler, were in the backroom, while the more elaborate bedding of the Brahmin, Hari Das, was against the far wall with his leather bag of magic tricks. Leysen himself stayed at the Grand Hotel, three blocks away on Main Street.

$243 from the devil snake for a minute's work. Smiling, Leysen locked the bills and coins into his iron strongbox. Then, since, as usual, none of the local banks would do business with him, he placed the iron box into his brass-bound trunk which he locked as well. The Hindoos had already received half their pay. The other half would come when they reached Sacramento at the end of the tour. Never pay a performer the full amount up front. They would just disappear – especially these Indian thieves.

Leysen turned away. He could not watch while Ashok fed the cobra a live mouse. He never wanted to see that slimy beast except at a fight.

There were several plans always running through his mind for the time when the cobra would either die or lose. Finding another cobra was out of the question. Magic and juggling alone would not draw enough money. He had to be prepared to add something unique; or be ready to cut and run.

Before a planned fight, the cobra was kept away from food for at least three days because after eating, the cobra would become listless and would only look for refuge if threatened. How long the snake could live in that wicker basket, Leysen didn't know.

At the beginning of their tour in Georgia, there had been two of the cobras, but one had stopped feeding for some reason and had finally been ripped to shreds by a dog in Alabama. That had been an expensive minute, but now only a distant memory. That was before Hari Das had joined them with his Hindoo magic act that kept public interest up while the cobra digested its meal.

Leysen watched the Brahmin across the room sitting cross-legged before a foul multi-armed brass idol that looked like a spider with human legs, a candle burning before it.

Hari Das had been on some sort of holy Hindoo pilgrimage to see the world when all his money had been stolen in Montgomery. He had come to Leysen to join the troupe in order to recover enough money to resume his travels and return to his home in Bangalore – a place Leysen had never heard of.

Hari Das cut a well-dressed graceful figure that had given Leysen access to some higher class hotels and homes that would never allow the snake within five-hundred feet – but the Brahmin was a strange quiet one who kept to himself. There appeared to be a wall between the Brahmin and the other two Hindoos. Something about a caste system – but that was unimportant. All that mattered was the cash.

"Watch that candle, Hari Das, I don't want this place burnt down," said Leysen.

Hari Das turned his head, his half-closed soft brown eyes shadowed. "Yes, Sahib Leysen, I understand." His words were carefully spoken, precisely paced, as though in a language strange to him. "Shiva, the Auspicious One, will protect the building for us. She has promised." He suddenly jerked his head back toward the idol and bowed lower, gritting his teeth.

A possible fatal mistake – certainly if the two thieves had overheard. Hari Das silently cursed himself in words that were not Hindustani. Shiva was a *male* god. One of the Principal Six. No genuine Brahmin would ever make such a mistake – it would be a fatal blasphemy.

He glanced cautiously back at Leysen who had only grunted and turned back to shuffling papers.

Hari Das was troubled. The girl with the green eyes, the only female in the warehouse – the green eyes that saw everything. There had been a Mexican *bruja,* a sorceress, in his ramshackle town who had eyes like that. Eyes that saw everything and that could kill with frightening spells. Was she one? Could she give him away?

To provide cover while he collected his thoughts, Hari Das began to murmur the *Aum Namah Shivaya*, the holy mantra of Shiva, all adoration to Shiva, over and over, while slowly bowing and raising his head.

He had seen more than just the green eyes in the crowd. To make his run, Hari Das would need all the money in Leysen's strongbox. He would try to pick the outer lock when Leysen left and the two thieves took their siestas.

***

"Dear Kyame, dear daughter," said Mama, smiling at her over the clean wash as she folded each item, her green eyes sparkling. "I fear you will never be an ordinary woman. You will grow up to read people, not to love them; to perceive things that a thousand other women would never know to look for; to search diligently for knowledge denied to even college professors and learned clerics; and to always be loyal ..." She suddenly began to cough. Her smile was forced as she choked back another cough. "Now, Kyame, help me fold all this. We must be ready to leave for the train when Papa comes from getting the money order at the bank."

But then Mama began to cough again, harder and harder, until tears were streaming down her cheeks. Hastily grabbing for a towel, Mama buried her face in it, coughing and gasping for air. She staggered against the wall, finally slumping down into a chair. Her breathing slowed, smoothing, becoming normal.

Kyame had rushed to her, to hold Mama's heaving shoulders. "Mama, Mama, please stop! Please stop!" That was when Kyame first saw the blood on the towel and the thin red trickle dripping from her lips that ran down Mama's chin.

Kyame sat up, sobbing. She held her face in her hands in the darkness of the night. The town noises, a soft whinny of a horse, faint in the background through the half-open window. She became aware that Papa had come to her and was holding her closely in his arms – just as Mama would do whenever Kyame had been scared in a new town where everyone was a stranger and people would point at her, whispering behind their hands, whispering about the *poor theatre girl*.

"Mama," she whispered, feeling Papa's reassuring whiskers against her cheek. "Mama's coughing … and the blood." She felt Papa's arms tighten around her, his quiet voice murmuring in her ear.

When, after several minutes, Kyame laid back into bed and Papa had pulled her covers up to her chin, she recalled Solomon Royale once visiting backstage in Abilene and telling her that she would bear the curse of being different all her life. Sometimes the curse would be good, he had said, and she should remember those times. And, he had insisted, forget all the rest.

***

"I do not search the stars for hire, Sahib," said Hari Das in his slow careful way, bowing and nodding to the man and his wife. He was resplendent in a silken green tunic, white turban and tight white leggings. The crowd on the stubble dry grass behind the Grand Hotel was growing with several women present. The women would sit on chairs provided by the hotel, while the men would stand.

There! The girl with the green eyes, one of the Impossible Piddingtons he had learned. Maybe an ally and not an enemy. Certainly someone who knew how to keep secrets, of which he, Hari Das, had many to keep.

It had been the stroke of genius that had broken his sleep last night. Sitting up abruptly in the sullen darkness, Hari Das realized he had the means to distract Leysen and the rest while he ran. And it had been there right in front of him all along. The Nag, the cobra. He had slept better last night than he had in any of the three months with the Leysen Hindoo troupe. And he had picked the lock of Leysen's trunk. Next to try the strongbox. The girl had moved closer with her drawing box, declining a chair offered by one of the men. When their eyes met momentarily, she smiled, then began to open her box.

Tom Leysen was eagerly collecting the 50¢ payment that allowed entry within the roped-off space where Hari Das would perform his high-caste magic, as the special blue handbill had promised.

Kyame watched the Brahmin as he moved gracefully behind a table constructed from two saw-horses over-laid with a carved mahogany plank. Just like what she, blindfolded, sat on while on stage -- only not with any carvings. She felt a touch at her shoulder and looked up into Papa's smiling eyes. He had held her close before they had gone down to breakfast at the Louis Hotel where they stayed at the other end of town. The Grand Hotel would not allow theatre people into their rooms. They had talked about Mama, sharing some memories of her beauty, kindness and wonderful laugh. It had helped erase the agony of her dream.

"Had to come, Daughter, after seeing your drawings," said Papa. "Watch his misdirection with the cups and balls."

Hari Das evenly spaced three inverted colored wooden cups, each with small handle-like projection on top across the table. A stack of blank paper and other things that Kyame couldn't see clearly were piled at one end of the table.

The crowd quieted when Hari Das raised his hands, pronouncing what sounded like a solemn blessing on the crowd in a language that Kyame couldn't recognize.

He raised each of the cups to show that they were empty and that nothing was concealed under them. Then one, then two and three small white balls appeared magically at his fingertips. The balls seemed to jump invisibly from under one cup to another cup, vanishing, multiplying; then he tipped two of the cups over with only a touch of his finger to show the cups empty. Hari Das lifted the remaining cup to display not the three white balls, but a single large yellow ball. The white balls had vanished!

The Brahmin bowed to the strong applause. He held the yellow ball at his fingertips, letting it roll across his fingers from hand to hand. A woman gasped. Suddenly there were two balls at his fingertips, yellow and red, then a third green one appeared as out of thin air, and -- a fourth, a blue one! The applause grew, then exploded when Hari Das held up both hands with four colored balls held between the fingers of each hand.

Kyame gasped. "How?" She looked up at Papa who was grinning and applauding with the crowd.

"Beautifully done, Kyame," he said, "I've never seen a better multiplying ball routine."

Hari Das smiled, bowing his turbaned head. After placing the balls into a leather bag, he began to roll the papers into tubes, held in shape with a string around the middle. He handed the tubes to a woman in the front row.

"Please, memsahib, please confirm for everyone that there is only the paper and nothing else," he said, in his slow cadence of speech. He bowed when she returned the tubes to him after affirming to the crowd that it was just three papers rolled up.

Hari Das carefully stood the three tubes in a row across the table. He instantly righted a tube that a light breeze had blown over, his quick hand moving almost invisibly to Kyame.

"I don't know what's coming," Papa whispered to her.

Hari Das gazed slowly around the crowd to build expectation. The green-eyed girl was watching his every move. He was pleased that he had surprised her with the cups and balls -- but now.

As he lifted the first tube to show that nothing was there, Hari Das caught a glimpse of a tall man stepping back into the shadow of a tree. The Brahmin's heart stopped. How had they found him so quickly?

He forced a slow smile as he raised the other tubes one by one to demonstrate nothing was there. Then quickly, he raised and tossed aside the tubes, revealing a live baby chick under each one. The crowd roared with surprise.

He reached out, picking up one of the chicks as the other two began to wander around the table pecking at the wood. He closed both hands over the chick -- and squeezed.

A woman cried out, "Don't kill it! Don't kill the poor thing."

Hari Das slowly opened his hands to show an egg, the chick had vanished! Quickly he repeated the stunt two more times, leaving three eggs on the table. With the audience laughing and applauding, Hari Das started to ...

"Hey, damn fine, Hari Das," a man called out from the back. "I knew a black magician who called himself George Jefferson Jones down in Alabamy who did that same chicken trick. You know George Jones? The murdering George Jones? We lynched his murderin' black papa and uncle ... and we got a rope waitin' for young George. Any tree will do." The tall man stepped from under the tree out of the shadows. "Like this one."

"The hell it will!" A lean bearded man in a gray frock coat stepped out from the crowd. "There will be no lynchings in this county while I'm sheriff. And no talk about lynchings either. So, you shut your mouth and move on, sir. I see you on the street even whisper the word lynch, I'll have you in a cell in two minutes. Understand me, mister?"

"Easy, Sheriff. He raised his hands in mock defense. "Easy". Name's Richard Griffin, by way of Birmingham, Montgomery and Houston."

Kyame turned to see the tall man begin to move toward the rear of the crowd, a wide grin on his face.

"I'll keep my mouth shut, Sheriff," said Griffin. "There's not going to be any trouble 'tween you an' me. I'm leaving on tonight's train. But," -- he pointed at Hari Das who stood frozen -- "you might want to check that fake Hindoo. Those chickens aren't his biggest trick. You had any robberies lately?"

When the sheriff turned back toward him, Hari Das suddenly threw up his hands. He shouted something Kyame could not understand.

"I curse you, man, with the curse of Shiva, the destroyer. You blaspheme my blood, my heritage, my gods. I curse you, Griffin, to ..." The crowd began to scramble away as Hari Das, his calm face transformed into a mask of hatred, thrust both hands toward the tall man, the thumb and two fingers extended on each hand. Raising his voice again, Hari Das spoke again first in a strange language, then, "Curse you to the abyss of Nag, the instrument of Shiva, you and all your family. Nag will find you!"

That's what the book on India had said that George Jefferson Jones had stolen from the bookstore in Montgomery. He had to hide from the lynch rope by making himself into a man who could walk among the white men. He had been mistaken for being Spanish a couple of times, but now he had no chance without the creation of Hari Das, the Brahmin who spoke only limited English.

The red handbills of the Royal Elite Troupe of Hindoo Faqeers had suggested his escape. The black man, George Jefferson Jones, had to become a believable Hindoo within three days, before the Faqeers moved on, before he could be swung by a rope from the closest tree.

He had memorized some common expressions in Hindustani from the book to use, but that was all he knew. The strange language he shouted was just gibberish. He spoke slowly, carefully to keep his words free of a Southern accent and slave slang. He had stolen some garments from an importer's shop, learned to wind a turban from another book and three days later presented himself to Tom Leysen as Hari Das, stranded Brahmin magician on a holy pilgrimage.

In the end, Hari Das owed his chance for escape to a dead cobra.

"Nothing wrong with being a fake Hindoo, Kyame," said Papa as they stepped back to let the agitated people pass them. "Let's see if Hari Das will talk to us. I don't like lynchings or people who talk about them."

Hari Das had disappeared by the time the Piddingtons had worked their way through the remnants of the audience. Tom Leysen had also disappeared. A small chick was pecking at the ground behind the table. Two colored balls, red and yellow, lay against a rock. Kyame picked them up.

"You know anything about this Hindoo magician, Piddington?"

Kyame turned to see the sheriff. She glimpsed a pearl-handled revolver under his frock coat. His silvered beard framed his lined face. His blue eyes were sharp but friendly. His large hands were gnarled and callused like he had broken rocks with them.

"Show folk know each other, don't they?"

"Sometimes, Sheriff, but I've never seen this troupe of Hindoos before. Hari Das is one of the better magicians I've ever seen."

"Uhm ... I don't care about stage names and such," said the sheriff, "that's part of the stage game. My father was an actor in San Francisco for a while when I was a boy. Name's Layne, Smith Layne." He held out his hand.

"John Piddington, Sheriff Layne. My daughter, Kyame."

Kyame took Sheriff Layne's hand. "What are you going to do, Sheriff?"

"Hari Das, or whatever his name, is a fine magician," said Layne. "I'll give him that, for sure. Can't even guess where those chicks came from.

"Right now, I'm going to make sure that man Griffin is on the train tonight. Hindoo troupe's down in the empty dry goods store, end of Main. Haven't got any robberies since they've been here; and Leysen and the Hindoos haven't caused any trouble. Had some people complain about having a cobra in town, which I guess I could call a public nuisance … but really, Miss Kyame, I can't do anything, just yet."

He tipped his hat and walked away.

28

Ashok snickered. "As I thought, Nagpal, our great Brahmin is a fake. He is only a black man running for his life."

Rinsing his mouth, the juggler spit out the water. "So, what is the harm in that? He brings in good money while your snake rests. He is of no matter to me. When can we break into Leysen's trunk?"

"Not until Sacramento. Then run to San Francisco. There is an Indian community there where we can hide and live."

Nagpal nodded. "So, we must be true to our salt until then. May the power of Shiva truly be with Hari Das."

***

The shadows played checkerwise across the Brahmin's face. Hari Das stood in the lumber storage rack behind Mitchem's Dry Goods two doors down from the hotel. Where now? Griffin would follow him. He could never get away. And Griffin would find others to join the hunt. Hari Das was now too easy a target, but where now?

"You dropped these two balls, Hari Das," said Kyame. "I think you will need them."

He started and whirled to find the green-eyed girl holding the red and yellow balls out to him. She was smiling, as was the man beside her.

"I'm John Piddington, Hari Das, and this is my daughter, Kyame. You are an excellent magician. I've never seen a ball routine like yours. And the chicks and tubes are a masterpiece.

"Would you join us for lunch in our hotel room?"

***

He had placed his white turban on the dresser away from the food. George Jefferson Jones shrugged. "I may as well be hung for a sheep as a lamb. Got to find a way out. Got to find a way to live."

"You have extraordinary courage, George," said John Piddington. "I don't know what happened in Alabama; but I don't like the word lynch any more than the sheriff."

Kyame collected the soup bowls, empty cheese plate and bread basket. She stacked it all next to the door. Then turned to look at the defrocked Brahmin.

Jones looked at Kyame. "Where I lived, I'd a been lynched just being this close to a white woman, Miss Kyame. Ropes everywhere, it seems. Everywhere." He struggled to smile. "I was so short of money that I'd drink bartender's mistakes." He wiped his moist eyes with a napkin. "My God, what can I say? Impossible Piddingtons? Yeah, you really are to treat me like this. To take the chance."

"You've had terrible luck, George," said Piddington.

George Jones looked at the turban then across the room at Papa. "No, sir, not luck. I think it's Shiva, reaching out with one of his arms to destroy an imposter hiding behind his religion. Shiva, the destroyer.

"As I've traveled, I tried to study everything I could find about the Hindoos, their religions, their castes, but it is all so confusing. I just couldn't keep it all straight, so I kept my mouth shut. Even then, I called Shiva *she*, once. God, that could have done me in right there. Hari Das is a yard wide and an inch thick."

"It's still only bad luck, Mr. Jones," said Kyame.

"Kyame," said Piddington, "I have an idea. You recall that showman, ah, his name I can't remember, that we met on the train who talked about Buffalo Bill's plans. Putting together a worldwide traveling show?"

"Yes, Papa."

"George, with your permission, I'll go send a telegram to Bill Cody's manager and suggest he consider Hari Das for his show." Papa stopped. "You'll have to use another name."

Jones smiled. "Odd. Really odd. I was thinking about another name only last night. I slept well last night and a name seemed to jump out at me. Jaiman Karkar. The victorious one. How about that?"

Kyame clapped. "That would look so good on handbills. So mysterious."

Papa stopped at the door. "How many tricks are in your repertoire, George, in your bag? Card tricks, too?"

"Yes, I can do many card tricks. I have about ten tricks that would fit a Hindoo routine ... and could add maybe three or four more. No torture tricks. I don't believe a Brahmin would do such things."

Papa grinned. "Why not show Kyame a few while I'm gone."

***

Returning, Papa stopped at the door to watch as Kyame smoothly palmed a card from the bottom of the deck.

"Your daughter, Mr. Piddington, learns very fast," said Jones. "An excellent hard-working student. She has the long-fingered hands needed for a good card worker."

Kyame split the deck and shuffled, letting the cards riffle together in whirring waterfall finish. She looked up at Papa.

"This is fun, Papa."

"The telegram is sent. I don't expect a response for a few hours at the earliest, Jaiman Karkar. And now Kyame and I must begin preparing for our show."

"Sir, Miss Kyame, I am in your debt, deep debt. You are the first white folk who have trusted me as a black man, not as an Indian."

***

Once away from the hotel and moving quickly in the shadows behind the buildings, George Jones worked his way back toward the rented store front. He knew what he had to do. It would disappoint the Piddingtons, after all their kindness, but there was no choice. He stopped. There were three men coming around the corner of the bank ahead into the alley. One of the men was Griffin.

Jones pressed back up against the side of a shed -- and held his breath.

"We're not going to swing, Griffin, just so you can string up this black man. Got to be more in it than that, by God, 'fore I'm throwin' in."

They stopped a few feet away from the shed.

214

"I understand," said Griffin. "Tom Leysen been doing pretty well with his Hindoos and should have four, maybe five hundred dollars in that strongbox of his. You help me with Jones, you take the money and run. Come up to my room over there at the boarding house. I'll lay everything out. Can't miss. I get my man; you get your money."

Jones listened until their footsteps finally faded away. Now he had move even faster.

***

Tom Leysen dropped the cash into the strongbox. Hari Das, if that was his name, had delivered another $46 to the treasury. But now he had to move the troupe on. That damned Griffin had fouled Julesburg right up just when public interest was picking up. Nagpal's juggling and fire-eating show planned for tomorrow would have brought in another $50-60 and then the snake would be ready again. He glanced out at the darkening clouds. Rains coming up. He locked his trunk and started for his hotel.

Didn't want to get caught when the rain started. Plan out what to do over a couple of whiskies – the best cure for a rain storm.

Jones watched Leysen walking rapidly up the street as he heard the first rumble of distant thunder. The two Hindoos would be sleeping. There was no one in sight as the streets emptied with the threat of a heavy rain storm.

Jones ran.

***

There was a train leaving Julesburg for Denver at 4:18. Jones had to be on it. But the lock on the strongbox wouldn't open. He wiped his sweaty hands across his leggings to get a better grip, a better feel on the lock-picks. He inserted the tension tool to keep the internal lock in position; then he tried another pick, raked it slowly inside the lock to line up the levers. He had counted seven levers holding the lock closed. Most lever locks had only four.

Nothing. A groan from the other room. One of the dacoits was stirring.

Jones took a larger pick with a wider foot from his pouch. And raked again -- slowly, slowly. The lock moved slightly. Gently, don't lose the setup! He could feel the sweat spreading across his face. He raked cautiously and felt the lock finally give with a soft click.

Jones filled a small cloth bag with gold coins, then counted out $97 in bills, only what was owed him. As tough as Leysen had been, he had given Jones cover when he needed it. George Jones couldn't take everything.

He closed the leather bag. The elegant Hari Das was wrapped up inside with the tricks. He smiled when he had dropped the red and yellow balls in. A white girl had saved them for him. Maybe, there was a chance, somewhere. Maybe it wasn't Shiva touching him.

George Jefferson Jones stood with a black slouch hat, worn boots but clean shirt and pants. He had washed what he thought of as his "black clothes" three days ago. He threw the bag over his shoulder to free his hands. This would be his last run to freedom – or to the end of a rope.

The rain had started, drifting walls of windblown water moving down the streets blotting out everything. Jones huddled under the eaves against the wall of the shed behind the bank. Water was soaking up into his boots as he ran toward the boarding house.

***

"That lightening looks vicious, Papa. I hope no one is out there."

There was a loud rolling series of crackling thunder followed immediately with brilliant bursts of light. Kyame screamed and jumped back as a bolt of lightning suddenly flashed in front of her exploding against a tree across the street in front of a church.

Papa held her tight. "Stay away from the windows, Daughter. There's not going to be a show for us tonight it appears."

***

George Jones stood dripping just inside the back door of the boarding house. The owner's office was just to the right and empty. Jones, with his one free hand, turned the register pages. Griffin was upstairs in no. 6. It was 3:40. Still time to get to the station. Train probably would be late in the storm anyway.

With each step upward, Jones stopped to listen. Nothing could be heard over the roaring of the winds and the pounding of the rain on the roof and walls. He moved faster. No. 6 was at the end of the upstairs hall.

Jones gently turned the knob and pushed. The door was locked, but he had the passkey from the owner's office. The lock slid silently open. He heard voices suddenly in no. 7. He turned the knob again and gently pushed. Griffin was asleep on the bed, his bare feet sticking out from under the blanket pulled over him. His hat was over his face, apparently to block out the flashes from the lightning.

Kneeling down, Jones slid the leather bag from his shoulders to lay it by the door. Then he placed the wicker basket on the floor that he had carefully carried with both hands squeezing the lid tight. Sliding it across the floor, he pushed it closer to the bed. He loosened the lid. Jones could feel the cobra shifting inside. It started hissing, low angry growling hisses.

From watching the snake several times, Jones knew once the lid was raised, the cobra would rise up before striking. He had only a few seconds to get clear of the basket and out of the room.

Griffin muttered something, shifting, moving his legs.

Now! Jones lifted the lid free and jumped back. He grabbed the leather bag.

He caught a last glimpse of the cobra flowing out of the basket across the floor as he closed the door. He hesitated. Jones turned back and relocked the door with the passkey.

When he reached the bottom of the stairs he heard a cry from upstairs and pounding on a door. George Jefferson Jones ran down the hallway, threw the passkey on the owner's desk and went out into the driving rain. The station was only five blocks away.

***

As swiftly as it had appeared, the storm was gone leaving the air filled with clinging dampness and the sharp tang of ozone. A small blue crack in the black clouds was forming near the horizon. Two more lightning bolts had struck somewhere in town but now all was quite. Even with the rain, however, two buildings were on fire.

Hearing two knocks, Kyame went to the door. A boy wearing a damp Western Union cap at a rakish angle held out an envelope.

"A telegram, Miss, for Mr. Piddington. Don't know how the thing got through the storm. Wires're down all over." Papa reached over her shoulder to give the boy two coins that he squeezed tightly in his fist. "Thanks, Sir."

Kyame watched as Papa torn open the telegram. He grinned and handed it to her.

Piddington, it said, send the Brahmin, Cody.

"Look's like things are quieted down out there, Daughter, let's see if we can find George somewhere and give him the news."

Wearing boots and wrapped in black rain slickers, Kyame and Papa walked down Main Street as Julesburg began to come back to life. Crowds were gathering near the two fires with men running to join the bucket brigades trying to douse the flames.

"Let's head over that way, Kyame. Maybe I can help pass the water."

As they approached the nearest fire, Kyame pointed to a group of people gathered behind the burning building.

"There's the sheriff, Papa," she said.

Piddington saw that the bucket line was fully manned for the time being. "Okay, let's go see what he's looking at."

Sheriff Layne was kneeling next to a charred heap, poking at it with a stick. He looked up as the Piddingtons joined the group of men, the women had left, holding their hands to their mouths. He flipped the stick away as he stood and shrugged.

"Lightning just fried'm," he said. "Wouldn't know it was Hari Das if his leather bag weren't there. My God ... would hardly know that pile used to be a human being but for the bag. Must have gotten the full blast of the lightning bolt."

A burnt portion of the leather bag lay just beyond the burnt seared corpse of George Jefferson Jones.

"Why was he here, Sheriff, out in the open?" asked one of the men.

Kyame walked away from the group, her stomach churning. He had been so filled with hope that a new life might be possible. She saw two shoe-prints under the eaves of the boarding house. But the rains had washed everything else away. They were two right shoes. Must have been running, the prints were so far apart. Running to where?

She looked up when she felt Papa's hand on her shoulder.

"He didn't need to run, Daughter," said Papa. "George only had to wait a few hours to learn about Cody's response. I wonder why."

She thought of their earlier conversation with George Jones. Bad luck? Or...

"Papa, maybe it was Shiva, after all," said Kyame.

29

Kyame Piddington lazily observed the passing flat farm lands, the occasional wagon moving on distant roads. Her slumber had been interrupted by a sudden jolt as the swaying train passed over uneven switch points. A roiling cloud of black locomotive smoke swept across the windows.

It would be about another hour to Wichita where the Impossible Piddingtons were to present their second sight act for four days at the Wichita Opera House. It would be the first real theatre that Kyame had ever been in. Papa had been confident that Wichita could generate enough extra money to add to their savings account for her schooling back east.

She looked over at Papa reading the newspaper. He immediately felt her eyes and looked down at her, smiling.

"Papa, why does God hurt good people?" she asked.

"You wake from a nap with a question like that, Daughter?" Papa laughed. "That is one of the most profound questions that can be asked. Why now?"

Kyame pushed herself up against the seat back.

"I saw someone out there" -- she motioned toward the windows -- "fall off their wagon when their horse stumbled. It looked bad. Why did God hurt them?" She hesitated. "Why did God destroy George Jones' hopes?"

She recalled Solomon Royale, the disillusioned preacher from Abilene and now an irreverent reporter in Lawrence -- and wondered. If someone trained to understand and yet abandons God for whatever he can find, what is there in the belief? She admitted there were days and sometimes weeks when God seemed so far away as to not exist at all to hear her prayers. Solomon had even stopped praying, though he had tried to make a joke of it.

John Piddington folded his paper. The paper was three days old with the brief note on the death of Solomon Royale buried in the corner of the last page -- but it could wait. Piddington felt an emptiness, though Royale had been in their lives for only a few days. He had sent cuttings of some of his articles from the two papers he had worked on -- well written Piddington thought. Royale had kept careful track of the movements of the Impossible Piddingtons, so the large envelope of articles was always a pleasant surprise. But the sad news could wait.

The green eyes of his pretty thirteen-year-old black haired daughter, so like her mother's, glistened with intent interest. She was growing up so fast, learning so fast in ways no ordinary girl could. But she had to, now that Laura had been dead for over two years. But Kyame always had challenging questions.

"Well, I ...." he started.

"My God, John Piddington!" A deep baritone boomed behind them.

Piddington looked up and immediately stood, his hand outstretched. "Cadwell! Jonathan Cadwell. Where did you come from? It has been too long, J. W., too long."

Kyame saw a tall bearded man dressed in a black pin-striped suit with waves of light brown hair cascading over his high starched white collar almost down to his shoulders -- with deep compelling brown eyes. He would be a challenge to draw but her drawing box was in the rack overhead. But his face was secured in her memory for drawing later.

Then his disturbing eyes turned to her.

"You are Kyame?" Cadwell asked, his voice softened.

"Yes, sir, I am."

"You have your mother's mystic eyes and her beauty, Miss Kyame. I have known your father and mother for many years."

"Daughter," said Papa, "this is J. W. Cadwell, the greatest mesmerist in the country and … a trusted friend."

Kyame put out her hand that was instantly enveloped by Cadwell's. She was aware that he had waited for her to extend her hand before he extended his -- the simple courtesy of a gentleman, her mother had once taught. He removed his hat and bowed to her. Cadwell's skin was soft, not the hard calluses of most of the men Kyame had met as they had traveled from cowtown to cowtown with their act.

Trusted.

Papa rarely used that word for anyone.

"Can you sit with us, Mr. Cadwell?" she asked, pulling her feet and skirts back to clear the way.

"That is most hospitable, Miss Kyame." Cadwell settled his long frame into the seat opposite, placing his hat beside him.

He smiled at her. "I was there when your mother named you. She saw your name while dreaming a vast dream of heaven. One of the angels, the prettiest that she saw, was named Kyame.

"Right, John?" Cadwell looked to Papa for confirmation.

Papa nodded.

Kyame saw the conductor suddenly appear at the door into their shifting and rattling car. The train was increasing its speed. He was running his left thumb over the heavy crystal of his watch after the manner of all railroad men.

Instantly, Kyame became uneasy. The man looked frantic as, moving down the aisle, he examined each face.

"Trouble, conductor?" asked Cadwell as the conductor came abreast of them.

"Palace car thief. Stole some expensive jewels from a lady up front. But then he just disappeared. *Disappeared.* Can't find anyone to fit the lady's description."

Kyame brushed both hands across her skirt as she looked to her left toward the window. Her ready signal.

Papa touched his belt in acknowledgement.

Using their silent second sight code that had become almost a second language between them, Kyame signed: "Man -- three rows ahead -- left -- had beard -- no beard now -- black coat -- was gray." Her message required only seconds.

Cadwell frowned in bemused interest, his eyes flickering between the Piddingtons.

Papa nodded. Leaning toward the conductor, he whispered, "Conductor, I believe your thief is three rows ahead of us on the left. In the black suit."

Cadwell looked first at her then Papa. "John, does Kyame have Laura's artistic memory?"

"In spades."

"Then, conductor," said Cadwell, turning, speaking softly. "That's your thief."

"But how do you know?" His voice was strained with panic. "I've got to find the bastard before Wichita or I lose my job. The woman he stole from is the division manager's wife."

"He came on the train dressed in gray," said Kyame. "And with a beard. Now he has no beard and is in black."

The conductor glanced quickly back and forth between Kyame and the men. "How ...?"

Kyame let her eyes go wide, her green pupils surrounded by white, her fingers spread as she passed her hands slowly before her face. She raised her chin as though striving to pluck a scent from the air. The technique she had rehearsed with Papa countless times. To color her statements with the mysterious, he had explained.

"Because, sir," said Kyame, "I *see* him. I *see him* with the jewels."

Startled, the conductor stepped back.

"We'll back you up, conductor. John?" Cadwell shifted his coat to loosen it around his shoulders.

Papa nodded.

"Sit very still, Daughter," Papa warned, as he stood.

"You gentlemen ... heeled?"

"I am," said Cadwell. A small pistol appeared in his hand.

The conductor nodded and turned back toward the front of the waggling car as Papa and Cadwell followed. Kyame swallowed when the conductor suddenly staggered against a seat back as the car swayed, then pulling himself up straight, he stopped beside the man in black.

"Sir, may I ask you to stand?" said the conductor. His face was glistening in sweat.

"Damn you, no! You bother me, conductor, and I *will report* you in Wichita," snarled the man in black. "Filthy Jew!" He turned away to the window.

"Stand, you miserable thief," boomed J. W. Cadwell, "and keep your hands away from your body. Further, man ... further! I have no patience with blackguards who steal from women." Cadwell pressed the muzzle of his pistol hard against the man's neck. "One bullet will end your worthless life!"

Kyame trembled; the fierce rage in Cadwell's voice was terrifying.

"Search him, conductor," said Papa. "He won't make trouble."

The jewels were in a black bag stuffed into a concealed slit in the back of his reversible coat. The conductor extracted a fake beard from an inside pocket. With a short length of rope given him by Cadwell, the conductor, who gave his name as Samuel Weiss, tied the thief's hands to the back of the seat.

Cadwell offered to sit with the bound thief to Wichita while the conductor returned the jewels.

Weiss wiped his face with his handkerchief. "My God, I owe you ... and your little girl. Who are you?"

Cadwell answered. "My friend and his remarkable daughter are the Impossible Piddingtons, and I, I am J. W. Cadwell ... the mesmerist."

The thief looked up at them over his shoulder. "Oh, Christ, of all the rail cars I had to walk into!

30

"I carry the rope, John, to demonstrate the impossible, when it is appropriate," answered Cadwell. "You know the stunt ... with the knots."

Papa nodded.

They were seated in the dining room at the Wichita Harvey House as Kyame finished her apple pie. The Santa Fe railroad had issued special passes to them for free travel for three months in recognition of their help to Conductor Weiss in capturing the notorious palace car thief, Ben Allison.

To Weiss's intense relief, both Piddington and Cadwell had credited the conductor with organizing the capture. An extra single-sheet was already selling on the Wichita streets describing Weiss' heroism and his receiving a $250 reward from the A. T. & S.F. railroad for capturing Allison.

Kyame had been impressed when Cadwell had asked her permission to smoke his cigar. No man had ever done that before. She was always just "the girl". She swallowed her chunk of hot pie too fast in order to respond.

"Certainly, Mr. Caldwell," she said, clearing her throat. "I like the fragrance of good tobacco." Kyame really didn't, but remembered that Mama had said that once and the man had seemed particularly pleased. Mama had confided to her later that she could tolerate the aroma of a good cigar, but never the stink of a pipe.

Impressed, Papa raised his eyebrows, as did the mesmerist.

Cadwell took a moment igniting the cigar. Once it was burning evenly, he raised it as a toast to Kyame.

"She is so close to Laura, my friend. You are deeply fortunate."

To be compared to Mama. Kyame glowed happily.

***

Excusing herself, Kyame had taken her drawing box out to the hotel porch to sketch the passing people, and to begin work on her portrait of Cadwell. "I want to do eyes today," she said, kissing Papa goodbye, and waving to Cadwell.

The mesmerist watched her as she disappeared into the lobby. "My God, John, your daughter is remarkably like her mother. May I make a suggestion? Margaret and I have never had children, so perhaps I am overreacting."

"I'll listen to anything you might say, J. W., anytime," said Piddington.

"Teach Kyame to handle a gun," said Cadwell, "at least a derringer. If you'll allow, I'll buy it as my investment in her education. As she matures, becoming a beautiful woman, she is certain to attract some difficult attention. Kyame should be able to defend herself."

After a moment, Piddington nodded. "Her mother carried a derringer. Maybe it is time for Kyame."

***

Henry B. Allen

The Allen Boy Medium

with Professor J. W. Cadwell presiding.

Coming to Wichita in three days under the auspices of

The

Anti-Death Alliance,

Arad Gilbert, president.

The powder blue handbills were everywhere. Great wonders were promised at the Mechanic's Hall from the ten year-old boy spirit medium for physical phenomena.

Kyame wanted to see Henry Allen in action. She knew about great wonders. She did them herself -- if she read Papa's signing correctly.

Papa was at the Opera House to finalize their arrangements and had agreed to Kyame's accompanying Cadwell.

"Watch J. W. closely, Kyame. He knows how to get up an excitement." He smiled. "Then we will get up one of our own."

Cadwell went first to the offices of the Wichita *Eagle*. Within a few moments, a young reporter, Eric Masterton, was following at his elbow.

When Masterton asked her name, Kyame answered, "I am of the Impossible Piddingtons."

"I've heard of you and your father ... and what you all did on the train. So ... you can read my mind, Miss Kyame?" His smirking smile irritated her.

"When the time comes, Mr. Masterton, when the time comes I promise I *will see* your thoughts."

Like a co-conspirator, Cadwell smiled over the reporter's shoulder, nodded then tipped his hat to her.

With Masterton in tow, Cadwell walked down crowded Main Street toward Kosierian's, the largest jewelry store in Wichita.

"What do you plan to do there?" questioned the reporter matching Cadwell's long stride, with Kyame following trying to keep only a step behind.

"To steal him blind, Mr. Masterton," smiled the mesmerist.

The reporter's mouth dropped.

Kyame grinned when Cadwell winked at her. Whatever, this was going to be something she would have to carefully describe to Papa later. No school could teach her like J. W. Cadwell.

***

Arthur Kosierian stood almost six inches shorter than the mesmerist with evident suspicion in every inch. Kyame sensed the jeweler's smile was perfunctory. The store was empty of customers.

His hands flat on the glass-topped counter, the jeweler said, "Sirs ... and miss," glancing quickly over the counter at Kyame, "How may I be of service?"

Cadwell bowed. "Your merchandise is most impressive, sir. I should like to steal all of it."

Kosierian's mouth dropped. "What? What is this, Masterton, a miserable joke for your paper? Remember, I'm an advertiser … and there are other papers in this town."

Cadwell leaned forward across the counter and drew two fingers of his right hand lightly across the spread fingers of the jeweler while continuing to speak on the elegant quality of the jewelry, his baritone soft and sincere.

Kosierian finally exploded. "What is going on?"

Cadwell smiled. "Your fingers are now pasted to the glass, sir. You cannot remove them no matter how hard you try."

The jeweler frowned and snapped, "I … !" His eyes flew wide. He twisted his shoulders, his wrists but his fingers wouldn't move.

Kyame was astonished.

The reporter stepped to one side and began scribbling furiously.

"I could rob you of everything right now, Mr. Kosierian, if I chose to," said the mesmerist, his voice strengthening. "*If* I chose."

Kosierian's face was flushing a purplish-red. "I ... I would shout for help," he barked, still pulling and twisting his arms. "There's an armed policeman just outside." But his fingers remained locked to the glass.

"Ah, you could," said Cadwell. "But," he commanded, "*you* cannot speak." With his index finger, the mesmerist slashed a quick line in the air before Kosierian's mouth.

The jeweler opened his mouth. Kyame could see the muscles strain in his neck -- but there was no sound!

Kosierian looked frantically around pulling at his fingers, trying to speak, to shout, but there was only silence.

The jeweler looked, opening and closing his mouth, thought Kyame, smothering a giggle, like a fish trying to gulp air.

"Enough, Mr. Cadwell, I believe you have proven your powers," said Eric Masterton, his own eyes wide with amazement.

Cadwell looked at Kyame who was struggling to suppress a laugh. "Enough, Miss Kyame?"

"Yes, Mr. Cadwell. Enough."

Turning back to Kosierian, he said, "Then, sir, at the young lady's direction … you are free." He snapped his fingers.

The jeweler fell back against the wall, gasping for air.

Kyame laughed. Yes, J. W. Cadwell knew how to get up an excitement.

31

"Papa, what did he do?"

John Piddington had been laughing at Kyame's excited description of J. W. Cadwell's visit to Kosierian's. He had called it "a beautiful stunt".

"J. W. is a master of the voice, Daughter. That is the key secret of mesmerism. He can bend audiences like no one else I have ever seen. J. W. first suggested, then convinced the jeweler that what he had said was true, that the man's own fingers were fastened to the glass, that he had no voice."

"Could he do that to me?" Kyame's voice was anxious. She had described how terrifying Cadwell had been on the train with the thief.

"He could, possibly, but he never would. He would never do anything to upset you, Kyame. J. W. is someone on whom you can always rely. He proved his friendship when your mother died." It had been Cadwell who had loaned him the cash to keep food on the table after Laura's final struggle with consumption had drained away all their money.

Piddington suddenly smiled. "Would you like to learn mesmerism?"

Kyame eyes went wide. "Me? Is that possible?"

"Let's ask ... if you really want to", said Papa. "J. W. taught Mama."

***

Cadwell's face was drawn. "The Allen boy is too ill to travel, John, so now I have no medium for my show in three days, which means forfeiting the purse -... $1,000."

"Purse?" John Piddington sipped his beer. Kyame was in their hotel room working on her portrait of Cadwell. The Opera House was ready for their performance that night.

The mesmerist leaned across the table. The dark saloon was quiet, almost empty.

"Things have been growing tight," said Cadwell. "The public interest in the spiritual, in mediumship is waning. Too many mediums and too many exposures. There has always been twenty fakes to every genuine medium, but only the fakes are ever described in the papers, which has convinced the public that fakery is all there is.

"And, even mesmerism doesn't draw as it once did."

"Your book teaching mesmerism is still selling?" asked Piddington. His friend's face was uncharacteristically apprehensive.

Cadwell barely nodded. "That volume is in its 25th edition, John. It's provided a steady though moderate income for many years. But even that will end at some point. I first wrote that book ten years ago, but now it's 1893. The public's interests are changing with the approach of the new century."

The two men were silent as they drank.

Cadwell drew on his cigar for a moment then said, "That $1,000 is the purse for a contest between the Allen boy and Darcy Y. Fox, a Wichita banker *cum* psychical exposer. Fox has destroyed three other physical mediums in the past few months ... all whom I knew well. Fox claims he will, under the same test conditions, duplicate and explain anything that Henry Allen does with the spirits. The audience is to decide who wins.

"With the interest from the contest, once Henry won, then the income from the following séances would make Wichita most attractive.

"But ... no Henry B. Allen." Cadwell hesitated, then leaned closer, to whisper, "John, do you think Kyame could learn the rope tie routines in time ... in three days?"

***

Diminutive, thin-faced with a thick shock of white hair, Arad Gilbert frowned. The lawyer vigorously shook his head.

"An untested medium for physical phenomena? A little girl, no less? Professor Cadwell, Mr. Fox will devastate the believers of Wichita with his one-sided victory. He has refused to accept any delay.

"Darcy Fox is not a gentleman ... but he will still win. His rowdy followers will pack Mechanic's Hall. Only the strongest experienced test medium could possibly overcome all the obstacles."

Gilbert shook his head and stood. "No, sir. The Anti-Death Alliance will not and cannot sanction such a contest. Nor will it contribute to a purse that would only serve to fill Mr. Fox's already large pockets.

"Good day to you, sir."

Cadwell was fuming, as a young man edged past him to hand Gilbert a sealed note. Gilbert waved the clerk away, then broke the seal.

Damn coward.

But the mesmerist observed Gilbert turn pale as he read the note. Their eyes met as Cadwell closed the office door.

***

"Gilbert is a damn coward, John." Cadwell leaned against the wall of the hotel room. With her father's encouragement, Kyame had gone for a walk to the Opera House and would return within about ten minutes. "And I am now holding the bag for the $500 as well. None of Gilbert's followers will contribute. Fox is to put up the other half.

"Will Kyame do it? It is difficult and unfair to ask her, particularly in so short a time."

Piddington smiled and leaned back, tilting his cane chair back against the wall.

"Kyame thinks you are the 'prettiest man' she has ever seen … after me, naturally. And she has drawn your portrait, which I will leave her to show you. It's remarkably good."

Cadwell smiled.

"And, J. W., she wants to help. You can start when she returns. Our routines for the Opera House require minimal rehearsal. I have discovered enough local dope and gossip to fire up our performances the next couple of nights, so her time can be focused on learning the necessary mediumistic rope ties.

"And … I also have an idea to suggest for climaxing our show tonight that may help both of us."

Cadwell pulled a chair up as Piddington leaned forward.

32

"Is Henry Allen a genuine medium, Mr. Cadwell?" Kyame asked, as they took a break in her rope-tie training. Her wrists were becoming reddened from the scraping of the ropes on her skin. She was getting faster in escaping the ties and then retying herself, but still not as efficiently as the mesmerist needed.

Silently, Papa watched them from across the hotel room, smiling occasionally in support.

It was a matter of her progressively gaining a little more slack with each turn or twist of the ropes, which were smooth finished cord that would allow some loosening in the knots, no matter how tightly they were tied.

The mesmerist hesitated, then answered, "Frequently, Miss Kyame, but not always. But the expectations in the séances are for constant success, so Henry has learned what you are learning … only not so quickly."

"But why not miss, Mr. Cadwell, why not fail sometimes? It would make things look more real," Kyame said, looking over at Papa. "Papa and

I miss intentionally every now and then. It always scares people because I become more real." She fluttered her fingers in a mock occult movement.

Both Papa and Cadwell laughed. "Yes, of course, you are right, Miss Kyame, regarding the second sight, but mediumship is not so forgiving and supportive. The believers, once snared, want spirits on schedule for constant reassurance. Sometimes the disembodied ones are in a weakened state, so the manifestations are limited … but that cannot happen often. Not with someone like Darcy Fox around.

"And Henry is good, with or without the spirits. It is unfortunate that you cannot meet him at this time."

As she settled back into the chair to be tied once more, Kyame asked, "If the ghosts only want to help us, why do people have to pay to talk to them?"

Cadwell stopped, the ropes hanging over his hands. He smiled. Kyame Piddington was so intense, so many questions. She wants to know everything -- and she is tough along with beautiful. To have a daughter like her, Cadwell smiled.

The mesmerist stretched the ropes to remove kinks. "Ghosts are the same after death as before. They expect to be paid, through the medium, for their work. As the great Count Cagliostro said a hundred years ago, 'The spirits do not come for nothing'."

Kyame thought for a moment, then nodded as Cadwell began to encircle her wrists with the rope.

***

Thanks to the heroics of the Impossible Piddingtons described so vividly in the train stories carried by all the Wichita newspapers, the Opera House was already full half-an-hour before the 8pm show time with late-arriving men and women grouping around the sides of the theatre.

Papa had somehow learned some local secrets, as he always did; Kyame didn't know how. He promised he would start showing her how that was done, but that was for later.

Kyame was blindfolded and seated on a raised chair in the center of the stage. Thus, reading Papa's silent signals through the fake blindfold, she identified objects shown to Papa that she could not see, announced the serial number on a bond handed to Papa, just as she had in other towns; coloring her statements with smokey acting.

But -- when Kyame warned a Mr. Joshua Lennox against his buying pasture land because the stream flowing through it was tainted, the audience was astonished; when Kyame laughed about the twins to be born and identified the traveling salesman who was their father, not the woman's husband, the place rocked with shouts and laughter while a man quickly ran out of the theatre.

Smiling, Papa had tightened his right fist and shook it slightly.

Kyame glowed. It was going good.

With the evening getting late, on cue from Papa, she hopped down from the raised chair on which she had been sitting and, removing her blindfold, walked to the edge of the stage.

Papa was slowly walking down the center aisle away from her with his back turned.

Kyame said, her voice rising in power, "There is death here. *Death. I feel him.*" The Opera House went instantly still, as if everyone were holding their breath.

As she saw the expressions of belief spread across the audience, Kyame let her eyes go wide, her fingers splayed as she wove her hands before her face. "Yes … yes, there is someone here who has passed on. Who is ... Oh, Papa! Papa! The man is coming toward me! He is coming! Coming!"

Papa turned back toward her.

Kyame pointed toward the far corner of the audience then let her hand move across the audience toward the center aisle, as though tracking something.

"What is it? What does the girl see?" several women were asking, twisting around to glance behind them. Others stood to glare suspiciously up at Kyame then behind them.

Suddenly a woman screamed. "He's here! He touched me! The ghost touched my arm with his cold fingers!"

Papa ran the last steps to the stage. As he came close to Kyame, he winked, and made a fist in his right hand.

Kyame had her hands over her face, her wide eyes visible between her fingers.

"Who was it, Joan ... who touched you?" a woman called across the turbulent audience.

"It ... it was Jake, *My Jake come back!* Only he knew where to touch my arm."

There was a sudden strong movement toward the side exits and the double doors in the back of the Opera House.

"Don't move, Daughter," Papa whispered. "Let the piece play out. Let them convince themselves. You've done enough."

Papa looked closer at her sparkling green eyes, smiled.

"And don't laugh."

33

"A marvelous convincing piece of work, Miss Kyame," said Cadwell. "Beautifully executed."

"And, John," the mesmerist turned toward Piddington who was sipping a cup of coffee on the other side of their hotel room, "you evoked the spiritual presence with real skill, like you did the spirits every day."

"Bringing the 'ghost of the North' is easy enough when the setting is in place", said Piddington. "Just bring your flat hand down toward the right person and the air you move will feel cool and wash over the person's hand or arm if they are within about three to four feet. That woman was only two feet away, so she felt a strong breeze with the passing of Kyame's ghost.

"The woman supplied most of the ghost of her Jake from her own imagination."

***

"Professor Cadwell." The three men waited for the mesmerist to swallow the piece of steak. "We apologize for intruding in your breakfast, sir."

Dabbing his lips with a napkin, Cadwell said, "Please join me, gentlemen. How may I be of service?"

As the men settled into the three chairs around Cadwell's table, he signaled a waiter. As the waiter poured coffee, one of the men placed an envelope on the table.

"I am Jared Thomas, sir. We are local merchants who are loyal members of the Anti-Death Alliance. We are followers of the divine truth of spiritual harmony.

"The appearance of Miss Kyame Piddington last night was stunning. The woman involved has not yet recovered from her joy at being touched by her late husband. We believe Miss Piddington may be an appropriate representative of our truth in the conflict with Mr. Fox. We want to give you this contribution toward the purse, as a demonstration of our sincerity and support."

"Perhaps, Mr. Cadwell," said another of the men, "the purse should be increased to more than one thousand dollars?"

The other two men nodded in agreement.

"I agree the Piddington girl may prove stronger than I first imagined," said Arad Gilbert. "I will approach Fox with the suggestion of a larger purse. That will appeal to his greed, if not to his good sense."

He rose to shake hands with J. W. Cadwell

***

Kyame sat next to Papa as he finished reading the newspaper after breakfast. He had already pointed out the front page write-up on their evening's show with the headline "Ghosts Walk with the Piddingtons at the Opera House". Kyame had been described as a "beautiful young medium of power".

"By heaven!" Piddington suddenly folded the paper to read carefully. "Kyame, the Dalton gang raided Coffeyville two days ago and tried to hold up two banks, the First National and the C. M. Condon & Co. bank. Remember that experience?"

Kyame pursed her lips. The memory of Papa locked in that safe still appeared as a nightmare on occasion. "Yes, Papa, I do. What happened?"

"Townspeople killed four of the gang and one got away. But, oh my, Marshal Connelly and one other man were killed by the Daltons."

"The Marshal? What about Deputy Macallen?" Her eyes went moist. Marshal Connelly had been impressed with the solving of the hotel robbery and murder. He had been such a kind man. Why does God hurt good people? Kyame still couldn't understand.

"No mention of Juice Macallen, so he must be all right. But what a horrible and stupid episode. The Daltons used to live in Coffeyville. They were recognized immediately, even in disguise." He shook his head and turned the page.

"I could recognize the Daltons, too, Papa," she said slowly.

He looked over the page at his beautiful daughter, his eyes softening. "Yes, of course, Kyame," he said gently. She had grown so much since that time at Ellsworth. She was consuming books like candy everywhere they found them and never stopped asking questions. So like her mother. She would memorize the books then read them later in her mind. It saved money and weight.

Piddington had to read books the old-fashioned way.

Kyame's eyes refocused into a dreamy reverie, seeming to retreat from the dining room to where?

"Kyame, I apologize for interrupting, but what book are you reading now?"

Her eyes instantly came alive. "H. Rider Haggard's *King Solomon's Mines*, Papa. I found it on the train, but it is missing some pages. It is so exciting. I want to see Africa, Papa. And I want to find other books that Mr. Haggard has written."

Piddington nodded as his daughter returned to the world of Allan Quartermain, Haggard's white hunter hero. He turned his attention back to the drab world of the newspaper.

***

Kyame finally had her portrait of J. W. Cadwell finished. His eyes had been very hard to capture -- but Papa assured her that she had done it.

But Kyame was troubled. She had watched Papa look at the women walking across the lobby, one or two reminded her a little of Mama, their hair, their dress -- their happiness. There was a deep distant longing in Papa's face Kyame hadn't seen before, as though she wasn't even there. She didn't know what it meant -- what she should do? Kyame was worried. Had she done something wrong? She held Cadwell's portrait tightly -- her drawing didn't seem so important any more.

Nothing did.

***

Mechanic's Hall couldn't hold the expected crowds, so the contest had been moved to the Opera House. With the admission price raised to fifty cents, the purse by agreement between Fox and the Anti-Death Alliance had become $2,000.

Peeking from behind the curtains, the crowds were the largest Kyame had ever experienced with rows of people standing along the walls jammed ever tighter together. She could feel the rising clamor sweep like a tide over the kerosene stage-lights, the smell of the kerosene mixed with human sweat and hundreds of unwashed bodies.

J. W. Cadwell had told her that no matter what happened he would always be in her debt for her courage and her generous support. And he promised to teach her mesmerism, if she wanted.

But what Kyame needed most now was the assurance that Papa still loved her, still needed her. She had seen him talking with one of the women.

34

Darcy Y. Fox was the ugliest man Kyame had ever seen. Hard cruel blue eyes, a slash of a scar across his forehead. He was bald, his head shining in the glow of the kerosene lamps. His breath was foul with whisky and garlic as he leaned over her to inspect the knots and ropes that bound her to the chair which was itself nailed to the floor of the stage.

Fox would use the same chair for his demonstration, but first the "miserable homeless spirits", as Fox called them, had to appear or there would be nothing for him to duplicate.

Kyame didn't like his confident smile as he backed away.

"I got it," Fox shouted to his supporters seated close to the stage. They cheered until others in the audience rose to shout at them to "quiet down or leave".

A cabinet with its hanging black curtains was rolled forward by four men until Kyame was surrounded, with only the front still open to the audience. A small table with handbells, tambourines, tin plates and a full glass of water stood about three feet away, apparently out of her reach, even if she could get free.

J. W. Cadwell stepped to the footlights. His voice boomed to the last row.

"Ladies and gentlemen, we meet tonight to test whether the precious harmonial truth of Spiritualism can resist the foul attack of materialism." Fox's supporters started to boo, but Cadwell's hard glance silenced them. "Based on your collective judgment, a purse of two thousand dollars in gold will be awarded tonight to whomever *you*," -- his hands swept across the audience --"decide deserves it.

"Let us begin. Is the medium secured to your satisfaction, gentlemen? Mr. Fox?"

Even Fox seemed momentarily cowed by Cadwell's stage presence.

"Yes, Professor Cadwell, we are satisfied that the young medium cannot move."

"Close the curtain. Spirits, come to us, tonight; come to us in our need. Come now!"

***

Once the curtain was closed, Kyame quickly slipped her left hand. Cadwell had taught that speed, speed and speed were paramount in order to mimic the spirits. Once free with the added slack, the rope encircling her left leg loosened as well. Reaching out toward the table, she grasped the stack of tin plates and tossed them over curtains out of the cabinet.

The clatter of their hitting the stage sent cries and screams through the audience. Then she struck the table three times with the tambourine and threw it out of the cabinet. Then sat back into the chair, regained the slack and groaned – the signal. She dropped her head, her eyes closed.

Barely ten seconds.

"Open the curtains!" Cadwell ordered. As the committee and Fox pulled the curtains back, the mesmerist pointed toward Kyame's slumped form. "Test the medium's bonds. Is she as you left her?"

The chairman of the committee turned toward the audience and nodded.

"Louder, sir, the people in the rear cannot hear you nod."

"Yes, Professor, she is as we left her. The ropes and knots are untouched ... by human hand!"

"Mr. Fox?"

Fox grinned. "Yeah, the girl's done her job well. Get on with it."

The curtains were closed again. Kyame drank the water and threw the handbells out of the cabinet. And sighed.

Twelve seconds.

Again, the curtain was thrown back. Again Fox and the committee confirmed the knots and ropes were as before. The curtain pulled shut.

Kyame slipped the slack on her left hand, rotated her right hand which came free. Moving even faster than during the rehearsals in the hotel room, her heart pounding, she removed the ropes from the chair, wrapped them around her left arm, pulled the curtain open and walked out to shouted astonishment of the audiences. She saw that the men in the front rows were not cheering or applauding.

Eight seconds.

She saw Mr. Gilbert standing and applauding, his smile was wide. Papa, standing in the wings, made a hard fist with his right hand and signed quickly, I-love-you-Daughter.

Kyame glowed. Everything was all right.

Cadwell took the ropes from her and gave them to the committee.

"Now let our young medium rest for the second test while Mr. Fox attempts to duplicate the presence of the spirits." He leaned over to Kyame to whisper, "Wonderful, Miss Kyame. Henry could not have done it better."

Darcy Y. Fox, grinning eagerly, was tied to the chair by the committee. Cadwell agreed that he was tied as had been the medium.

Though taking almost a minute longer than Kyame, Fox successfully duplicated everything Kyame had done. The front rows cheered lustily while most of the audience sat in silence.

The second test was to allow Fox himself tie the medium in any way that did not endanger her health or life. Then Professor Cadwell would tie Fox.

Fox's breath sickened her even when Kyame turned her face away from him. He skillfully countered each of her attempts to gather slack until she was truly tied tightly.

Cadwell challenged Fox. "My God, man, you're torturing her!" He pointed to Kyame's swelling wrists starting to turn blue. "Injuring this girl is not part of the contest!"

The audience was on its feet, shouting at Fox, while the men in front stood cheering him on.

Fox stepped to the footlights, his hands raised to quiet the angry audience. "I bear this young girl no ill will. If she requests my tying be loosened for her comfort, I will do it.

"Ask her!"

The audience went quiet, as Cadwell turned toward her, and Papa watched from the wings, his face drawn and apprehensive.

Suddenly, Kyame hated Darcy Fox with everything in her. More than she had ever hated before. Her anger swept like a raging fire through her. She wanted only to destroy him in any way she could.

"No!" she cried. "He can pull the ropes *tighter* if he wants. I will have the spirits here tonight! And they will haunt Darcy Fox forever!"

Fox turned pale when he saw Kyame's young face contorted by hate. Then, taking a breath, he smiled and shook his head.

"No, the ropes are tight enough. But ... I *will* add one last thing without touching the ropes."

Fox beckoned to a man in the front row, who quickly came forward carrying a black cloth. Taking the cloth, Fox shook it out.

"I propose to wrap the medium in this cloth and tie it shut at her neck and at her feet. If she can create the manifestations under those conditions, *any of the_manifestations*, I will admit defeat at once! No vote need be taken."

Frowning, Cadwell looked over at Kyame. The committee looked at her. The audience stood to look at her.

Fox sneered at her.

***

Kyame felt something spreading through her, a warm confidence she had never felt before. Her anger cooled into implacable determination. Yes, yes she would do it.

She just didn't know how.

"Let Mr. Fox continue, Professor, gentlemen. It is time for the spirits to convince *everyone*."

Her gentle voice carried to the furthest reaches of the quieted audience. Papa looked strangely at her. Even Kyame didn't recognize her own voice.

***

As Cadwell closed the curtain he saw Kyame close her eyes, only her head was visible, the black cloth wrapped tightly around her and tied at her throat and ankles. She made no sound, no signal. He stepped back a step, then two and turned to join the committee at the footlights. He glanced over at a distressed John Piddington and frowned.

Piddington shook his head, his face deeply drawn in worry.

***

A silent moment passed, then another. The audience began to shift in their seats. Even the men in the front rows were leaning forward.

The murmuring grew.

"Merciful God, release the dear girl, she is suffering too much! Give the foul fiend his blood money," a woman pleaded before the audience. "You're killing her!" she screamed.

Then everything and everyone went silent.

The curtain was drawn back and Kyame stepped through, free of the ropes and black cloth. Her hair was tousled and tangled, falling down over her eyes. She took a step, nearly falling, recovered, then, pushing her hair away, Kyame pointed toward the audience who cringed before this wraith, then toward Darcy Fox.

"I have enough, enough of this. I will not come again tonight." The voice was husky, mature, not the voice of a young girl. "I return now. And you" -- she extended both hands her fingers spread toward Fox -- "you will burn in the Hell that you deserve. We will be waiting for you … Darcy Fox."

Several women screamed.

Kyame turned slowly back to the cabinet, pulling the curtain closed behind her. A moment, then another.

"Open, please!" called Kyame, her voice in pain.

Cadwell, followed by John Piddington rushing from the wings, Fox and the committee dashed to the cabinet. Cadwell threw the curtain back.

"My dear God!" he cried, stepping back in amazement.

Kyame was still tied tightly, wrapped within the black cloth, tears streaming down her face, her hair exactly in place as though just brushed.

Cadwell unfolded a knife from his pocket and began cutting the ropes, pulling the cloth away, seeing Kyame's wrists and hands swollen and blue.

"Get her out, J. W., get her out," Piddington cried. "My God, Kyame, this is too much, too much. Dear Kyame!" He turned toward Fox. "By God, man, if she is seriously hurt, I will kill you tonight!"

Fox stepped back, his face pale, his supporters frozen in silence.

With the last of the ropes cut, Piddington scooped up his daughter, kissing her repeatedly on her cheeks, her forehead, and carried her off stage, tears streaming down his cheeks.

35

J. W. Cadwell roared in anger. "Darcy Fox gets the purse! Gilbert, you damned fool! You agreed to give that bastard the purse regardless of the results! This young girl went through utter Hell for nothing ... for you! You miserable fool! Why man? Why?"

Arad Gilbert cowered against the wall of his office, the furious mesmerist towering over him. The wooden box filled with gold coins was on his desk. Fox had paid immediately and walked off the stage, clearly shaken.

"I ... I had to pay off a loan at Darcy Fox's bank. He sent me a note threatening immediate foreclosure on my home. This contest was the only way I could get enough money in time. You must understand. You must."

Piddington stood with Kyame at his side behind Cadwell. He started to speak, but stopped when J. W. motioned to him.

"Well," said Cadwell, his voice suddenly soft, unthreatening, "we can understand your plight. But that box weighs so much, Gilbert, that you can't lift it alone. Try. We will help, eh, John?"

Piddington and Kyame began to smile.

"Yes, J. W.," said Piddington, "we will help."

Arad Gilbert looked at Cadwell, then at Piddington, he avoided looking at Kyame. He sucked in a deep breath and strained to lift the box. Gilbert couldn't move the box of gold. It was as though the box was welded to the desk. But he had just set it on the desk -- only a few moments ago. What was happening?

Cadwell smiled again. "The box is so heavy that you don't even want it any more, do you, Mr. Gilbert."

Gilbert looked confused. "Ah, ah, I ... I ... guess not." Befuddled, he shook his head.

"Then Mr. Piddington and I will take it away, so you won't be troubled with the box any longer. You will sign a note giving the box to us ... won't you."

Gilbert slowly sat down at his desk, his eyes wide, his face slack, his hands and arms moving as in a dream. He handed the note up to a smiling, supportive Cadwell, as Piddington picked up the box, winking at Kyame.

***

"That was masterful, J. W.," said John Piddington. "How long before Gilbert realizes what has happened?"

Cadwell laughed. "About the time Darcy Fox slaps him around when he doesn't deliver the money as promised."

They had split the $2,000, with Cadwell insisting the Piddingtons take $1,500, the extra $500 as a personal gift to Kyame.

They stood at the Wichita train station with two trains waiting, The Impossible Piddingtons toward Denver while the mesmerist was headed east.

Cadwell bowed to Kyame. "Miss Kyame, you are the most courageous young woman I have been privileged to meet. Your mother would be truly proud. I still don't understand how you did it.

It appeared to be a spirit speaking through you, but I have never seen that manifestation before. But there are now believers in Wichita where there were none before."

Kyame responded with a small curtsy. "I still don't know either, Mr. Cadwell. I only know I never want to do it again. I never want to feel that terrible hate again. I can't really remember what happened, until Papa picked me up."

Papa had bandaged her sore wrists once they had returned to their hotel. Papa's arm felt so good around her shoulders that the pain in her wrists simply vanished.

"So, John, we will meet again in three weeks in Little Rock?"

"Yes, J. W. Looks like there may be some good opportunities there ... but as Kyame said ... no more spirits."

They laughed.

Cadwell started for his train, then paused and turned back.

"And, Miss Kyame, we will begin your instruction in mesmerism. I will send you two books for your early study. And I am most pleased with my portrait. I plan to put it on my playbills in the future ... and on the cover of my book should there be a 26th edition."

She curtsied again, smiling. "Yes, Professor, I look forward to learning your strange art." She smiled again. "You do have a most interesting face."

***

With their train straining forward, John Piddington settled into his seat, unfolding his newspaper.

Kyame asked, "Why does God hurt good people, Papa, by letting them believe in spirits that aren't there? Not always, anyway." She touched her lips as if to wipe away something. "The Bible even says mediums are bad and are like wizards. That minister last year in Ellsworth said that, something about Leviticus. Have I been bad? Will I go to Hell?"

Piddington stopped to look over at his frowning daughter.

"Kyame, you are seeing the world as few young people ever see it. You are asking profound questions years sooner than most people." He smiled. "You are so special to me, dear Daughter. But I didn't start asking those questions until I was twice your age."

"Then what are the answers, Papa?"

36

"You cannot lift your hands from the table," murmured Kyame Piddington with all her practiced suggestive sincerity. "They are welded to the wood."

"But I can, Miss Piddington," laughed Max Early, reporter for the Atchison *Globe* -- and did, laughing louder. He pushed his glasses back up his nose and brushed his dark hair back into place.

His smirking grin irritated her.

Kyame hesitated.

Why could she not control this man? Several months ago in Little Rock, J. W. Cadwell had instructed her: "Under no circumstances hint that you doubt your ability of fully mesmerizing those you have been trying.

"Keep cool, for no matter how discouraging your prospects of success may be," he had said, "by persevering you may get the best subjects of a lifetime within the next ten minutes."

But under her direction, or operation as Cadwell had called the initial inductive process,

Early *had* forgotten his name, that critical preliminary step toward achieving mind control that Cadwell had emphasized before attempting physical control. Or had Early really forgotten? Had the reporter just been faking it to see what she would do, as a crude joke for his column?

Barely holding her anger in check, Kyame smiled, then laughed.

"Yes, and you do remember your name Mr. Early, do you not?"

He nodded, still grinning.

"I think we have been joking with each other. Your reaction suggests you have played games with mesmerists before," she said. "It's too bad, Mr. Early. It could have been an interesting experiment ... a useful one for your paper."

She leaned back against the cushion of the sofa. The lobby was empty and Papa was late.

Over the months, she had had some successes in her mesmeric practice. Her best was when she had convinced their train conductor as they had approached Omaha that a team of oxen were drawing his train, not a locomotive, and that the beasts had to be fed immediately when they arrived in Omaha.

The moment the train stopped in the Omaha station, the conductor had immediately begun a frantic search for feed for "my starving team" to the raucous laughter of the train crew and everyone on the station platform -- until Kyame had snapped her fingers to finally break her control over him.

She had stopped laughing herself when Papa had whispered to her that J. W. would have been impressed with her technique, but not with the humiliation of someone doing their job. Kyame had immediately apologized to the conductor, but his bitter anger toward her had continued throughout the rest of their trip.

But she *had done it*!

Professor Cadwell had urged her to use her new knowledge at every opportunity. "*Constant* practice is the *only* valuable practice," he had instructed. "But beware of fakes who will lead you on to your embarrassment and their delight."

At the end of their last practice session in Little Rock, while waiting for Papa to return from the bank, Cadwell had, with her permission, lighted his cigar and reminisced about Mama.

"Your mother, Kyame, was a uniquely beautiful and gifted woman. You are very much like her, but your artistic talents are far beyond hers. I also detect a growing, ah, intensity in you, something your mother also did not exhibit.

"But ... your mother could connect with a mesmeric subject faster than anyone ... including myself. She couldn't explain why, it just was."

But now that short fat reporter, Max Early, was laughing at her.

Of course! -- *now* she realized. Cadwell had said that a good subject must be in a negative or passive mood, not excited. Max Early had been suspiciously eager to meet the mysterious Kyame Piddington, one of the two Impossible Piddingtons, too eager, she now understood, to be a successful subject. She should have calmed him down before trying.

She had been stupidly careless.

Kyame was relieved to see Papa finally appear at the arched lobby entrance.

Now, her thirteenth birthday several months in the past, Kyame no longer wore her black hair down her back as she used to, but arranged it in a loose bun that encircled her face. And the last of her girlish short skirts had gone to the local church. Papa had said that once she began the monthly evidence of becoming a woman, she should dress as one and would have her own room adjoining his.

Kyame was already taller than her mother and her dresses with their sweeping skirts were beginning to fit her -- better.

She liked that.

Papa had smiled at dinner last night. "You are becoming a truly remarkable young woman, Daughter."

But Papa was not smiling as he approached.

"Ah, Mr. Piddington," said Max Early rising, "I have been most charmed by your beautiful daughter. Though" -- he smirked -- "I seem to be beyond her mesmeric powers ... for the present."

Kyame could see Papa force a smile on his face. "Kyame is still learning that enigmatic art. My thanks for acting as a patient subject."

They shook hands and Early left the lobby.

Once the reporter was out of sight, Piddington turned to his daughter.

"We are ruined," he whispered as he sat beside her. "The account I had set up at the Little Rock bank has been embezzled of most of our savings. The police have captured the bank manager involved, but our money is gone." He closed his eyes and bent his head. "I am so sorry, dear Kyame. That was to have paid for your schooling in September. Now" -- his face drawn with worry, Papa looked at her -- "now we must work harder to regain your opportunity. I will see you in art school in Boston in September ... some how."

Kyame held back the tears of desperation that began to form. Papa was desolate, his face grey with worry and she just could not add to his burden. She wrapped her arms around his neck and kissed him on his cheek.

37

Max Early nodded to the bell captain's whispered message as he left the hotel. The Piddington girl was a looker, with two, maybe three more years and a couple of extra inches in the right places -- well, anything might happen. But the Piddingtons were in serious -- possibly useful -- distress.

Kyame Piddington hated him. He could sense her anger even though she concealed it passably well. A clumsy mesmerist -- he grinned -- but there was something special about her. The Piddington girl wasn't going to be clumsy for long; she had grit like no girl he had ever experienced.

Early stepped back to let a carriage pass before he crossed the street to the newspaper offices. He beckoned one of the paper's runners, a Negro boy in a green uniform a size too big.

"Suh?"

"Take this note to Dr. Baldwin." He quickly scribbled a chiastic message. He did not have to sign it.

"Yes, suh," the boy answered and was gone.

Early looked around him, the busy streets, the new construction, the burgeoning opportunities for the right people. He opened the door to the hectic news room. The Piddingtons may make bigger headlines than they ever have dreamed.

Max Early wasn't grinning.

38

JOHNSTONE

IS

THE MAN WHO KNOWS !!!

The Man Who Knows stood before a large colored lithographic portrait of his lean features with his hypnotic eyes centered against a brilliant red background. His face was surrounded by a smokey question-mark. Alexander Johnstone, a sinewy six and a half feet tall, towered above the assembled reporters, doctors, merchants and one or two clergymen. *Johnstone* **is** *the Man Who Knows* was in white across the bottom and top of the large poster. Johnstone wasn't smiling on the poster, nor as he stood before the crowd of Atchison's most prominent skeptics.

"What about St. Louis, Johnstone?" Max Early challenged. That brought a rumble of approval from the crowd.

Johnstone smirked. "What about St. Louis, Mr. ... ah?"

"You're the man who knows, so tell me." The reporter stood for emphasis.

The crowd twittered with anticipation.

Johnstone frowned. The standard garbage -- they were eager for his failure -- but not this time. He passed a long-fingered hand across his brow, frowned more deeply, then stabbed his right finger toward the reporter.

"You, are ... Early, are you not, Mr. Early?"

Max Early was silent as he sat down.

The crowd went silent as well.

"Mr. Johnstone." A small balding man in a worn black suit with a minister's collar raised his hand. "What about that widow in St. Louis? Are not the police looking for you?"

"As you can see, I am easy to find, sir," said Johnstone, bowing to the minister. "And I will not waste any more of my time pulling your names out of the ether this morning. I can't halt an express train at every milk stop.

"And, no, the police and the district attorney were at the St. Louis station to see me off. The widow involved, a garrulous woman with an unsteady mind, apologized for suggesting that I might take advantage of her and her savings. The money had vanished but the bank confirmed that I was not involved."

Aggie Phillips, a detective sergeant, stood and identified himself. "Mr. Johnstone, I have nothing against theatre people and we will have the Impossible Piddingtons performing at the Music Hall for another two nights. They do a very nice and mysterious show.

"But, sir, the widow Elliott died shortly before you left St. Louis, and I have received a warning telegram from the St. Louis police that we should keep our eyes on you while you are here.

"Why would I receive such a message if your leaving was as agreeable as you suggest?"

The detective remained standing.

"Sergeant Phillips, you have your job, and I, I have mine." Johnstone radiated sincerity. "If we each do them, then there is nothing further to discuss. Agreed?" Johnstone's voice was warm, even friendly. "I will provide complimentary tickets for the entire Atchison detective organization to my shows in this great city so that you and your colleagues can be personally present to protect the public morality."

Johnstone stepped toward the policeman, extending both his hands in a gesture of openness. "I will even break my basic rule and allow you personally to explore back-stage as much as you like before a show, if you wish.

"I do, however, require strict privacy to prepare myself for the psychological strain of reaching into the minds of my audiences, to see beyond, on their behalf, so I pray that you will allow me that precious time."

The crowd nodded almost in unison.

Max Early only grinned.

Phillips sat back into his chair. "That's ... that's very generous Mr. Johnstone. I will accept your offer on behalf of the office."

***

John Piddington, sitting at the back of the crowd, considered the long lanky mind reader. Johnstone was a notorious glass-ball worker, probably the best one in the business who could charm the goods out of any woman. Johnstone's style was as smooth as his reputation for shady dealings was deadly. But, Johnstone was wealthy while he was now nearly broke. He would watch the Johnstone operations more closely.

Piddington had been surprised that he had not encountered any of Johnstone's advance men in the past week -- walking the cemeteries, checking town directories in the library, perusing church rolls, copying out property records, etc.

With the information properly organized and delivered with compelling style from the stage, audiences couldn't believe the seer could know their lives in such detail. Good advance men, or women, who understood when to dig and when it was safe to buy the necessary information, were worth every penny they were paid to an act like Johnstone's.

A wayward advance man could threaten to queer a psychic's reputation to gain more coin, but no one would be stupid enough to take on Johnstone. The backstage rumors were that the mind-reader had killed four, perhaps as many as seven, men who had crossed him whether it was up in the Klondike gold fields or in an alley behind a theatre.

Piddington knew advance work; that was a basic secret of all second sight mental acts including the Impossible Piddingtons; that and, he smiled, a beautiful talented daughter who had learned to convince anyone she could see into their minds.

Johnstone was famous for being the celebrated "man who knows" who could answer any unspoken and unwritten questions on any topic of human concern, and challenge anyone to prove he was not accurate. He had a standing offer of $2,500 to anyone who could prove he used any paid confederates. Johnstone was a showman in a class by himself. His level of advance work would require at minimum three people and almost two weeks of work.

But there had been no one.

Why?

There was some digging to do.

39

Alexander Jason Johnstone's basic credo was: First you eliminate your enemies -- then gut the friends who could give you away.

He scowled at Max Early.

"Say it all again, Early, I want to savor the flavor, before I spit it out."

"Your two sneaks quit just after they arrived last week. I talked with them, set them up, opened some doors ... and then Delgado, the wop, didn't like the way the police looked at him and got on the next train out. Harris, it turns out, had an old wanted poster hanging in the police station from a piece he pulled in Kansas City two years ago. Fleeced a widow ... sound familiar?"

Johnstone smirk twisted his long face. "Those two were good at digging out what the sheep thought was safely buried. I couldn't care less about anything else they had done. I've probably done worse in my own life." He suddenly leaned toward the reporter who flinched without thinking. The crystal gazer's eyes were pure murder. "But, they ran away with my money in their pocket, so I'll find them. They'll wish it had been the police when I get finished with them."

"But ...." Johnstone stretched out his long legs, leaning back in the high backed cane chair. "But, I need some material until Fanny Albright gets here from Cincinnati to take up the slack." He stood. "Tell me about the Piddingtons? They have a good rep. Not on the big time, yet, but good."

Max Early grinned. "I think I may have something for you, Johnstone, in that direction. With some suitable financial incentive ... and other thoughts."

Johnstone shrugged, laughed, a handful of twenty-dollar bills appeared suddenly at the tips of his long fingers. He flicked his wrist and dropped the wad on Early's lap.

"That's the rule, Early. Squeeze when you can; lick the shoes when you can't.

"So give," he snarled, pulling his chair close and sitting down, his face only inches from the reporter's.

Early grinned -- and tossed the bills away to the floor.

Kyame studied the approaching man as Papa always instructed. Read the people, he had said, see what you can gain before they open their mouths. Speak with confidence, it won't matter if you are wrong, just adjust, and manage the situation. A beautiful young woman is usually challenged only by another woman.

The man, whose name, Joe Springler, Kyame had overheard coming into the hotel dining room, was clearly down on his luck; though he tried to convey a joyful confident attitude. The heels of his boots were worn flat, his gold signet ring had been clipped of some of its gold at least twice and was missing its stone, but his shirt and starched collar were new. But his tie had been badly pressed, probably by him.

Some luck perhaps, but not much -- not enough. His cut of steak had been much less than Kyame was planning to eat for her dinner.

Though not defeated, Joe Springler had surrendered for the day. When he thought no one was watching his jaw sagged a little.

Kyame had been seated at the table next to him. Papa was a few minutes late; but he had instructed her to study anyone around her then compare her assessment as the truth might become evident -- then analyze how she ....

Apparently sensing her, Springler looked over and politely acknowledged her. He turned away to watch with envy as the waiter poured champagne for a young couple two tables away.

Kyame decided.

"Mr. Springler, your champagne is losing its chill," she said, gesturing toward his water glass, her fingers fluttering near the glass. "You really should drink it before it goes flat."

Springler looked over, his eyebrows raised. "My name, Miss, you know my name?" He looked at the filled water glass.

Kyame smiled. "The champagne, you ordered a glass, a bottle would be too much you told the waiter. Keep you from a good night's sleep. Sleep, Mr. Springler. Drink your champagne and relax. Just relax. The waiter said it was a very good vintage."

She could see in his face, his muscles softening, her suggestion beginning to take effect. Not like Max Early; Joe Springler yearned for peace.

He reached for the glass -- glanced at Kyame, smiled, raised the glass in a brief toast to her, then took a deep swallow.

His relief was so visibly intense that Kyame turned away. She felt she was intruding into his privacy.

But she had done it! Her induction technique had been perfect!

But champagne, she thought, it always tasted so bitter. Maybe you had to have an old tongue to enjoy it.

***

The folded note handed him by the desk clerk was brief:

"Piddington. See me. Dr. Baldwin's office. One hour."

AJJ was scrolled with a wide-nibbed pen in the corner.

***

John Piddington had to smile as his green-eyed daughter excitedly related her mesmeric experience. Springler had emptied the glass in three swallows, and had left his dinner with a wide grin on his face. Piddington raised his glass of water in formal acknowledgement.

"Water into champagne, Daughter, an inspired piece ... almost Biblical."

"Oh, I hadn't thought of that," Kyame said, her eyes suddenly going wide. "Papa, do you think that's what He ...?

"No." He shook his head in emphasis.

40

Standing, Johnstone threw the five twenties on the table in front of John Piddington.

"You are a professional, Piddington, a good one. I won't waste words or insult your intelligence. As you have already noted, my advance people are not here ... for various reasons. I need your help and as much of your local information as you can *spare* from your own needs. You have two nights left, then I open for a week." He reached back to pull a chair to the table. "I deal only in cash ... that hundred on the table ... a hundred minimum for each night until my backup advance man arrives from Cincinnati. More ... if your dope is on target."

Piddington looked at the cash. He had no alternative. That hundred could help cover the hotel and leave a little to start rebuilding their financial reserves. With Johnstone in town, the Impossible Piddingtons would likely draw smaller crowds for their last two days.

No choice. He took a deep breath. Kyame would understand.

"I have notes at the hotel," he said, "that would cover your first night. But I would have to do more mining in the files ...."

"Then do it. Leave the notes here with Baldwin. He'll have an envelope with the money each day. You know what's needed."

Johnstone jabbed a long forefinger at him.

"*Each day* ... Piddington." He drew an envelope from his jacket pocket and dropped it on the bills. "I want the goods on the names in there first."

As John Piddington got up, Johnstone also stood, a dominating eight inches above John Piddington. "You go heeled, Piddington?"

"No. I don't own a gun. Never wanted one."

"Get one." Johnstone's narrow face moved, more a smirk, than a smile. Then his face softened. "If I had a daughter as beautiful as yours, Piddington, I would always have shotguns ... in both hands ... ten gauge with heavy lead."

***

302

Piddington returned an hour later to leave an envelope with a portion of his notes at Dr. Baldwin's office. Baldwin's nurse was indifferent and dropped the envelope into the center drawer of the doctor's desk.

The small nickel-plated five-shot .32 revolver, a woman's pistol the gunsmith had said, felt awkward in his pocket. Like many men who traveled the West, Piddington had fired enough guns in his life, but never carried one -- guns had always brought turmoil, rarely resolution.

Kyame was edgy around guns, uncomfortable. He didn't want to upset her -- but at some point, he needed to ensure she could handle a small pistol. J. W. Cadwell had been right. That was life, good or bad.

Johnstone had raised an eyebrow at the .32. "Couldn't even scare anyone, let alone hurt anyone with that toy, Piddington," he sneered, laughing.

John Piddington didn't like the feeling of becoming Johnstone's armed stooge.

But there was no choice.

***

Kyame quickly sensed the growing tension in Papa as they entered the hotel dining room for a private afternoon ladies-only performance that he had arranged on short notice for a flat $60 fee. Papa had tried for $75 but the hotel manager, Sam Bradford, would not consider more than $60.

"Women won't drink enough to justify $40," Bradford had said. "A ladies-only show ... ah, but if you get the Ballinger crowd in here, then, $60."

Somehow Papa had done it.

This would be different than the performances in the music halls. An audience of all women -- that had always been an uncertain situation in the other towns. And the routine of this show would need to be different. Kyame would have to interact with the audience in new ways that they had only barely rehearsed earlier that morning.

Kyame compressed her lips, then, seeing the ladies settling into their chairs, she smiled as Papa stepped back to allow her to precede him into the interim theatre.

Their awkward one-hour rehearsal in their room had not been smooth. Papa had been pressing; the burden of the loss of her school money was wearing heavily on him.

"We will have to fill our performances with stunts rather than the more telling personal revelations. If the right women are there, I can feed you some interesting materials. If they are not ...."

Then he had explained his arrangement with Johnstone, a man Kyame had instantly disliked when she first saw him towering over a gathering of men in front of the telegraph office across the street. His barely restrained expression of contempt for the men around him, as if they were fleas to be brushed off. It grated against her. Max Early was in the group, laughing loudly enough for her to hear. Kyame turned away, as Early turned toward her at Johnstone's pointed instigation, his long fingers thrust toward her.

Much of the inside Atchison information that Papa had dug out, he had sold to The Man Who Knows, so their own performance was weakened in turn. Tears had filled her eyes hearing of Papa having to do business with someone so --

so vile and ugly as Johnstone solely to enable her to go to school.

So evil.

Papa only shook his head when Kyame had offered to wait for another year, or two years. He squeezed her shoulders, kissed her on her forehead, then left to dig more.

I-love-you, Daughter, Papa had signed as he had walked away across the hotel lobby.

But Kyame was determined that Atchison would know the Impossible Piddingtons were still in town.

She shuddered at the thought of Johnstone. Evil. His whole being was just -- evil.

41

Looking about the rearranged hotel dining room from the next to last row of chairs, Mrs. Phyllis Bentley grew increasingly troubled as the father-daughter duo of the Impossible Piddingtons seemed to pull secret thoughts from the heads of the other women, seemed to know personal information they should never have known. The strange girl, dressed in a shimmering teal blue gown, her face outlined in silver lace; Kyame, tall, beautiful, graceful -- but, after all, just a *theatre girl* -- not someone *she* would ever want in the Bentley family -- and the girl could see even when blindfolded, see things that Phyllis could not see even with her own ey..., wide open. Kyame Piddington was a frightening, threatening presence to any church folk.

That's not right, not good.

The Good LORD never intended any human being to have such powers; they rivaled His own. He would truly "smite them down" with his righteousness as Parson James had insisted only yesterday at the church tea when someone had asked him about the powers that the Piddingtons and now this man Johnstone seemed to have.

But Phyllis had to be here, because Eudora Ballinger, the wife of her Stuart's boss, the president of the First Bank of Atchison, had firmly suggested that she should be.

"The wife of a rising financial executive should be seen, Phyllis dear, not hidden away in a nursery," Eudora had said so sweetly, with her underlying threat.

Eudora was a Spiritualist and believed there were spirits everywhere; but her word was law at the bank. All of Atchison knew that the founding capital of the First Bank of Atchison came from her family, not her husband's.

Horace Ballinger had revealed, most confidentially, only two days ago to Stuart Bentley that the bank would be opening its first branch in Kansas City at the insistence of its largest customer, the Santa Fe railroad, and that he, Stuart, was being strongly considered to be the senior manager for the new branch. An opportunity of greatest ....

John Piddington was approaching her! Phyllis shrank back in her chair, but he kept coming.

***

Piddington stood slightly behind the attractive young woman who was obviously agitated by his approach. She insisted on looking away, probably hoping he wouldn't notice her. He had already signed the name Phyllis Bentley, Kansas City, and the number 14. He stood in the X-position, arms crossed to the left and slightly behind the target, to identify Bentley to Kyame.

The show was going reasonably well, but Johnstone had taken most of the best information he had dug up. It was Kyame who was causing the women to titter and whisper among themselves as she sold his information with determined confidence. Her smokey acting had never been so effective. And today, she would close their show, her way, for the first time. This was the right audience for this step in her career.

"You must relax," murmured Kyame, "Mrs. ... Mrs. Bentley ... is it? You block your own thoughts … you weigh your heart needlessly, ma'am."

Kyame suddenly stood, her arms stretched out toward the woman, her fingers spread, her blindfolded face appeared to Phyllis Bentley like the mask of a pagan priest. "I feel your anxiety regarding … a larger city … to our east."

Phyllis Bentley gasped. She could feel Eudora's accusing eyes on her -- but she had never said anything to anyone, never, never -- never!

The secret was so important. The best site for the bank's planned construction in Kansas City was a prime location, near the Santa Fe regional offices and an expanding business district. A rival bank was selling the property. If its management knew the Ballinger bank was the buyer, either they wouldn't sell at all, or at a price that would be doubled, or most probably even more. According to Stuart, Horace Ballenger had personally committed a specific date, the 14th, in two months to open the bank to the Santa Fe President -- there could be no delay. The Santa Fe railroad was considering placing a two-million dollar loan with the Atchison bank, and they had insisted on having bank offices close by. Stuart would handle the loan, if all went well.

How could the Piddington girl know? Oh, dear God. Was this pretty witch going to destroy Stuart's career, their future chances, just for a moment of entertainment?

Kyame stepped closer to the gathering of women who had gone silent at Phyllis Bentley's pale face, her hand to her mouth. Some shifted away from Kyame as she approached.

Then she stopped.

"Papa, please give me a pencil and paper. I will write the city I see. It is too important, is it not, Mrs. Bentley, to speak out loud?"

Phyllis nodded weakly, her hands shaking.

Kyame wrote very quickly, folded the slip of note paper and returned it to Papa.

When Phyllis Bentley opened the folded slip of paper that John Piddington handed her, she saw Kansas City written in small letters. She felt a wave of dizziness as she instantly crushed the paper and shoved it down into a pocket.

"Am I correct, Mrs. Bentley?" asked Kyame gently. "The other ladies would like to know."

Mrs. Bentley was really scared for some reason beyond the mystical bent of their show. Kyame would ask Papa about Kansas City later. She decided not to use the number 14. So pale, Mrs. Bentley looked to be on the edge of a breakdown.

"Yes, Miss Piddington, you are correct ... though I cannot understand how."

As the women murmured, pointing at Kyame and then at her, Phyllis avoided Eudora's eyes. If that girl could know, who else could?

Removing her blindfold, Kyame caught Eudora Ballinger's eyes. She curtsied slightly.

"Mrs. Ballinger, my father and I are honored that you and your close friends have come to this afternoon's ladies entertainment."

Eudora nodded curtly, still wondering about the Bentley woman and her loose mouth.

Kyame gestured slowly across Eudora's eyes as she moved closer to the seated woman. The women sitting closest at first leaned away, then, their eyes on Kyame's ensorcelled face they leaned forward.

"Please relax, Mrs. Ballinger, it has been a wondrous day ... has it not?"

Eudora nodded slightly, her eyes going wider, her jaw going slack.

"Just relax, there is so much that you can experience." Kyame studied the woman's face carefully -- the first test. "Your name is not Ballinger, however, is it, ma'am? In fact, you have forgotten your name, have you not?" She spread the fingers of her right hand and moved them across Ballinger's eyes, as though stroking velvet.

Eudora Ballinger opened her eyes wider with her realization. "I ...I am ...am ...." She fell silent, her face twisted in confusion, fear growing in her eyes.

Kyame saw Papa bow his head, smiling. Kyame had her.

Kyame also noted Phyllis Bentley's growing smile, color returning to her cheeks.

"Ma'am, as you look at me ...." Kyame became aware that three women sitting closest to Ballinger were also going into the trance. She suppressed a grin. Good. Better than good. "As you look at me, ma'am, when I clap my hands twice, I will begin to fade from your sight, until I become invisible to you. When that has happened, you will stand and ask the other women, 'Where is Miss Piddington? and 'Where has the girl gone?' I will remain invisible to you until I snap my fingers."

Kyame noted carefully as Ballinger's jaw dropped slightly and her face go pale. She clapped her hands once.

A silent moment -- another.

Kyame clapped her hands the second time.

Eudora Ballinger rose slowly from her chair and turned to face the gathering of hushed women.

"Where has Miss Piddington gone? Has anyone seen the girl?"

A sharp gasp swept across the room.

John Piddington was grinning so widely he had to turn away.

In the back row, a woman reporter from the Atchison *Times* was frantically scribbling and flipping pages on a pad.

"But, Eudora, dear, Miss Piddington is standing in front of you", one woman offered from three rows back.

"Who? What did you call me?" asked Ballinger, turning around. Kyame was standing less than two feet from her.

"The girl has left the room for some reason. Can't you see that?" she snapped in exasperation.

The other three entranced women had also stood, asking if anyone had seen the Piddington girl.

Phyllis Bentley's careful smile had become a wide grin of relief. Stuart would not believe this.

"Now, ma'am, ladies, please be seated," Kyame spoke gently. The women settled slowly back into their chairs, their backs stiff, upright, not touching against the chair.

"Ma'am, ladies, you will begin to feel cool refreshment flow like clean mountain water throughout your bodies, cleansing, restoring, filling you with hope, forgiveness, and joy for the future."

Kyame noted the changing expressions on the faces of all four women. She nodded to Papa's raised eyebrow. It was time to close.

Kyame stood in front of Eudora Ballinger.

"Ma'am, you now recall your name. It is Eudora Ballinger, is it not?"

"Yes ... I am Eudora Ballinger ... ah-h ... Miss Piddington."

Remembering J. W. Cadwell's strong admonition against too sharp a conclusion to a deep mesmeric trance, Kyame said, softly, "The waters flowing through each of you are slowly receding; you *will remember* my fading into nothing; you *will recall* through the rest of the day the refreshment of the clear cool waters; and now, as I count to ten, you will return to this room and to the company of your friends.

"Mrs. Ballinger, you *will* *give* your handkerchief to Mrs. Bentley when I snap my fingers."

As she counted slowly to ten, Papa came to stand beside her.

"Wondrous, Daughter," he whispered. "Mama could not have done better."

Kyame smiled as she said, "Ten", and snapped her fingers. Eudora Ballenger immediately rose, walked to the back rows as each eye followed her.

"My dear Phyllis, please accept this silk brought from Vienna with my warmest compliments," Mrs. Ballinger said, and turned back to her seat.

42

"Piddington is better than any two advance men I've ever used," said Alexander Jason Johnstone. He dropped the notes back on the table. "Of the six names I gave him, he already has good dope on three. That will get the job started.

"Drop an extra couple of hundred in his next envelope."

Dr. Baldwin nodded and closed the door behind him.

Max Early grinned. "Coupla hundred is one thing, yeah. But you want real work from Piddington; you need real incentive for him to stay in Atchison."

Johnstone stretched out his long legs.

"Yeah. When Fanny gets here tomorrow, Early, she'll start watching the pretty daughter." He read the notes. "Christ, Piddington must be the real thing to get some of this stuff."

Both men laughed raucously.

***

Jeremy Marotta owned three dry goods stores in Eastern Kansas, hotels in Topeka and Wichita, and was building a foundry and machine works just outside Atchison, on the banks of the Missouri river. He had built his first fortune in the conflict of the Klondike gold fields as a merchant not a miner. He had fought and killed his share of men in that accursed place – but reading the note that he had found in his coat pocket caused him to turn pale with anger. It wasn't his reputation the blackguards threatened, it was his wife's. And it wasn't money they wanted.

Laughing, Jack "Wolf" Barnato threw the cards across the table. "Too many queens for my poor jacks to handle, Whitey. You beat me all hollow this time."

Whitey Rhodes, whose eyes, beard and hair were coal black, grinned as he swept the table clean of gold coins and paper money. $452 – a workingman's salary for a year. "Down payment on what you've taken off me the last three days, Wolf."

The other two men at the table threw their ante on the table, sipped their whiskies, and waited for Rhodes to deal.

Smiling at his friend's joy, after all losing to a good friend was only a loan anyway, the cash would all come back later, Wolf Barnato leaned back to light his cigar. Reaching into his pocket for matches, he found a note with the matches. Frowning, he couldn't recall putting anything into his match pocket other than matches.

Seeing Barnato's face becoming red with rage, Whitey Rhodes stopped dealing. "Wolf, you with us? Something wrong?"

Scooping up his money from the table, Wolf snarled, "Out. I'm out."

Barnato stormed away, settling his black jacket on his shoulders, he slammed the door behind him. The money demanded didn't bother him; he could make that up easily — it was the threat, the arrogant threat.

***

Glancing quickly about the office, Chief of Detectives Johnston Lyle's hands shook as he plunged the note back deep into his pocket. How could anyone know? All that was buried, buried deep, locked away eight years ago. How could he stop them, buy them off? Whoever it was, they didn't ask for money. How could anyone know, unless they could speak to the dead?

***

"Ain't no more gravy in the grift, John," said Maze Edwards. "Spirits just don't pay like they used ta. Too many exposures by those damn traveling magicians like Kellar and Herrmann ... and by those more damnable turncoat mediums like Van Vleck. Even if most of the exposures aren't even the real thing, I couldn't tour publicly anywhere without some smug fool writing up exposures in the local paper same day I set up shop."

Kyame cocked her head, smiling. "You don't believe in the spirits you raise, Mr. Edwards?" she asked with mock innocence.

Maze Edwards grinned at the green-eyed girl. "Once, at the beginning, young woman, I saw what I knew to be something from the other side. Then ... then, well, I fell over the fact that there was more profit in fake spirits than in the real ones ... there being more of the former than the latter, you understand.

"And, Miss, I am Maze to any Piddington. I owe your papa there enough that even buying him the biggest farm around wouldn't be enough."

"Then, sir, I am Kyame to you."

John Piddington shook his head. "No, you owe me nothing, Maze, and never will.

"Kyame, when this gentleman is not playing with words, stories and accents, Maze Edwards is most accomplished spirit medium around, otherwise Eudora Ballinger would not rely so much on him ... and tell him so much to our benefit."

"Ah, dear Eudora." Smiling, Maze Edwards raised his glass in salute.

He turned to Kyame who was wrapped in a deep green robe sipping hot tea, the glow of the afternoon show only just fading from her mind, their final performance in Atchison tomorrow night. The evening was just taking hold outside their windows.

"And you, Kyame," he grinned. "You went invisible on Eudora! Not even my spirits can do that. What a glorious piece of business that was! Not even old Cadwell himself ever pulled that stunt ... that I know of anyway. Damn, beautiful girl, you are a piece of work yourself. That took genuine courage."

Maze Edwards stood, placed his empty glass on the table and picked up his hat. "Need to be slipping away. Wouldn't want Eudora to know we have ever seen each other, so I best be moving like a shadow in a coal mine."

John Piddington stood, his hand extended. "Thanks for your help, Maze. The Kansas City input was just what we needed."

Edwards tossed his hand. "Nothing, John. I'll keep my ears open in case something else bubbles up from Eudora and the spirits.

"But just be careful of Johnstone when he opens later this week. I'd get right out of town. He don't buck *no* competition.

"And," emphasized the medium, "he might be pulling in some of his toughs for his Mid-west tour ... seen him do it in Seattle.

"Sends those goons to 'encourage' other glass-ball acts to leave town on the first train. Scared even Carmi and his Hindoo troupe right out of Seattle. You know Carmi is tough as wrought iron and has the nerve of ol' Satan himself, but not when his wife was threatened.

"And you, Kyame," Edwards pointed at her. "You be careful. Rumor is Alexander Johnstone once made some money as a white slaver out on the Oregon coast, shippin' white girls to Asia."

Taking a breath, John Piddington lightly brushed his hand against the small pistol in his coat pocket.

***

Laughing, Kyame tapped on the connecting door between their rooms, then entered. She handed the Atchison *Times* to Papa, pointing to the advertisement:

'Minister requires a young man to take charge of a span of horses of a religious turn of mind.'

Papa chuckled. "He doesn't say what denomination the horses need to be. Apparently it doesn't matter about the young man."

Kyame felt warm inside. It was good to see Papa smile and laugh -- even a bit. But they had not played their regular evening chess game for two nights.

But then Papa rose and was gone again.

Kyame hesitated, then decided.

43

The envelope he had obtained from Dr. Baldwin held $300 in twenties. John Piddington bit his lip. In two days, he had gotten $500 of Johnstone's money, working as the mindreader's miserable stooge. He felt disgusted.

Kyame. Kyame. She would understand, she always did, but she would plead even more with him to stop; he realized that, but he couldn't ask her to wait another year. And Laura -- he could almost feel her tearful scorn.

But now there was something else.

The information that Johnstone most wanted couldn't be used in a public performance. As hungry as Johnstone always was for spectacular material, he certainly wouldn't risk getting shot by Wolf Barnato, or by an enraged policeman.

If anything, Marotta's fury at the revelation of his wife's bigamy; Lyle's deceit, framing his own brother-in-law for murder while a sheriff's deputy in Texas; and Barnato's abandonment in Arizona of his wife and only child to Apache raiders while he ran away -- all that could only be used in private readings, if even then. There were times, times when even The Man Who Knows had to back off a few steps.

Along with casing the Kansas and Missouri towns they had been performing in over the past few months, Piddington had picked up bits of material, rumors, idle talk in hotel lobbies, court houses, and, occasionally, saloons, about Barnato's and Lyle's treachery, along with insights about others on Johnstone's list of the state's prominent targets in other towns; but he realized, as explosive as the accumulated materials had proven to actually be, there was an ethical limit, a line he wouldn't cross himself.

But, confound it, man, you just fed that stuff to the biggest crook on the stage -- knowing he *would* use it, *somehow*.

Piddington abruptly turned down a narrow street behind the towering brick and stone Atchison county court house. He stopped in the darkness to lean against the stone wall, to take a breath, to take stock.

What is going on? There is more in play here than just a week of stage shows in Atchison.

Like playing chess with only one piece and you don't know which piece.

Those other three names on Johnstone's list -- those three men together probably owned half the property in Atchison with some across the river in St. Joseph as well, and, they were all investors with close ties to the Santa Fe railroad. A quick perusal of county records had shown that, along with information he had found in other towns.

John Piddington never threw anything away from his mining the rich communal veins.

Everyone has something to hide, not all of it illegal or immoral, oftentimes just awkward or embarrassing. That latter material is fair game for a mental act. Audiences enjoy having fun at the expense of the wealthy and pompous.

But what was going on -- here

44

Wolf Barnato carefully seated the two heavy shells into the derringer. Brass-jacketed .44's with soft slugs of lead that could splatter a man's skull. Only a small gun with a hard recoil. Barnato didn't like big guns as they tended to make big holes in the wrong people. With the derringer, you had to get very close -- that made sure it was always the right person.

He fitted the butt of the little pistol into the extension rod of the hold-out, then compressed the rod's spring until it clicked, the gun now locked against his left forearm. If he needed it, with a slight pressure of his left elbow against his hip, the hold-out would deliver the gun into his left hand in less than a second; the first .44 slug would be on its way in another second. The setup had never failed him.

The left sleeves of all his jackets were slightly larger than the right to accommodate the smooth hold-out action. Tailors had quickly learned to stop asking why.

His reputation for always being heeled had held off some serious situations at various tables between St. Louis and San Francisco. But he had been thinking of moving his operations East, to New York City, Philadelphia and Boston, and maybe the ships to Europe.

The note detailed where he was to bring the money, what kind of bills, how it was to be packaged, and a brief warning: come alone or the Barnato story would be in the *Globe* and *Times* the next morning.

Barnato didn't care about the men around the tables; his cards did all the talking. It was his family, and more hers, who would attack him. Clara had four brothers meaner than any Apaches who would come after him with axes if they thought he had run out on their little sister and their beloved niece.

Christ, he had been going for help, not running away. There was a trading post less than a mile away where several gunmen were always hanging out.

There had been nine Chiricahua Apaches in the band, all armed with Army rifles. He'd left two loaded 12 gauge shotguns and a loaded .44 revolver with Clara. She could handle guns. *She* knew he wasn't running away. She needed to hold off the Indians for less than an hour. Only a lousy hour! But -- damn!

Barnato had the package in his right coat pocket with three twenty-dollar bills on top of twenty-five carefully cut strips of newspaper. As he held out the package to the blackmailer, he would turn his body to conceal the gun appearing in his left hand.

Wouldn't be the first time.

With the loss of Clara and little Susan, his world had become a deck of cards and a bottle. He could never have made it as a sod-buster anyway -- but Clara had hated his gambling, even when he poured his winnings onto her kitchen table night after night. They had decided to move away, to California, to maybe San Francisco for Susan's schooling, and so that Wolf could get a job more satisfying than nights at a green baize table.

The man Barnato really wanted was the gutter scum who had dug up the Arizona story. If he's not there tonight, then Wolf would hunt him down

45

Wrapped in a black coat with a black silk scarf tied closely around her head, in the gathering darkness with the sun already gone behind thick storm clouds in the West, Kyame walked a block behind Papa. Her black double-barreled over-under .41 Remington derringer was in the pocket of her coat. She quickened her step when she saw Papa suddenly turn into a street at the court house.

***

Smiling, he watched the gambler coming toward him, cautiously cross Commercial Street, avoiding the lights that were just coming on in the windows of the businesses along 5th and Commercial. He turned to move to the designated exchange point, behind the Methodist church at the gate to the cemetery. He wondered if Wolf had that damn derringer up his left sleeve.

He would assume the gambler did – the safest bet going. His own gun was in his left hand. Barnato probably wasn't carrying the money.

Didn't matter – this time.

***

Kyame stopped. Papa was gone. Where? She turned back to Main Street. Where? Lights were coming on along Main. A man dodged around the lights as he moved rapidly away from the crowds on the sidewalks and started down 5th Street. An uneasy feeling swept through her, that compelling feeling that Professor Cadwell had told her to always trust -- Kyame stepped quickly into the street to follow.

***

John Piddington watched Wolf Barnato almost running along the street and up on the sidewalk, then the gambler made an abrupt turn down 5th Street away from Commercial. There was a church in that direction, two blocks down. It was unlikely that Barnato was late for a game in that neighborhood.

Piddington had collected the story of Barnato's abandoning his wife and child from several sources; when the Impossible Piddingtons had performed in Wichita, Ellsworth, Dodge City, and even in Denver. The story might not even be true, but Johnstone had Barnato on his list.

Piddington moved down a parallel street, starting to walk faster once he was away from Main.

***

"On time, Wolf. Good. The money. Then get out."

Barnato could only see a long dark form behind a tree growing against the cemetery wall.

The gambler turned slightly, holding out the package out with his right hand, feeling the derringer snap into his left. The dark form moved closer.

The single shot shattered the stillness!

46

At the sharp crash, Kyame started, then saw a form drop to the ground, another bending over it, taking something. Someone was running up the street, she heard the footsteps.

The dark form moved quickly away, casting a long moonlit shadow on the church wall. Then it was gone.

Cautiously, Kyame moved closer, her hand closed around her derringer. When J. W. Cadwell had taken her to a Wichita gun-shop, Kyame had politely rejected the nickel-plated engraved derringer with mother-of-pearl grips first shown her. She selected instead a plain blued-steel weapon with checkered hard black rubber grips.

She could hit nothing the first ten times she had fired the hand-pistol. It bucked and almost jumped out of her hand, but before they had left Wichita, Kyame was hitting three out of five bottles at fifteen feet. Now it was four out of five, but she still wasn't sure she could actually shoot a man.

Kyame heard a door open nearby. Someone stepped out with a lantern.

**

John Piddington heard the shot as he rounded the corner. Someone was bent over a fallen body, then the lantern appeared, and the form quickly disappeared into the lowering darkness.

Another form, smaller, was limned for a moment against the lantern, then it stepped back into the gloom.

My god, it was Kyame! She had followed him!

"Run, Daughter, get away from here!"

She turned instead to run to him.

"Papa, Papa, are you all right?"

He put his arm around her shoulders. "Yes, but neither of us should be found here. Let's get back to the hotel. Over this way, Kyame, away from the church."

"What is happening?" she asked as they walked rapidly. "That man who came here ... who was he?"

"Wolf Barnato, a gambler. I'll try to explain back in our rooms."

***

Kyame's tears wouldn't stop.

"No, Papa, please, not for me, *please.*" Papa's arms were tight around her. "Let's cancel the last performance and leave ... like Maze said. We can work out some new stunts. I'll work some extra matinees with my mesmerism.

"Johnstone has been selling lucky tokens for 25₵ outside the Music Hall. They can't cost more than a penny to make. I asked at a blacksmith shop. We can do that, too.

"Please, Papa, let's run, run now."

The hard knock at the door startled them both.

While Kyame wiped her eyes, Piddington went to the door. Sgt. Aggie Phillips held out his badge. Max Early stood behind him.

"John Piddington, I have come to arrest you on suspicion of killing Wolf Barnato."

Piddington shook his head. "Sergeant Phillips, I don't even know Wolf Barnato. I've never met the man." He heard Kyame sob behind him. He turned. "Just a mistake, Daughter, don't worry."

"Piddington," said Early, "Barnato was shot in the head with a .32, and Sayers, the gunsmith, says you bought a .32 a couple of days ago. Where is it?"

Piddington looked hard at the reporter, then pulled his jacket off the coat-rack, removed the pistol from the pocket.

"Here, Sgt. Phillips, I've never fired it."

Phillips cracked open the pistol. "One bullet missing, sir, and" -- he held the barrel to his nose -- "and it smells of powder. It has been fired, Mr. Piddington."

Kyame gasped.

Frowning, John Piddington shook his head. Nothing made sense.

"I won't cuff you in front of your daughter, Mr. Piddington ... but we go now ... and no funny business."

Kyame saw Max Early leering at her from behind the detective's shoulder. It made her feel dirty.

"I won't be gone long, Daughter." Papa put his arms around her. "See Maze for a lawyer's name," he whispered. "I've been set up by Johnstone. I don't know why."

He stepped back, put on his jacket, and walked through the door with the detective holding his arm.

Her tears stopped. "I love you, Papa," she said. "I'll take care of things."

Max Early leaned back and closed the door, an ugly grin on his face.

Within minutes Kyame was gone.

47

Maze Edwards cursed under his breath. "No way, Kyame, that your father could have done that. No way. I'll get a friend over there tonight. And, young woman, I pay the legal fees, no arguments."

Kyame smiled, nodded, squeezed his hand, and closed the door quietly behind her.

There was work for her to do.

***

It was six in the morning. Kyame had not slept -- maybe sleep next week, or never, whatever time it took. She quickly swallowed a glass of milk, a piece of cheese and a chunk of bread before walking to the police station.

"I have the advantage, Sgt. Phillips" said Kyame, confidently, "of knowing with certainty that my father never shot anyone. Therefore, I know that someone is out there trying to use my father for some terrible purpose." She leaned forward in her chair. "I mean to find out what is going on."

***

After leaving Maze Edwards, Kyame had returned to the scene of the killing, using matches to examine the ground, and walk where she thought the dark form had gone.

Kyame returned again as the sun came up, to look again. There had been a short hard rain during the night that had washed away the soil around the tree, exposing the roots.

There were three, no, as she peeled them away from the trunk, five wet strips of newspaper, all cut the same size. Kyame carefully folded them into the pocket of her coat.

***

Maze's lawyer had assured her he was looking for a judge to set bail; but one wouldn't available until the afternoon.

Aggie Phillips was impressed. He had read in the papers about Kyame Piddington's mesmeric powers and had seen her once on the stage at the Opera House. Her quick green eyes went straight through him. His own daughter was two years older, but he could not imagine his Christine on any stage -- or challenging a policeman.

"This is what we have, Miss," said Phillips. "Chief Lyle is in full agreement with my direction. Fact is he pushed for the arrest ...."

"Who is Chief Lyle?" Kyame interrupted.

"Chief of Detectives, Kingston Lyle, my boss."

"For how long?"

Phillips frowned. "Two years, came from ... just a minute, I'm the detective here."

"You were about to tell me why my father sits in a cell back there," demanded Kyame, her jaw set.

"To begin with: the .32 pistol with one round fired; the .32 hole in Barnato's head; the $300 in twenty-dollar bills in your father's coat pocket; the twenties scattered around the body, almost $600 worth; and a witness who saw the whole thing, saw someone grabbing up the money.

"Then there is the blackmail note in Barnato's pocket from someone demanding a thousand dollars in twenties; the fact that your father has been seen around town asking questions." He pressed his hands on his desk. "Among other things, of course."

"Who is the witness?" Kyame asked.

Phillips hesitated. "Miss Piddington, I fully understand and respect your feelings. If the Chief had not insisted, I would not have taken your father in yet."

"Why did your Chief insist?"

The detective hesitated. It *had been* strange for Lyle to be so immediately interested, so insistent.

"There's pressure to keep Atchison 'clean of crime'," said Phillips. "Pressure from business groups, churches, newspapers, just about everybody. If there's a crime, we have to have someone in jail right quick."

"Even innocent people in jail ... how clean is that?" Her voice dripped sarcasm. "And the witness?"

Phillips shook his head.

***

Kyame had too much fire in her eyes. That was going to lead to trouble, but Maze was impressed nevertheless.

The three names Piddington had given Kyame: Barnato, Lyle and Marotta. Strips of newspaper just the size of twenty-dollar silver certificates. The blackmail note found on Barnato. Maze agreed that John Piddington was being set up for something.

"Lyle has only been here for two years. Where did Kingston Lyle come from? Sgt. Phillips wouldn't tell me."

"I'll do some asking, Kyame. But, be careful, like I warned. Johnstone is not someone to hassle. I know you'll take any risk for your father, but be careful of which risk you take."

***

When the woman opened the door, Kyame asked, "Excuse me, ma'am, but did you see anything of the killing last night right over there near the church? I'm collecting material for a story for the *Times* about responsible citizens."

Kyame had dropped her voice slightly, hoping it would sound more mature. She was at least four inches taller than the woman.

"Why?"

"Your name, ma'am, so I get it right in the article."

"Lethbridge, Mrs. Richard Lethbridge, ah, Sybil Lethbridge ... but my husband should really be here."

"Did he see anything? It is a trying day, ma'am," said Kyame, her voice softening. She passed her hand before the woman's eyes, like stroking velvet. "So very trying, Mrs. Lethbridge, you really should rest ... sit down, relax and just rest yourself for a few minutes. You need rest. Your mind needs rest. It can be so tiring ...." Kyame saw Lethbridge's jaw slacken. "But Lethbridge, that's not really your name, is it? You have forgotten your name."

Kyame took her arm and led the dazed woman back into her house and sat her on a sofa. "Lean back and sleep, hearing only my voice. You are surrounded by only peace and safety."

Mrs. Lethbridge fell back, her eyes shut.

***

It was the woman, not her husband who had taken the lantern out to see what was happening. She had looked out the window just moments before the shot when some large animal had run across their porch. It had startled Mrs. Lethbridge who was up waiting for her husband to come home late from the Santa Fe train station.

A tall man had been standing by the tree when another man, apparently the gambler, Barnato, had come up. Barnato had extended a package toward the other man, who then shot him. She had gone out on the porch with the lantern to see if someone had been hurt.

A reporter had suddenly come up to her out of the dark and told her Jack Barnato had been shot and that he had seen a Mr. John Piddington do it. He said he would go for the police.

The reporter was Max Early -- on the scene *before* the police. How did he know? He had warned Mrs. Lethbridge not to mention his being there to anyone. It was a murder investigation, he cautioned, and she needed to be very careful who might learn about her. Not even her husband should be told. Lethbridge had promised she would say nothing about him to anyone.

Kyame left Mrs. Lethbridge in a deep sleep with a suggestion that she could not recall Kyame's visit unless Kyame's voice allowed her to, and she would not recall the name Piddington. She was to awake, fully rested, in thirty minutes.

48

They sat diagonally across a long table from each other at the Atchison lending library -- the only place Maze felt was safe for them to meet. He had to be certain none of the Ballinger crowd could connect him with the Impossible Piddingtons. He had several books piled in front of him while Kyame had several newspapers scattered around her.

"I am not a medium so much, Kyame, as I am a rented friend, someone who will listen without criticism for as long as the client needs. Listening is always the key. Listening is the cheapest form of flattery. People always tell you more than they are aware of." He quickly glanced around room and leaned toward her. "I checked the medium's Blue Book for Atchison, the joint collection of information shared by all mediums.

"According to the Book, Lyle is from Tulsa, Oklahoma. He was a senior sergeant on the police force there, but was forced to leave after only two years. He was from Texas before then. Had a shaky reputation, the law was whatever he decided it was, but some of the people liked his toughness, his results. That toughness got him in some kind of trouble. I don't know what, but maybe that trouble has followed him here.

"In his casing the town, your papa must have found something about that."

When Kyame explained her session with Mrs. Lethbridge, Maze grinned. "You are definitely a piece of work, Kyame. I'm not sure it is legal to alter a witness' recollections ... but legal doesn't matter in this case."

First glancing around the library, Kyame started to speak, paused, frowning. She shook her head.

"Papa and Mrs. Lethbridge both said they saw the dark form picking up something from the ground. But what if that dark form was putting something *down* on the ground, like twenty-dollar bills, not picking them up?

"Maze, what if Barnato had come with a package of fake money, newspaper strips the size of twenty-dollar bills? He was armed, the derringer was found in his left hand. He came to kill the blackmailer ... the dark form guessed that that was what the gambler would do and shot first. Then the dark form scatters the money and takes Barnato's fake package away to make it look like Barnato had brought the money demanded. The newspaper strips I found were missed in the darkness."

The medium agreed. "That could work. And it would also suggest that the blackmailer did not want the money, he simply wanted Barnato dead ... for some reason. That part doesn't make much sense."

"So," Kyame said, "we have a Chief of Detectives with a shaky reputation who wants to immediately throw Papa into jail before the sun is up; a reporter who is on a murder scene maybe before the murder ... and a tall shadow running away." She cocked her head. "Are Lyle and Marotta also being blackmailed? And the other three on Johnstone's list ... them, too?"

***

Fanny Albright threw the Atchison *Globe* on the table, the large black headlines already condemning John Piddington as the killer of the well-known gambler, Jack Barnato. The by-line was Max Early.

350

"Early, even for you, isn't this getting a little too obvious?" she said. "The man hasn't been in the hands of the police for even 24 hours and you're ready to hang him."

"We want to keep him where he is, Fanny," Early snapped. "That's where he can do us the most good. I don't want any judge to put him back onto the street too soon.

"You just do what you are told, lady."

"What about his daughter?" Albright persisted. "She is still out there. I hear she's a tough one."

Johnstone closed his valise and settled his coat on his shoulders.

"She's only a theatre kid," said Johnstone, "with no friends in town. Forget her. No straight citizen will believe anything she says." His lean face was rigid, then relaxed. "More important things now ... stage manager and the dancers are already over there setting things up." The seer grinned. "My favorite time ... time to start shaking the coin from the locals."

The seer pointed at the woman. "Fanny, get digging. Use Piddington's local notes for a start. I need more material for tomorrow's show and for the matinee in two days.

"And, keep your eyes open for that Piddington girl. I just want to know where she is." He swung the valise off the table.

"Come on, Early," said Johnstone. "I need to get to the theatre for final setup." The crystal gazer laughed. "You can interview all the cops backstage as they protect the public morals." He was still laughing as he left the room with Max Early trailing behind.

Albright shook her head. Nothing felt right, but Johnstone had her paper, had goods on her, and it would be too risky to challenge him. That glass-ball worker would find her wherever she ran to. Better the police than -- him.

She left for her own room.

49

Maze had agreed to see what he could find on Max Early, while Kyame, who said she would wait in their room, had decided instead to go after Johnstone. He seemed to be the center of everything, whatever all that was.

Papa had talked about Johnstone before the mindreader had arrived in Atchison. He said that with his oriental staging, dancers, and illusions, he was the greatest showman on the stage, greater than Hermann the Great, Harry Kellar or any of the big-time magicians. But -- The Man Who Knows always left a trail of rumors and missing men behind him. But, Papa had suggested, how much of that talk was professional jealousy spread by competitors, trying to knock off a major challenger; and how much truth, no one knew.

Kyame was determined to know.

***

Kyame watched Johnstone and Early leave the hotel together. With the Impossible Piddingtons canceled, Johnstone had moved his opening night up a day.

The sun was low, the gas streetlamps were being lighted, and lights in the some of the buildings along Main Street were flickering on.

Kyame was dressed in a pair of Papa's old trousers with the cuffs pinned up, one of Papa's black shirts and Papa's dark blue woolen cap. She wore soft black kid gloves, her best. They were like a second skin.

Kyame had learned the Johnstone troupe had rented half the third floor of the hotel, with a guard on the third floor landing at the top of the main stairs to discourage anyone from intruding into the private mediations of the mystical Man Who Knows.

The alley was empty and without light. Kyame stumbled in a pothole, falling to her knees. She froze, listening. Nothing.

She moved to the building, letting her right hand slide lightly along until she found what she was looking for.

Kyame piled up two boxes, then clambered up. She was barely able to reach the bottom rung of the iron fire escape. Hand over hand, Kyame pulled herself up until she could get a foot onto the lowest rung. After a minute's rest, she moved rapidly up to the second floor windows just as the lights in the room went on.

Kyame dodged back into the shadows as two forms indistinct behind the curtains, but obviously a man and a woman, moved near the window. She would have to cross the fire escape landing to reach the rungs on the other side of the window, to get up to the third floor.

Kyame waited, as the couple stayed by the window, the sky continuing to darken.

She pulled Papa's watch from her pocket, holding near the glow of the window to see. It was 7:30. Johnstone's show started at eight and would run until 10:00 or a little later, according to Maze.

There was time, but she had to move. A man had wandered behind the hotel to urinate against the building, then he moved back to the street. If he had looked up, she would have been silhouetted against the last of the light in the sky.

Kyame dropped to her knees, flattening herself against the rough planks of the landing, and, like an inch-+worm, moved, braced on her elbows and knees, lowered, moved and lowered again across the landing.

Once clear of the window, she stood, gripped the rungs and resumed climbing.

Of course, the window at the third floor landing was locked. There was another window about two feet away. A narrow ledge projected from the building. Stretching, hanging on to the fire escape ladder, Kyame thought she could reach and pull herself over to the window. If it was locked, then she would pull back to break the window at the landing as gently as possible.

She planned to make her evening visit look like a cracksman, a sneak thief looking for cash and jewels. Part of Johnstone's publicity pitch recounted the numerous valuable gems given him by the crowned heads of Asia and Europe, so there was an obvious draw for a bandit.

As she pushed, the window slid upward, a few inches, then stopped, wedged in place. Too narrow to get in. She pushed the window back down, then pulled herself back to the landing.

Kyame steadied herself against the wall and pulled the small crowbar from her belt.

Tap. Harder. Tap! The window cracked. Tap! Pushing against the window glass with one gloved hand, she tapped still harder, pushing the broken glass back into the room. She shook her hands and arms to free herself of any glass slivers.

Kyame waited.

Silence. Some voices from the street, but no reaction to the sounds of broken glass.

She reached in and up to unlock the window, then pushed it up. Another moment and she was in.

Kyame went to the closet. That would identify which room it was. This one had only women's clothes and light gauzy costumes. Must be the dancers.

She moved to the adjoining door to the next room. It was locked.

Papa had started teaching her the rudiments of lock-picking, but this was no time for practice. Kyame wedged the crowbar into the doorjamb, leaned into the iron bar and began to pry the door away from the jamb. She pushed harder. Suddenly the lip of the crowbar slipped loose from her grip and clanged to the floor! Kyame froze, not breathing.

Nothing. No sounds.

Gripping the iron bar tighter and wedging it deeper into the doorjamb, she threw all her weight onto it. The door flew open.

***

Aggie Phillips nodded to the now colorfully robed and turbaned seer.

"Everything to your satisfaction, Sergeant?" asked Alexander Jason Johnstone, his eyes outlined with black mascara, his cheeks and lips highlighted with rouge. "I must pass to the stage for my final preparations."

Phillips had never seen anything like the twin pretty dancers wearing almost nothing as they smiled warmly up at him, brushing up against him as they moved silently on their toes to the wings. The strange equipment, elaborately painted boxes, backdrops suggesting the walls of an oriental temple, and the great sparkling crystal ball set on a golden tripod in the center of a carved ivory and ebony table.

He had just never seen anything like it.

"Ah ... yes, Mr. Johnstone, yes, everything looks ... satisfactory."

"Then, Sergeant, I will ask you and your men to take their seats and enjoy the show."

***

Kyame let her fingers move slowly across and around the carved box. First pulling the curtains shut, she had lighted a lamp, then turned it low. From the closet and the top drawers of the dresser, there was no doubt, this was Johnstone's room.

The drawers yielded only silk drawers, ties, and numerous shirts, along with some magazines and a manuscript for a book on oriental philosophy, obviously copied from somewhere.

The closet was filled with more suits and more expensive suits than Papa had every owned in his life. Some gorgeously colored ceremonial robes and a jeweled turban hung to one side.

Two steamer trunks stood open. The small compartments inside were empty, except for one drawer that was locked. A hard twist of the crowbar broke it open. Jewelry and some paper money that she pushed down into her pocket. Knowing the backstage world, Kyame was certain the jewelry was only glass, but a thief might not.

"It's very hard to make realistic mistakes," Papa had warned her, "so you must put your mind into the other person's thinking."

So, a thief would just grab everything that looked valuable and sort things out later. She stuffed the jewels into her other pocket.

That's when she saw the box. It sat with other boxes and apparatus in the largest drawer of the second steamer trunk, but it was obviously of better workmanship and made of exotic black and white wood. It must be for something special.

Her fingers found nothing in the empty box. She pressed the carved rosette design; it didn't move. She pressed again, as she twisted the design counter-clockwise. There was a sharp click.

Kyame carried the box over to the lamp where she saw one side of the box had moved a fraction of an inch. Her fingernails under the edge of the side, she pulled gently -- the side of the box opened up.

It worked like the well-crafted Jap Box once shown her by one of the magicians with whom they had shared the bill in Julesburg, Colorado.

Silk handkerchiefs were packed into a secret compartments in the long side of the box. With the release of the wall inside the box, the magician could produce scarves and handkerchiefs from the previously shown empty box. With only a quick pressure of the magician's fingers against the wall, the box could be almost instantly shown empty again.

Johnstone's black and white box was bigger than any Jap Box Kyame had seen. In its concealed compartment it held a thick sheaf of papers. Some $50 and $100 dollar silver certificates which she stuffed into her pockets -- but more importantly, documents with Max Early's name on them;

letters, three photos, form papers that looked like receipts. The lamp was dimming, running low on oil. She found pins on the desk in the room and pinned everything together. She stuffed the packet of papers down the front of her shirt and buttoned it to her neck.

Kyame opened the opposite side of the box the same way to discover a thick stack of hundred dollar bills. She took everything, but let a $50 dollar bill fall to the floor near the forced door. A thief moving in haste would never notice dropping the bill.

She closed the box and returned it to the steamer trunk. With the loss of the jewels and the fifty on the floor, perhaps Johnstone would not think to look further.

Some people, Professor J. W. Cadwell had instructed her, think themselves so clever that they cannot conceive that anyone could match them. Those are the easiest to con, he had said smiling. He always looked for them, as they made such lucrative targets.

The Man Who Knows sounded like he could be one of the mesmerist's favored targets -- and now hers.

50

Maze Edwards' jaw dropped as Kyame laid out her swag. "You are a piece of work, from bark to core, young lady."

Kyame cocked her head; her smile was lethal.

In his investigation, Maze had already determined that Max Early might be a bigamist, or worse. The reporter also had other problems. The medium was waiting for some telegrams for confirmation of sketchy information in the Blue Book.

Kyame tapped a receipt from Sayers Gunsmithy. "Early bought a .32 pistol *the day after* Papa showed his gun to Johnstone. That's how Barnato could be shot with a gun the same as Papa's.

"I think Mr. Sayers is an honest man. I think if Sergeant Phillips asked him, he would admit to firing Early's .32. Then Early had the guns switched when Papa and I were out of our rooms. Wouldn't have been hard to do; I know that now from experience."

Maze laughed and nodded.

"And," continued Kyame, "the papers I found show that Early owed Johnstone over $3,000, and it was due to be paid off in two months, so Johnstone *owned* Early, as he apparently owns other people."

"Who then killed Barnato? Not Early. I don't believe he has the guts to kill," said the medium. "There is no violence in his background ... as shady as that is."

"I agree," said Kyame. "It had to be Johnstone himself, but we could never prove that. No one would ever testify against him ... if any of those stories about him are true.

"But we only need to prove that Papa couldn't have done it." She set her jaw. "Then we leave town."

"Why then was Barnato killed?" asked the medium.

Kyame was quiet for several moments, unmoving, her eyes half-closed, then she said, "The only thing I can think of would be to use Papa to get more data for the local blackmailing, like that note found on Barnato; then put him out of the way so that there could be no later connection with Early or Johnstone.

"They could use the information Papa found any time they wanted. Blackmail never spoils on the shelf … so the sheriff in Dodge City told me … unless the targeted person dies. So, Barnato was blackmailed in order to set up Papa as his killer, to discredit Papa if he tried to challenge anything later.

"And it appears," she continued, "that Johnstone ensured that Early was always the front man, the stooge for the evil work." Kyame pursed her lips. "But," she said, "what about the others, Lyle and Marotta? There must be more at play … but maybe, with Johnstone out of town, whatever that might be would be delayed."

"Agreed. Johnstone will be back, some way." Maze Edwards extended his hand to her. When Kyame took it, he squeezed gently.

"You have freed your father, Kyame." He turned back to her as he reached the door of the library meeting room – a room that Edwards had reserved earlier for a Spiritual Teaching Class that he later canceled too late for anyone else to use. "What about the money you found ... and the other materials?"

Kyame grinned. "I'll keep the money as any good thief would, except to repay you for your legal expenses for Papa. The Man Who Knows surely knows he dare not try to prove anything."

Maze shook his head. "No, no repayments, that's my contribution. You took all the risk. You keep all your, ah," he grinned. "All your research findings."

***

Alexander Jason Johnstone, The Man Who Knows, was deathly pale with cold fury. Fanny Albright stood as far from him as his hotel room allowed.

"Quit cursing that girl, Jason," she said. "You bet on Max Early and it was a dead bet. Even his 'solid' witness, that Lethbridge woman, couldn't remember anything, never even heard of the name Piddington; and then with that gunsmith Sayers ... there was nothing left to hold John Piddington. So, fold'm and move on for God's

367

sake. Early's in jail and isn't going to talk about anything. And ...."

Johnstone looked up at her, the black and white Jap Box in his hands. He slammed it on the floor and stamped it to splinters.

"Shut up, you miserable filth," he snarled. "I will not be beaten by a damn fourteen-year-old girl! She will pay for my having to cancel the run in Atchison ... and losing a squeeze opportunity worth tens of thousands. I'll still squeeze Marotta and Lyle somehow, and the others will pay as well. They all will pay! I will find them and *they will pay*!"

A cold smile flowed across the seer's face then vanished. Color began to reappear in Johsnstone's lean face. He nodded.

"Time to retreat, regroup and plan the counter-attack." As his men came into the room for the luggage, he turned to Albright. "I'll call you when I'm ready. Understood?"

Fanny Albright nodded as she edged out of the room.

***

There were three at the table: Papa, Driver Robson, the attorney hired by Maze Edwards, and Kyame. Kyame wore her shimmering teal blue performance gown; it was the best she had. With the Johnstone cash, she would buy another, in another town.

Alexander Jason Johnstone had abruptly closed down after one show and had left Atchison. Max Early was in jail. The Atchison *Times* was running large headlines celebrating the embarrassment of the *Globe* that had run Early's loud accusations. And Sergeant Phillips had warned Johnstone, though they could not charge him with anything, the seer was never to come back to Atchison County.

Johnstone's response had not been made public.

"My client, Miss and Mister Piddington," said Robson, "could not be here for reasons I believe you fully understand. But he did want me to deliver this bottle of champagne for your celebratory dinner this evening."

The lawyer signaled their waiter, who stepped quickly to the table. After displaying the label to each of them for approval, he carefully opened the bottle with a restrained pop and poured Kyame first.

With all glasses filled, Papa raised his glass, then smiled, "This is real champagne, Kyame, not your mesmeric vintage."

She laughed and nodded. "Yes, Papa, the real thing ... the best kind." The impressive label had said Dom Pérignon, 1887. Kyame would remember that.

Papa raised his glass to her, as Driver Robson raised his.

"To you, dear Daughter, who brought me freedom ... to 'The Girl Who Knows'."

Kyame raised her glass, but shook her head.

"No, Papa. To 'The *Woman* Who Knows'." She smiled as she sipped. This champagne wasn't bitter at all.

***

Sacramento was still almost an hour away as Kyame balanced the large book on her lap. The dim faded gilt words on the torn loose spine said:

The Colle Wor of Shakesp. Papa watched as she murmured the words to herself.

Frowning, Kyame said, "Didn't Shakespeare ever laugh, Papa? Is this really English?"

"What are you reading, Daughter?"

"Hamlet, ah, Act 2, scene 3. I really can't make any sense out of it. One of the actors in that touring troupe we saw back in Lincoln last week said they had cut Hamlet and couple of other Shakespeare plays down because people wouldn't sit through the whole thing ... and they changed some of the words to American so their audiences could understand what was going on."

"Well, Shakespeare requires study and reflection, Kyame. Mama always preferred his sonnets and poetry to the plays." John Piddington smiled. "Reminds me of an Italian laborer who was working on a road near our house back in Ohio. You were seven or eight years old then."

Kyame closed the dusty book that she had found in a trash can in the waiting room in Ogallala. She laid both her hands across it and leaned toward Papa, her green eyes so intense that

Piddington felt he was looking into Laura's eyes once again. There was a catch in his throat when he spoke again.

"I once went by and saw him resting on a pile of cobble stones reading Shakespeare. When I asked, he said it was to learn English. When I pointed out that no one spoke English that way anymore, the laborer responded, 'Too bad, signor, too bad. It is the way English should be spoken ... with that gentle rhythm in the words.'"

Papa placed his hand on Kyame's head and smiled. The hurt of their coming separation numbed for just a moment. "Shakespeare is worth the effort to understand, Daughter. Not a cut-up version or an American version, but his words from his pen ... and his heart. Mama would lose herself in his sonnets while we traveled."

"I think, Papa, I will start with the sonnets and leave Mr. Hamlet for later." She looked up and grinned. "A lot later."

51

The last performance of the Impossible Piddingtons had been two nights previous at the Palace Theatre in Sacramento. As they had started a few weeks before, with Kyame's height and developing maturity, Papa had placed her sitting on a chair that in turn rested on a table in the center of the stage. He invited volunteers from the audience to come to the stage to form a "human wall" around her to ensure that Kyame could not receive any help from back stage. The position, though apparently more exacting, more scientific, actually provided Kyame with a much broader view of the audience from under her blindfold. She had to be careful that, sitting so high, that no one could glimpse her eyes under the blindfold -- a mistake that could give the whole game away. Kyame kept her head bent slightly, carefully observing the position of the people around the table.

The change in her position had initially increased the stress in her performance, but by the end of the first week, it had become routine and she could concentrate on her smokey acting.

Halfway through a performance in Eugene, Oregon, a man had stood in the audience and loudly challenged her, even with the human wall and blindfold, to continue with her back turned to her father. As Papa had already signed two subjects ahead, Kyame stood, whirled, her flowing skirts flaring, as she turned her chair. She continued to thunderous applause.

As Papa had before, when they had met with other interesting challenges; he inserted that move of suddenly turning her back to the audience into the act. Adding her own touch, Kyame would apparently almost step off the table as she shifted her position which would draw immediate outcries and warnings from the audience – while subtlely convincing the audience of the genuineness of her blindfold. The best misdirection, J. W. Cadwell had once suggested to her, was a well planned accident.

"Always, Kyame," said Papa, "always be ready to learn from your audience they often have great ideas."

***

But now it was time. As much as he had willed the large station clock to stop, Kyame's train to St. Louis and then on to Boston was starting to take on life. John Piddington would be continuing on south to San Francisco to a position with Montgomery-Hill Bank while his daughter's journey would be alone, back across the country to the Boston School of the Arts on Boylston Street. She looked so tall, confident and beautiful – so much the image of her mother.

"Papa, I'll be all right," said Kyame, her smile, small, sad and without its customary brilliance. "It's time for the train ... and for me to stand on my own feet.

"But I'll miss you, Papa, so very much. I'll miss ... miss everything, walking on a stage with you ... making the people scream." She tried to smile but the tears started down her cheeks.

They embraced – then Kyame walked across the platform to the train, the steam enveloping the engine, then roiling back across the six passenger cars.

She handed her carpetbag up to the porter who quickly disappeared up the steps into the car.

Papa had insisted on her traveling First Class at least to St. Louis. Kyame turned back to look at Papa who was wiping at his eyes. She returned his wave. With the assistance of the conductor, Kyame mounted the stairs and looked back as Papa waved again. She had to stand back as the conductor came up the steps.

"Please go inside, Miss," he said. "We are leaving now."

Finding her seat near the center of the car and pressing up against the window to see Papa, Kyame felt the train begin to move. Papa walked along keeping parallel with her until the train gained speed and he fell back out of her sight. Her last glimpse was of Papa waving, then making that hard right fist of approval that had so often caused her heart to glow.

I love ...

But Kyame lost his last sign as the train drew away.

Kyame had never felt so suddenly alone, as she turned back in her seat, to turn to her new life.

She wondered if the Impossible Piddingtons would ever walk on a stage again.

A

Brief

Intermission

To Allow Some Reflection

On

The Coming of Second Sight

"I rested my head in my hands, and in my excitement laid down the first principles of second sight."

Jean Eugene Robert-Houdin

Memoirs of Robert-Houdin

1859

The origin of second sight, of the demonstration of the transfer of unspoken thought without using the natural senses from the mind of one medium or priest to his partner, dates back at least to the publication of Reginald Scott's *The Discoverie of Witchcraft* in 1584, which includes an implication that two-person thought transfer dated even earlier than that.

Second-sight as a stage act, however, dates to over a century before the time of the Impossible Piddingtons in the 1890's. In 1781, Philip Breslaw, a German magician, advertised "the communication of thoughts of any person to another without the assistance of speech or writing". Three years later, the French performer, the Chevalier Joseph Pinetti, had his wife "seated in one of the front boxes with a handkerchief over her eyes". With her husband in the audience, she would then "guess at everything imagined and proposed to her by any person in the company". Pinetti claimed their demonstration was a genuine exhibition of preternatural powers.

But it was the brilliant French conjuror and inventor, Jean Eugene Robert-Houdin, with his eleven-year-old son, Émile, as the blindfolded medium, who, with his development of the first practical silent code, created the modern second sight act. The father-son duo first performed second sight publicly in Paris at the Théâtre Robert-Houdin on Thursday, February 12, 1846.

Even with the extraordinary range of illusions and automata developed by Robert-Houdin throughout his celebrated career, *La Seconde Vue,* the second sight, remained one of the magician's signature presentations.

The innovative Frenchman never revealed his methods of second sight.

The basic scenario of the second sight act is that the two performers appear to communicate mentally with each other; they do not necessarily claim they can read the minds of anyone else in their audiences. On occasion, the medium, under deep trance, can apparently see the future.

The medium on the stage is described in Washington Irving Bishop's 1880 booklet, *Houdin and Heller Second Sight Explained*:

Robert-Houdin and his son, Émile,

performing *La Seconde Vue,* second sight. 1846.

"The clairvoyant is usually a young lady, interesting in manner and dejected in appearance, as if distressed by some constant strain on the nervous system. The clairvoyant also presents an appearance of passive submission, as if in fear of some all-powerful controlling influence, and, even when possessed of robust vigor, she assumes an air of having no will of her own, and exceeding timidity.

"The clairvoyant is blindfolded completely."

The point is to suggest helpless innocence on the part of the medium on the stage, which helps gain the sympathy and more effectively engage the belief of the audience.

The use of some sort of clever verbal code to convey information in a second sight act was quickly surmised from the time of Breslaw and confidently explained in books and newspapers -- yet the second sight acts continued to mystify as the performers created increasingly subtle codes and signaling techniques to finally achieve, with Robert-Houdin, the performance of portions of the act in complete silence which negated the very idea of codes.

Some innovative second sight performers in the late nineteenth century began to utilize complex coding systems in which subtle movements were coupled with a phonetic system in which sounds, not words, conveyed a broad range of information under even the most demanding conditions.

The original phonetic systems were based on combinations of forty sounds, e.g., th, ing, ish, oi, ou, where the meanings were derived from the sound and from their relative position in a series of sounds.

Modern phonetic coding systems which utilize only thirteen sounds are even more flexible. As the sounds seem to the audience as only incidental to the performance, the spectators come away with the impression that the performance was performed in complete silence.

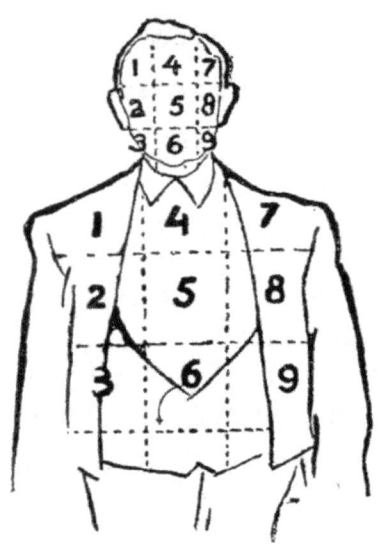

Silent Code Signaling Chart

Zero was signaled by touching

the back of the neck or head. Numbers signaled

referenced memorized lists of common objects,

which could run to three to four hundred different items.
(1905)

In the career of the Impossible Piddingtons, Kyame and her father have been given coding capabilities that actually did not fully evolve in the profession until the early 20th century with Julius and Agnes Zancig, billed as "Two Minds With But

386

a Single Thought", who convinced even investigating scientists in the 1920's that their powers were genuine.

As adaptable and quick as the modern codes are, to become proficient, to be able to speak silently, demands a regimen of daily multi-hour practice by the two performers working together, to the point where, as Kyame learns, the line between the trick and the genuine becomes remarkably thin.

But the success of second sight as entertainment is not due to ever more clever coding or advanced technology, but to the same techniques of showmanship that Breslaw, Pinetti and Robert-Houdin would immediately recognize. Given the mysterious transfer of information, how can the performers then sell that information effectively in order to amuse and convince their audiences, i.e., the "smokey acting" as Kyame comes to call her delivery of the details that Papa has coded to her.

Kyame is taught one of the principal techniques of presenting second sight early on by her father. And that is: be wrong, miss, get close but not precisely on target. Papa signs a pocket watch, but then signs that she is to miss; so, following Papa's coding, Kyame describes the watch in some detail but then calls it a lady's compact.

She has clearly "seen" the object, but the thought conveying the image was confused or distorted by ... well, whatever the audience will believe, e.g., someone coughs loudly; someone noisily leaving the music hall; or any disturbance that would deflect the attention of the audience itself. As Papa instructs Kyame, miss productively *on purpose* -- never by accident.

After all, only tricksters, con-men and politicians claim to be right all the time. Therefore, if the Piddingtons occasionally miss, the audiences come to believe that their powers of mental communication, of second sight, must most likely be genuine.

And the audience must perceive a process, an effort being made by the performers to communicate that, conceivably, is based not only on a strange talent, but on hard work and sustained study. The suggestion of risk and perhaps pushing the human envelope near its limits can add to the tension felt by the audience.

Kyame might be perceived by the audience as a young psychic woman who needs mature experience to be able to sort out and understand the extraordinary images she is receiving from her father; and, perhaps, from other people in the audiences. Thus Kyame's "smokey acting" is critical to reinforce that perception and to ensure the success of the Impossible Piddingtons.

And, as the mesmerist, J. W. Cadwell, instructed her, it is only through constant practice that her ability, not only to mesmerize, but to be a convincing psychic personality can be attained.

By the time Kyame Piddington reaches fourteen, she has become an experienced professional performer of psychic illusions, effects which, sometimes, not even she can explain.

Her presence only becomes more compelling at sixteen after two years of selling her art to Boston dealers, while perfecting her mesmeric techniques.

Part 2

The Boo How Doy

[the hatchet men]

52

New York City

Sunday, April 14, 1895

Kyame Piddington watched William Steinitz move slowly, arthritically, from board to board, leaning heavily on a stout black cane. Hers was the last chessboard of seventeen in a public simultaneous exhibition. The boards were arranged in a large U-shape with the open area in the middle for the chess master and former World Chess Champion to move from board to board.

Kyame was the only woman sitting at one of the boards, or, for that matter, anywhere in the large game room. When she had put her five-dollar gold piece down on the table in the foyer of the Manhattan Chess Club, the Club secretary had frowned as he reluctantly picked it up.

They had advertised twenty boards at five dollars a board in the principal New York newspapers, but Steinitz' loss of his championship title to Emanuel Lasker a year earlier in June, 1894, had apparently reduced interest in the exhibition.

Lasker, not even half Steinitz' age, had defeated the "Bohemian Caesar" with ten wins to five for Steinitz and four draws. The match, played in New York, Philadelphia and Montreal, was over more quickly than anyone had expected. Steinitz had issued a challenge for a re-match, but Lasker had not yet responded.

It was simple. The Club had told Steinitz he would receive a hundred dollars for an afternoon's work while the Club's prestige would be further enhanced with the demonstration. It was very simple; the Club needed Kyame's money even if she didn't sit at a board. The Secretary did not want to make up the difference from the Club treasury.

Kyame had felt the stares and frowns of the men as she gathered her skirts to go up the stairs to the game room -- and the undisguised lust of some of the younger men as she moved by them. She had begun feeling those stares at fourteen, but she had been a *theater girl* then, only a cheap *theater girl,* not an educated young woman, a young college student deserving respect.

When Kyame entered the game room, William Steinitz stood in the middle of the large U-arrangement of the tables smoking a black cigar.

He was oblivious to the shuffling commotion of the men settling at their assigned boards.

The chess master was short, 4-5 inches shorter than Kyame. His face, hidden behind a bushy reddish-brown beard, was crowned by a massive forehead that could have been taken from one of the Greek sculptures used in Kyame's school for composition practice. His intense brooding presence was intimidating.

Kyame had drawn black against Steinitz's Ruy Lopez opening. It was the first chess opening that Papa had shown her three years earlier when he had begun teaching her how to play chess.

***

"Just avoid the really dumb mistakes and always work to develop your position, Daughter. Never move the same piece twice at the beginning," Papa had instructed as they waited backstage to begin an evening performance. "You will always be in the game then, long enough to learn more."

In the four years of the Impossible Piddingtons, with her maturing skill with her 'smokey acting" most of their audiences had come to accept Kyame Piddington as psychically endowed -- and a young woman, maybe, to be feared. Of course, without Papa's silent signaling and his "digging up the dirt", there would have been nothing. Even she, with Papa's careful teaching, had learned the techniques of dirt digging in their final year together.

How she so missed Papa now and that sudden surge of excitement as she would walk on stage, feeling and seeing the frightened awe in the faces of the people – especially certain women, those mothers who would not let their children play with her because she was only a *theater girl*. Kyame had taken special joy in scaring them, if she could.

Papa had discouraged her attitude. "We need all the paying customers we can get, Daughter. Don't scare them away," he had admonished her after a show in Decatur, Illinois, in which Kyame had driven two women screaming out of the music hall by promising a vivid doom to their children – a doom not signaled by Papa.

Papa's disapproval had weighed heavily on her, bringing tears -- but she recognized that he had been right.

It was two years now since Sacramento, the last time the Impossible Piddingtons had walked on stage, two years of her study in the Boston art school that Papa had worked so hard and saved to give her.

When she had seen the Steinitz exhibition announcement in the Boston *Herald,* Kyame had immediately purchased a train ticket. To play William Steinitz, even for only a few moves, was something she had to do, to be able to share a special experience with Papa.

Papa had answered her first question, back then, waiting back stage as they had stood, prepared to begin their performance, telling her that William Steinitz was the greatest chess player in the world.

Chess had triggered an immediate excitement in her. She and Papa, and others, had played daily ever since those first backstage lessons.

After a few months at her school, the Boston School of the Arts on Boylston Street in Back Bay, Kyame had been able to sell some of her drawings and paintings first at school exhibitions and then to the Vose Gallery over on Newbury Street, which meant that Papa could keep more money for himself. Her art appearing in the windows of the Vose had immediately boosted her artistic reputation in Boston.

Papa had been working now as a loan officer at the Montgomery-Hill Bank in San Francisco for two years, but in their letters it was clear that he longed to return to the stage at some point.

Papa had confided in one of his letters to meeting a woman, Eliza Abbott, who seemed special but in a way different from Mama. But when she and Eliza had met once in Boston, Kyame had refused to acknowledge her.

***

First arriving at her board, Steinitz' attitude toward her had been muffled, somewhat hostile. But when Steinitz had first moved his king's pawn and Kyame had responded immediately to the first four standard Ruy Lopez moves, he had nodded, then awaited her fifth move, the move that might begin to differentiate this Ruy Lopez exercise from the hundreds of others he had experienced and studied.

His broad muscular shoulders and arms made him appear even shorter but lent an overpowering presence at the board, leaning forward on his cane. Steinitz had been born with a clubfoot, Kyame had read, so the power in his shoulders had come from using crutches and canes all his life.

He was sixty. She was sixteen. Lasker, his conqueror, had been twenty-five.

Steinitz stood sideways to her as though not looking at the board at all, humming softly to himself. But she knew he had simply memorized the position of the pieces on the board and did not need to look at it.

Just as Kyame did not need to look at her board -- either.

Her fifth move, she took his pawn with her Queen pawn, to clear a diagonal for her King's bishop to the far side of the board.

It had pleased him.

"When in doubt, my dear," whispered Steinitz, "take a pawn. A pawn is worth a little trouble." The adjacent players leaned closer to try to hear his words.

Steinitz shuffled away, to stop at the small table that held his lighted cigar in an ash-tray. He paused, to enjoy his ever-present black cigar for a few puffs, then shuffled back to board one.

Kyame's response was the same that Steinitz had used himself against Mikhail Chigorin in Havana in 1889; a game, however, that Steinitz had ultimately lost. She had memorized Steinitz' seminal book, *The Modern Chess Instructor* -- a copy of which was in her bag under her chair.

***

Now fifteen moves later, as Steinitz approached, Kyame pushed her Queen's bishop forward to bring more pressure through the center. He had forced her earlier to sacrifice a knight and three pawns to break through into his inner defenses. But she had blocked him on two occasions from penetrating within a dangerous proximity to her king. But now he was threatening again.

Eight of the boards were now empty, victories for the master; and she was into her seventeenth move.

She looked up into Steinitz' deep dark eyes.

Joy.

She had tried to understand what she was seeing in his eyes when he would come to her board. She now realized that it was plain joy; to him it was the chess that was his only world, the only place for the deep joy of his eyes. He was not crippled in his chess world, only in that *other* world. Kyame knew now she could finish the portrait of him that she was sketching while he was moving along the other boards.

Four more moves and now there were only six still playing. There had been one draw, board five, who sat back smugly smoking a wretched pipe. Kyame could almost tolerate good cigar fragrance, but never the reek of a pipe.

Kyame abandoned the strategy of the Havana game to thrust her queen forward. Steinitz would have to either take her queen and thus open a clear rank for her rook; or leave her queen in position and capture her black bishop. She could support her exposed queen within two moves.

It was time to attack his throat.

The chess master paused, nodded, whistled softly and took her bishop, then shuffled away.

Kyame's momentary elation was quickly squelched. She had misjudged. Oh, confound it!- It would take *three* moves to support her queen.

Two more resignations left only four players. Then with stunning quickness only two: the man at eleven hunched closer to his board; and Kyame at board seventeen with her queen gone and Steinitz' relentless white horde advancing, progressively sealing off ever more of the board.

Three moves to mate it looked like, but only if she didn't recognize the key pivot of his assault, his innocuous knight.

Kyame sent her last rook to his doom, capturing the knight, expecting an exchange that would buy her maybe 2-3 more moves to live.

She watched as board eleven dismissed his king with a final flippant thrust of his forefinger; a look of disgust distorting his face. Clearly, the finely dressed man with green brocade waistcoat and starched white collar thought he would triumph over the little Jewish chess master in front of him.

Served the over-dressed ass right.

But then Steinitz was in front of her. A moment, then another.

"A most intelligent move, my dear," he said, all eyes on the two of them. "May I propose a draw? My exchange will render us both incapable of mounting a stimulating attack."

Kyame was stunned. She had hoped to last maybe ten moves. She had lasted thirty-six and gained a draw.

"I agree, Herr Steinitz. Our positions have become sterile."

He looked carefully at her. "A most apt word, Miss ...?"

"I am Kyame Piddington, sir."

He turned toward the cigar table.

"Sir, would you honor me by signing your book?" Kyame reached into her bag of drawing materials.

Steinitz turned back as Kyame withdrew the chocolate-colored book with the brilliant metallic gold chessboard embossed on the cover.

"I would be pleased to do so, Miss Piddington."

"And, sir, please accept this from me." She tore her penciled portrait of the chess master from her sketchbook.

Steinitz looked at the portrait as the crowds began to gather around them. "It is now I who am honored, Miss Piddington."

He withdrew a pen from inside his suit coat and wrote across the title page of the book. Waiting a moment for the ink to dry, he closed the book, and returned it to her. He bowed and shuffled away into the crowd, his rolled-up portrait in one hand.

Kyame opened the book.

"Miss Piddington. To a unique artist from one who aspires to art, yours sincerely", followed by his small cramped signature, "W. Steinitz".

Kyame glowed. Papa would be so proud. The book would be her Christmas gift to him.

53

Wong Woon shook himself furiously awake. Foolishness! Weakness to allow his thoughts to escape without control. A *kunchen*, an all-knowing one, one gifted with the Message of the Wind, telepathy, could sweep up the thoughts with his hand and fling death stones, the mystic *torma*, across his life. His followers in the Bing On tong should believe that their master never slept -- let alone had terrifying dreams.

Straightening his tie and shaking his head clear, Wong pushed away from his chair, cursing softly as he stood. Almost time for his new customer to arrive.

As he had awaked, Wong had caught himself momentarily thinking again of himself as the despised and filthy Gedun Drup, an escaped petty thief from a meaningless village in Western Tibet, instead of the feared tong master, Wong Woon.

His long suppressed Tibetan youth erupted without warning whenever, in his dreams, the mammoth white dog with red-rimmed eyes emerged from the unearthly brilliance of the moonlit Lamayuru Valley to walk toward him once again; its massive slobbering jaws open, its breath curling in the cold air. The size of a pony, the dog, once seen, forever scarred the memory.

Seeing the fabled dog had been the most terrifying experience of his life. The hungry red eyes had seared his puny soul until, stopping only a few feet from him, the dog had silently turned away to enter into a closed windowless shed -- and vanished.

Gedun Drup had soiled his clothes with fear, staring after the dog. But, Wong Woon knew as he settled his suit coat on his shoulders -- that it had not been a dream; not a *tulku*, a creation of magic; not a *tulpa*, a phantom. Not then. He could still smell the foul heaving breath of the horrific dog.

Not a dream.

Gedun Drup had been wide awake, waiting to rob a passing merchant just coming up from the lake his goods strapped on the back of a pack horse tied behind him. The merchant passed without knowing Gedun Drup was there. The waiting thief had been paralyzed with terror.

***

Alexander Jason Johnstone, The Man Who Knows, stepped back, flicking his handkerchief to remove the bit of blood splattered on his cuff. He had seen men killed in the gold fields, he had done the killing himself on appropriate occasion; he had seen men beaten on the streets of New York City, he, also, had done the beating when it was necessary. But never had he experienced any queasiness in his stomach before this moment in a San Francisco warehouse.

And the stink of Wong Woon's cigarette, like burning plums, only a foot or two away turned his gut.

Two men stripped of their clothing were tied down on their backs on wide planks extending between packing crates three feet off the floor. Their arms and hands secured tightly to their sides with green fish-line, their bounds becoming obscured by the swollen purple flesh; their legs spread apart and strapped in place with wet green leather, which squeezed the legs down to the plank ever tighter with each passing moment as the leather dried.

Some minutes earlier, when Johnstone had first arrived, one man was Caucasian and the other was Chinese. Now, after being flogged with bamboo flails by two heavily muscled Chinese highbinders stripped bare to the waist, each stroke lifting away a layer first of skin, then flesh, there was little skin color left to differentiate between the two.

Both men had attempted to hold their tongues against their rising agony, but finally the bloody mass that had been white released a scream that caused even Johnstone to shudder. The bound Chinaman began to shriek, then squeal, finally to bawl an inhuman sound that the seer had never heard before, even in the dregs of Skagway, Alaska.

The immaculately attired Chinese gentleman standing next to Johnstone flicked away the ash from his cigarette before taking another long drag. The tong master, Wong Woon smiled up into the tall crystal gazer's eyes, his smooth dark features marred only by a red scar running from his left ear to his chin; his hair cut *kidi,* in the American manner, short, close to the head -- not the humiliating long braided queue of Imperial Qing style. Wong's beaverskin derby, deep blue vested suit with white spats across his glistening shoes all came from tailors on Market Street that even Johnstone could just barely afford.

"It is Ming tradition, the tradition of the Bing On tong, Mr. Johnstone," said Wong Woon, gently, confidentially, "to beat betrayers on their

407

thighs for a time as instruction for their future behavior." He bowed his head. "We believe profoundly in tradition."

As the screaming went silent for a moment, the two bound men gasping desperately for air, Wong Woon said, still smiling, "Ah, sir, it seems the lesson has been understood. How so rewarding for everyone."

Wong tossed his hand and the beating stopped. The two muscled highbinders bowed and disappeared into the darkness of the far reaches of the warehouse. Two other men dressed in silken black wound with the white sashes reminiscent of the Ming, began to cut the beaten flesh loose from the planks.

The Caucasian, a Chinatown Methodist missionary, the Rev. William Kearney, had rounded a corner of Bartlett Alley in the heart of red-light Chinatown at a poor moment, just in time to observe a young man from his drifting flock, Ah Shok, buying from an opium dealer, who was a member of the Bing On.

When he had furiously objected to the transaction, the missionary found himself suddenly dragged from the street through a narrow open door and into a dark room. He regained consciousness tied naked to a plank.

Wong Woon directed that both men receive instruction. He had derided Ah Shok as only a pathetic rice-Christian -- Chinamen who believed in the white Christian preaching so long as the mission supplied them with food. Ah Shok needed to learn to be more circumspect with his opium buying.

Wong Woon bowed slightly to the much taller Johnstone. "My deepest apologies for having taken your esteemed time in observing this teaching opportunity. Now let us enjoy refreshment in my private office and speak of important mutual concerns."

He flicked the stub of his cigarette away, then he extended his flat hand, the fingers pressed together, toward a door without markings.

Johnstone nodded and followed, careful to stay a half-step to the rear where he could follow the movements of Wong Woon's highbinders, his hatchet men, the *boo how doy*, as they formed a rough half-circle behind him.

The seer did not enjoy the feeling of not being in control -- of being absolutely powerless.

But the price and quality of Wong's opium were worth some trouble

54

John Piddington threw the pencil back on his desk, shifting his shoulders to loosen their tightness at the end of a long day hunched over tally books, examining client accounts, tracing funds movements.

"You look fatigued, John," said Harvey Atherton, vice president of the industrial loan group at the Montgomery-Hill Bank and John Piddington's immediate boss for the past two years.

"Is there a concern I should know about?" Atherton settled casually into a chair against the wall.

Piddington shook his head. "There doesn't appear to be, Mr. Atherton, just some odd coincidences regarding the Rosner accounts that keep turning up."

"Harry Rosner? What could possibly be a problem with him?" the banker asked. "Not two nights ago, I attended a most elegant dinner and reception at his marvelous mansion on Russian Hill for John Mackay, the last of the four Comstock Silver Kings, to celebrate the start of Mackay's laying the Trans-Pacific Cable to

Hawaii. Everyone was there, even old Adolf Sutro ... and the wonderfully elegant, Mrs. Langtry."

Harvey Atherton shook his head, grimacing. "I almost acquired a number of shares of Mackay's Trans-Pacific Company," he said softly, "but for my wife ..."

He stiffened and looked back at Piddington. "Granted," Atherton said finally, "Villa Illuminaire, the Rosner mansion, cannot approach the matchless grandeur of the Hopkins or Stanford mansions on Nob Hill, or the old Flood place for that matter; but the oysters Kirkpatrick were ...."

Harvey Atherton let his eyes rise toward a heaven filled with oysters baked in bacon and strong goat cheese.

"Other than being very aggressive and a bit sharp in his dealings that, ah, inconvenience his competition, I cannot imagine why we should be concerned with Harry Rosner's credit with the bank."

Standing, Atherton stepped toward Piddington, jabbing his forefinger at him.

"Remember, John, I fully supported your proposing Harry Rosner last year as a client. The President agreed and was impressed with your analysis."

Atherton stepped closer, dropping his voice. "All our loans with him are comfortably collateralized, are they not, John? He is your client and one of the specific reasons you have moved up in the bank's organization so quickly ... ah, given your theater background."

After two years and building up the bank's industrial loan portfolio, it was *theater* again. He missed dear Kyame so much, relished her weekly letters -- he missed their walking out on a stage.

"The collateral is quite safe, Mr. Atherton," he said. "It is just the flow of funds that seem, well, unusual. But our present loans are certainly safe."

But for how long, he reflected.

"I received a note from Mr. Rosner's attorney, Mr. Elliot Blackwood, this afternoon that caused me to begin this analysis."

"And you did not immediately notify me?" Stepping back, Atherton tried to sound ruffled.

"I needed to assemble appropriate data before putting Rosner's request and my recommendations on your desk, sir."

Atherton nodded. "And when will you be doing that?"

"Friday morning ... at your earliest convenience, Mr. Atherton."

Four days.

"Ten-thirty o'clock," said Harvey Atherton, turning away.

John Piddington watched the vice president walk rapidly toward the rear exit from the bank. He was a son-in-law of the president, but possessed a good financial mind, but a much too cautious mind, and an even more suspicious wife.

Harvey Atherton had agreed to support Harry Rosner as a Montgomery-Hill client only after Piddington had, in detail, ensured the collateral was fully sound and the titles of the properties were completely clear, and had analyzed Rosner's proposed use of the funds, the acquisition of a portion of the equity of the Occidental and Oriental Steamship Co., a growing San Francisco firm with Southern Pacific Railroad capital already banked.

A reasonable attitude, certainly, given Rosner's growing reputation for wildness, for abruptly moving his accounts through a number of California banks; but five documents saying the same things are not necessarily more secure than a single document well-researched.

The issue that now alerted Piddington, after analyzing Rosner's past funds flows and investment pattern was that it appeared that banks tended to cease operations once Rosner had his accounts pulled out. Too many times to be coincidence, and now Harry Rosner wanted to substantially raise the limits on his line of credit with Montgomery-Hill Bank backed by only the same collateral, a group of warehouses on the San Francisco wharves, which would significantly expand the exposure of the bank.

On each of his two expeditions over the past three months to the warehouses, Piddington had found them empty, in disrepair, with little evidence of recent usage. Yet, when the loans were first extended, the warehouses had been full of goods and frenetic shipping activities with dozens of Chinese stevedores sweating the loads off ships into the warehouses and onto wagons.

One oddity he had observed was that the workmen all wore white sashes. Piddington had never seen that before -- but his developing knowledge of Chinatown customs was still only superficial.

But now the warehouses were standing empty, as empty as the banks that Rosner had touched before. A few discreet questions to men, not Chinese, working the docks indicated that the warehouses were rarely used; and usually, if at all, only at night.

There was more digging to do. Piddington smiled as he closed the rear exit door behind him and started down the alley his jaw set.

It *was* theater, again.

55

When "The Man Who Knows" appeared six month ago for a two week run at Keith's Theater in Boston, Kyame had skipped classes to occupy a seat at the back of the balcony. She had never actually seen Johnstone work and wanted to study his celebrated methods.

At the close of almost two hours, Kyame was in awe. As others began to leave, she remained seated in order to reflect on what she had just observed.

Never had she experienced a more powerful and convincing illusion of mindreading and clairvoyance. The richly robed and turbaned seer was silken smooth with his perfectly timed humor, which in turn, had strengthened his later exotic crystal gazing which had brought repeated gasps of astonishment from the mostly female audience that had completely filled the theater.

As she expected, Johnstone had narrowly missed twice, once giving a man the number on his mortgage deed, a document that had been in a bank vault until ten minutes before Johnstone's show started. The man insisted that the number had never been written down and existed only in his mind. The seer had correctly revealed seven of the nine digits of the number.

And then a few minutes later, when he mixed up the names of a mother and mother-in-law, he dropped a risqué joke that had the audience laughing and the ladies blushing for several minutes.

The Man Who Knows was the best stage performer Kyame had ever seen.

As she went down the stairs from the balcony, Kyame knew she had detected some of Johnstone's techniques, but she had no idea how the mortgage deed effect could be done, or how his floating ball was done, or how he had produced two doves from an empty glass bowl held by a woman in the middle of the audience.

The magic illusions, colored with oriental settings, music and dancers were overpowering -- and Kyame did recognize the dancers from Papa's and her encounter with the Johnstone troupe over two years earlier in Atchison, Kansas.

There was the constant subtle suggestion from Johnstone's clever patter that maybe, maybe there was more to the illusions than just magic tricks. Johnstone was truly The Man Who Knows, a master of the art -- but Kyame still hated him, hated him with all her heart.

Now according to the current issue of *Variety* she was reading while sipping early morning coffee in the Everett House hotel lobby, Alexander Jason Johnstone was in San Francisco to start a three week run at the Alcazar Theater in a few days.

She wondered if Papa would slip in to watch -- even once. They had traded letters speculating on Johnstone's methods for the Boston show, but Kyame was still not sure how the mortgage deed stunt was done -- barring, naturally, the use of a confederate, which seemed very unlikely in this case.

Replacing the coffee cup, she saw it was nearing time to leave for her appointment. When he learned she would be in New York City, J. W. Cadwell had asked if she could visit a close friend of his to pick up a small package.

The previous evening, when Kyame had asked the hotel concierge about the address, he was uneasy.

"Doyers Street ... that is a short sharply curved street that is called, if you will excuse me, is called the street of murder. Doyers is not a safe location for any white man … and particularly not for a white woman alone, Miss Piddington," he said, shaking his head. "It is the territory of the Yee Hung Oey, the Society of Righteous Brothers -- a fearsome group of Chinese brutes. And, most particularly at night.

"If your visit is not truly urgent, Miss Piddington, I would strongly recommend that you not go at all."

Kyame left with the map drawn by the concierge.

56

Looking out his great bay window, Harry Rosner rotated the champagne glass in his fingers. As the evening darkened, over on Nob Hill hundreds of lights in the great mansions were coming on. Rosner's own butler, a reformed burglar just out of prison named Quincy, was busy moving through the rooms lighting the lamps of the Rosner mansion, Villa Illuminaire.

The great Nob Hill house of the Townes, where he and his wife were invited tonight, along with the Huntington, Stanford, Crocker, Flood and Hopkins palaces, each with their forty, fifty or more rooms, were all carefully furnished even if some of the rooms were never used, just lighted.

Edward Searles, a former interior decorator, who had inherited the more than $70 million Hopkins fortune when his wife, Mary, the widow of Mark Hopkins, had died four years before, had joked to Harry during the Mackay reception that he still couldn't find his way around the Hopkins mansion; his wife Mary had insisted on too damn many rooms!

But, Rosner mused, at least Searles could live in it, unlike Mark Hopkins who had died shortly before his wife's outrageous mansion was finished. But Searles was only interested in the furniture, boring Harry with endless aesthetic nonsense. Only a few days ago, Searles had finally abandoned the Nob Hill fortress with its seventy-foot tall chimney tower for a sedate thirty-room stone mansion on New York City's Fifth Avenue.

Rosner's own place, three floors with its 17 rooms -- he sipped more of the champagne -- but only the first floor was completely furnished, and only one room, their master bedroom and his office, was furnished on the second floor. The rest of the second and third floor rooms held only a lamp sitting on a packing case at each window.

No visitor was allowed up the great red-marble main stairway. Quincy's principal duty during social gatherings was to firmly discourage curiosity.

He took a deep swallow. There would be gallons of champagne tonight, Mrs. Towne would see to that.

Cassie came up behind him. "Harry," she laughed, "save your appetite. Drink their inventory, not ours."

He grinned, kissed her lightly on the forehead to avoid smudging her makeup.

"One glass left in the bottle. Couldn't let it go flat." He stepped back. "You do look most fetching tonight, Cassie. I have never seen that gown and ensemble before."

Cassie whirled to allow the flowing red lace flare out. "It's the latest Trilby fashion, Harry. Most of the women will be wearing something like it tonight ... and tomorrow night, and after that. Everything is Trilby these days because of the play and that mesmerizing novel. Trilby this and Trilby that ... even Trilby cigars and, my God, even Trilby diapers!" She laughed. "So, give me a sip. I plan to eat a horse tonight."

Rosner gave the glass to his extraordinary blonde wife, her enticing blue eyes sparkling with mischief.

"Atherton needs *close* attention tonight," he explained. "Things getting a bit tight, Cassie, but still doable ... very doable."

"I understand," she said, "I will ensure that Atherton is ... amenable to our needs." She brushed her hands down her hips to smooth out invisible wrinkles. "There's a rumor, Harry, that Ed Searles is giving the Hopkins monstrosity to the San Francisco Art Institute. He doesn't want it when he has a couple of East coast Hopkins mansions to play in." She laughed. "Ed doesn't even know how much Hopkins cash he inherited. He's spending until someone tells him to stop."

Her husband frowned and put down the glass. "Wish that were our problem."

Cassie smiled a slight quirky smile. "Searles is an artistic fool with at least seventy million. You are a genius with dangerous debts ... and me. So," she grinned, "you're ahead of the game."

Her face suddenly quieted. "All this about Trilby ... but we really need a Svengali, don't we." Her smile faltered. "But even Svengali would not be enough, would he?"

Harry felt chilled. It was unnatural for Cassie, his beautiful Cassandra, to be somber. But she was right. The timing was getting very tight and a little magic wouldn't hurt.

His arm around his wife's bare shoulders, Rosner looked back out the bay window. The endless beckoning, taunting lights over there on Nob Hill with only darkness between him and them, no path was marked out to get to that summit.

The familiar scenario that came to him when he couldn't sleep: of crossing a deep gorge on a single wobbly plank bridge that could give way any time but with a huge pile of radiant gold heaped on the other side, waiting.

They would walk further out on that wobbly board tonight.

57

The carriage slowed as the cabbie tightened the reins, the horse slipping on the ice-capped cobblestones. He turned, to lean back toward Kyame who was wrapped in a heavy blanket, her breath clouding about her head.

"Pell and Doyers, Miss. I don't go anywhere into that." He pointed toward the narrow dark street with steam rising from a few silent Chinese street vendors braving the hard chill. "Ain't mucking with those Chinee … the Righteous Brothers would soon's chop your head off as look at you." He bent closer. "You sure this is the place you want, Miss?" The harness rattled as the horse shifted its shoulders, stamping its hooves in the cold.

Kyame threw back the blanket and stepped down. She squeezed the railing as her shoe slipped on the ice. Turning, she held the fare up. "Yes, this is the place. Thank you."

He tipped his peaked cap and snapped his whip. The horse thrust its shoulders into the harness and the two-wheeled hack began to move away, its iron-tired wheels clattering over the street.

Gathering her long coat around her, pressing its high fur collar against her cheeks, Kyame walked up Doyers Street to the nearest vendor, boiled rice and fish-heads, a small man in a blotchy blue padded cotton jacket with a high neck, who stood, slapping his arms across his chest to keep warm. As she approached, his gelid stare became deadly. He frowned, his mouth turning down until its ends almost touched his chin – and abruptly showed his back in contempt.

The concierge had warned that Doyers was the center of tong warfare; that if anything happened, *no one* would or could come to her aid – but the address of Professor Cadwell's friend was 28 Doyers Street.

Walking past the fish-head vendor, Kyame saw a bent gaunt woman of indeterminate age tending two tea pots with a rack of small brown clay cups. A cup of hot tea would be encouraging – even just holding the hot cup would help offset the harsh wind that blew down Doyers, tossing papers and sending a round piece of cardboard skidding across the street. Except for the five vendors she could see, there was no one walking on the street.

Kyame knew she was being watched closely; she could feel it. The fish-head vendor was just coming back into his stall, when she looked back. He dodged his head away at her glance.

Kyame nodded to the heavily bundled woman and pointed to a cup.

The woman hesitated, then poured the tea.

Kyame dropped a nickel into the vendor's extended boney hand. The heat of the cup quickly warmed both her hands.

"Dr. Mar Tan, ma'am, do you know him?" Kyame asked sipping the steaming green tea. She raised her cup. "Oolong?" she asked.

The woman suddenly raised her eyebrows, pointed toward a small red sign hanging over a door half way up the right side of the street.

"Der, ladee," she said.

"Xie xie," thanked Kyame, which exhausted her knowledge of Mandarin Chinese. She swallowed the last of the rich oolong tea and returned the cup.

***

Kyame knocked according to Cadwell's instruction and pushed on the door, but it was locked. She looked up and down the street. No one was near her, except the unseen watching eyes that caused her skin to prickle. A gust of coarse wind blew her long coat away from her skirt.

A woman with a small boy trailing her suddenly appeared, crossed over the cobblestones to the other side to silently disappear.

Kyame knocked again; twice quickly, then twice slowly, the knock instructed by Cadwell. After a moment, she heard a soft click.

The skullcap of the small aged man who peered around the edge of the door was heavily embroidered in gold and silver. He looked up, to examine Kyame closely through thick glasses. His weathered dark face was deeply lined, a wisp of white beard fluttered in the wind. He was dressed in a black silken jacket and pants with black slippers.

"What you want, ladee?"

"Dr. Mar Tan, please. I come from a friend of his."

"Who you, ladee?"

"I am Kyame Piddington … from Boston."

Another larger hand appeared on the door as it was pulled back.

"Professor Cadwell notified me that you would be coming, Miss Piddington. I am Mar Tan." His English was without accent.

The doctor was the same height as Kyame but a hundred pounds more in weight, his thick neck overflowed the stand-up collar of his green satin jacket. His broad face was lighted by a wide smile. His black satin skullcap had two rows of diamond-shaped pieces of deep green jade sewn around it.

"You are most welcome, young miss, please come in ... please excuse the suspicion of my humble servant."

***

With the Lung Ching tea, the tea of the legendary Dragon Well, poured into blue and white porcelain cups and crisp brown biscuits on a raised white porcelain dish -- and his servant gone -- Mar Tan leaned back into his cushioned rosewood chair, his cup at his fingertips.

The woman was as beautiful as Cadwell had described to him. Her inquisitive jade eyes caused his loins to tighten. There were those in Chinatown, even just a scarce block away, who, with a whisper from him, would pay heavily to possess such a woman, to sell her to the court in

Peking, or the slavers in Shanghai or in San Francisco -- or to hoard her beauty, away from prying eyes.

Mar Tan bowed his head. "So you played chess with the great Steinitz, Miss Piddington," he said. "I envy you the opportunity. To engage, to interact with the truly great, is by itself a life-forming experience, a special grant of the gods. May I ask the outcome of your encounter?"

"A draw ... after 37 moves," she said, with a small smile.

Mar Tan leaned forward, his eyebrows raised, his smile wide. Her modesty was -- most seductive. "Draw! A draw against the great Steinitz? I salute you, young miss ... yes, you are as my good friend, the Professor, described." He swallowed the last of his tea and rose. "Please excuse me for a moment. I must bring the package for which you have come." The ponderous doctor waddled to the far end of the room.

Arrayed along ledges mounted on the paneled wall behind Mar-Tan's richly carved trestle desk of dark pearwood were a large blue jade disc with a hole in its center mounted in a carved ebony stand; then a graceful milk-white jade vase holding one large purple blossom; and, she caught her breath, a jade sword on a purple sandalwood stand, the blade a milky green, a cream-white hilt inset with multiple colored bits that caught the light, the pommel carved in jade so deep a green that it approached black.

My god, it was glorious! She ached to touch it.

Among the exotic woods available at her art school, Kyame had found a small piece of purple sandalwood. She had carved it in the shape of a man's open hand. It had sold immediately at the Vose gallery on Newbury for three dollars.

Returning to his chair Mar-Tan held a small package wrapped in brown paper, He watched the light animating her eyes for a moment.

"Jade is the stone of heaven, Miss Piddington," the doctor said. "The hands must be stroked with the jade daily; the stone expects it ... some scholars say, the stone *needs* it."

Pushing aside a stack of three books, he placed the package on the desk between them.

"The large jade disk, Dr. Mar Tan, I've never seen anything like that. What is it?" Kyame asked. "The hole looks to be about a fifth the diameter of the disk. Is that important?"

Mar Tan's eyes opened wide. "My good friend, the mesmerist, said you had the most zest for knowledge of any young woman he has ever encountered."

He went to the disk and carefully brought it back to the table. He positioned it in front of Kyame.

"This is a *Bi* disk, young miss, from the Zhou dynasty of Chinese history, almost three thousand years ago. It is carved in the traditional rice pattern; each grain of rice carved is identical to all the others; as the stars in the heavens. The *Bi* disk is the ancient Chinese symbol of heaven, a symbol we still use.

"Rice is life, so eternal heaven must be filled with rice, thus the rice pattern," the doctor said. "In those days, it was thought that burying jade with a dead body would stop the purification of the flesh ... and jade was also used to stop up the body orifices to ensure purity ... thus allowing the person to enter heaven fully whole and untainted.

"That," Mar-tan said, "naturally, but sadly, is no longer believed; but the *Bi* disks are still venerated, even by modern physicians as myself."

"Whose grave did this disk come from?" Kyame leaned closer to the disk. "It is so

433

handsomely carved, that the person must have been of some importance."

Mar-Tan was impressed. "Ah, again you are most correct. This came from the grave of a senior minister to the emperor."

"May I?" Kyame extended her fingers toward the *Bi* disk.

The doctor nodded.

The stone was like cool glass to her touch, a gentle power she had never felt before, even compared with the Greek marbles at school. So smooth that the stone felt soft -- so gently soft. The workmanship -- she could not detect any corrected errors among the uncounted grains of rice, as there always was in her own carvings. To carve a stone this hard three thousand years ago must have taken weeks of patient grinding and polishing -- must have been with jade dust, the only thing hard enough.

And without detectable mistakes? Truly amazing, a transcendent work.

She leaned back.

"Marvelous, Dr. Mar Tan, marvelous. The artist surely was a genius. My thanks."

He grinned. "I am told by our mutual friend that you are a most excellent artist yourself. You will then appreciate what is in this package. The Professor instructed me to give this to you ... as a gift from him, in remembrance of a certain time when you, as he explained, with little training called the spirits for him under most severe conditions. He said you would come to understand the connection, but asked me to explain the object."

He slid the package across the table to her.

Removing the brown paper revealed a green and gold silk box about three inches square. Kyame gasped when she raised the lid.

The *Bi* disk was of pellucid crystal carved in the classic rice pattern around the central hole. Bound around its circumference was a broad gold band. Rendered in gold at the top, a dragon and tortoise were joined in violent combat -- their eyes sparkling green gems. A gold chain of large links was attached behind the battling icons.

After a few seconds, Kyame said, "I can't believe it."

"The *Bi* disk is from the Han Dynasty, almost two thousand years old. It was mounted in gold a hundred years ago in Hangzhou by an artisan of the Imperial Qing court. The two

435

animals represent your life: the dragon representing power and the tortoise long being.

"The exercise of power can destroy years; but to preserve life before all else will mean loss of power, of meaning. So, the dragon and tortoise fight, always, for eternity, for supremacy."

"Their eyes?"

"Emeralds from the mountains of the region that was once called Upper Burma. Emeralds from the heart of the holy mountains of Kachin are believed by many to grant far-seeing abilities, to grant the second sight."

**

Once back in her room at the Everett House, Kyame opened the silk box once again. The beauty of the disk and chain was beyond anything she had ever seen.

Dr. Mar Tan had been amused with her sudden quiet, her wide eyes. He had refused to say anything about its value, only that the crystal *Bi* disk carried special responsibilities that she would come to understand in her years ahead. He politely refused to identify who had been the original owner of the disk two thousand years ago.

When she placed the gold chain around her neck and looked into the long mirror on the door of her room, the *Bi* disk shown like a star from heaven. The green eyes of the fighting icons sent off different sparkling patterns with each of her movements. Mar Tan had said that the crystal disk would become more beautiful the more it contacted her skin.

She should, the astrologer had insisted, never take it off.

58

"I'll be jarred! You're right, John Piddington. It doesn't make righteous sense." Jeems Humbrick dropped the pages of numbers and dates back on the table, and then reached for his stein of Bavarian ale.

Humbrick was a wine and spirits importer, a customer of Montgomery-Hill Bank and a good friend. He imported Bavarian beers to bring superior German culture to lawless San Francisco, as he frequently explained to his many customers.

"But," he said, poking a thick finger at Piddington, "you still don't have the reason for the numbers. They don't make sense, but they don't prove anything ... yet. You don't have the why."

John Piddington brushed away the delicious foam from his lips. "I know. I'll dig deeper, as deep as I have to in order to understand what Harry Rosner is up to."

Humbrick leaned across the table. They were in his office at the rear of his spirits shop at the corner of 5th and Market Streets; the only sounds coming through the walls were occasional shouts, of barrels being moved and a sporadic clinking of glass against glass.

"John, *mein gutes Freund*, when my barrels and cases of spirits arrive on the wharves not five blocks from my door, I know the longshoremen help themselves to a case or two. It's part of the price of doing business in this town. It is stealing, in one sense, but not bad stealing so long as it is only a case or two. My goods arrive unbroken.

"However, my *special* liqueurs, cognacs, brandies and wines come by a different, unannounced route ... and if those are sampled, then *it is* stealing.

"Do you see?" The German frowned. "I fear you have raised your beautiful daughter to have the same sense of virtuous outrage that I see on your face now."

Piddington laughed. "Yes, Jeems, she reflects her mother's teachings as well as my own. But, based on her letters, Kyame has grown more practical, as she has matured as a woman."

Putting his stein back on the table, Humbrick chuckled. "Practical? A dangerous word, John ... an excuse for anything ... especially in a beautiful woman."

Humbrick spread the papers in front of him. He tapped the papers with a pencil. "I have been in Frisco-town for thirteen years, John. You, only two years, though you are rapidly making a good name for yourself. But in all my time nothing has changed ... nothing can be trusted.

"San Francisco is a gambler's town, John, always has been and always will be. From the time of the Gold Rush, it is still only a miner's camp with all the rules of a miner's camp ... of which there is only one ... get before you are gotten." Humbrick stopped to listen to the sounds coming through his walls, then looked back at Piddington.

"Harry Rosner is a San Francisco gambler, like *die Scharlatanen* ... the charlatans up there on Nob Hill. Take before you are taken. If these numbers here are right and the story you think they tell is right, John, then Rosner is an embezzler and a fraud on a most interesting scale ... but he is still just a Frisco gambler, a hustler. If he wins, then he can build his temple on Nob Hill beside the Huntingtons, the Townes and the rest, who are also Frisco gamblers and hustlers.

"But if Rosner draws the low card," the merchant said with a slow Germanic shrug, "then he deserves whatever happens."

"But Jeems, what about ...?

"The innocents who lose their money in the banks he's apparently looted?" Humbrick shook his head. "If this were Kansas City or St. Louis ... or even New York City ... I would have some sympathy. But this is San Francisco, mein Freund ... only a fool would blindly obey the laws here. No one should come here who does not understand that."

Humbrick suddenly stood. "I will return. I need to investigate the sudden silence out back."

John Piddington leaned back and shook his head as his friend's large lumbering body disappeared through the door.

A sudden silence?

Harry Rosner was a malignant crook who had to be taken down, his pelf seized, somehow -- in spite of a pliable police department, indifferent prosecutors, a purchased mayor -- and, he frowned, the untouchable tongs.

To not fight Rosner would betray Kyame's respect for him. And that, John Piddington would never risk -- regardless of the cost. He would find a way to do it himself, if he had to.

First, however, he had to find why Rosner needed the money to take such risks. Certainly not to just be able to flaunt wealth on gold-encrusted Nob Hill, as one source had suggested.

A visit to Rosner's mansion might prove interesting. Unlike others of his ilk, Harry Rosner did not maintain an office in the financial district, nor did he employ anyone except when he needed them for a specific purpose. But Rosner would have to steal almost the whole of California just to match the estates of the Big Four and the Silver Kings in San Francisco.

And the Big Four estates became richer daily through their iron-fisted monopoly of all California transportation. Nothing could be shipped in the state without the estates of the Big Four, operating as the Southern Pacific Co., taking a major piece of the profit out of every bushel or box shipped anywhere.

Piddington had enough information to demonstrate with reasonable certainty to his superior, Harvey Atherton, that Montgomery-Hill should not take any further credit risk with Rosner -- but he needed Rosner's why to conclusively convince Atherton and his father-in-law, Oliver Hill.

As John Piddington left, familiar noises had resumed in Jeems' back room.

Silence could be threatening to anyone.

***

Jeems Humbrick watched his friend disappear down Market Street with a great sense of uneasiness. The merchant walked across Market up 5th one block to drop a small unaddressed envelope into a vase of roses. The woman looked up from trimming a bouquet. Second vase from the end, second row. Her nod was barely perceptible as she continued to snip the rose stems. The note would be at Room 635 at the Palace Hotel within an hour.

Humbrick knew the docks, the piers; he was on them almost every day. He knew a broad range of men who were customers of his liquors and beers. As he walked back down the hill toward his store, he knew that John Piddington was right about Rosner -- but there was something still missing. John needed to be watched for his own protection -- if it wasn't already too late.

59

Harry Rosner threw his pencil down on the papers on his desk. He looked over at Cassie reading by the window who raised her eyebrows.

She laid her book aside. "Problems, Harry?"

He nodded. "Some problems are starting to develop faster than I feel comfortable with. For one, my personal notes to buy into the Occidental and Oriental Steamship operation of the Southern Pacific will start to come due in three weeks. That's $65,000. I cover or I lose the shares ... *very* publicly." He shook his head. "That would effectively destroy my growing reputation as the 'brilliant financial wizard and smart trader', as the *Call* and the *Bulletin* keep printing.

"That would also begin to unravel my political connections ... to say nothing of Wong Woon and our tong friends. The Bing On tong has no patience for losers."

Rosner stood up and smashed a fist into the palm of his hand.

"Second: I have a meeting in four days with the broker, E.H. Harriman. He is working with Kuhn, Loeb & Co. in New York to refinance the Union Pacific Railroad, to take the company out of receivership proceedings when the markets collapsed two years ago." He leaned toward her. "Cassie, a dollar in the UP now could become worth a thousand in three, maybe four years. The UP is the only viable potential competition to the Southern Pacific."

She smiled at her husband's growing enthusiasm. There was always another deal coming up that dear Harry had to get into. But --

"Then," said Rosner, his voice cooling, "there is the second payment on the lease for Villa Illuminaire ... $90,000, due in five weeks.

"Then the investment payment to the Bing On ..."

Cassie came to look down at the pages of numbers. She laid her head on his shoulders and hugged him. "So, my smart trader, how much do we really need, now? Worry about the Union Pacific later."

Rosner smiled up into her mocking eyes. "I need that $250,000 credit expansion at Montgomery-Hill to keep us even, to buy time while I close on other opportunities."

She nodded and returned to her book, a collection of poems by Joaquin Miller. "Let me know when I am needed."

Harry already knew the answer to that.

60

"You are Earth Tiger, Miss Piddington." Dr. Mar Tan had pronounced over their final cups of tea, once Kyame had given him her birthday, January 5, 1879. "There are five Tigers of the five basic elements; but Earth Tigers ... Earth Tigers climb moonbeams; move with the frightening sound of a shadow; with the invisibility of a thought. You are *Keng Yin,* young miss. There will not be other Keng Yin until" -- Mar Tan hesitated for a moment -- "ah, 1938."

Then he stopped smiling, wiped his mouth with a silken blue cloth and whispered, "Your birth has placed at your core the soul of *tsyh ker,* the assassin, young miss." Mar Tan hesitated at Kyame's instant frown. "However, not that soul of an ugly wanton killer; but that of an implacable, methodical enemy. You will be feared." He continued. "You are *woo shyr,* a traveler between the worlds of the here and the not-here.

"You have beauty at your fingertips and in your eyes. Those who only see that will be in deep regret."

***

Kyame inserted a finger to hold her place in the just published novel, *The Red Badge of*

Courage, a book that she had purchased in New York. She no longer memorized books to save weight and money, but there were some works that she still wanted permanently in her mind, to draw on instantly as needed. Now, for the most part, she just bought, read and put the volume in the bookcase next to her desk in her room at school. The bookcase was overflowing.

She leaned back against the seat, the train rattling north back to Boston through the barren wintry morning landscape of Connecticut. She touched the crystal *Bi* disk that hung from her neck beneath her ruffled blouse at the juncture of her breasts.

It had *only been* to do a favor for Professor Cadwell that she had sought out Dr. Mar Tan, but her life had been changed. She knew it, but couldn't yet understand how. Had she been born in March or later in 1879, the doctor explained, she would have been a Rabbit, and, though artistic, pleasant and generous, utterly harmless.

She shook her head. Was that Zodiac stuff real? How could it be? Papa had been evasive whenever they had discussed astrology in various hotels and trains during their travels.

The doctor had presented her with his card upon her leaving. "With the disk, Miss Piddington, you have become one of us, one of the Righteous. As is our esteemed friend, Professor Cadwell."

The card had the doctor's chop embossed in heavy red ink with his address in English. He had said that now that he had met her, he would have her personal chop carved and sent to her.

She reflected. Papa was going to enjoy this letter. They would be discussing Chinese astrology for weeks.

But what had changed in her life?

***

"Smokeless powder, Miss Piddington."

James Wells picked up the two metal cartridges from his work table and loaded her black metal over-under double-barrel Remington .41 derringer.

Kyame had first taken the Boylston Street trolley out almost to the end of the line to reach the Wells Gun Shop when her derringer had misfired during one of her shooting practices in the woods back of the school. A passing Boston policeman, investigating the shots, had recommended Wells to look at her hand-pistol. The gunsmith had

448

corrected the problem in less than five minutes --
and had refused payment.

"You will never pay for anything in this
shop, Miss Piddington. I have had little beauty in
my life since my wife and child died of the typhus
two years ago. Your coming through my door
brings out the sun."

Kyame had only smiled. Wells was a young
man with the saddest eyes she had ever seen.

Wells beckoned her to the indoor shooting
range at the back of his shop. He laid the loaded
pistol, its muzzle pointing down-range, on a table.
A large iron plate suspended from the ceiling
across the back of the range leaned forward at a
45-degree angle to the ground, to deflect any errant
slugs directly into the loose dirt in front of the
target.

"The black powder shells for your
Remington .41 give you a probable lethal range of
maybe 15 feet, Miss Piddington; but to be certain,
the reliable range is only the width of a poker
table. Much further and the slugs will just bounce
off anything reasonably solid like a heavy coat."

He picked up Kyame's derringer as she
stood just behind his left shoulder.

"That round wood target is ten yards. Watch what better chemistry encased in a brass, not a copper shell can do," he said.

The sound of the shot was different, higher pitched, sharper -- it seemed to her. But the section of wood that flew off the target was no assumption. Wells' second shot was the same. The wood target had two jagged gaps in it at a range where she couldn't have even hit it with her black powder shells. And there was no acrid smoke lingering in the air after each shot, as with the black powder, but still a distinctive pungent odor.

Wells saw her eyes light up and smiled. A beautiful young woman who liked guns -- a true blessing of the gods.

"The recoil is harder, as you would expect, so you will need to brace yourself when you fire, until you learn the recoil strength," he said as he handed her the empty pistol, swung open at the top to allow reloading.

Kyame pressed two brass shells into the open breech, pivoted the double-barrel back into position. When Kyame heard the pistol snap closed, she ran her fingers lightly over the barrel back to the hammer to ensure everything was in place, in what had become a habitual action for her.

Kyame held the small pistol tighter than usual, sighted over the top barrel at the damaged target and squeezed gently.

The recoil was bone-jarring, far greater than she was accustomed to. The slug whacked the iron plate high and to the left.

Kyame took a breath. Her elbow twinged with pain. Her derringer was a different gun with the change in powder.

She grinned at Wells, rubbing her arm. "Heavens! That was a real kick."

Taking her position again, now knowing what was coming, Kyame squeezed gently. With her arm held more tightly against her body and her wrist stiffened, the slug clipped off a bit of the top of the target.

"I'm starting to get some feel for it ... I think." Kyame snapped open the derringer, extracted the spent shell casings, and placed the opened pistol on the table, the muzzle pointing down range.

"I agree," said Mills, smiling. "Here is a box of twenty shells, with my compliments, to practice with, to strengthen that feeling."

An hour later, Kyame had cleaned her derringer, reloaded it with the smokeless shells, and placed it into the pocket of her coat.

The wooden target was in shreds.

She placed the money for two boxes of twenty cartridges each on the counter but the gunsmith pushed the coins back. Kyame bowed her head. She was never to pay, but she always tried.

"Mr. Wells, when was the load of the .41 cartridges changed? I hadn't heard of it 'til I walked in your shop this afternoon."

Wells grinned. "I had them made, so this afternoon would have been the earliest you could've known. I've been working with Smith & Wesson on their cartridges for other guns, so they did the work for me on this one. They're good people out there in Springfield."

"What is my maximum range now?" After a moment, she added, "Lethal range."

"Forty feet with good accuracy. The bullet-drop beyond that distance is pretty sharp." Wells said. "The slug will certainly penetrate a thick coat at twenty-five feet.

"If your weapon was not constructed of heavy forged steel throughout, Miss Piddington, it could not have safely absorbed the increased recoil and higher temperature ignition of the new powder. A lot of the hand- or muff-pistols for sale now would blow up in your face with a smokeless powder load.

"But," he cautioned, "a gun is always a last resort … cautious thinking is always the better weapon."

"I'm always cautious, Mr. Wells," said Kyame, as she closed the door behind her.

Well, she reflected, as she walked into the reddening sun, almost always.

61

"Two o' these and you'd hug a wildcat. By God, if you wouldn't," grinned Harry Rosner, raising his glass in a feeble toast. Their discussion was not going well and he needed it to be successful. Desperately needed success. Cassie's seduction of Harvey Atherton at a secret tryst had proven successful, but Atherton couldn't move until a loan officer named John Piddington finished his investigation. Bank rules, you know, and all that, Atherton had explained, pulling his pants up, as Cassie had re-buttoned her torn Trilby gown.

Cassie had done her job, as always -- but there would be another day's delay at least -- and the malevolent Chinaman across the table wanted his cash now.

Wong Woon did not smile as he took a small sip of the glass. It was a repulsive barbaric concoction of strong alcohol with apple cider. The mixture was called a "stone fence" -- apparently it was the favorite drink of the famous sham cowboy, Buffalo Bill, and his admirers -- of which Wong Woon was not one.

The tong master frowned. The white race wipes away life with their foolish devotion to drink. Drunkenness was a futile life. Anything that impaired the intellect was to be shunned. The traditional teachings of his Tibetan childhood were clear -- and true. Even the contemptible Han people of the China coast understood that.

His Han-like features and the Han name he had taken had saved him from some of the cruel discrimination of the coastal towns -- until he spoke with the mountain accent. Then Wong Woon would have to fight. Rather than speak better Han, he had learned English.

"The only reasonable profit, Mr. Rosner, is the maximum profit ... anything less can only be counted as acceptance of failure," Wong said. "I do not see a maximum profit from your proposal. You ask that I provide you with support today, while you provide me with ... nothing, until when? Ah, yes, I am to wait for three days for you?" He replaced the glass on the small table between them. He sighed as he shook his head. "I have other demands on my resources, Mr. Rosner."

At Wong Woon's raised eyebrow, the highbinder in the shadows who had been blocking the heavy back door stepped quietly forward, his black flat-brimmed hat pulled low throwing his eyes into darkness. A small polished iron hatchet hung from his woven belt.

Rosner could feel the threat growing. He touched the derringer in his vest pocket. "I understand your impatience, Wong Woon. I understand that your time, and your people's time, is valuable, and I will provide additional funds to compensate appropriately."

Wong picked up the stone fence, stood, and threw it against the wall, glass and liquid exploding across the room.

"We have done pieces of good business in the recent past, Mr. Rosner," said Wong Woon, so calmly that it chilled Rosner's bones. "Therefore, I will give you one more day to arrange affairs with a fifty percent increase in my fee." His black eyes went cold. "We will meet at my private office tomorrow at four in the afternoon. If you are late, then Kwan Duck will come ... to guide you.

"Do not disappoint me."

***

Harry Rosner wiped the sweat from his face and neck once the door clicked shut behind the immaculately dressed tong leader and his shadowy *boo how doy* escort. They had met this time on neutral ground, the back room of Rosemary's Grill and Bar on Battery Street, a small place that favored sweet boys and so would not draw anyone who concerned Rosner.

They had both arrived and would depart from a back door onto a narrow wooden bridge leading down to an alley. Wong Woon would arrive first and leave first. What Rosner might encounter if he didn't follow instructions, needed no elaboration.

Only with the increased funding from Montgomery-Hill Bank could he even his account with the tong, replenish his opium inventory and be able to walk away to drain another bank, to continue his steady progress toward his goal.

The Bing On tong had entered his calculations via an earlier deal that had needed a physical push, to gain Rosner the options on some of the water rights of the land sections that would supply San Francisco's growing needs. There were many tongs in Chinatown, but Wong Woon was the leader most feared on the docks. The whispered rumor was that he was not even Chinese but that was a question that Harry Rosner would never even breathe aloud. So, it had been to the Bing On that Harry had turned.

Cassie had warned that Wong was Satan himself, but, Rosner understood, even Satan had his proper place in San Francisco society.

But the oath, the oath of the Bing On, to which he had been 'encouraged' to submit, that evil ritual was nothing to joke about.

At their first meeting, Wong Woon had smiled warmly and suggested the oath carried greater commitment than a mere white man's handshake.

Harry had allowed his finger to be pricked, then squeezed to produce a large drop of blood that he smeared across the document of their agreement. After which he had intoned mechanically after Wong:

By this red drop of blood, I swear,

The secrets of this tong I never will declare,

Seven gaping wounds shall drain my blood away,

Should I to alien ears my sacred trust betray.

The grim smiles and cold eyes of the surrounding highbinders ensured that the oath remained clear in his mind.

The Big Four, Stanford, Crocker, Huntington and Hopkins, had controlled the Central Pacific Railroad and later the Southern Pacific and so had gained control of California.

But all Harry Rosner wanted was to stand astride San Francisco itself, to become in fact the smart trader that many thought him to be now -- without getting a hatchet buried in his head in the process. He dropped a fifty dollar silver certificate on the table and walked out into the damp late afternoon.

62

Kwan Duck laughed, a slow dieseling sound. "A singsong woman's puppy, sir. That is the weapon he carried. He placed his hand on it. I will cut that hand off, should he touch the little gun again ... if it pleases you."

Wong Woon nodded and leaned back into his carriage. Strangely, the Tibetan white dog had suddenly come to mind. The animal had no name as no one wanted to talk about its terrifying presence, a position he could understand too well.

But -- the white walls of his *fan t'an* parlors, the white of the tables and chairs, white, the color of bad luck for the gamblers ...

The color of the dog.

63

John Piddington needed the why of Harry Rosner's actions to explain to Harvey Atherton why Rosner's account should not only *not* be expanded, but actually shut down and closed instead. He slowly opened the door, replacing the lock-picks in his pocket. Rosner's mansion, Villa Illuminaire, should have an answer -- otherwise he would have to stall Atherton further -- which almost certainly would cost him his job.

The mansion was dark. Rosner and his wife were at a charity meeting at some church to raise funds for orphaned mariner's children. The only light Piddington had observed as he moved cautiously through the formal gardens toward the rear of the house was at the far corner in the back, probably the servant quarters.

He moved the slide which covered the front of his dark lantern, allowing a narrow flickering shaft of light into the darkness to reveal a kitchen storage area. Tins of cooking oil, boxes of flour and sugar, a vat of butter turning rancid, bins of dried vegetables and wedges of cheese under glass covers.

A zinc-lined squat barrel of something. Two other similar barrels, but empty were pushed back against the wall.

John raised the lid of the barrel. His light revealed small reddish-brown cones wrapped in waxen white paper. He picked one up and crushed it to a chunky powder in his hand.

The scent -- he couldn't be sure with the myriad other smells in the small room, but it could be opium. Two years or so earlier, a friendly reporter in Sacramento had shown him some captured bulk Indian opium at police headquarters when Piddington had done a handcuff escape in the jail there just before finally dropping show business to return to banking. But the drug then had been packed in small waxed calico bags, sewn shut.

Though Piddington had learned the bitter flavor of opium in Sacramento, only a damn fool would ever taste an unknown powder, when it could be rat poison -- or something even worse.

He put two more wrapped cones into his pocket and brushed his hands clean. Opium or something stronger? There was a doctor near his rooming house who could confirm it. The doctor sold opium as a cure for the morphine habit.

Rosner was not running the kinds of risks he was solely for opium; especially in San Francisco where opium den addresses were exchanged at church suppers, even though opium sales had been forbidden by city ordinance since 1875. No matter. So exciting to visit, a smiling matron had once informed Piddington, to understand "their" culture, naturally, and reach out to such lost souls yearning for salvation.

But this was wrapped and molded Chinese style, if it was the drug. Why a barrel, when, according to a talkative police detective who was a customer at the bank, opium dens were easily identified in Chinatown -- unless Harry Rosner was supplying the white man's trade, the other mansions.

John shook his head. Didn't make sense.

For the risks and the heavy damage Rosner had done to the other banks, and the lives involved, there had to be more than that. With the right money, in the right place, Piddington knew Harry Rosner probably wouldn't be arrested even with a dozen barrels of opium or whatever in his basement.

There must be something else, something that could bring Rosner more serious trouble. John covered the lantern and stepped carefully between the boxes toward a narrow stairway.

64

Kyame, the telegram said, Your father at risk stop Maybe his life stop Will not confide in me but has total trust in you stop Come at once stop We need your help

Eliza Abbott

Kyame had not liked Eliza Abbott the one time they had met. Abbott had become the woman in Papa's life; had eased his loneliness but Kyame could not warm to her. Eliza was the daughter of Creed Abbott who owned a large dry goods store on Columbus Street in San Francisco. Eliza worked as the lead bookkeeper in the family store.

Papa had even suggested, during their one visit together to Boston eight months ago, that he and Eliza were discussing recreating The Impossible Piddingtons act again. It was clear that he yearned for the stage again -- but his announcement had deeply disturbed Kyame. The act was only for Mama or her -- not for a stranger.

Abbott was an attractive and intelligent woman; Kyame would grant that -- but nothing like Mama. She could not imagine Papa even noticing Eliza Abbott if Mama were still alive.

Eliza had tried to be friendly, expressed honest interest in her art, but Kyame had repulsed her efforts at friendship. She understood Papa's need to have someone other than a daughter in his life, but …

Her telegraphed response was brief:

Miss Abbott: Coming. Kyame Piddington.

Kyame sent a second telegram to J. W. Cadwell to inform him of her departure for San Francisco and the reason. If Papa needed her, then school and everything else meant nothing.

She was on the train the following morning, the signed Steinitz book in her trunk, the *Bi* disk hung from her neck beneath her green velvet jacket.

65

Up four steps, another door that squeaked as he opened it. He froze -- listening. After a moment of silence, Piddington moved ahead.

Momentarily opening the dark lantern revealed he was in a spacious dining room. He quickly closed the lantern when its yellowish light flashed across the room off the multiple framed mirrors on the walls. Moving silently he stepped along the wide parquet central hall populated with busts of chubby angels and austere women on short marble plinths into a front parlor.

Cold moonlight lit the room, throwing distorted elongated shadows across the floor; large dark paintings glistened in carved gold frames.

He opened the four drawers of a small desk. It appeared to be made in French style, at least in the semi-darkness. Empty, but for a stack of Rosner's business cards. There were no other storage areas visible in the room.

Piddington silently crossed the large mosaic of California mountains that dominated the entrance hall floor. The widely celebrated spiraling stairway of luxurious African red marble, according to the social columnist of the *Examiner*, with polished brass railings rose grandly to his right.

Passing under an arched entryway, Piddington entered the formal living area. A broad red marble fireplace rose to the ceiling, the hearth extended at least four feet out into the room.

Smiling, Piddington shook his head. Good God, there was space in this room amongst the many pieces of shadowed shapes of furniture for forty or more people to wander around -- without getting into each other's way. It was like an opulent waiting room for a train station.

A few minutes of searching showed there was nothing personal in the room. All six drawers of a sideboard were empty, other than for a few linen napkins.

He stopped at the arched way to look back into the vast cold hall. The setup struck him. It was only a stage setting. Everything -- the parlor, the dining room and now the living room, the whole first floor was just a stage setting. No personal pictures, the Rosner's had no children, and not even a portrait of his famously beautiful wife, Cassandra.

And, he suddenly realized, no books -- no books of any kind. Not even those trophy volumes that the wealthy Frisco gamblers prominently exhibited -- to display the intricate tooled leather bindings and their implied good taste -- without, naturally, ever opening them.

So, what the hell was Rosner's play? A quick smile at the pun.

Jeems could be right, Piddington considered, as he cautiously climbed the marble stairway to the dark second floor. Rosner could be just a Frisco gambler covering some wagers that had turned sour. Piddington had heard indications from other bankers at lunches, suggestions that Rosner had some "serious" personal notes outstanding, but no one breathed any details.

Or, maybe, the man was on a winning streak and simply wanted more. Gambling isn't always bad news.

But, as John Piddington reached the second floor landing, by God, Rosner wasn't going to cover his bets with Montgomery-Hill money *and* the Piddington reputation.

***

Empty!

The four large rooms on the street side of the second floor hallway were all empty. Nothing, absolutely nothing -- except for a large unlit brass lamp sitting on an empty whiskey packing case in the central window in each room -- and, no sign that the rooms had ever having been lived in.

The whole Villa Illuminaire, nothing but a stage set?

Piddington stopped breathing.

Steps!

Someone was on the main stairs. He stepped back into a bedroom and quickly moved to a closet, leaving its door slightly ajar.

After a few moments, Piddington saw the bedroom door opened by a short muscular man, whose bald head glistened in the glow from his lamp. He wore only rolled up shirtsleeves with no collar attached, blue suspenders held up baggy black trousers.

The man went to the central window, lit the large brass lamp sitting on the packing case and left, closing and locking the door behind him.

John Piddington left the closet to listen at the door. There were muffled footsteps, then another door closed and the click of a lock.

Then -- nothing. No sounds of anyone descending the marble steps.

Nothing.

Piddington quickly picked the simple lock of the door and slowly drew the door open.

There were no lights.

The servant may have gone down some backstairs -- but, in any case, Piddington knew he had to get moving, to get out of the house.

But not before examining the third floor as well -- and the last room at the far end of the second floor. He had to turn away from that room when he had heard the movement on the stairs.

Piddington stepped out into the dark silent hallway. Quickly moving up the stairs to the third floor, he discovered the same as on the second floor. Each room empty, but with a lamp lit in each room. The servant must have lighted the lamps on the third floor first. The steps he had heard were the butler, or whatever, coming down from above, not up from below.

But, an uneasy chill went through him -- none of the third floor doors were locked.

Piddington moved to the far end of the hallway, where the one room he still needed to examine was one floor below. There was a steep narrow stairway set into the wall, thickly carpeted obviously so the passing servants would not disturb the family.

But what family?

The mansion was virtually empty. Reaching the second floor, the stairway was blocked by a closed door. Piddington slowly turned the knob and pulled. The door moved silently. Still with his dark lantern screened and relying on moonlight through windows at each end of the hallway, he stepped into the hallway.

The crunch of stepping on balls of rolled newspaper was like a siren going off! The old traveler's trick of spreading wadded-up newspapers around your bed in a hotel room so that no one could approach you without giving themselves away.

Suddenly he was blinded by a lamp thrust into his face.

"You!" snarled the butler. "I knew some weasel was in the house! Knew I could find you! Don't think you're goin' to leave this house, man!"

He swung out of the dark.

The club slammed Piddington back against the wall just grazing his head and smacked hard against his left shoulder.

His arm went numb. Piddington dropped his lantern.

"You ain't leaving here standing up!" The butler swung again.

Piddington dropped down under the soughing wind of the passing club, then drove his deadened shoulder into the stomach of the butler, throwing him back hard against the wall. The butler lost his grip on his lantern as it smashed against the wall, the hallway instantly going dark which left only the shadowed moonlight.

Piddington staggered to his feet to run toward the main stairway, his left side without feeling, his arm hanging loosely.

At the bottom of the stairs, Piddington could hear his attacker coming rapidly down the stairs behind him. No time for cleverness, Piddington ran for the front door.

Dear God! It was unlocked!

He threw it open and ran down curving stone stairs to the street -- and kept running, his arm swinging like a dead chicken wing.

***

Quincy started after the fleeing figure -- then stopped.

The butler backed slowly up toward the front door. He closed and locked it. Cold

473

perspiration dripped from his jaw -- but not from chasing the intruder.

He took a breath. There were three more rooms yet to light.

***

Kwan Duck stepped back into the shadows. The face of the running man, who passed within only a few feet of him, was clear. He could deal with Rosner's man Quincy any time Wong Woon desired. The tong master wanted Harry Rosner to know he was being watched; otherwise Kwan Duck would have been invisible, only one of the shadows cast by moonlight.

66

Harry Rosner reminded John Piddington of a card trick he had once seen in New York. A card mechanic, Elliott, a Dr. James Elliott, was sitting at a square table in the lobby of the Holland House Hotel on Madison Square, with three stylish young men at the table. A crowd of on-lookers stood in a circle around them, John Piddington among them.

Elliott asked each of the three men to name the poker hand they would most want in a tight situation, but they could not be the same hands, as, as Elliott pointed out, with a sly grin, there was only one of each kind of card available.

The first requested four aces; the second a straight flush in Spades, 9 to King; the third a full house, Kings high.

Incredibly, Elliott then dealt, face-up, each of the requested hands from a shuffled and cut deck of the hotel playing cards.

He dealt his own hand face-down.

Waving off the applause of everyone, Dr. Elliott then, one at a time, scooped up each face-up hand, turned it over and left a pile of five cards face-down in front of each of the three men.

"Now my hand ... the dealer's hand." Elliott grinned, taking a long draw on his cigar. He slowly turned each of his five cards over. It was a royal flush in Spades, 10 to Ace.

The crowd gasped in awe. Someone immediately challenged, "Hey, that can't be, Elliott, you've already dealt some of those cards."

"Have I now?" said James Elliott with a mischievous smirk.

With his hands obviously empty, Elliott then reached across the table to slowly turn over each of the other three hands. The audience, and John Piddington, shouted in astonishment. All of the three of the requested strong hands had mysteriously transformed -- into nothing; just a high card surrounded by four miscellaneous cards, a five in one hand, a Jack in the next and a seven in the third. The requested cards shown only a few seconds earlier were gone!

"Never," said Elliott, jabbing his cigar toward the cards, "never assume anything until you have seen the dealer's hand."

So, reflected Piddington, as Eliza continued to gently rub his aching shoulder with liniment, what hand is Harry Rosner playing? Is he the dealer or the sucker? And what was in that second floor room he never saw?

Eliza stepped back. Taking a cautious breath, she said, "I telegraphed Kyame, John. I am worried about you, but you won't let me help."

Frowning, John looked up. "Her answer?"

"Kyame is coming."

"Oh, God," he whispered. Laura would never forgive his putting their daughter at such risk.

67

His golden turban lay on the dressing table, his flowing multi-color silken robe hung from a coat rack, but Alexander Jason Johnstone, The Man Who Knows, had not yet removed his makeup, his features, gleaming with sweat from two hours on-stage, vivid with rouge highlighting. But his eyes, enlarged by mascara, were deathly furious.

"No shipment!" Johnstone raged about the dressing-room. He smashed his large hand mirror across the edge of the table, sending glass shards flying across the room.

Jumping back, the Chinese messenger cringed against the door, his hands raised to protect his face against the glass.

"Sir, sir," pleaded the messenger. "I only bring the words. Please, sir."

Johnstone towered high over the terrified messenger.

"When?" The mind reader gripped the messenger's shoulder. "By god, man, I will crucify anyone ...."

"I know not, sir. Master Wong Woon, himself, will contact you later tonight. Please, sir, I go."

Johnstone was silent, his fists squeezed tight. The small Chinaman remained frozen up against the door. The crystal gazer's cooling fury was still at a dangerous edge.

He needed the purified Balkans opium by six o'clock tomorrow evening or he would have his own customers enraged. But he could not risk irritating the Bing On tong. Even with his own militant resources, Johnstone could not match Wong Woon's murderous strike capability.

His anger finally contained, Johnstone resumed his chair. "The cause of the delay in delivery?"

"Master Wong Woon has said that a banking manager is blocking the transfer of necessary funds to an intermediary, sir. That will be dealt with most swiftly, sir."

"What banking manager?"

"I am not privileged to convey that information, sir."

"What bank?"

"Montgomery-Hill Bank, sir, on Stockton Street."

68

A frisson of throbbing excitement spread over her body. Her heart still pounded as, several steps behind, Kyame had followed Mama back to the dressing-room. Even as Mama held her flowing skirt up with one hand to allow her long stride, her gown of shimmering teal blue-green swept behind her.

As Papa had instructed, Kyame had waited for Mama to leave the stage and for the audience to begin to move toward the exits before she started to move toward backstage. Papa did not want Kyame to be easily identified with The Impossible Piddingtons. Papa had gone to the manager's office to collect the evening's ticket money.

It was just the third time that Kyame had sat in the audience in order to relay Papa's signing to Mama up on stage when Papa moved beyond Mama's sightline from under her blindfold. That could happen when The Impossible Piddingtons appeared in large halls. No one suspected a little nine-year old girl sitting innocently at the end of the first row on the center aisle. But tonight, tonight Kyame had delivered key signs to Mama even when two cynical men had stood right behind her seat to scrutinize Papa's movements at the back of the Opera House.

"Can't be a verbal or a silent signal code, Nate, can't be," one said. "No way that woman up on that stage, and blindfolded, by God, could see or hear Piddington all the way back there. Hell, *I* can barely see him now."

The man, Nate, swiveled his head, twisting around, looking up at the filled balcony, then back, as Mama had delivered Papa's information, as relayed from Kyame, with great anguish, hesitation and struggle to strong applause.

Finally Nate nodded, as both men sat down. "Frank, I guess you're right. Nothing in that book I bought covers anything like what these Piddingtons do. Thought I had'm though, with that special hunter watch, but that green-eyed witch up there missed on it and called it a compact. Sose, are they real, man, are they genuine mindreaders?"

Kyame had relayed Papa's signals while she had stretched in her chair to look ingenuously back up at the two men behind her. She had signed two situations while the two suspicious men were only a foot away.

481

Once the dressing-room door was closed, Mama had embraced Kyame, squeezing her tightly. "Marvelous, darling daughter," laughed Mama as she stood back to reach for a glass of a water. "You executed under pressure which shows how mature you are becoming, Kyame. Signing while they were almost looking at you was perfect timing."

The dressing-room door opened. Papa came in, his face grim, with two men close behind him. Men that Kyame had never seen before. She frowned -- except maybe they were the ones she had drawn yesterday?

The leading man, who held a small gun against Papa's back, was short in a worn gray business suit with a black beard wearing a weathered derby; but Kyame could see that the beard was fake. When the other man came further into the room, Kyame suspected he was a woman dressed as a man in a black frock coat and wide-brim hat down over her eyes.

Kyame smiled. The woman's fake mustache was off center. She saw Mama smile in return. The woman was wearing gloves and holding a small gun that quivered in her hand.

"Sit, Piddington. There," directed the man, as the other closed the door. He grinned. "Now, Impossible Piddingtons, I am going to give you a little problem to solve with your great powers. If you miss, you give us all of the ticket money in that yellow envelope in your pocket. If you succeed, you still give us the envelope." The two laughed.

Mama smiled. "And what, sir, *and miss,* is your great problem?" She cocked her head coquettishly to one side. "Your names, perhaps ... Joshua and Lily isn't it? Or perhaps you have another question?"

Lily had started when Mama had said miss. "Josh, how could she know that? We never ..."

"Shut up!" Josh turned to face Mama. He had paled but still held the pistol steady, now shifting the muzzle to point directly at Kyame. Then he grinned. "Hey, good trick. If we had time you could tell us how you did it. So, great oracle, what is the serial number of my gun?"

Mama signed that Papa and Kyame should stay quiet. "Do you know it? Or do I have to think for you, Joshua ... ah, Mercer, though you call yourself Malone in this town. Not so?"

"Oh, my God, Josh, let's get out of here. She's a witch for sure." Lily backed against the door. Her face had gone white with fear.

Kyame watched Mama's face go quiet as though she were reading her book of *Shakespeare's Sonnets* on the train, letting the words wash over her mind. Then Mama raised her eyes. "The number is 10145 ... A. 10145A." She looked at him. "I am right am I not? Check Josh, don't guess."

Joshua Mercer hesitated, then dropped his eyes for an instant to examine the serial number. Papa suddenly leaped from his chair to smash an empty water bottle over his head. Mercer dropped like a rag doll to the floor.

Kyame lunged for the woman's gun, knocking it from her hand. Kyame quickly scrambled for it under a chair.

"Oh, God, don't shoot. Please don't shoot." Lily was trembling, leaning back against the door. "It was a joke, a silly joke Josh thought we could try. For God's sake, don't shoot."

Kyame handed the pistol to Papa who had Joshua's gun in one hand.

"The sheriff, Kyame, fetch him quickly, please," said Papa.

***

When the dressing-room had emptied of the sheriff, one deputy and the two clumsy robbers, Papa turned to Mama.

"Laura, the names, the serial number ... how did you do it? I signed nothing."

Mama gently placed her hand on Kyame's head. "Our beautiful daughter is faster than we are, John. She signed the names to me. You couldn't see it. You had drawn those two people yesterday, you said, Kyame."

"Yes, Mama. Once they were in the room, I could make out their ears. I had heard their names when I was drawing them, so I remembered them.

But Mama, how did you get the serial number? I wouldn't even know where to look on the gun."

"Yes, Laura, how did you do that?"

Mama looked at the two people she loved most in the world. She would have thrown herself on the gun to save Kyame or John, as she knew they would have to save her.

Puzzled, she shook her head.

"I don't know how I was right ... but all I wanted to do was to get Joshua to look down at the gun to give you the chance, John, to use that bottle I saw in your hand. Odds were that he didn't know the number himself. Didn't matter if I was right or not ... but, I *was* right." She shook her head again. "Strange ... I don't know how."

***

Kyame stretched and shifted to work out the cramps from sleeping curled on the seat. It was still black outside the window as the train rumbled through the night.

When she had told that story of her family at a tea party in a teacher's rooms at the Boston art school, there had been no reaction at first, as though she had been describing life on another planet.

Finally, the teacher, Mrs. Crewe, who taught etching, said, "How quaint the west seems to be, Miss Piddington, like out of a dime novel I once read." Then one of the other students began describing the first time she had ridden a horse on her grandfather's estate in Maine. It was as though Kyame didn't even exist.

She had no close friends at school. There was one girl, a second-year sculptress named Angela, who had invited Kyame to meet her parents at a school art show. Her father was a tough-handed carpenter who had traveled as an actor once. But Angela had to leave school when her father no longer had the money.

The students all seemed too young and foolish, who had never faced anything more threatening than an inconvenient rain storm -- even the boys who flirted with her seemed childish.

How lonely Kyame was for Papa and their wonderful and frightening times together. The memory of that strange event with the pistol had suddenly come to mind as Kyame had shaken off the sleep. Mama had been so full of life then, so ready to laugh.

Kyame realized that her closest friend now, other than Papa, was mesmerist J. W. Cadwell – and maybe that gunsmith on Boylston Street.

***

Kyame was hungry. She pulled down her lapel watch. 6:34 AM – half hour to the breakfast stop. There was nothing out the windows except the shadows of passing telegraph poles and occasional distant lights of farmhouses as the horizon was beginning to lighten. There was little sense of time, the days passed as just monotonous repeats. The swaying car with the steady chirrups of the wheels on the track had lured her into a few hours of restless sleep, but no more.

She and Papa had done numerous overnight trips to reach their next performance stop, but back then when she was younger, she could stretch out across a single seat to sleep – but no longer. She smiled. Another life change.

The train could not move fast enough for her to reach Papa. For Eliza to come to her meant something must be seriously wrong.

She tried to get back into the latest Stanley Weyman romance adventure spread on her lap, *The Red Cockade,* but the words just wouldn't sink in. Kyame always enjoyed the latest Weyman

488

swashbuckling novel with his flawed heroes and doubtful heroines. Papa had once said that flaws in a man were all right, so long as they were productive flaws.

She leaned back against the headrest and closed her eyes.

***

Thirty minutes to eat and return to the train. Kyame followed the jostling mob of travelers toward the station restaurant. Glancing at the message board by the main station entrance, she was astonished to see "K. Piddington" listed.

"I am Kyame Piddington. You have a message for me?"

The clerk sorted through the telegrams spread on his desk. Finding one, he passed it through the brass-railed window. It read:

palace hotel market street stop room 635 stop if you need aid.   J.W.

Kyame stuffed the telegram into her pocket and moved quickly through the surging wave of hungry passengers. J. W. Cadwell's setting up San Francisco support was comforting. She only hoped she would never need it.

Coffee, heavily salted scrambled eggs, greasy pork sausages across a greasier rasher of thick bacon, fried potatoes and more coffee, a glass of water. Then back to the train.

Aid? What was J.W. expecting her to find?

69

"Elected? Only fools seek elected office," snarled Harry Rosner, tossing back his brandy in a single lump. "Once I arrive, once the deals deliver, I will control the elected fools. It's the manipulation and organization that does the work."

Cassie shook her head -- her man was hopeless in this condition. Quincy's description of the intruder had been frightening enough, until he had described the hatchet man watching them. Harry had then downed three glasses of brandy without stopping.

Harry picked up the crystal brandy decanter -- then stopped as Quincy came into the living room.

"Messenger from Wong Woon at the door … the back door."

Rosner, his face still flushed from brandy and frustration nodded.

**

Silhouetted against the gibbous moon, dressed in black with the white sash of the salaried-soldier of the Bing On, the stout broad-shouldered Chinaman bowed as he extended a sealed envelope.

"I am Ah Chang, sir," he said in clear English. "This is my master's message. He expects no answer." The informant bowed again and vanished into the night.

Cassie waited as Harry broke the heavy seal and opened the message. His eyebrows went up, his face went pale.

"Holy Christ, Cassie, an all-out tong war. The Hip Ying tong has moved into the wharves and has killed three Bing On soldiers. They've posted *chun hung* posters on the blank walls in Bartlett Alley declaring the Bing On tong to be dogs of the gutter, agents of the Qing, and challenges them to let the dogs howl.

"To let the dogs howl means a fight to the death, without quarter." Rosner grimaced. "The tongs only take prisoners temporarily anyway."

Cassie shuddered. "What happens to us, Harry, to our life, if the Bing On loses?"

Rosner looked for the missing brandy decanter, but gave it up.

"I have a noose around my neck, the other end of the rope is held by Wong Woon. If he loses, the noose closes, and we lose the opium cash flow," – he took a deep breath as he glanced around for the brandy -- "we lose everything, Cassie, everything."

Harry Rosner looked at her, focusing on her beautiful blue eyes usually so filled with fun, but now filling with fear.

"And," he added, "the Hip Ying will certainly come looking for us since I have been providing funds to help finance the Bing On commercial enterprises that the Hip Ying would seize … the white mansion opium trade above all.

"Frankly, my beautiful wife, we should pack what we can carry and prepare to run."

"When does the battle begin?" Cassie asked, her hand at her breast.

"Now. Tonight."

"Is it possible to pray about a tong war?" she asked, a crooked smile on her face. "That's where we are at, isn't it?"

**

Ah Chang moved rapidly through the alleys and backstreets of the affluent white neighborhoods of Russian Hill. If anyone saw him, he knew he would be ignored as only a laundryman or less. He stopped at the corner of Columbus and Green Streets.

Only a few carriages were moving slowly down Columbus away from him while a group of four men, white men, were walking away from him on Columbus. Ah Chang stepped quickly to a coal chute that opened into the dark alley. He lifted its cover a few inches and dropped an envelope into the blackness.

He turned back into the alley and vanished. He must be back in Bing On territory within a half an hour to loyally take up his notched hatchet or be looked on as a traitor to his tong. With eight notches on his hatchet, Ah Chang would be a marked man by the Hip Ying.

He started to run.

Traitors to the Bing On did not die quickly.

But captured secret operatives of the Qing Emperor's Board of War intelligence service, the True Eyes, did not die for days.

Ah Chang knew his envelope would arrive within the hour at Room 635 at the Palace Hotel. Not even the Imperial Chinese General Counsel, Li Wang Yu, in his handsome twelve room mansion on Stockton Street knew of the presence of the True Eyes in America.

The firm Manchu bureaucratic rule was that the True Eyes were never to operate outside the

Empire's borders. But the Empress Dowager Cixi had overruled the Board of War and the Emperor Guangxu. She clearly saw the tongs as anti-Qing, sources of cash and support to rebels in the South, and therefore to be penetrated, disrupted and destroyed wherever they operated.

The tongs, even those who hated each other, would join to kill the Chinese General Counsel within minutes if any of the tongs caught even a whiff of a direct consular involvement with the hated True Eyes, the Imperial slayers who wore the Manchu circle, who poisoned the rebel republican movement, who murdered the rebel leaders.

70

Kwan Duck watched carefully as his sub-leaders assembled their salaried-soldiers, the white-sashed boo how doy. Ah Chang had been late arriving and brought disturbing news. The Tough Brick tong had traveled from Sacramento to join the Hip Ying against the Bing On tonight.

Backed by its own influence over access to many of the San Francisco wharves, two months earlier the Bing On had seized control of the lucrative Sacramento slave girl trade from the Tough Brick. If the Tough Bricks wanted singsong girls they had to pay the Bing On price which would cut their profits by almost three-quarters -- an intolerable affront to the proper way of culture and cash flow.

Wong Woon had been anticipating some Tough Brick response, but had held back from a direct attack in Sacramento, preferring to protect his position in San Francisco. The Tough Bricks and Hip Yings had always hated each other and had fought a few months ago, over a single, but most unique, slave girl -- but not tonight.

Ah Chang had learned that for their support to the Hip Yings, the Tough Bricks would recover the slave girls and take over the Southern wharves, leaving the rest of the Bing On assets to the Hip Ying.

Wong Woon had laughed when Ah Chang finished his report. "That arrangement would last for two days, perhaps," Wong said, "before they would fall on each other's necks and in the end lose everything to the hovering Bo Sin Seers tong who would move in to collect the remains.

"Ho! Good, Ah Chang!" Wong Woon had grinned. "We can solve two problems tonight."

***

Their preparations completed, Kwan Duck led his hatchet men from their headquarters, the Hall of Far Reaching Virtue, an unmarked warehouse. They wore silken jackets made of the five colors of the Ming, white sashes and the red turbans in memory of the rebel fighters in the failed Tai Ping Rebellion.

The pepper men would be in the front rank, backed by vitriol throwers, then the assault lines of hatchets and swords. For two days, the soldiers had ground their hatchets, swords and meat axes to razor sharpness. The remainder of the Bing On boo how doy were armed with iron clubs sharpened to points at both ends. All carried slung shots at their hips, short lead-filled leather cylinders for close-in work.

Forty-six men moved to Kwan Duck's order.

Kwan Duck looked back at his men. *"Loy gee, hai, dai!* Come on, you cowards!" he snarled. "I will kill anyone who retreats!"

He was answered by a loud roar and cheer: *"Ah ga la! Ah ga la!* Strike him! Strike him!"

They marched for Clay and Dupont Gai, the agreed battleground. The lowering crawling night fog blended with the smoke of chimneys and braziers in the abandoned streets to smear away the outlines of the marching men. There would be watchers but only at a safe distance.

There would be no white police anywhere near Clay and Dupont. But no white men would be molested if they came near the battle. If any whites were killed in a tong conflict, there was too much risk of igniting a race war that the Chinese had no hope of winning.

All tongs had agreed.

***

The chants of the Hip Yings and the Tough Bricks rose in volume as the torches and red turbans of the first of the Bing On came into view.

The chant was punctuated by the rhythmic clashing of the swords and hatchets.

Once the warring tongs were arrayed on each side of Dupont, Kwan Duck shouted, "Let the dogs feed well tonight!" The Bing On surged forward, screaming insults.

Ah Chang led his men at the division between the two enemy tongs, to split them, sending Lee Kay and his seven pepper men two steps ahead.

The pepper-men ran forward, throwing small paper bags of finely ground hot red pepper into the eyes of the front rank of the Tough Bricks and immediately pulled back into the ranks; two of the retreating pepper-men fell with knives in their back.

The vitriol throwers ran through the fleeing pepper-men to lob acid over the adjoining ranks of the Hip Ying with long handled ladles scooped from sloshing acid-filled buckets carried by support-men armed only with slug shots.

Ah Chang ordered his hatchet men forward, as gunshots sounded, two of his sword-men fell at his feet. He buried his hatchet in the neck of the first Hip Ying to oppose him with one hand, swinging his slung shot across the head of the next.

Jumping over the bodies, Ah Chang swung his hatchet again and again, ducking under a meat axe that sliced through his turban.

A quick glance to the left. The Bing On front line, howling with eagerness, had already penetrated past the first line of Hip Ying hatchet men to press rear lines against a brick wall.

In spite of the screams and yelling, Ah Chang suddenly heard three loud claps from his left, the sign of desperate trouble. One of his men, Lee Shan, was struggling to fend off three Hip Yings. Ah Chang slashed his way between two Brick men to drop one of the Hip Yings from behind, severing his head completely, then kicked hard into the groin of the second, as Lee Shan dispatched the third by burying his sword into the top of the man's head.

Lee Shan nodded his debt and plunged back into the battle, first killing the Hip Ying groveling in pain on the ground with a quick swipe of his sword across the man's throat.

On the roof, two floors above the street battle, Bing On snipers began to fire into the densely packed and shifting fighting. They aimed at the rear of the mass of surging men, the most likely location of the enemy. In the fog-smeared flickering yellow of the street gaslights and the torches carried by both sides, it was difficult to clearly identify the tong fighters -- but they fired anyway.

The Hip Ying snipers hidden three floors up across Dupont began to fire down on the now visible Bing On snipers.

Ah Chang suddenly discovered no one in front of him. He had broken through -- the two enemy tongs were separated.

Shouting to his men to sweep to the right, Ah Chang swung his hatchet to crush the skull of a support-man carrying acid to the Brick vitriol throwers. Ah Chang dropped his hatchet, picked up the bucket and rushed at a small group of disoriented Tough Bricks. Swinging the bucket, he lobbed the vitriol into the air over their heads, drenching the men with the burning concentrated sulphuric acid.

As they screamed in agony, more of Ah Chang's men swept in to decapitate them.

Recovering his hatchet, Ah Chang pressed forward. A Brick appeared before him. Instantly swinging, he felt the hatchet slip in his hand, its shaft covered with hot blood and sweat. As Ah

Chang's blow glanced off the Brick's shoulder, the hatchet came loose in his hand.

As the Brick raised his sword, Ah Chang was knocked to the pavement by a bullet in his left shoulder. He felt the wind, the breath of death, from the sword stroke swish over his head, then the Brick falling across him, his severed neck pumping blood across Ah Chang into the cobbled alleyway. A Bing On swordsman jumped across the body.

"Ah Chang?" the man shouted, hesitating.

Ah Chang waved him on.

He knew he had been shot by a Bing On sniper, but no matter. Ah Chang grasped his hatchet -- a stupid thought suddenly ran through his mind. He would need a longer shaft for his hatchet for all the notches he would be cutting after tonight.

Rising, his left arm hanging painfully at his side, Ah Chang gripped the shaft tighter and swung again and again.

***

Wong Woon stood in the shadows of Lime Alley watching and hearing the battle rage hardly forty feet away. He was losing men, at least eight that he could see; he saw Ah Chang go down from a friendly bullet; blood-covered Kwan Duck was whipping his men forward on the left flank.

No matter.

For some to be hit, even killed, by a fellow salaried-soldier was to be expected in any tong war. Since arriving in America five years earlier and taking a Han name, Wong Woon had fought in too many wars to remember, to erase his homeland status as a despised Tibetan, to gain unquestioned and feared respect. There could never be any thought of his returning to China. As blood filled the air, killing became indiscriminate as the men tired and the killing lust gripped their souls.

No matter.

The stronger the Bing On appeared, the easier it would be to steal new recruit replacements from new arrivals on the ships and from the other tongs, even from tongs who came from foreign China provinces. The boo how doy wanted always to be on the winning side, the lucrative side. Anyone could be replaced.

And Wong Woon loved no one.

***

Kwan Duck had trapped the last vestiges of the Hip Yings against a back alley wall. His men moved in, ignoring cries for mercy, chopping away the crumbling human wall, arms, hands and heads littering the alley.

In an adjacent alleyway, Ah Chang and his men were butchering the last of the Tough Bricks.

When the dogs howl, no man lives.

Leaping back from the Brick as he fell, Ah Chang whirled, his hatchet at the ready, his useless arm swinging out as he did. He was inhaling blood lust, tasting it, embracing it. A great cold wave of disappointment swept over him.

There was no one left to kill.

***

Wong Woon looked at his watch. Thirty-five minutes. One of the longest tong wars of his experience.

Kwan Duck staggered toward him, his broad face smeared over with blood, two large slashes across his great heaving chest. The boo how doy leader raised his meat axe in salute.

"Master Wong, the dogs have howled, as you wished."

Wong bowed in acknowledgement. "Collect our sleeping soldiers, Kwan Duck. Leave the rest for the rats."

He turned away. No one would know the cost of battle to the Bing On. As Wong Woon

504

walked into the darkness he reflected that it had been a most fruitful evening with two problems solved.

71

Kyame Piddington yawned. It was another dull evening as the train struggled up the long grade leading to the Rockies. It would be slower progress but in the morning coming down the other side of the mountain pass, San Francisco and Papa would be only two more days away.

Her fingers grazed the *Bi* disk concealed under her blouse. She was hardly aware of it about her neck any more, yet she still felt -- different.

Kyame closed her eyes.

72

Detective Will Irwin of the San Francisco police wiped his mouth after vomiting his breakfast of ham and eggs -- then threw his sodden handkerchief into the gutter of Dupont Street. Bloody chunks of human beings, once men, were strewn along one side of Dupont and into two alleyways. They were only Chinamen, yes -- but still human. Without winds to disperse the odors, the wretched stink was suffocating.

"Sacramento, Will, look at this." The uniformed cop had pieces of red and white paper in his hand.

Irwin took the small thin white paper. It was a tong membership certificate. White was Sacramento, red was San Francisco. Other colors were rarely seen.

The harness bull waved his hand toward an accumulation of human parts.

"All those Chinee have white papers -- and those" -- he pointed down the street to the left -- "have red. So, they wiped each other out? Doesn't make any sense."

"It doesn't." Before arriving, Irwin had learned that the street word had it that the Bing On fought two combined tongs over slave girl trade, or at least control of the slave girl business.

"This gruesome mess suggests that the Bing On annihilated both tongs in one night," said Irwin, "but at what cost to them?"

The cop, Mark Hansen, nodded. Hansen had walked these streets and alleyways of Chinatown more than a few times. Never any trouble, because he was white. A Chinaman in a blue police uniform would probably be dead in minutes.

Hansen knew the Bing On never left their dead or dying behind, so no one could know what losses they might have suffered. Wong Woon was no fool -- that was for sure.

"What's the count, Hansen?" Irwin asked.

"Best we've been able to tell -- we haven't matched up all the hands, arms and heads -- there were about 25-30 red sheets and 18-25 white sheets. So," said Hansen, "if the higher numbers are right and the Bing On had an equal number of hatchet men, then you have over a hundred hatchet and sword wielding killers going at each other here last night. The dogs howled, for sure."

Irwin looked away, as if he could get a breath of clean air, not the oppressive rotting odor of human flesh mixed with the coppery odor of blood-filled gutters, and the pervasive smell of partially eaten human entrails against the clinging stench of urine. The first of the police to arrive an hour ago had driven off the feasting dogs, cats and rats.

"Collect the body parts, leave the blood for the locals to wash away. Dump the celestial garbage in the harbor for the fishes. There is no usable evidence here ... but get everything out of the pockets. I want to confirm which tongs were here."

Hearing iron wheels on the cobbled street, Irwin looked around as a two-horse police patrol wagon drew abreast of the detective.

"Message for you, Detective," the driver said, "from the station."

Irwin took the sealed official yellow police envelope and waited until the wagon had moved away. The driver and his partner were pointing at the chunks of bloody humanity.

"Hey!" the driver yelled toward Hansen. "You ain't puttin' any of that miserable muck into this wagon."

Inside the envelope were two fifty dollar silver certificates with x's in white ink across both of the eyes of William Seward on each bill, turning the former Secretary of State's image into a buffoonish cartoon.

Wong Woon's order: clean up and get out.

Detective Will Irwin no longer cared which tongs had fought. He slipped the envelope inside his tightly buttoned suit jacket. As he walked down Dupont toward his personal carriage, Mark Hansen glanced over at him, an eyebrow raised.

Irwin nodded.

Hansen stuffed the collected red and white papers into his pocket and walked away. All the membership papers would vanish within the hour, as ordered.

73

John Piddington stood in the shadows watching the carriages approach to disgorge their glittering cargo onto the broad steps of the Villa Illuminaire. Lights filled all three floors of the mansion, and together with eight gas-fired torches standing the height of streetlights writhing in the evening breezes created daylight on the mansion's circular courtyard approach. Multiple liveried Chinese attendants ran from coach to coach. Another gaudy reception probably paid for with Montgomery-Hill cash.

He had only one more day to pull his report together for Harvey Atherton, but it would be conclusive. The bank could not extend more credit to Harry Rosner; rather, it should call the loans it had outstanding immediately. Even then the bank would have to book a loss on all the loans.

Piddington had learned from a Mills & Beecher broker over a gossipy lunch that Harry Rosner was late on his scheduled payment to M & B to complete his purchase of allotted shares in the Occidental and Oriental Steamship Co.

Rosner was always a few days late on everything, the broker had confided over his third beer, but the speculator had always made the required payments in the past -- but this was the elephant payment, the final thirty percent in one lump. If he missed this one, the broker broke into a leering grin, Rosner would forfeit the shares and lose what cash he had already paid in.

There were also the spicy rumors that floated through the saloons about the gorgeous Cassie Rosner, but Piddington ignored them. He and Kyame in their travels had known actresses with scandalous reputations who were in fact more chaste than the ministers' wives who had criticized them.

Piddington realized that Rosner's final payment on Occidental and Oriental of $215,000 would more than exhaust the balance of his existing Montgomery-Hill line of credit. How then would the speculator handle the payments to M-H? M-H had to call their loan before Rosner could make the payment to Mills & Beecher.

***

His left shoulder stiff and sore, his almost useless left arm supported by his hand thrust in a white sash, Ah Chang was about to leave his post across from the glittering Rosner mansion. He had, as directed by Kwan Duck, allowed himself to be seen periodically from the front portal of Villa Illuminaire.

His replacement, Low Yet, was just approaching through the trees behind him, when Ah Chang caught the movement of a white man half a block away as the man had shifted out of the shadows then dart back into the darkness.

Who was watching Harry Rosner other than the Bing On? His instructions from room 635 were to gain understanding of the Bing On relationships with the white money men – but not to interfere, just get the names.

***

Piddington moved down the block to skirt the walls of Villa Illuminaire and find the small Judas gate at the back. Even with the many guests, he could move up the servants' stairs to the second floor, search the room, and be outside again within fifteen or twenty minutes. Rosner and his wife and their servants would be preoccupied with their guests. He did not detect the quiet shadow moving thirty feet behind him.

A short shrill whistle cut the night.

***

Ah Chang took a breath and cursed softly. The call for additional support from his relief as Low Yet could not leave his post to track the white man who had clumsily exposed his presence again. Ah Chang wanted to watch the white man alone, but now he could not be seen by the other Bing On observers. He was supposed to be returning to the Hall of Far Reaching Virtue in Chinatown.

***

Piddington opened the back door and pocketed his lock picks. He moved through the storage room and paused to listen at the door into the kitchen.

Voices.

A door opposite, away from the voices opened with a slight push. Another store room -- with three of the familiar barrels partially filled with small brown cones of opium. The drug doctor had confirmed to Piddington the brown powder was opium of a very high quality. Probably no guests would be allowed near this -- at least not without payment.

Maybe.

Piddington moved to the door and cracked it open barely an inch. An empty narrow corridor that -- as he pushed the door further open -- led to a steep narrow stairway. He moved silently up the cushioned stairs, the noise from the reception growing in volume.

The house was radiant in light including the second floor that had no shadows, the combined hiss of the many gas lights easily audible.

Piddington moved quickly to the door of the room.

Locked.

It wasn't a standard bedroom lock. He took two rarely used picks and after several minutes of patient probing and turning, the lock clicked open. He locked the door behind him.

He started in the small office just off the bedroom. Nothing in the desk drawers, none of the drawers were locked, nothing in the closets, nothing in the drawers of a long table that ran along one wall.

Piddington stood in the middle of the office and slowly rotated, looking for a break in pattern, something that didn't tally.

He stopped. There it was.

The thick green book was out of place among the others on the shelf. No books anywhere in the house but only here on one shelf in Rosner's office.

The green book concealed a locked dispatch box. Again a few minutes to beat the strange lock, clearly a custom design for Rosner. If so, he needed a better locksmith.

Opened, there were share certificates in Occidental and Oriental -- totaled 20,000 shares. A sheet listing a payment schedule to someone, and a list indicating payments coming to Rosner from the Bing On tong -- brown-money was the line item.

Lists of people, all men, all -- my God, Harvey Atherton among them! Though his own memory was exceptional, it couldn't match Kyame's. She would need only one glance and have everything, numbers and names, locked into her mind. A suddenly surge of longing to see his daughter swept through him.

Piddington sat down and began to quickly record the numbers and names and the dates -- he could figure the relevance of the dates later.

In fifteen minutes he had everything and knew he had to get out quickly. He was pushing his odds as it was. At the bottom of the dispatch case there was a small circular piece of green jade with a hole in the center. A souvenir? He left it.

***

Ah Chang pressed further back against the wall. Too long, too long for the white man to be in there. Not a thief. A thief would be in and out in only a few minutes, possibly with his pockets filled with cones of the Balkan opium handled by the Bing On and Rosner.

Balkan was the most powerful raw opium available, with a double or higher concentration of the drug. After purification by the Bing On, the power to induce an opium trance increased even more, by two or three times. The initial customer price was ten times the Indian, Turkish or Chinese product. Ah Chang had notified 635 that Rosner was helping to finance the flow of the Balkan. Once customers became addicted to it, nothing else could satisfy them and then the customer price would double, quadruple, or more.

So -- finally, he comes, the errant white man.

Ah Chang moved back. 635 will want to know who this man is. He turned to run, to arrive at the Hall near the proper time.

As Ah Chang disappeared, three black shadows behind him moved quickly. The white man was gagged, blindfolded and tightly bound

517

within barely a minute. No sounds. He was thrown over the shoulder of the largest of the shadows. They vanished into the night, rapidly leaving the brilliance of Villa Illuminaire behind.

74

The Man Who Knows boiled with fury. Alexander Jason Johnstone had customers waiting to load his pockets with gold, while Wong Woon sat quietly smoking. The Chinaman's windowless office with its small fireplace only added to the oppression Johnstone felt.

Two sharp knocks, then the door opened.

Kwan Duck noted Johnstone. "We have captured the banker, Master Wong," he reported in Chinese. "At the place of the white ...," he paused, looking again at Johnstone. "He is the one I saw earlier running from the house."

Wong Woon nodded. "Prepare him for instruction."

***

The white man's eyes were filled with fear. Still gagged the man could make no sound and could not move. Once his naked body had been placed on the table, the three soldiers had left to seek out Kwan Duck.

Searching the piled clothing of the white man, Ah Chang had quickly removed papers from the man's pockets and stuffed them inside his shirt.

Kwan Duck suddenly appeared.

"The master has ordered this white man to be instructed. Ah Chang. Lead these two men to properly position the *student*."

Kwan Duck left laughing at his joke.

Ah Chang bowed in obedience. These would be the last lessons the white man would ever learn.

***

Johnstone smothered his surprise at seeing John Piddington tied and stretched naked on the board. A look of recognition momentarily lit up Piddington's eyes. Good God. The seer had never liked Piddington and his snotty daughter, but this, for God's sake, not to be thrashed to a pulp by Chinese thugs.

Wong Woon, stylishly dressed in blue pin-stripe, settled into his chair, placing his derby on a small side table. He flipped his hand.

Two highbinders stepped forward, each holding a long bamboo flail. One ripped away the gag in the white man's mouth.

John Piddington had never before experienced a surge of sharp pain like that which swept over his body like a tidal wave from the first lashing of the bamboo flails. He gritted his teeth to squeeze back a cry of pain. Johnstone and the Chinaman just sat there watching him.

Johnstone, that miserable devil incarnate.

***

"Do you know this man, Mr. Johnstone? I detect recognition in his eyes when he saw you."

The rhythmic thuck! thuck! of the flails striking and stripping away bare flesh continued.

The seer nodded. "John Piddington. Used to perform a second sight act with his daughter. I hired him couple of years ago to do some background work for me in the mid-west."

"And his daughter?" Wong asked, an eyebrow raised.

"Back east somewhere. I heard Boston. Some kind of art school."

Piddington's sudden unbridled scream of acute pain shook Johnstone, his face draining of color.

"Come, Mr. Johnstone, to my office. You are clearly discomforted by Mr. Piddington's traditional instruction." As he led the way, Wong Woon said, "You are aware ... that Mr. John Piddington was the bank manager blocking the flow of funds that has inconvenienced us both.

When his instruction is complete, then the funds will be available, and you will have your goods, most promptly."

***

Through a curtain of rising pain, blood running across his face into his mouth, John Piddington watched Johnstone and the Chinaman leave. Johnstone had glanced back, his lean face pale.

The screaming he heard had been his own, Piddington realized. He seemed to be floating away from the sweating highbinders swinging their flails. There was no longer any feeling in his body. It was overwhelmed with the agony of the repeated blows. Again. Again. He gasped for air, exhausted from screaming.

John Piddington's last clear thought, as his mind disintegrated into shards of grotesque pain, was of precious Kyame, eleven years old, looking up at him, her green eyes shining, asking him in that hot hotel room in Kansas: "Papa, is what we do, right?

75

Maid of Athens, ere we part --
Give, oh, give me back my heart!

Lord Byron's quaint lines kept repeating in his head. Cassie had recited portions of Byron's *Maid of Athens* as she had unbuttoned her gown, slowly revealing -- beyond any shape or anything in Harvey's dismal marriage experience. Ah -- ah.

* * *

Harvey Atherton had to wait some moments before rising from his desk. Consuming lust had spilled over his body. Thoughts of his planned assignation with Cassie Rosner tonight stirred his loins, an awkward erection further tightening his already tight trousers.

He shook his head and coldly began to think of his endlessly complaining wife, of her father whom Harvey had to face in a few minutes, and then his plain, complaining flat-chested wife again with her crude incessant whining. Moments of such visions and thoughts, gradually restored his body to normal.

***

"So, Harvey, you want to increase the bank's bet on Harry Rosner's business acumen?"

Oliver 'Hickory' Hill lighted a cigar, rolling the tobacco at the tips of his fingers to get an even glow from the flame, his cold brown eyes holding Atherton in thrall.

"Wasn't Piddington going to confirm some suspicions he had regarding past Rosner deals? Where is Piddington? He is normally the first one in the bank.

"I like that young man." Hill tossed the match into a large stone ashtray on his desk.

Atherton coughed. "I have grave news, Mr. Hill. Mr. Piddington was killed last night by ruffians attempting to rob him. He was cruelly used before dying trying to defend his honor."

Hill was instantly on his feet. "Why was I not immediately informed this morning?" he shouted. "My God, man, a colleague is murdered. You act like it was nothing. I saw enough death in the trenches at Petersburg to never want to see it again.

"His family, damnit, Atherton, what family does he have? The bank will pay for any funeral the family requests. Human beings work for me, Atherton ... not *ciphers* like you apparently think."

Atherton went pale. He hated his father-in-law and having to put up with his repulsive daughter as wife, but the position was too important to him to, to do anything Hill demanded.

"Sir, he has only a single daughter, at school in Boston. I sent a telegram to her as soon as I learned of the tragedy, requesting instruction. I could not do more, sir," he pleaded. "Not more at this time. My deepest apologies for not notifying you sooner."

Atherton hated his enforced groveling, this sniveling posturing. Getting that personal piece of the Rosner fortune promised by Cassie in the deals coming up would finally free him of Hill, he sought a word, ah, the Hill disease.

Hill returned to his chair. He nodded. "Keep me informed, Harvey." He rearranged papers on his desk. "What is her age, Piddington's daughter?"

"I believe sixteen or seventeen, sir."

Hill shook his head. "That is too early to lose a father." He leaned back, the chair creaking as it always did. "So," he said, as a cloud of smoke formed about his head, "tell me about that rogue, Harry Rosner."

***

As Harvey Atherton wrote the telegram his body began to glow and tighten. The message said: Cassie stop Deal signed stop Full credit request granted stop Cash immediately available stop Fourteen percent interest stop Lowest possible for one year. Harvey. The address was one that Cassie had assured him was her *most* private address.

***

Laughing, Harry Rosner tossed back the whiskey in a lump when Cassie finished reading the Atherton telegram aloud. He refilled his crystal shot glass again.

"We're clean, my love. Clean! Clean!" He laughed. "Fourteen percent? Who cares? By the time of the first payment next year Montgomery-Hill won't even exist." He downed the second shot in a swallow.

Smiling, Cassandra Rosner walked closer to her husband to look down on him, stretched across his favorite red leather chair.

"Clean? Not quite yet, dear," she murmured, her smile soft and inviting. "When can I kill

526

Harvey Atherton? He utterly disgusts me. Like those other fumbling bankers."

Her mischievous blue eyes glittered.

76

Looking through the window as the train slowed, the presence of Eliza and not Papa on the station platform filled Kyame with cold dread. Eliza's face was pale behind her hastily applied makeup. She did not smile when Kyame stepped from the train.

"Oh, my God, Kyame!" Eliza burst into tears, rushing to her. "They've killed your father ... they've killed my John!"

Papa. Papa. For a moment, Kyame couldn't breath. She felt Eliza's arms close about her. She couldn't move, couldn't speak. Her first thought was that she could never give Papa the signed Steinitz book and tell him about her playing the greatest chess master in the world. She would never hear his laugh again, his hand of approval on her shoulder. Papa, Papa, I need you. Her tears began to flow.

Kyame reached out to hug Eliza.

***

Creed and Marsha Abbott offered Kyame a room and compassion. She hesitated -- then accepted. They gave her space; didn't intrude when she sat silently beside the fire with a cup of coffee cradled in her hands; food spread on a sideboard -- and withdrew.

Remembrances tumbled through her mind, slowly at first, then the avalanche started, tears flowed, she sipped coffee, eyed the food, then finally rose to cut off a chunk of still warm roast beef and ate it with her fingers, then returned to her chair to sip more coffee.

The one person she most loved, most needed, who was the one person who had validated her life -- had been brutalized almost beyond recognition. Eliza had fainted when the police had shown her John Piddington's battered remains.

Kyame took a deep breath. Her world and her heart had grown cold.

It was done. Life was done. Papa could not come back. Mama was gone. With them both gone, it was her decision now, her life. Like the youth in Stephen Crane's novel, was she now about "to be measured"?

She had to start over.

Kyame would start with the police. And would move to Papa's room that would now be her's -- until -- until.

Creed Abbott had committed to paying her rent and board for as long as she needed.

**

Detective Will Irwin stood as Kyame entered his office. He smiled. The girl was tall, quite attractive and well dressed in sweeping blue and white, with some style, better than he had expected. That damned Chinaman in the derby, or any other moneyed celestial, would move serious pelf to possess this white woman.

Just a thought -- as, smiling, Irwin extended his hand. "I am terribly sorry about your father, Miss Piddington," said Irwin, settling back as she accepted a chair. "When would you like to claim your father's body? There is nothing, unfortunately, that we can learn for our investigation from his remains."

"Tomorrow morning, Mr. Irwin. My father will be cremated here in San Francisco. There will be no funeral. He traveled so much that any place would be the same to him." Kyame watched the policeman shuffle the papers on his desk. He seemed nervous. "What do you know of his death, Detective? Who did it?"

Irwin hesitated. "Chinese, perhaps, the mode of death suggests that."

"The brutality suggests that? Why was he killed?"

"We don't know," Irwin said. "Maybe he saw something that he shouldn't have; maybe a couple of highbinders thought he had money on him ... maybe." He raised his hands in a helpless gesture.

"What Chinese?"

"One of the tongs."

"How many tongs are there?"

"No one knows. No white man. It changes almost daily."

"So, Detective, you and the police obviously will do nothing. Is that correct?" Kyame remained expressionless.

Irwin said, "There were no witnesses, Miss Piddington ... the beat ... the attack took place somewhere else and your father's body was placed where the harness bull on the beat could not fail to find it." He restacked the papers again. "There are never any witnesses to a tong killing."

Kyame stood. "Tomorrow morning for my father's body," she said. "I expect nothing ... neither aid nor assistance from the Frisco police in punishing the brutes who killed him.

531

"But, Detective Irwin, I promise" -- her voice going cold -- "they will be punished ... and any who aids them. No matter *who* that might be."

Kyame had resolved, as she had started up the steps of the police station that she would hunt down and kill the murderers herself, regardless of the law.

Dr. Mar Tan had been right -- the law is mindless and useless.

77

A reddening sun was setting, just touching the rhythmic sinuous ocean. Roiling clouds and a low haze, framed by the cliffs of the Golden Gate, were colored a matchless iridescent copper. The small fishing boat bobbed jauntily with each movement of the waves.

A young man, part of a group of men standing at the docks smoking and talking, he gave his name as Jack London, had offered to row her to wherever she wanted.

He had a kind face and warm smile, and seemed to understand the depth of her grief -- so Kyame trusted him. He had refused her offered payment.

Kyame held the urn holding Papa's ashes tightly in her arms. She would scatter his ashes in the spotlight of the sun. She tried to smile. Papa would have liked that touch.

"Careful, miss," London said, as she stood in the boat. He put out a hand to steady her as she momentarily lost her balance.

Kyame removed the stopper from the urn and dropped it over the side. Holding the urn with both hands, she raised it up toward the sun then turned it over to let its contents fall into the ocean, moving the urn about to spread the bits and dark powders. A soft breeze swept some of the ashes away into the waves.

Then Kyame tossed the urn high out into the air over the waiting sea, sat down and sobbed.

She didn't hear the splash.

***

As London helped her up onto the dock from the boat, he said, "You did well, Miss Piddington. You honored your father more than a church full of fusty dour bishops. God bless you." Then he grinned. "May I have the honor of buying you a beer?"

Surprised, Kyame had to smile. She nodded. She would start her hunt tomorrow -- if it took the rest of her life. Even if, in the end, it took her life, too.

Jack London was a struggling writer, Kyame discovered as she sipped the cold beer. Only a few things published, but his ideas never stopped.

She smiled. "Like my art. It seems never enough time for all the ideas. Please send me any of your work. I consume books."

London laughed. "Agreed, Miss Piddington. I will try to slake your hunger for the well written word. Do you care for poetry?"

534

"Yes."

"What kind?"

"Short."

London exploded in laughter -- and Kyame finally felt a laugh rising in her. She wouldn't laugh again until she had Papa's killers dead at her feet.

78

Kyame stepped from the rising room onto the sixth floor. It had been an amazing, almost magical experience.

From the moment she had stepped down from the two-wheeled taxi in the Palace Hotel's Grand Court, someone had been at her elbow to lead her from the graveled and noisy Grand Court where six floors of white balconied galleries rose above her reaching to a vast opaque glass dome directly overhead. Eight other carriages were picking up and discharging passengers in the circled Court with room for still more.

Massive carved doors were opened by two white liveried bellmen, one of whom then led Kyame across the opulent lobby crowded with fashionably dressed women and elegantly attired men to the bank of four rising rooms. The rooms were raised by hydraulic pistons to the highest levels of the seven floor hotel.

The white-and-red liveried Negro operator bowed as Kyame entered a room richly paneled with dark carved woods set off by fantasy landscape paintings on each wall. Fresh flowers in large wall-vases filled the room with rich fragrances of roses, lilac and others that Kyame couldn't recognize. Extending his hand to suggest she sit on the low black leather sofa against the back wall, the operator slid the door closed, then moved a brass handle. A gentle wheezing sound, then she felt the floor begin to lift under her like a magic carpet.

The operator bowed again, as he slid the door open on the sixth floor.

"Odd numbers to the left, Mademoiselle", he said. He had had to jog the control twice to bring the floor of the rising room precisely level with the sixth floor. "Please watch your step."

The engraved sign on the door at room 635 of the Palace Hotel said: Anglo-Oriental Marine Insurance Co. Kyame knocked, then pushed the door open.

***

Eliza would have been good for Papa, Kyame was coming to realize. As Kyame made adjustments to Papa's arrangement in the room that was now hers, Eliza would tell her about Papa's life in San Francisco, his quick advancement at the bank, their life together and the life they had planned.

Kyame placed the Steinitz book on the nightstand where she would see it first in the morning. She explained the book when Eliza asked.

"Steinitz? Even I know the name. You played him? Who won … may I ask?" Eliza was hesitant, still unsure of Kyame's feelings toward her.

Kyame thought back to those first lessons back stage. She took Eliza's shoulders and smiled. "Papa. Papa won." Then she described the experience.

"Oh, Kyame, you were the center of his life, of his thinking, his greatest pride," said Eliza, packing Papa's clothes to make room for Kyame's in the closet. "He so glowed when speaking of you. He would share parts of your letters with me, pointing out how much like your mother you were.

"Oh, Kyame, he loved you so much." Eliza sat on the bed. "I feel like a child. I can't stop crying."

The two women had sat together and cried together.

***

The door opened. "Good morning, Miss Piddington," said the woman at the small cluttered desk. She was Eurasian with high cheek-bones and a dazzling smile that lit her large dark eyes. Rising, she was dressed in dark red in the flowing Trilby style of full billowing sleeves, rich brocaded skirt and no corset. "Please come in. Our mutual friend, J. W. Cadwell, said you might be calling."

She pointed to the warming teapot. "I am Kum Yong Sinclair, Miss Piddington. May I offer you a cup of most excellent Gun Powder tea? It arrived on the clipper this very morning.

"My superior will join us in a moment."

***

"I am Judson Rowland, Miss Piddington. Please be seated. My most profound sympathies on the loss of your father." He raised a cigar. "May I? Tobacco is my worst habit."

"Of course, Mr. Rowland," said Kyame. "Why would Professor Cadwell send me to an insurance company?"

Kyame had been struck by Rowland's presence when he had entered the room to accept a cup of fragrant tea from Kum Yong and first introduced himself.

Tall, quite handsome, silver at his temples with a closely-trimmed silver-grey beard, finely tailored, but lethal in some undefined way. There was a very slight bulge in his tailored jacket under his left shoulder. A pistol?

"J. W. warned me that you could be very direct." He smiled. "You are here because we are *not* an insurance company. We only look like one. We have no clients, nor seek any." Rowland replaced his cup and smiled. "The Palace Hotel is usually half empty anyway and with 755 rooms too big for anyone to observe everything. And, as many travelers prefer the lower floors, being up here on the sixth is the appropriate place for a quiet office like ours with an excellent view of San Francisco from all the windows."

"But," Rowland had beckoned Kyame to follow him into his office, "the Palace is the greatest hotel west of the Mississippi. Various members of the Big Four estates, including Collis Huntington himself when he is in town, and the Southern Pacific management, are almost always to be found in the grand barroom downstairs."

Letting the cigar burn for a moment, Rowland leaned across his desk, his smile fading. "I will explain, but what I say must never be repeated. Do you understand, Miss Piddington?"

Kyame had noted that the papers on his desk had not been moved recently -- the lines of dust showed that. A stage setting had been her first thought on entering Rowland's spacious office carrying her cup of tea.

Kyame went cold. "I know how to keep secrets, Mr. Rowland ... my father taught me."

Awkward and embarrassed, Rowland acknowledged her answer.

Kum Yong had locked the outside door and joined them. To break the difficult silence, she laughed. "There are some families, Kyame, who will hire a carriage, drive down Montgomery, cross Market and swing into the Grand Court of the Palace to be grandly handed down by the doormen. Then once inside the Palace they depart by the nearest exit. They can't afford to stay at the Palace ... they just want to be seen entering the hotel."

"True," said Rowland. Kyame's face was still cold and suspicious. "But along with being expensive, the Palace unfortunately can be very noisy ... as you can hear even now, six floors up. Noise from passing cable cars; clatter of drays over the cobbles of Market Street; and that unending echoing procession around the central Grand Court below our door."

He put the cigar down. "My sincere apologies, Miss Piddington. I stupidly overstepped my caution.

"So, let me explain this office. President Grover Cleveland and Secretary of State Richard Olney are preoccupied with the Spanish occupation of Cuba … and the brutalities being committed there by the Spanish Army under General Valariano Weyler.

"Secretary Olney, however, is quite aware of other parts of the world … most specifically China. The Qing Dynasty is dying of corruption and incompetence. It is only a matter of time before the Empress Dowager and her ilk are overthrown. But the Qing are no threat to American commercial activities in Asia.

"The alternatives to the Qing, the radical rebel republicans are as corrupt as the Imperial government, if not more so; but more violent, and they may prove in time to be much more threatening to American interests.

"Secretary Olney is fully aware of Qing and tong activities from his previous position under Cleveland as Attorney General."

With the conversation safely underway, Kum Yong excused herself to return to the outer office.

"A small informal group," Rowland said, "has been formed by the Secretary to watch the Chinese developments, in China as well as in America; to make temporary common cause with the Qing intelligence operations in order to better anticipate what might be coming."

"Why then am I here?" asked Kyame, placing her cup on Rowland's desk. "What is my involvement?"

"Your father was killed by the boo how doy of the Bing On tong."

Kyame gripped the arms of her chair. "Boo how doy?"

"Highbinder, killers. Literally the expression means sons of the hatchet, Miss Piddington. The attack on your father does not appear to have been an accident.

"We have a source inside the Bing On, who is a member of the feared ... justifiably feared ... Qing intelligence group called the True Eyes. The True Eyes report directly to the Empress. Our contact's name doesn't matter at this point."

Rowland paused.

"He witnessed your father's murder."

"Where are the Bing On, that I can begin to kill them all?" Kyame's face was pale, her eyes cold, her hands began to tremble.

Rowland stood. He shook his head. "No. You would certainly fail in that and ... there is more than just the Bing On involved.

"They apparently have a white face in the person of a notorious financier and speculator, Harry Rosner. We don't fully understand the relationship, but apparently your father was getting close ... and that was why he was killed without mercy.

"If I may say, Miss Piddington, your father was an extraordinary man. Without his courage, we would not have these."

Rowland removed several papers with penciled notes from a drawer. He spread them before Kyame.

She recognized Papa's handwriting. She nodded.

"Our Qing contact removed these papers from your father's pockets before the Bing On searched him. They appear to be data taken from Harry Rosner's private files. Your father was captured by the Bing On as he left the Rosner mansion on Russian Hill.

"Rosner appears to be providing funds to the Bing On to finance opium smuggling, the profits of which, some anyway, are going back to China to support the rebel organizations."

"So what does Rosner get in return?" Kyame asked.

"Killers on call ... at least that, and probably a piece of the opium profits as well. His business dealings are always at the far edge of legal.

"But, *legal* here, Miss Piddington," Rowland emphasized, "is an illusion of law and stability, much like a *Pi Ying Xi,* a Chinese shadow play."

Judson Rowland walked around his desk to stand at Kyame's side.

"We will go over these papers so you can understand as much as we do. Then, based on J. W.'s input as to your own courage, I will be asking you to put your life at risk to help finish what your father so nearly achieved. Stop Rosner, stop the Bing On, delay the financing of the radical rebel movements in China."

Kyame smiled for the first time since she finished her beer with Jack London only a few hours earlier.

"I am glad I came, Mr. Rowland. But there is one thing. What about the police? I don't trust them."

Rowland's smile morphed into a thin smirk. "Police? Some of the Frisco detectives are owned by tongs or industrialists or politicians though we don't really know who owns who." Rowland exhaled, twirled the cigar in his fingers. "Indeed, Miss Piddington ... what about the police? They are of no value to us."

Kyame nodded. "I will deal with them ... if they get in my way."

79

Clarissa Towne whispered behind her crystal champagne glass to Cassie Rosner, as they watched the black-haired young woman pass under the tall arched entryway into the luxurious Rosner living room.

"Who is she, this Carolina Victoria Falconer? She looks ..."

"Judge Adolfus Sloan suggested her to me," said Cassie, as she stepped away to start toward the young woman. "He was quite excited about her. Said Miss Falconer would be most appropriate, given the widespread interest in Trilby. The judge is most handsome and most persuasive, as you know, Clarissa. Please excuse me."

***

Using his extensive quiet city contacts, Judson Rowland had arranged for Kyame to appear at a formal dinner and reception at the Villa Illuminaire honoring Collis P. Huntington who had just arrived from New York.

The sole surviving member of the infamous Big Four, Collis P. Huntington was looked on as the most hated man in California because of the monopoly held and ruthlessly enforced by his Southern Pacific Co., as well as Huntington's personal ownership of the governor, state legislature, half of the San Francisco newspapers, and most of the California legal system. But the moment he crossed the California border, he became the richest man in the state, which muted the hatred, as necessary.

Rowland had asked Kyame what name she would use, since they couldn't risk any possible recognition of the Piddington name.

After only a moment, Kyame had said, "Carolina Victoria Falconer."

***

Carolina Falconer had been executed for murdering two men in Boston when Kyame had first arrived at the art school on Boylston Street. Falconer was described in the papers as a beautiful assassin with the richest purple prose of which the many reporters were capable.

The defendant had started a small business which had grown steadily, prospering beyond Falconer's dreams. Because she needed new capital to continue to grow, Falconer had to take on first one then a second partner. They in turn tried to steal her business away by openly violating the terms of their agreements.

Operating in a world of limited women's rights, Falconer had little to fight back with, even with the men's illegal actions. She could not find a lawyer to take her side against them and saw her hard-won success being drained away into their pockets.

She had poisoned one partner, and, when assaulted by the second, she nearly decapitated him with a meat cleaver.

Falconer fascinated Kyame, who skipped classes to attend the raucous trial. She discovered that Carolina Falconer was indeed beautiful, with a compelling smile, gentle blue eyes, well-read, intelligent -- and utterly unrepentant.

Kyame instantly liked her. Sketching Falconer, her belligerent strength, her calmness as the prosecutors fed the all-male jury with salacious visions of a malevolent witch taking the lives of two honest Boston businessmen.

Kyame had found vastly more character in the face of Carolina Victoria Falconer than in any of the Greek marbles at school.

After Falconer had been found guilty by a unanimous jury verdict, Kyame had pushed her way through the curious crowds to reach out her hand to the passing manacled murderess.

"I heard you, Miss Falconer," Kyame had said, their hands slipping apart as the harness bulls pulled their prisoner away. Falconer's hands were soft, the hands of a musician.

"God help me ... at least someone did," responded Falconer and disappeared into the crowds.

***

"Yes, Mrs. Rosner, I am Carolina Victoria Falconer. I work within the shadows of the human mind."

"Let me introduce you to my guests, Miss Falconer."

Kyame shook her head. "That's not necessary. Their names will come to me as our minds touch."

Cassie frowned. Good God! A mindreader? Judge Sloan didn't ... Were there really such people?

Kyame was dressed in the rich teal blue-green gown she had worn in their last show as the Impossible Piddingtons. Nothing Trilby – she felt the popular style was inane and impractical – and artistically silly.

Kyame had tailored the gown to fit her more closely, Eliza had helped, and to lower her neckline to match San Francisco requirements. About her neck hung the crystal *Bi* disk with its warring icons. She wore a flowing green silk scarf draped over both shoulders that hung down her back to her waist. The scarf partially concealed the lower part of her face.

***

In the Boston courtroom, Kyame had listened as the judge had fulminated loudly against Carolina Falconer, throwing Biblical quotes at the guilty defendant like rocks at a ritual stoning. Falconer had never flinched in the face of her theocratic condemnation.

"There may be a God, your Honor," Falconer had declared to courtroom in answer, "but He is not the god you describe. He is not *your* god."

The circumstance had reminded Kyame of the ministers in various towns who had preached against the Impossible Piddingtons as possessing powers beyond the pale of Christian forgiveness, subverting the powers of the GOOD LORD Himself.

Granted, Papa had often intentionally provoked the pulpit outbursts – they were good for business. But the Bible and the image of a loving

Christian God to Kyame seemed ever more distant and diffuse with Papa's murder.

***

The laughter of the Rosner guests was settling. As a good host, Harry Rosner had entered into the spirit of the evening. The mayor and two prominent lawyers had succumbed to the mesmeric spell cast by the strange black-haired witch. After transforming the men into mules braying at each other, Kyame had them sing Verdi passably as a trio though none of them spoke Italian.

With everyone's eyes on him, Rosner volunteered to become a subject of Miss Falconer's demonstrated mystic and amusing mesmeric powers.

When Kyame induced Rosner to squawk like a duck and waddle like one, the crowd collapsed in laughter, with some men raising their champagne glasses to cheer, "Harry, Harry!"

Cassie began to choke from laughing at her waddling husband. She struggled to regain her breath.

As the crowd noise slowly abated, Kyame whispered into Rosner's ear, "You will turn away and forget me whenever you see me, whenever I clap my hands twice. Only my voice can control you. You will obey when I whisper. Nod if you understand and will obey. At the count of three."

Kyame stood back to start the applause as Rosner emerged from his trance. He first nodded toward her and then stood, a stupid grimace on his face.

"All right, all right everyone, what did this marvelous young woman do to me?" he said, an awkward grin on his face. He noted even Collis Huntington, not known for a sense of humor, was laughing.

Cassie rushed forward. "I'll explain later, my dear little duck." At which the crowd roared again.

Kyame raised her hand, then extended it toward Huntington. "Will you join me, Mr. Huntington? I am fascinated by your mind. Would you allow me to touch it?" Then she smiled. "And I promise no more birds, animals or trios."

Huntington's eyes went cold. He sat for a moment without moving.

Kyame beckoned with both hands, fluttering her fingers and smiling.

The tycoon stood and nodded. "I admit I am fascinated by how you gain such ... such personal information on your subjects, though they have never met you before. Just how *your* mind works, Miss Falconer, is most intriguing."

Huntington sat in the subject's chair as Kyame had first called it forty minutes earlier.

When someone called out, "Careful, Mr. Huntington, she doesn't have you signing checks for her," the guests laughed and even the tycoon managed a brief, but concerned smile.

"Please relax, Mr. Huntington. I want none of your money… I want to see into your mind. I know you have many questions running through your mind … the condition of those two bridges on the Chesapeake & Ohio railway which seem, if I understand, to be crucial to your decision to buy that financially troubled railroad."

Huntington's eyes went wide. "How the devil could you know that?" he demanded, starting to stand.

Judson Rowland had given her detailed backgrounds on Huntington and others likely to be at the reception; private details, not public.

Kyame quickly placed her hand on his shoulder.

"Because I need to reach past those troubling concerns into the calmer portion of your mind. Let me give you special rest, Mr.

Huntington. It won't be funny to all these people, and may even be boring, but let me ..."

Kyame began the first passes, gently touching the banker's forehead, his eyebrows then down to his eyelids, pressing through his wiry beard to stroke his cheeks. Stroking velvet, as she always thought of it.

"Let me pour rest like a cool relaxing stream, like a wilderness waterfall, through your mind. You love the wilderness." She noted his jaw loosening, going slack. "Are you feeling the cool water, Mr. Huntington... as you close your eyes?"

Cassie Rosner gasped with the rest of her guests as Huntington's eyes closed under the Falconer spell. Cassie was concerned, even afraid. This woman was like no other she had encountered before. As close as she could watch, Cassie could not detect any trick. There could be no confederates. That glittering crystal disk Falconer wore, her subjects seemed dazzled by it – that must be her secret. Cassie had never before seen anything like Carolina Victoria Falconer.

"Rest, Mr. Huntington, down to your toes, out to the tips of each of your fingers. Rest." Kyame touched his forehead again. "The bridges are not the problem, Mr. Huntington. It is Roscoe

... Roscoe Lewis, a manager at the C&O office in Baltimore who is the worst problem.

"Watch him closely, sir, very closely."

The crowd murmured in confusion. What was the woman saying?

"Now begin to wake, Mr. Huntington, wake as I count to five. You will feel refreshed as you have never felt before."

Kyame counted slowly as the observers moved closer. She touched the glittering *Bi* disk at her breast.

"Five," finished the mesmerist.

Collis Huntington opened his eyes. He smiled up at Kyame. "Never felt better, young woman. Never. Not even the best whiskey at the Palace bar ever made me feel like this. Marvelous, Miss Falconer. Marvelous."

As Huntington returned to his chair, Kyame curtsied to acknowledge the rousing roll of applause across the room.

"My thanks to Mr. and Mrs. Rosner for inviting me ... and my thanks to each one of you for opening your mind to me.

"I now return control of your minds to yourselves." Her mischievous smile triggered a second round of applause.

***

While the rest of his guests continued to drink, Harry Rosner escorted Kyame to the front door, pressing an envelope into her hand. He had at first baulked at her $200 fee, but Judge Sloan had guaranteed she would be worth it.

With her black evening coat wrapped tightly around her, Kyame whispered. "Harry, return to your guests and tell them you saw me off in my carriage. Go now."

Rosner stood confused for a moment; he blinked several times, then nodded mechanically and turned away, as Kyame quickly mounted the red marble stairs.

***

Quincy looked up from serving a tray of smoked salmon to catch a glimpse of a black form disappearing from the landing of the main stairway. He looked for a place to leave the tray to follow.

"Quincy."

It was Cassie Rosner. He went to her immediately.

"Something fishy, Mrs. Rosner," he said. "Thought I saw someone going upstairs. Need to follow. Just to be sure."

557

Cassie nodded. "You know what to do."

***

At the top of the stairs, Kyame stood with her face buried in her hands. Papa, Papa, show me where to go. So little time. She turned to the right, running to the room at the end of the hall.

Locked.

Papa was better with lock picks than she ever was, but another moment and the lock clicked open.

***

Quincy took the stairs two at a time. He slipped at the landing on the marble polished slick as grease, recovered, then started up again.

***

Kyame opened the dispatch case in the thick green book. The book didn't fit the pattern of the house. No visible books, no library. So, why books in here if not to hide something?

She thumbed through the papers, recognizing some of what Papa had noted. There were more documents now. Several new papers, with dollar amounts and recent dates. Even one from today.

With the papers locked in her memory, Kyame restored them to the dispatch case and the book. She blew out the lamp and moved silently back toward the bedroom door. She hesitated. The nightstands – maybe.

Along with a small book of poems, there was a pistol, a small .32, on Cassie's side. Moving around the bed Kyame thought, what an interesting marriage.

A gun on his side as well, but no book. A large heavy .44 single action Army Colt. She had fired one of these cannons once at the Mills Gun Shop. An ugly weapon with an ugly recoil and a loud noise that made very big holes in people and targets.

Wait. Her fingers touched a small address book obscured under the gun. She lit the lamp and held the book under it. Kyame flipped slowly through the pages, memorizing each of them. Then blew out the lamp and replaced the book under the gun and closed the drawer.

The lock on the bedroom door suddenly clicked, the door opened slowly.

Kyame pulled her scarf up to conceal her face, pressed up against the wall with her derringer out and cocked. She waited. A glimpse. It was the butler, Quincy, with a Bowie knife in one hand, a dark lantern in the other.

**

Quincy listened. Nothing. He moved toward the boss's office. Standing instructions. Office first -- kill anyone who is ever found there, no noise.

He opened the flap of his lantern at the door to the office. No one. He whirled. A rustling sound behind him.

Christ! The Falconer woman! He saw the little black derringer in her hand and started to laugh. Damn slug couldn't even reach him across a room this size.

**

Kyame squeezed the trigger, bracing for the hard recoil. A short sharp bark. Quincy's leer of contempt went slack as he staggered a step, slumped against the bed and rolled to the floor, a .41 caliber hole in his forehead.

Steps!

Kyame stepped back into the partial shadows cast by Quincy's fallen lantern.

Harry Rosner suddenly appeared at the door.

"Good god, Miss Falconer! What are you doing here?" He shook his head in confusion. "I saw you leave. I ...I saw you leave the front door only minutes ago." He looked around, finally seeing the body sprawled against the bed, blood flowing down across the carpet.

"Quincy! You killed ..."

Kyame clapped her hands twice.

Rosner stopped, his eyes widened, then his mouth closed, he turned mechanically, then silently left the room.

Harry Rosner would not recall seeing her. But he would see her in his dreams. His rejected memories would surface there in some grotesque form. Experience had taught her that. How long her post-mesmeric suggestions would control him, Kyame didn't know.

Neither did J. W. Cadwell. Depended on the mind of the subject, he had said during one of their practice sessions years ago in Little Rock. Experiencing high stress could shorten the time, he cautioned, as could too frequent invoking of the suggestion. But Cadwell warned there was no reliable rule, a day, two days, maybe even a week. Just don't take chances.

In Kyame, Cadwell's planted suggestions had lasted less than half an hour -- but, Cadwell had explained, she had too strong a mind to be controlled, too active a spirit.

Wrapped in black, Kyame moved quietly through the house, paused near the empty entrance hall, the noise of Cassie's party getting ever louder, then out the front door and into the night.

***

Kwan Duck, turning from relieving himself in the trees across from the brilliantly lit mansion, was too late to detect the swift movement of the woman wrapped in black.

80

"Quincy has a big hole in his head, you heard the shot, and you saw nothing, Harry?" Cassie was incredulous. "No one but a phantom or an invisible ghost could have shot Quincy and escaped without you seeing them. You were there on the second floor for God's sake. According to the police, all the back doors and windows are still locked from the inside."

"I saw no one." He shook his head as if to clear it. "There was a wraith, a shadow, maybe, that I glimpsed." He shook his head again. "I don't know."

The mansion had emptied quickly of guests once Quincy had been discovered. Police had arrived in thirty minutes. Detective Will Irwin and three uniformed cops were searching the house and grounds for any signs of entry.

"Harry, who could enter this house, kill Quincy and vanish?" She knew the answer before he spoke.

"The boo how doy of the Bing On ... Wong's salaried soldiers," he answered. "They want to be sure I know they are out there until I pay Wong Woon tomorrow. I have all the cash from Montgomery-Hill."

"Then pay the bastards, Harry, whatever it takes. Next time it will be us!" Cassie threw her coat around her shoulders. "And I will finish my role with Montgomery-Hill Bank, as well."

81

Judson Rowland left the room, quietly closing the door on Kyame who wrote rapidly, dumping her memory onto a stack of blank papers. When Kum Yong had placed a full steaming tea pot and a plate of shortbread cookies on the desk, Kyame had glanced up and smiled.

As they sipped their own late night tea, Kum Young asked, "Her memory, Mr. Rowland, Kyame really can remember everything?"

"According to J. W. Cadwell she can," said Rowland. "Even better than her mother who apparently also had prodigious talents of memorization."

She shook her head. "I have difficulty remembering my grocery list." Kum Yong started at a short sharp knock at the office outside door.

Opening the door, Rowland found the sixth floor liveried Palace Hotel butler, a silver tray extended with an envelope on it.

"A telegram for you, sir. It arrived a moment ago."

A network of pneumatic tubes ran throughout the hotel, ensuring prompt delivery of any messages to any of the 755 rooms.

Rowland placed a coin on the tray and closed the door. He looked up from the telegram that had been sent from a strategic clerk he had placed in police headquarters.

"The Rosner pattern continues it appears, Kum Yong. Harvey Atherton has been found with his throat cut on Geary near Eddy. He was robbed."

"Key bank managers regularly seem to die following loans to Harry Rosner," he said. "John Piddington's speculations are making more hard sense."

82

His battered valise filled with hundred-dollar silver certificates marked with President James Madison's grim image, Harry Rosner stopped at the Palace Hotel barroom, with its mirrored walls and soaring arched windows -- and its golden circle of regular moneyed drinkers.

Collis Huntington was surrounded at a large table, at one elbow by John C. Kirkpatrick, longtime manager of the Palace, at his other by silver king, John Mackay, and then by several bankers, politicians and speculators each pitching their schemes.

Passing near the table Harry heard Huntington say, "Gentlemen, if it rained twenty-dollar gold pieces until noon every day, at night there would still be some men out there begging for their suppers."

Catching the tycoon's eye as he approached the bar, Rosner nodded, touching the brim of his hat. He felt his personal prestige move up a notch when the others in the barroom noted that Huntington nodded and smiled in acknowledgement.

Rosner settled at the long bar next to Paul Dresser, whose firm handled the investments of numerous wealthy families, though not in same position as the Nob Hill collection. Dresser was always eager for the latest underground information that might benefit his clients and quickly offered to buy Harry a beer or one of bartender William Boothby's famous cocktail creations.

A beer, Boothby, signaled Rosner. At once, the immaculately dressed Boothby placed a foaming mug before the banker. "Good to see you, Mr. Rosner."

"How is your campaign progressing?" asked Rosner as he sipped and licked the foam away.

"Progressing very well," said Boothby. "All indications are that I will sit in the next legislature come the election. My friends have been most generous, as have you, sir." He withdrew to deal with another customer.

Dresser leaned closer. "Nosing with Collis P. Huntington, I hear, Harry. Reception go well last night? A beautiful female mesmerist, no less. Did she have a crack at hard-headed Collis?"

First swallowing the cold lager, Harry laughed. "Reception went well. Huntington -- away from that foul New York office, can be a charming presence. And yes, Carolina Falconer put him into a mesmeric trance that he was still talking about long after she had departed." Harry shook his head, like he was trying to loosen something inside. He said nothing about Quincy

"Headache?" asked Dresser.

"No, just an odd feeling." He sipped his beer and said casually, "You've heard about the Montgomery-Hill tragedy?"

"Tragedy?" Dresser leaned closer. "I know one of their loan officers, Piddington, I think his name was, was beaten to death by highbinders. Damn shame a man can't safely walk down a Frisco street."

"There's more, Paul. Harvey Atherton was found robbed, with his throat cut over on Geary."

Dresser's eyes flew open. "Harvey! Good god! He's a key man at Montgomery-Hill. He's Hill's son-in-law. I have some of my clients' coin at M-H. What's ol' Hickory going to do?"

"Fight off the run, I assume. Bank should be strong enough," said Harry, as he swallowed his beer.

"Run? What run?"

Dresser wasn't drinking any longer.

Two other bankers Harry recognized slid their drinks down the bar to join their conversation.

"Run?" one asked. "Where?" asked the other.

A small bank, Fidelity Union, had failed only three days earlier when news slipped out that a major loan had gone bad. Depositors stormed Fidelity's offices on Columbus demanding their cash. The bank's coffers only had enough cash to cover demands for two hours -- and when the bank couldn't raise enough through emergency loans from other banks fast enough, the doors closed, the owners bankrupt.

Glancing about the boisterous barroom, Dresser whispered, "Who knows about this, Harry? What is the status?"

Two more drinkers sidled up the group and stood at its edge.

Harry shrugged, sipped his beer. "Only a handful of people," he said to Paul Dresser, the group pressing closer to hear him. "Some smart people are moving now, but ... once the news gets out, it will be an avalanche.

"Remember." Rosner tapped the bar for emphasis. "Hickory Hill took a big position in

Mackay's scheme with the Hawaii cable, but that couldn't start paying off for months, if not years, if ever. Bought a good quarter million in bonds, I understand. His pockets may be stretched thin now." He finished his beer. His voice lowered to a bare whisper, he said, "I'm already out."

Harry picked up his valise.

"Have an appointment with a client. Have a good day, gentlemen," Rosner was satisfied as the bankers abandoned their drinks, moving through the doors ahead of him.

***

Wong Woon finished counting. "So, Mr. Rosner, we are now even ... for a time. I understand your butler has recently met with misfortune. My condolences. The police are, I am sure, diligently investigating."

Harry frowned. "They haven't found a thing. Quincy was shot with a .41 pistol. The back doors and windows of the house were locked from the inside and the front entrance was filled with guests. Can't figure how, why or who did it."

"Your guests included the impressive Mr. Huntington. I congratulate you." Wong dropped his smoldering cigarette into a red jade ashtray. "The goods will be delivered to you and one other client this evening ... at the usual place. Don't be late. There will be additional profits to share within a week.

"Now, Mr. Rosner, I have other demands on my time."

***

Once the door closed behind Harry Rosner, the tong master lit another of his sweet-smelling plum cigarettes, as he leaned back into the deep cushions of the divan. The piles of cash on his table were a rewarding sight, but there needed to be more.

Rosner was becoming unnecessary and awkward. The killing of Atherton was an act of cold stupidity. Oliver Hill had too many connections in Washington, D. C., connections that could prove to be inconvenient.

Holding the Frisco police and others in check locally would suffice for another month, maybe two, but Wong Woon did not want a vigilante or federal police force pushing their way into his operating territory.

Recognizing he could never return to China, Wong Woon had decided to become American, thus his dress, hair style and command of English. But he needed more to get away from being perceived as only a high-toned laundryman. He needed contacts beyond the likes of Rosner. Seizing Rosner's share holdings would be a necessary start.

He blew the smoke from his mouth.

Blaming highbinders was a convenient solution for mindless politicians looking for quick answers to the city's problems. The Chinese had always been convenient solutions to white political failures.

Pushed the wrong way, Wong mused, exhaling through his nose, and provoked by Rosner's impetuous act of murder, a race war could develop in San Francisco which the Chinese community could not hope to win -- even if all the tongs came together.

Which was the biggest joke of all.

83

"That appears to be Rosner's pattern," said Kyame, rubbing her eyes after completing her memory dump, then she went back to make corrections and to look for patterns. There had been no sleep for her -- she wanted none. "Stretch his credit well beyond the backing of the original collateral; immediately take the full amount in cash under the expanded credit line; a key banking manager dies; a run starts and the bank fails ... and somehow Rosner's note is never found in the wreckage of the bank's operations."

Kyame pushed away from the wall to walk around the room, her arms crossed. "Then do it again and again. Based on the data from Rosner's box and notebook; he started all this over two years ago and has ruined six banks so far while amassing a fortune."

"And maybe a seventh, Kyame," said Rowland. "A run started at Montgomery-Hill Bank this morning, Rosner's current credit source. And Harvey Atherton, the vice president at M-H in charge of Rosner's account, was killed last night. His throat was cut. He was your father's former boss.

"The list of names from that address book you found who later turned up dead is certainly strong supporting proof."

The room was silent as Kum Yong watched the two predators move silently on each side of the room with each comment building on the previous one.

"Based on what I've just examined, the glue that holds the Rosner scam together appears to be the opium, or do you see it differently, Mr. Rowland?" asked Kyame.

Rowland stood with his hands on his hips, looked over at Kyame. She had stopped to lean against the wall.

"I think you have it, Kyame. I think Rosner works like this."

Now Rowland began to pace around the office, jabbing his forefinger into the air. "Cheat a bank and use the funds to buy into legitimate investments; then eliminate the bank and key people, and do it again; more loans and more investments with no pay-backs required ... and no embarrassing records.

"But, like any honest investor, not all the Rosner plays pay off ... so something else has to cover ongoing expenses like the lease on Villa

Illuminaire, so the opium trade. That brings in a tong, the Bing On, and maybe the highbinders are involved in eliminating bankers as necessary."

Rowland motioned toward an easy chair. "Kyame, get some rest. There is more coming, but we don't know just when, yet."

Kyame sat down and started to stretch out, then stopped. "Therefore, if we destroy Rosner's opium operation, we destroy the brilliant Mr. Rosner." She smiled. "That's a happy thought."

She closed her eyes and was immediately asleep.

84

Ah Chang could just see a slice of the crystal clear blue sky over San Francisco harbor. For a brief moment he could feel again the crisp breeze off the waters, the wondrous odors of rotting fish, salt, and...

The moment was gone.

Wong Woon stood over him, as he had the day previous. Kwan Duck and his highbinders had alternated slow tortures, burning cigarettes pressed onto his genitals and his face, with hard beatings with the bamboo flails; then a small inhalation of opium that numbed the worst of the pain and water to slake his thirst -- then Wong Woon would interrogate him again about the True Eyes.

With Ah Chang's determined silence the tortures would resume.

Ah Chang thought he would burst in pain when Kwan Duck crushed his testicles sometime in the lost past.

Wong Woon's anger had exploded when he first learned that Ah Chang, his trusted lieutenant, had left a message for some yet unidentified contact. It had been intercepted at a flower stall on 5th Street. Ah Chang was supposed to have been coming back from watching Rosner. When a Bing

On support man working as a laundryman accidentally observed Ah Chang in the wrong place, he had decided to watch, in case Ah Chang might need his help.

The recovered note gave the time for the opium delivery and the place. No name or address on the envelope, but the drop-point was watched until an attractive American-dressed Eurasian girl had appeared to buy flowers but had insisted on the vase and rose bouquet positioned two in from the end of the second shelf -- the drop-position. The flowers on the shelf were all the same.

An attempt had been made to follow her, but her trail was lost when she entered a hotel where the support men could not follow.

The owner of the flower stall, an elderly American woman, had died too quickly under interrogation to provide any information.

So, now Wong Woon focused on Ah Chang.

"So, Ah Chang, you are a fighter after my own heart," said Wong Woon. "Your hatchet is well-notched. I will grant you a last wish, the wish of a Ming warrior ... your head will be cut off with your own hatchet. You and the hatchet will be burned together. It is Ming tradition."

Wong beckoned to Kwan Duck. "Instruct without interruption ... but I want the number he mumbled a few minutes ago. Then burn out his eyes. I will send his head to the Empress."

The flailing resumed, as Kwan Duck rammed bamboo splinters under each of Ah Chang's finger-nails. Ah Chang's screams became higher and louder.

When Ah Chang fainted, water was thrown over him. Once his eyes opened, Kwan Duck began ripping the finger-nails from the right hand, shouting, demanding the number, the number, and the pain would stop. Ah Chang would be able inhale rich opium smoke that would erase all pain. It would carry him to paradise.

When Kwan Duck started on Ah Chang's left hand, the True Eyes agent felt his soul collapse. He felt the last vestige of his life ebb away, his face washed with his own blood, he could not endure more. The pain had to stop, to...

Kwan Duck lowered his ear to the battered mouth. "Again," he demanded, the blood in the mouth muffled the sounds.

"6...3...5."

Kwan Duck brought the many-notched hatchet down, severing Ah Chang's head with a single blow.

***

Wong Woon frowned. 635. A room number perhaps. A control point for the True Eyes? He nodded. Likely. Ah Chang would not have fought the pain for so long.

A hotel would be best for that purpose. People coming and going from many points. Easy enough to confirm. There were only three hotels in San Francisco with more than five floors. The Palace, the Baldwin...

"Send me the woman Li when she returns from the Baldwin Hotel," ordered Wong Woon.

85

"They killed Mrs. Allen ... they may have seen you, Kum Yong," said Rowland. "We must move the office again."

Kum Yong immediately began to gather papers.

"Do you recall anyone watching you?"

Kum Yong stopped. "There was a laundryman. He came outside the laundry to cool off. It's directly across 5th from Mrs. Allen's flower stall."

"Did you feel anyone following you?"

"No, I took the scattered way back as always. No one could have picked me up. I changed my coat and hat as well at the safe room."

Rowland crushed his cigarette into an ashtray. He finally nodded. "We move anyway"

Rowland turned to Kyame as she came back into the room from washing her face.

"The opium is delivered tonight, Kyame. Our contact in the Bing On left notes at two drops. We have lost one drop ... and possibly our contact, but we have the information."

"Good. I will be there," said Kyame.

"Remember, Miss Piddington," cautioned Rowland. "We have no legal status. We are outside the law."

Kyame's eyes went cold. "That is where I want to be."

"I will contact Olney to send more help," he said. "We seem to be approaching a break point in the affairs of Harry Rosner."

***

Wong Woon frowned as the woman Li left his office. Li was one of four cleaners for the fifth and sixth floors at the Baldwin Hotel. A family from New York had occupied room 635 at the Baldwin for the last three weeks. A district judge from Los Angeles had been the previous occupant for two months. There was a businessman from Sacramento before that. There was nothing at the Baldwin Hotel. The Palace and the Occidental...

Wong stepped to the door of his office and issued orders.

-***

Clouds enwrapped the low moon, leaving only a muted glow in the overcast darkening sky. Curling layers of haze were drifting in off the harbor waters that muffled the creak and grind of

582

ships tied against a dock somewhere as the tides shifted. Seagull cries echoed from every direction.

Kyame was wrapped in black; dressed in a black working shirt, black cavalry riding pants and black boots with soft soles. She moved swiftly through the shadows until positioned in a partially opened door in a warehouse opposite the target location. Her derringer was loaded and one pocket was filled with smokeless-cartridges.

Cautious thinking first, before the gun, James Mills had recommended. A soft smile momentarily lit her face.

Probably not tonight.

The low single-story building sat in the middle of a cleared unused pier. Part of the Rosner loan collateral, Rowland had pointed out in their planning. A sliding door at the side of the building stood open about two feet that revealed nothing.

No one could approach the structure from any direction without being observed from one of the building windows. There probably were lookouts stationed further out around the building.

A white seagull swooped close across her vision. Its sudden squawk caused Kyame to jump. She caught her breath and remained still, her heart rate returning to normal. Rowland had telegraphed for additional aid and asked her to simply watch and wait, not to try anything.

We are not legal, he had warned her again. Even the police could be against us.

A carriage stopped somewhere off in the thick haze. A single lamp suddenly appeared in a window and a dark form at the opened door. The door slid further open. Faint light came from inside.

That line from Stephen Crane's novel about the acts of hidden cowardice of his hero, the youth: "He had performed his mistakes in the dark, so he was still a man", intruded on her mind.

Mistakes in the dark. Kyame shook her head.

The jostling harness came closer. A two-wheeled carriage with one man stopped near the door. The inside light brightened.

Kyame cursed softly.

The tall lean silhouette was unmistakable. It was Jason Alexander Johnstone! She gripped her derringer and took a step -- then stopped and retreated.

As much as she hated the seer, it was Harry Rosner she had to bring down. Johnstone could be dealt with later.

The minutes passed, maybe fifteen or twenty. She couldn't really be sure. Two dark forms placed packages into the carriage and returned to the building. Johnstone reappeared, mounted the carriage and moved off, to disappear the way he had come. Johnstone came within easy range of Kyame's smokeless bullets but she waited.

The turn of Johnstone's wheels had scarcely faded when the jouncing springs of a wagon became louder.

Rosner?

Crouched down, Kyame moved a few feet from the shelter of the warehouse behind her. She wanted to be sure.

One man was hunched forward on the driver's seat of the small one-horse hitch wagon with some sort of design painted on the side. Silhouetted, Kyame could see the driver was in a heavy coat with a cap pulled low.

She moved closer.

A dark form appeared. He grasped the horse's bridle.

Someone said quietly, "On time, Mr. Rosner, excellent. There has been a slight change."

"Change?"

Kyame recognized Harry Rosner's voice -- and his sharp concern.

Rosner climbed down from the wagon and entered the building.

Kyame unfolded her knife, crept stealthily forward and knelt down next to the front wagon wheel away from the building. The man at the bridle was on the other side of the horse.

There was no way she could sabotage the wheel. She crawled forward to the harness traces to the wagon and began to cut about two-thirds of the way through the tough leather. Sensing a moving presence behind it, the horse shifted nervously, tossing its head.

Kyame froze.

Steps -- then the springs creaked as a box or something was dropped into the wagon-bed. Then new steps and another box into the wagon. Then a third.

She moved forward to cut into the reins. She brushed the flank of the horse to help settle it down. Kyame moved back to crouch by the front wheels.

"We are agreed then, Mr. Rosner."

"Yes, Wong Woon, agreed."

The door of the building slid to leave only a foot or so still open. Most of the light was blocked as Rosner rounded the back of the wagon too rapidly before Kyame could move.

Rosner stopped when he saw the form rising up beside the wagon.

"You?" He was stunned. It was that Falconer woman! "What in all hell ...?"

Kyame clapped twice as she moved around Rosner to retreat to the warehouse.

Rosner instantly stopped -- his mouth still open to speak. He shook his head. Something was wrong but he could not grasp it. There was something here, something he needed to warn Wong Woon about. But he couldn't remember what it was. Damnit! He just couldn't remember. It was only a minute ago!

Finally shaking his head, Rosner mounted up to the driver's seat, snapped the reins across the horse's back as the highbinder at its head released the bridle. The wagon began to move.

Rosner guided the hitch wagon around to start back toward the street; the wheels creaked over the planking of the pier. It would take half an hour of careful driving to get to his private storage area three blocks from Villa Illuminaire. The three barrels of brown gold in the back would carry Cassie and him for at least three months -- and clear the required lease payment on Villa Illuminaire.

But damn! What was flitting around inside his head?

***

Kyame saw Rosner still shaking his head as the hitch wagon vanished into the darkness. She didn't hear another sound until the massive arms were suddenly around her, crushing her chest, exploding the air from her lungs. Another pair of hands jammed a gag into her mouth.

"Master Wong will find you of interest, woman," growled Kwan Duck.

86

Harry Rosner pulled onto Jackson Street, the horse slipping on the frosty bricks. The wagon fish-tailed in reaction to the horse's erratic path.

Another block and Rosner turned onto Green Street. Nearing Russian Hill, he had to move quickly before the many parties began to disgorge the wrong people onto the streets; proper people who would quickly recognize the smart trader Harry Rosner, and wonder what he was doing and more, what was he carrying.

The agonizing headache returned. He snapped the reins. He had to move faster.

When the horse suddenly swerved, skidding, its forelegs spread as it struggled to recover its balance on the slippery brick street, Harry Rosner's memory suddenly returned.

"Oh, my Christ!" he suddenly snapped, his mind flooded with suppressed images, images that had taunted him in his dreams. It *was* that Falconer woman. That damned mesmerist had messed up his head. Good God, she had bedeviled him! The witch had made herself invisible to him.

Yes, he had seen her in his bedroom with a gun in her hand. Falconer had killed Quincy. Yes, she had never gone out the front door. He had seen her go up the stairs. Yes, he had just seen her outside Wong Woon's warehouse. She knew about the opium, Falconer could destroy him, whatever she was.

Rosner jerked in the reins to turn the wagon around. Fighting the tightened bit, the horse whinnied in protest, scrambling its hooves to regain its balance on the bricks.

With the wagon centered on the street and no opposing traffic, Rosner snapped reins again, and again, as the horse gained speed. Everything was at risk because of that damned woman with that crystal disk around her neck. That must have been her secret. He would wring that neck and rip that disk off himself!

Rosner pulled hard on the left rein to guide the now galloping horse around the corner, then a hard right would send him straight back to the pier. He would be there in a couple of minutes to warn Wong Woon.

As the horse pulled left in response, the wagon continued straight on, the wheels breaking free to slide over the icy bricks. Rosner fought with the reins to steady the horse, then suddenly the left rein snapped apart! He fell across the driver's seat, the leather of both reins still gripped in his hands.

Rosner grabbed at the arm rest of the seat to right himself when another, louder snap, like a pistol shot, sent the wagon teetering up on two wheels as the frantic horse dragged it along with one harness trace.

The end of the wagon whipped around to smash against a street light. The collision flipped the wagon up and over onto the sidewalk, three barrels of small brown cones wrapped in white paper flew out onto the street. As they tumbled down the street, one, then two and finally the third barrel cracked open, scattering the cones across the dark cobblestones.

Dazed, frantically throwing up his hands, Harry Rosner smashed head first into a brick wall, crushing his skull and snapping his neck -- silencing his tortured memories.

87

Recovering consciousness, Kyame found her blindfold and gag gone, and the cords removed from her legs and wrists. Her shirt had been torn open, the *Bi* disk lying on her exposed breasts.

Kyame saw she was lying on a silken divan in a windowless office, a small fire burning within a jade-encrusted fireplace. A well-dressed Chinaman in a pin-striped suit, American styled, with short hair, broad face and a leering grin was staring at her, her black derringer cradled in his hand. But was he Chinese? There was something different about him.

She pulled her shirt closed, buttoned it, her hand grazing the *Bi* disk.

"I am Wong Woon, Miss ...? You may sit up if you like." He laughed. He drew heavily on his cigarette, exhaling slowly. He had had to confirm she was actually a woman, not a man. Her aggressiveness was outside his cultural experience. No Chinese or Tibetan woman of class would fight against capture the way this woman had.

"A most silly weapon, Miss. A silly singsong woman's weapon, but you are not a natural woman. Your aggressiveness separates you from your sex. You will require careful instruction."

He suddenly frowned. "Your name!"

"I am Kyame Piddington. You butchered my father."

"Ah," Wong leaned back in his chair. "So I meet the mysterious daughter of the fool Piddington, the girl that friend Johnstone warned me of. He has a healthy hatred for you, Miss Piddington. But that will not concern him any longer."

Kyame quickly examined the room. The only door was barred from the inside with no knob, only a simple latch. No windows. A desk of carved polished rosewood. At another time she would think it beautiful. Two circular deep green jade scholar's screens stood on the desk. A large crystal ball on a gold dragon frame commanded the center of the desk. So clear, the crystal was almost invisible.

"You wear the crystal *Bi* disk adorned as the Qing would desire. A true *torma* stone. That will stay with me. An excellent piece worth ... but no matter. At another time the story of how you came by it might have been of interest."

Wong cocked the derringer and stood up.

"So, Miss Piddington, what am I to do with you? I could of course come closer and just squeeze the trigger. Killing you with your own weapon, but that is a traditional compliment for a valiant Ming warrior, not, as Johnstone called you, a snotty American girl." He walked to the desk, crushed his cigarette.

Kyame slowly stood. The barred door. The crystal ball. She moved to remain in front of tong leader.

"You would be dead before you moved six inches, Miss Piddington," Wong said, lighting another cigarette. "Your thoughts are transparent."

The stink of burning plum was turning Kyame's stomach. A flash of a memory of vomiting at a Kansas boarding house swept across her mind. She smiled. So very long ago.

"Amused? You have a curious warrior-calm about you, Miss Piddington. I have never seen that in any woman before. But, we must decide what to do with you."

Wong paused, as though to add up his options.

"I could just give you to Kwan Duck and my salaried-soldiers, who would enjoy your esteemed company." He bowed his head. "Or ... or, I could sell you to slavers in Sacramento who would in turn sell you into the silver fields of Nevada where your price, Miss Piddington, would be quite high.

"Or, to Bhan Gar of the Chee Kong tong for shipment to the Qing court as a court slave for the Empress Dowager. I understand that Manchu witch has grown fond of exploring young bodies like yours."

Kyame dove for the crystal ball, as Wong brought up the derringer and fired.

The unexpected hard recoil threw Wong's hand back, sending the slug over her head as Kyame threw the crystal with all her strength at the tong leader's head.

The hard thack! of sharp contact on the bridge of Wong's nose sent him over the back of his chair, the derringer flying across the room.

Kyame ran to the gun then saw a long silver letter opener on the desk. Another shot might have the whole tong waiting for her on the other side of the door, if they weren't there already. She shoved the derringer into her pocket and grabbed the silver blade.

Wong was stirring when Kyame knelt down beside him. Holding the blade with both hands, she plunged the letter opener down hard into his chest.

His eyes flew open in shock, as she jerked, twisted, wrenched the blade free. Hot blood splattered up into her face and over her hands. With both hands, Kyame plunged the blade down hard into Wong's chest again, twisting it, pulling the blade free. She struck again

Weakened and disoriented, Wong Woon tried to raise his hands in defense -- then fell back. Blood seeped from his lips, his eyes glazed and went blank.

Her hands squeezed tight on the hilt, she took a deep breath, then another one, and finally let her hands relax -- and released the blade embedded in the man's chest.

The tong leader was dead.

Wiping her bloody hands across Wong's shirt, Kyame stood, breathing hard. Her hand contacted the crystal *Bi* disk as she pressed her hand to her heaving chest.

Now, truly, was the time for cautious thought.

She could not risk encountering the highbinders. She would have no chance against them. Kyame looked first at the door then down at Wong's body.

Kyame knew what she was going to do. She would make sure the highbinders knew the Impossible Piddingtons had been here. Kyame could almost glimpse Papa over there by the desk, squeeze and shake his right fist to signal "good work" as he had in so many dusty music halls.

There was only one way out.

That was to vanish.

Kyame struggled to drag Wong Woon's limp body across a silk rug to the door, leaving a bloody trail behind. There was no knob, but above the simple latch was the short iron bar that, dropped into its iron slot, was Wong's guarantee of privacy.

Kyame listened at the door. Faint sounds but nothing that seemed close. But Kyame remembered the silence when she was captured.

She couldn't risk waiting. Kyame reached under both of Wong's arms and strained to raise him up on his knees in order to lean, to balance the slumping dead weight of the body against the door, the silver blade still deep in his chest.

Kyame raised the bar to unlock the door. She pushed the door back against Wong's weight until she gained a couple of inches of open space. Kyame wedged her foot into the crack to hold the door just open. There was no one outside. The one shot had not been heard. She balanced the iron bar vertically on its pivot.

Taking a handful of cartridges from her pocket, Kyame threw them across the room into the fire. She pushed hard against the door, to force her way through the narrow opening. When she stepped back from the door, the weight of Wong's body thrust it shut, the shock threw the bar off balance to fall into its slot.

The sharp clang of the bar falling confirmed the door was now locked securely from the inside.

The cocked derringer in her hand with only one shot ready, Kyame moved silently away from the sounds of the highbinders, to search for any means out – hoping the attention of the highbinders would be distracted when the cartridges began to cook off in the fire.

***

Kwan Duck thought he had heard a shot earlier, but the master had ordered that he was not to be disturbed with the white woman. But now Kwan was certain there were shots. One, two, then two at once, another!

"Come!" he ordered four salaried-soldiers hunched over a long table preparing opium pills for smoking.

"Master Wong! Do you need us?" Kwan Duck knocked again. "Master Wong!"

When there was no answer, not even a curse and an order to go away; he pounded again on the door as two more shots went off.

With two massive highbinders with him, Kwan Duck lunged at the door, ripping the bar from the wall. Kwan Duck pushed the door back.

Wong Woon was dead! The master's own silver knife in his chest! Kwan Duck searched the room. No one was there! There was no place to hide. How could that be? No windows, the door locked by the master from the inside, the shots fired only seconds before they battered down the door.

The white woman with the mystic *Bi* disk. Kwan Duck shook his head, cold fear gripped his heart. She was a *tulku*, a witch who could melt into the air.

88

Judson Rowland waited a few steps away until Kyame and Eliza had embraced, tears in both of their eyes. The train for St. Louis and then on to Boston was waiting.

Creed Abbott had been angry when Kyame had promised to find a way to repay him.

"You are family, young woman. You never pay any time you are in San Francisco. Don't ever say that again!" Then he had held out his hand. "You are John's daughter. He was a truly good man. I can see him in you."

Rowland came up when Eliza started back to rejoin her parents.

"I have notified Secretary Olney of your amazing contribution to wrecking the Bing On opium trade and Harry Rosner's involvement. We still don't know where Cassie went off to or just what her role might have been. With Wong Woon's death, the Bing On tong has dispersed, its territory already taken over by other tongs.

"There are a lot of humiliated people on Nob Hill and Russian Hill who are out sizable amounts of money because of Rosner."

He held out his hand. "If you don't mind, Kyame, may I call on you again? Your skills are unique."

Using one hand to hold her hat in place against a stiff breeze, Kyame smiled, as she took his hand. "I suspect I will encounter the tongs again somewhere. They seem to have long memories. So I need to learn more." She nodded. "But, yes, Mr. Rowland, if I may be of help again, call me."

The conductors began to bellow out: "All Aboard!"

"What will you be doing, Kyame?" asked Rowland, as he held her elbow to assist her in mounting the stairs up into the car. "The stage? J. W. says you could be an almost certain success as a stage mesmerist."

Kyame laughed and shook her head. "I think Carolina Falconer's career as a mesmerist is over. I want to take my art and see the world. But there is one thing," -- she paused -- "one thing I need to do."

Rowland raised an eyebrow, as a conductor came up swinging his lantern.

"Yes? And that is?"

"Learn to speak Chinese."

***

Wearily, Kyame dropped her luggage inside the door of her room. The days on the train had been difficult. Memories of Papa kept coming through her tears, through her dreams. She found even the destruction of Wong Woon and Harry Rosner did nothing to assuage her grief.

But, after many days, when Boston was called as the last stop, her tears had dried and her heart was still. And, she could now feel the intense satisfaction of that blade going into the tong master's chest.

To take a human life. She had never wanted that. Quincy had been self-defense, there had been no choice. She hadn't really killed Rosner. Kyame had wanted to publicly humiliate him, to destroy his reputation, but he was dead because of her.

And Wong Woon -- killing the tong master in the locked room had been a memorial to Papa. He had taught her to always look for the unexpected effect. He had been there with her -- Kyame was sure of it. Their last performance together; the last performance of the Impossible Piddingtons.

***

There was a pile of accumulated correspondence which her landlady had methodically placed in her room. On top was a small package with a New York postmark that Kyame opened first.

The letter from Dr. Mar Tan lay on top of a deeply carved round red lacquer case filled with thick red paste. Her chop was wrapped in crimson rice paper.

It was carved from red jade, about an inch square, about two inches high. A stalking tiger was carved in astonishing detail on top. There were delicate inscriptions incised on all four sides in Chinese which she couldn't read. The chop engraving itself on the bottom was a mixture of graceful flowing cursive figures, which she also couldn't read.

My Dear Miss Piddington, Mar-Tan's letter read, I have heard from Professor Cadwell of your San Francisco ordeal. Its sadness and its triumphs. Please accept my deepest condolences regarding your honored father. I know no words to help ease such a loss -- except to offer friendship in however form may be helpful.

San Francisco proved I was right in my estimation of you; you proved your soul of *tsyh ker*. I was right as well in my choice of a chop for you.

You now have a name to be recognized -- and if necessary -- feared.

My most humble greetings,

Mar Tan.

He had signed in both English and Chinese.

Kyame held the red jade chop in her hand, its smoothness invited her touch; the stalking tiger challenged her thoughts.

She broke the tiny red seal and opened the small folded note at the bottom of the package. Inside was a white card. Her chop was in thick red ink on one side, and on the other, her new name was written in English:

The Shadow of the Tiger.

The End

Appendix

Deck Estimation

From the Notebooks

of

John Piddington

August 10, 1892

This mental illusion illustrates the thought reader's redirection rather than a magician's misdirection.

If executed well, it will change the spectator's expectations of the performer in some significant way

The deck is shuffled by anyone. Performer riffles through the cards, not too fast, apparently memorizing their order, but actually he only notes the top card.

Put the deck back on the table and have the cards cut by the spectator "anywhere, anywhere at all". The top portion is placed away from the performer, the bottom half is left in front of him.

The performer picks up the top card of his pile, squints at the far pile apparently estimating the number of cards in it, and calls the card he had originally noted. The spectator turns over the top card -- naturally, the performer will be right. You will be rewarded with a murmur of astonishment from the audience.

The performer drops his stack of cards on the far pile and asks to have the deck cut again.

The performer already knows the top card on the deck -- he just looked at it. The performer does the routine again and is right again, except in looking at his cards this time he subtlely notes the second card down not the top card of his pile. The next time, his 'estimate' is wrong, but then he calls the second card down and is correct. The audience murmur will be louder.

This "miss" actually seems more impressive to observers than the mentalist getting the card exactly right again. And so on, adjusting the

606

misses, then quit before things get dull -- or too obvious.

Note: It is the apparent memorization of the deck and the estimation of the number of cards cut that gives this routine its logical validity. The demonstration of arcane knowledge rather than expertise in sleight-of-hand.

Without the estimation slant, after one or two hits, it can become very obvious to the audience what the mind reader is actually doing and the murmurs of admiration will turn quickly to laughter of ridicule.

If the presentation is well thought out and rehearsed -- and the performer quits soon enough -- the audience will credit the performer with a remarkable memory, a discipline that should be apparent in the performer's other activities as well.

Remember, that when you create an effective *illusion*, you also create a *genuine* impression.

***

March 23, 1893

The Squires Duplicated Name Effect

Though Ted Squires refused to sell his method to me, this is the effect that I put together for Kyame which was well received by reporters in several cities. Even Squires thought her presentation was effective, the one time he saw it

-- in Salt Lake City, I think.

Two squares of blank paper, about 2"x2", are folded into pellets. A spectator takes either one to write a name, a name that should be only known to the spectator, even a fake name if they choose.

Kyame has a blank pellet of the same paper and folded the same way, hidden in the left hand pocket in her skirt. As the spectator begins to write, she reaches into her pocket and brings out the blank folded paper, being careful that no one can see the pellet in her hand. All attention is focused on the writing spectator anyway.

When the spectator has finished writing and has refolded his paper into a pellet, Kyame takes it in her left hand, and as she walks to where the spectator has decided he wants his pellet placed, she switches the written pellet for the blank in her hand. After switching she holds the blank pellet high for everyone to see as she carries it to the place selected by the spectator.

Kyame then picks up the other folded pellet from the table and, as she reaches for a pencil, she switches the spectator's pellet for the blank one.

Now, with the spectator's pellet opened in her hand, Kyame apparently writes a name, actually reading the first spectator's written name. Kyame apparently writes the name she has in her mind with a pencil, though actually only lightly pencil-tracing the name already there, then refolds the paper into a pellet and hands the pellet with the spectator's name on it to spectator 2, while pocketing the blank pellet. Her hands can now be shown completely empty.

Kyame walks to where the first spectator's pellet has been placed and, with her fingers spread to demonstrate that her hands are empty, picks up and apparently reads the name written by the first spectator -- she sometimes rotates the blank paper to suggest to the audience that she is adjusting it to bring the spectator's writing upright, a subtle touch of legitimacy.

After announcing the spectator's selected name, Kyame drops the pellet into her pocket and walks over to where the spectator 2 has the first spectator's written pellet, thinking it is Kyame's written pellet.

Spectator 2 reads what the first spectator has written which, of course, is the correct name. He hands the pellet to Kyame, thinking it is hers. She then drops the pellet into her pocket as she takes her bows.

Both of Kyame's hands are empty at the finish and only two pieces of paper have apparently been used.

With the proper presentation the routine works to good effect; but how Squires himself did it neither Kyame nor I know.

Historical Note

Several characters in *Revelations of the Impossible Piddingtons* are historical, as Collis P. Huntington, the last of the Big Four, and the richest and most hated man in California – unless you had a deal to pitch; writer Jack London; and J. W. Cadwell, the most successful mesmerist in America. His feats of mesmerism described in the story are genuine and are taken from newspaper accounts of his presence in various cities during his tours, including his "robbing" a jewelry store with wide-eyed reporters at his elbow. He repeated this stunt at his hotel in another city when the registration clerk there had loudly ridiculed mesmerism and all mesmerists as fakes and frauds. Within moments the clerk found his hands glued to the counter and unable to speak to the high amusement of the men and women in the lobby.

The Second Novel
In the
Adventures in Second Sight
Series

The Shadow of the Tiger

Now in both
Amazon Kindle and
print formats.

Enjoy the first chapters.

Here is wisdom. Let him that hath understanding
count the number of the beast: for it is the number
of a man; and his number is

six hundred threescore and six.

Book of Revelation, Chapter XIII, Verse 18.

Lobby Bible (King James Version)

Hotel de Paris,

Monaco, 1896.

Let him consider his system wisely: that the
numbers of the wheel total the number of a man;

six hundred threescore and six.

V. B.

Monte Carlo Roulette Systems

1896

Principality of Monaco

Friday Evening, January 10, 1896

Hotel Hermitage

Behind the man the Dog's Head promontory, *Tête de Chein*, rising high above the shifting sea, was limned against a slim moon. Dressed in "climbing black" as he thought of his working clothes, he turned and looked back at the hotel wall. Third floor -- third balcony from the right. There were no night sounds, except an occasional muffled feminine laugh -- a gruff male tobacco cough.

Tonight was different from so many other nights. Tonight he did not steal for himself -- he didn't really need any more money to continue to live the life of which he had always dreamed -- in a small comfortable villa above the bustle of Cannes, above the inviting beach -- and above the ever tossing suspicious sea.

He grinned as he shook his hands to loosen his fingers, warm the blood. After tonight, there would be none of the usual problems of identifying the correct connoisseur to purchase the stones of particular distinction and notoriety that would lay hidden in his valise. Rather tonight, he shook his head, he did not really even steal -- it was more of a simple transaction.

614

He was performing an Imperial service for a fee of 150,000 gold Marks, a fee he had confirmed three hours earlier had been transferred into his special account in a small bank in Rome. In addition, any and all police records relating to his past work in one of the principal European countries would be expunged -- permanently. That promise was unshakable. It came from the crown itself.

All, he smiled, shifting his shoulders a last time, assuming a successful night.

But, had it not been for an awkward mistake four months ago, he would not even be here tonight, regardless of any fee. That mistake was sharp in his mind, in order to avoid any possibility of a repeat. He had trusted the wrong person, a misjudgment that had breached the wall of anominity he had erected with such care, and had enjoyed so many months.

Invisible in black, he moved silently through the tailored bushes and flowering shrubs to the base of the hotel wall. He recovered the short ladder he had left there in the early afternoon during a brief but hard rain shower that had driven everyone inside. It would raise him to the first ledge. From there he would find his way with "fingers and toes" -- as he had once explained to a beautiful, marvelously naïve French woman one night in Marseilles who had been easily convinced that he was a retired special intelligence agent of the French *Deuxième Bureau,* much like a dashing character from equally naïve romantic fiction.

He pulled himself up and over the railing of the balcony. There was some pain in his back – from too much relaxation. He grinned under his mask. True, he needed more frequent exercise, but not practice.

The moon, like a guilty accomplice, had withdrawn her light behind a cloud. A soft step, another, and he stood at the partially opened French doors. There were only the sounds of deep slumber of the man and his wife. He automatically touched his pocket to confirm the critical material was still in place after his rapid climb.

The door swung silently open. He knelt, then went to his hands and knees as he entered the room. His target was the suit coat that the Count de Dagoneti had worn earlier that day at the Monte Carlo Casino. The closet was on the other side of -- but no! -- the coat was thrown over the back of the chair at the dressing table. A gown was on the floor, silken to his touch. He smiled. They had been in a bit of a hurry. That is always best, for the first time of the evening -- then later, slower, more deliberate -- deeper.

He reached into the coat pockets one by one until he found the casino chips. He withdrew them, and replaced them with the chips from his pocket. Ten 1,000 franc new Monte Carlo chips out; ten 1,000 franc new Monte Carlo chips in.

The transaction completed, he turned to crawl silently back to the French doors. Once on the balcony, he drew the one door back to its original partially open position. He stopped at the railing to listen. Nothing. The night itself was complete silence, complete blackness. The moon remained hidden.

He was over the railing and down the wall of the hotel to the ground in less than a minute. He left the ladder behind the bushes and moved quickly through the closely trimmed greenery. Crouching down, he reached a spreading tangerine tree where he had left a black bag hidden in its lower branches. There would be no outcry, as no apparent crime had been committed; but, as he had painfully learned over the years: *it never paid to be careless.*

He quickly changed into black evening trousers and a white double-breasted dinner jacket, straightened his black tie, brushed the soil from his custom-made Italian patent leather pumps, and, smiling in anticipation, strode down the marbled walkway toward the Jardins du Casino and then on to the Casino itself where he was known as Baldur, the Count von Trotha, a suitably modest title to explain his wealth.

Von Trotha would be welcomed at the tables by the useful elite as a cautious but successful risk-taker, and for his generosity to the needy -- needy gamblers, that is.

A satisfying night that had been -- ah, no -- unsatisfying. He had seen some exquisite jewelry on the dressing table -- had even allowed his fingers to brush lightly over it -- but had left it. Now, he wished he had taken it. It would be accounted as just another robbery of the carelessly rich on the Riviera and would not cause his client any trouble; but, the deal had been *strict*, in, out and don't touch anything.

All right, then. He shrugged. The night was done, and the tables waited.

Riveria di Ponente

San Remo, Italy

Sunday, February 2, 1896

The patient rolling surf whispered its eternal message of indifference to humankind -- and to the body it rocked gently in the sand. Washed clean by the touch of the sea, there was a large ragged wound across the man's throat. He was dressed in an unbuttoned white double-breasted dinner-jacket and black evening trousers, but his feet were bare. Both hands lay open to the sky. His shirt pocket held a one thousand franc chip from the notorious Casino that dominated the cliffs a few miles to the west

He would be rocked by the sea for yet another hour before the first morning strollers would discover his body, as the sea pulled back, retreating from the recurring foolish problems of humankind.

Secretum secretorum

Tu operans sis secretus horum.

[The secret of secrets;

Thou that workst them,

be secret in them.]

1

Oval Office

White House

Washington, D.C.

Tuesday Morning, February 4, 1896

Shifting his burly body in his chair, President Grover Cleveland reached down, unlocked and opened the second drawer on the left in his desk. He withdrew the single paper there and, after pushing piles of documents aside, slid the deciphered cablegram across the desk to his former Attorney General, Richard Olney -- and now his Secretary of State for the past eight months.

As Attorney General, Olney had put down the violent Pullman strike of 1894, an act that had made legions of new friends, as well as adding a new range of implacable enemies, but which had clearly shown that though quiet voiced, Olney was a man of relentless, even merciless will.

Gray haired with a heavy gray mustache and two years older than the President, Olney had immediately made his mark in his new position by upgrading all foreign American diplomatic posts from Legations to Embassies, giving notice that the United States was diplomatically equal to all other countries -- particularly European.

Olney noted the grim expression on his friend's large mustachioed face. Grover Cleveland's broad smile could light up a room. But now the well-lighted Oval Office seemed dark.

Cleveland had weathered politics at all levels, mayor of Buffalo, New York, then Governor of New York then President from 1885-89, and now at 59, President once again, since 1893 -- the only Democrat to be elected president against a continuing flood of Republican control with his opposition gaining 100 seats in the House in the 1894 election -- a very public reaction to the continuing national financial troubles of 1893.

Cleveland was publicly noted by both his critics and supporters for being average, only more so than most men. And though his political enemies persistently attacked his policies, no one ever attacked his honesty -- or his willingness to listen.

Also, since July 1, 1893, with a secret shared only with his wife and with Olney, he had undergone difficult and risky surgery to remove cancer from his mouth. The recently inaugurated president had felt a roughness on the inside of his mouth, a roughness that seemed to grow. When it was confirmed as cancer, Cleveland wanted to keep the surgery absolutely secret, so it was carried out by

621

three physicians in the main cabin of the presidential yacht, the Oneida.

Utilizing a unique cheek-retractor enabled the surgery to be done entirely inside the mouth and thus avoid any external incisions. Cleveland's entire left upper jaw was removed and replaced by specially constructed replacement of vulcanized rubber that maintained the original contours of Cleveland's face, and, remarkably, his normal voice and pronunciation. President Cleveland addressed a special session of Congress two weeks later. No one in his audience had detected any change.

Tapping the paper, Cleveland said, "The English ambassador hand delivered that message to me half an hour ago, Olney. It is the subject of the utmost secrecy, even within the English government itself. Only the Queen and the Ambassador ..."

"And the code clerk at the British Embassy, sir," said Olney smiling. "Code clerks have mouths, too ... and sometimes grasping hands. We have had some experience with that ... from both sides."

Cleveland nodded agreement to his Secretary's clear point. "Yes, Olney ... certainly. I am assuming here a certain rigor in the English vetting of their embassy people -- but your point is acknowledged. As you see, the English Prime Minister, Lord Salisbury, is asking for our help in Southern Europe. He requests an answer from me within the week. But ... we have no help to give ... officially."

Cleveland pushed back from his desk, brushing his forefinger across his thin black mustache, a nervous habit as he collected his thoughts. He had a large map of Europe on a tripod against the far wall of the Oval Office which had been used in an earlier meeting. He tossed his hand toward it. "Salisbury requests we supply several intelligence agents to temporarily replace the agents that the English have recently lost. Six of them have been killed, in one way or another, in the past seven weeks. They have only one agent left operating in the area … in southern France ... he's located in Monaco.

"And Salisbury has no other agents available he can send, not for at least three months … and he wants to know why he has lost his people … and wants that information very quickly. He, as you can see in the note, is concerned that some kind of major threat is developing in southern Europe; but hasn't as yet been able to give it any shape, any details."

Receiving the cablegram back from Olney, the President dropped it back into the drawer of his desk and locked it. "Our problem is that the United States has no government vetted intelligence agents anywhere in Europe. And, except for that strange group you have assembled, Olney, your so-called Anglo-Oriental Marine Insurance Co., there is no one else I could call on … even assuming that there is anyone in that group who could meet the need. Whatever that need might be. Even the British Ambassador has not been fully briefed on the specifics."

623

Olney stood. "I will apprise Judson Rowland immediately of a possible need. Mr. President, may I be blunt with him? I would bet my life on his integrity."

Grover Cleveland looked up into the bleak dark eyes of his Secretary of State. He had trusted difficult missions to Olney before. He nodded. "Tell him what you feel he needs and get back to me with your thoughts." As Olney walked toward the door, the President added with curt emphasis, "Sooner, my friend, sooner than later."

Shadow of the Tiger is available at
http://amazon.com/dp/B00LP287CK

The third book, now in-progress, *Pi Ying Xi, The Shadow Play is* set in 1897 in San Francisco, Honolulu and Tahiti in which Kyame must learn to walk on fire to confront the war God 'Oro to save the lives of those whom she loves.

Other Books by Barry H. Wiley

The Thought Reader Craze, McFarland, 2012. A non-fiction study of the intense search by scientists, academics and others to establish telepathy as a fact of human nature and perhaps the first scientific proof of life-after-death. The book also tells the story of the men, woman and, occasionally, children who so successfully hoaxed the scientists; as well as the parallel story of the creation of the one-man minding act one Monday morning in 1873 in a Chicago saloon. The stage performers used the scientists to gain public credit, while the scientists used the performers to maintain public interest. In the end, the performers gained and lost fortunes, while the scientists gained and lost reputations.

Available in both print and ebook formats on Amazon and on the McFarland website.

A Spirit of Fraud. Set in 1876. A British occult Brotherhood under the apparent direction of the Archangel Uriel plans to seize defenseless America in the waning months of the Grant administration. Only the celebrated spirit medium, Annie Eva Fay, detects the threatening presence of Uriel's minions. Gaining the help of the Pinkertons, Annie moves to stop the Brotherhood. But Annie's spirits are all fake. Is the Archangel a fake as well? And will there be time enough for Annie to learn the truth?

The novel was reviewed October, 2014, on the online journal *Kings River Life Magazine* (www.kingsriverlife.com) which compared *A Spirit of Fraud* to *The DaVinci Code*.

Beyond The Tempest, a sorcerous tale of Bermuda. Bermuda. Pink sand, exotic beauty, mysterious history, a three billion dollar national debt, and a per capita murder rate twice that of New York even with the most draconian gun control law in the Western world: Ten years in prison without parole for possession of any gun, or any part of a gun. In *Beyond The Tempest,* the real Bermuda is a principal character in the novel, not simply a tourist backdrop.

Set in contemporary times, the novel tells the story of mentalist and former physicist, Kaarin Larsson, who is booked at the last minute into a venture capital conference in Bermuda to replace Tony DiMarco, celebrated memory expert who has been murdered twice, shot with a .32 and a .41 magnum at the same time in a deserted Bermuda cemetery. DiMarco's killers thus were risking hard time just holding the guns. But why two killers?

Kaarin is attacked by two killers her first night in Bermuda, one with the .41 and one with a knife. She knows no one in Bermuda – why her?

Together with Inspector Keith Haggard of the Bermuda Police Service, she searches for answers. Why are her friends Serreta and Sugar Alberts, magicians currently performing at the Pink Sands in Bermuda, also targeted?

But the constant underlying question that torments her nights, and her unguarded moments: *Is she human?*

Note: Research for *Beyond The Tempest* included interviewing the Bermuda Commissioner of Police, which resulted in his assigning an officer to show Bermuda as the police see it -- a remarkably fascinating afternoon in paradise.

Beyond The Tempest e-book is distributed through Smashwords to Barnes & Noble, Kobo, and Apple iBookstore, and a print version is available through Amazon and local bookstores.

Tales of a Thought Reader, 2016, a collection of five short stories with Stuart C.

Cumberland as protagonist. Cumberland (1857-1922) was the premiere thought reader in Victoria's Realm, performing only for the wealthy and royal of Europe, America, and the Near East. But even with his success, Cumberland had secrets he had to keep concealed to be able to walk the Salons of the elite.

While fiction, the stories draw on real events in Cumberland's remarkable life and career, including a remembrance, written by a certain doctor late of the Afghan army, about his friend, Sherlock Holmes, meeting Stuart Cumberland for the first time.

Available as a print and ebook on Amazon.

http://amazon.com/dp/B01A9TKWFE

For more information on the stories, books and blogs of Barry H. Wiley visit his website at www.barrywiley.com

Barry H. Wiley

Author Biography

Barry Wiley is a retired high-tech executive, having done business in 24 countries most recently throughout SE Asia.

His short mystery story, "The Great Houdini! Murder Case", was nominated for the 2015 Derringer Award, for the best in short mystery fiction; while his non-fiction book on psychical history, *The Thought Reader Craze* (McFarland, 2013) won the 2014 Christopher Literary Award.

Wiley's historical occult novel, *A Spirit of Fraud,* was compared to *The DaVinci Code* in a review in *Kings River Life Magazine*.

Among other short stories, he has had three short stories published in his on-going series featuring John Randall Brown, a retired high-tech executive turned professional mentalist. Think Thomas Crown as a fake psychic and a reluctant detective.

Barry Wiley has lectured on the history of mentalism and spiritualism at several venues from the Magic Castle in Hollywood and the Magic Circle in London, to the annual Meeting of the Minds of the Psychic Entertainers Association, and most recently at the Los Angeles Conference on Magic History.

He has also written a number of non-fiction articles for magic and history magazines in America and Europe.

www.ingramcontent.com/pod-product-compliance
Lightning Source LLC
Chambersburg PA
CBHW052339020726
47503CB00001B/30